BENEATH
the
SURFACE

Cover photo © 2001 Corbis Stock Market

Cover design copyrighted 2001 by Covenant Communications, Inc.

Published by Covenant Communications, Inc.
American Fork, Utah

Printed in the United States of America
First Printing: June 2001

07 06 05 04 03 02 01 00   10 9 8 7 6 5 4 3 2 1

ISBN 1-57734-828-1

Library of Congress Cataloging-in-Publication Data
Grossman, Jeni, 1951-
    Beneath the surface / Jeni Grossman.
        p.   cm.
    ISBN 1-57734-828-1
    1. Children of clergy--Fiction. 2. Mormon families--Fiction. 3. Young woman--Fiction.
4. Missouri--Fiction. I. Title

    PS3607.R67 B4 2001
    813'.6--dc21   2001028370
                                              CIP

BENEATH
the
SURFACE

a novel

JENI GROSSMAN

Covenant Communications, Inc.

Do not, as some ungracious pastors do,
Show me the steep and thorny way to heaven,
Whilst, like a puff'd and reckless libertine,
Himself the primrose path of dalliance treads.

—I, iii, HAMLET

DEDICATION

For my loving husband, Gary,
who always makes the next thing—and the next—*possible*.

ACKNOWLEDGEMENTS

I would like to thank all those who provided encouragement, support, and information during the writing of this novel: Janette Rallison and my sisters in the American Night Writers Association helped me shape and focus my writing. DeeAnna DeGroff, Joseph Peterson, and Megan Bradshaw (my creative writing students at Heritage Academy in Mesa, Arizona) were my early readers who expressed enthusiasm for the characters and story. Jessica Duke and Larry Gesell provided information about geology and law enforcement. My teenagers, Zach and Lindsey (excellent writers themselves), urged me on and let me borrow the computer after they were in bed. My husband, Gary, who always thinks I can do anything. And my parents, Virginia and Kenneth Grider, who instilled in me a love of words.

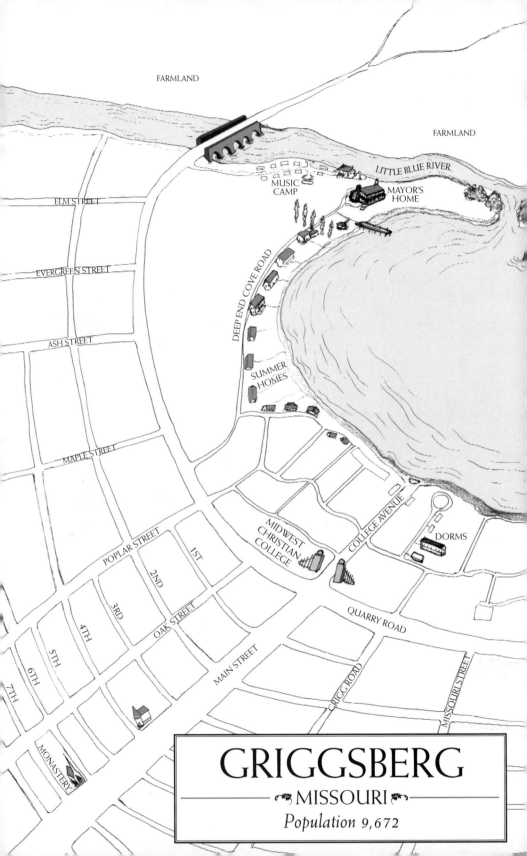

FARMLAND

FARMLAND

LITTLE BLUE RIVER

MUSIC
CAMP

MAYOR'S
HOME

ELM STREET

EVERGREEN STREET

ASH STREET

DEEP END COVE ROAD

SUMMER
HOMES

MAPLE STREET

POPLAR STREET

1ST

2ND

3RD

OAK STREET

4TH

5TH

6TH

7TH

MAIN STREET

MIDWEST
CHRISTIAN
COLLEGE

COLLEGE AVENUE

DORMS

QUARRY ROAD

GRIGG ROAD

MISSOURI STREET

MONASTERY

GRIGGSBERG

☙ MISSOURI ❧

Population 9,672

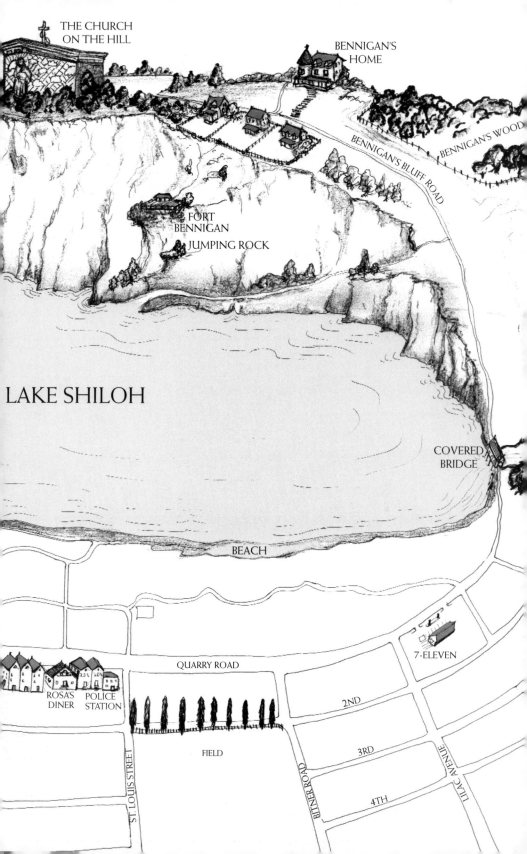

CHAPTER 1

The phone woke Hannah Dennison who had fallen asleep on the floor, her chin resting on an open book. Years later she would remember that phone call—and the discovery of the body in Lake Shiloh—as the end of her childhood and the false shelter of her own innocence. The second ring caused Hannah to lift her head slightly and stare at the page of Shakespeare framed by her elbows and arms, one forearm stacked on top of the other—it was the balcony scene of *Romeo and Juliet*. She used the cuff of her sweatshirt to rub off the little grease smudge her chin had left on the page. Her waist-long hair spread like tendrils of wild ivy over her plush bedroom carpet. During the third ring, Hannah unfolded herself from her tortured position. Her legs had been stretched out into Chinese splits in an unbroken line from her hips; her torso pressed flat on the floor above them. Madame Karanaeva had recommended that all her advanced ballet students sit in this position for fifteen minutes each day to perfect their turnouts and keep their muscles flexible. Hannah squinted to see the time on her clock radio. *Midnight.* She had held the painful position for more than three hours.

On the fourth ring, Hannah stood, testing her weight on her wobbly, overflexed muscles, and tottered over to the phone by her bed. On the fifth ring, wincing and moaning, Hannah picked up the receiver.

"Hannah? You okay?" came a gruff male voice from the phone. "It's Dale Farley."

"Yeah, Chief, just . . . suffering for my art," she replied, sitting gingerly on the edge of her bed, biting into the knuckle of her thumb.

"Your folks out of town again?"

Hannah looked at her clock again and realized that a phone call after midnight rarely brought good news. Suddenly she knew exactly why Dale Farley had called. "Have you got Gabe at the station, Chief?" She grimaced again, this time from having to deal with the antics of her twelve-year-old brother whom she had last observed sleeping soundly in his bedroom down the hall.

"Fourth time this summer, Hannah. Every time your parents go to one of them Christian pep rallies, Gabe seems to think he can do as he pleases. You need to call your Aunt Kate or get Jared or someone to bring you down to the station." Jared was Hannah's next-door neighbor who was old enough to drive. Aunt Kate lived across town.

"Can't you just send Gabe home in a squad car like you did last time?"

"I'm not going to do that, Hannah. I'm filing paper work on him for his own good. First step toward a juvie record, Han. He's too young to be hanging out down here on that college campus. You know how it gets over Labor Day weekend with all them college students coming back."

"So exactly what crime has Gabe committed, Chief?" she asked, protectiveness bristling up through her annoyance.

"I haven't actually caught him doing anything other than breaking curfew, but it's just a matter of time till I figure out what he's up to. We want to keep Gabe out of serious trouble, Hannah, so let's get your folks in on this and nip this midnight wandering thing in the bud."

Hannah was touched by the genuine worry she heard in Dale Farley's voice. The Chief had been a member of her father's church for as long as she could remember; most of his patrolmen were members too. In a concerted effort, they had kept Gabe's mischief off the police blotter, and the Dennison family name had remained unsullied all summer long.

Her father's church functioned as the center of the social and religious life in the small town of Griggsberg. His non-denominational house of worship called The Church on the Hill stood on the high end of Bennigan's Bluff; the stained-glass figure of Christ could be seen from anywhere in town. The church was the loom on which the threads of all their lives were anchored, then woven into a tidy, predictable pattern. *Loom.* That was a good word. In addition to providing its foundation, the church loomed over the town like a watchful presence.

Behind the forty-foot-high bluff snaked a good-sized river called the Little Blue. Between the Bluff and the town, a glistening lake curved like a kidney bean, meeting the river at both ends of the lake. Before it had accidentally flooded years before, the lake basin had once been a dusty limestone quarry. After the quarry flooded, forming the lake, Midwest Christian College had moved its campus from downtown Kansas City to Griggsberg. The shiny new college campus and the magnificent church above it had transformed Griggsberg into a bustling, prosperous college town.

Hannah had fallen silent as she considered how she would get down the Bluff to the police station to claim her brother without the whole town finding out he was in jail. "Okay, Chief, I'll throw on some clothes and find a way down there." She hung up the phone and massaged her calf muscles through the large holes of her favorite dingy-white, wooly leg warmers. Scattered on the floor by her bed were the five Shakespearean plays she had been reading over the summer for her honors English class. The test was on Tuesday, the first day of school. *Maybe Gabe will settle down once school starts up again,* she thought wearily as she stacked her books.

Without changing her grungy San Francisco Ballet sweatshirt that she always wore to bed, Hannah stepped into a navy blue pleated skirt and buttoned it at her slender waist. She couldn't find her Doc Martens in her cluttered room, so she grabbed her leather dance slippers with the black elastic bands from her dance bag. She snugged these on, then wove her unruly ash blonde hair into a single messy braid, secured it with the inky rubber band from the morning newspaper, and tossed it over her shoulder. From the glass dish on top of her father's dresser, Hannah picked up a large ring of keys and found the one to his Ford Taurus. No sense in bothering anyone at this hour. Although Hannah was still two months shy of her sixteenth birthday, she'd been driving the family car for more than a year whenever her parents left on one of their frequent trips to speak and sing at church conferences, to participate in political rallies, or to appear on

Christian television shows. *How else can I get bags of groceries up the steep roads of the Bluff?* she always thought to herself whenever she took the car. *Do they expect me to make a nuisance of myself whenever I need to haul anything home or get Gabe and me where we need to go?* She wasn't going to let a few pesky laws keep her from doing what she needed to do. Over the last year, Hannah had developed a secret pride in her ability to run a home and look after her brother during the frequent absences of the adults who lived there. She thought of these self-taught skills as her personal contribution to the family ministry. Knowing how to survive and get things done had freed up her talented, charismatic parents so they could go out and save the world.

Without turning the headlights on, Hannah backed the Taurus out of the garage and headed down the hill. *No sense in waking the neighbors.* In the rearview mirror, she caught sight of Gabe's wide-open bedroom window on the second floor of the house. One of his royal-blue curtains with the rows of red and yellow superman logos flapped in the breeze like a wagging tongue. She noticed for the first time how close the branches of the elm tree had grown to her brother's window, and made a mental note to get the saw out and chop them down. *Time to bust Superman out of jail,* thought Hannah bitterly as she rumbled over the wooden floorboards of the covered bridge. She switched on the headlights and drove toward the police station.

* * *

While Hannah had been asleep with her chin on her schoolbook, the town of Griggsberg below her was bustling with Friday night activity. Carloads of shouting college students sped up and down the streets of the campus and through the downtown area. Students who hadn't seen each other all summer were walking downtown on Quarry Street, talking excitedly or laughing and roughhousing on the campus lawn. They stopped to eat ice-cream cones at the little metal tables outside Baskin-Robbins, or walked further down Quarry Street for a large plate of onion rings or biscuits and gravy at Rosa's Diner.

Dulcey Martinez, Rosa's seventeen-year-old daughter, sat with her new boyfriend, Matt Moore, at the little speckled Formica table at the back of the diner. Dulcey had grown weary of the high school boys in town and was working her way through the best looking freshman boys at MCC.

As Matt made short work of a double cheeseburger, Dulcey carefully picked out the sausage bits from the plate of biscuits and gravy her mother had set before her. Rosa's daughter was lining up the little sausage pieces on the edge of her plate like a greasy necklace of taupe colored pearls. The creamy white, pepper-flaked concoction that Rosa ladled over flaky homemade biscuits was famous in Griggsberg. People even drove the nine miles from Kansas City for Rosa's late night specialty. The cops from the station next door swore by it, and the college kids referred to it as "comfort food." Occasionally, Matt took a break from the dwindling cheeseburger in his beefy fists to drain the remains of the large vanilla milkshake in front of him.

Rosa stood behind the counter pouring coffee for a policeman on his dinner break. She was a small woman with a once-pretty but now-tired face, a slightly thicker version of her petite daughter. Her long, coal black hair was done up in a lovely twist achieved by the artful placement of a single yellow pencil. When the officer's cup was full, another harried waitress snatched the coffee pot from her and headed toward the two booths full of college kids. Rosa put a check down next to the policeman and began clearing the heavy crockery plates from a table near Dulcey and her date.

"Eat, Dulcinea!" she said over her shoulder to her daughter as she carried a bus tub of dirty dishes past the booth. Then to the officer, "She eats like a baby bird! She thinks just because she is dancing, every bone in her body should stick out! D'you see how skinny she is? Stand up, Dulcey; show Officer York how skinny you are."

Dulcey sat unmoving, her back to her tormentors.

"Hey, you just let me know when she gets too thin," said York, about to deposit a large forkful of his own gravy-soaked biscuit into his waiting, watering mouth. The fork found its destination as he added, "I'll lock her up and she'll *have* to eat this *delicious* stuff, huh?" Even though he was talking with his mouth full, Dulcey heard his teasing threat and stiffened her back in response.

Dulcey knew that York had just been hired and that already her mother was training him to watch out for her. Over the years, without them even realizing it, she had trained all the guys at the station to watch over her headstrong only child. Matt laughed as Dulcey turned her body sideways to shield her plate from their view. "Let's get out of here, Matt. Mom wants me to eat an entire month's worth of fat and she's trying to get the cops to force-feed me."

Matt seemed amused at the affectionate tension surrounding Dulcey. He pointed toward a doorway at the back of the café that led directly into the Griggsberg Police Station next door. "So your mom's diner is actually a part of the police department, right?"

"You'd think so. Besides all her downtown business, Mom cooks for all the cops and anyone who gets put in jail." Now Dulcey was stealthily spooning the creamy white gravy into the empty red tumbler that had recently held Matt's milkshake. She finished the guise by plunging his straw into the white goo. It stood bolt upright with no problem. "Come on before she figures this out."

Matt tried to linger at the table, licking ketchup from his fingers. He was from Tulsa where his father pastored a large Protestant church, and he was interested in how things worked in the little town that was to be his college home for the next four years. "So your Mom feeds all the criminals that get put in jail here in Griggsberg, huh? She must be busy *all* the time," he mocked. "Are you aware that the brochure from MCC says it has the safest campus in the United States? How much crime could there be in a town of nine thousand people with three thousand of them being Christian college students?" Ever since early August when Matt had moved into the dorms to get a jump-start on a job at the college bookstore, he been learning all about Griggsberg.

"Give us some credit . . . Griggsberg has a few criminals," Dulcey said defensively. "In fact, you probably know one of the inmates in our little jail right now." Dulcey gathered her purse and jacket and pulled Matt to a standing position. "Didn't you tell me your dad went to seminary with Craig Dennison?"

"Yeah, they were roommates back in the golden olden days and I went to summer Bible camp every summer with his kids. Now don't tell me the police have got Hannah Dennison locked up in there! If they do, it would be for reading her Bible in school or something. That's about as bad as Hannah gets."

"Not Hannah . . . her brother Gabe. I saw Chief Farley pick him up earlier tonight over by the campus. He was downtown consorting with some of those wild preachers' kids from the college."

"No kidding. Gabe's just a little kid. They've got *him* locked up?" Matt reluctantly allowed Dulcey to propel him out the back door of the diner.

"Well, you know those preachers' kids. When they get away from mommy and daddy, they're *always* the wildest kids in town," she taunted Matt, flashing her dazzling, dimpled smile. As they left the diner, she called to her mother, "I'll be back before one-thirty to help you close, okay Mama?"

Matt stuck his head back in. "Thanks for the grub, Rosa. You're a great cook! I'll have her back in time to help you clean up."

"Just because I gave Dulcey the night off, don't you let her talk you into no mischief tonight, Matthew. I need her back at closing time. My dishwasher is out sick tonight and I need Dulcinea to wash pots and floors tonight. And you can scrub a few tables to work off that cheeseburger. Okay, Mijo?"

Once out in the dimly lit parking lot, Dulcey grinned and kissed Matt expressively. "Look at what I've got on under my sweater, Matthew," Dulcey said, hiking up her thin sweater to reveal a shiny black wetsuit with neon green stripes on the sides. "You are going to be my lookout while I go on a little underwater mission tonight," she whispered conspiratorially.

Matt had come to Dulcey's scuba certification ceremony a few days before. She had finished a summer of lessons given by the college instructor, Dmitri Karanaeva. At the ceremony, Dmitri made them all swear they would never dive in the deep part of Lake Shiloh because of the dangerous crevices and the old quarry equipment still immersed at the bottom of the lake. Dulcey, who had been the only girl in the class, had become furious when one of the divers let it slip that Dmitri was planning to take the guys down to explore the forbidden deep end of the lake in a few weeks. She had not been invited to the all-male rite of passage. Dulcey had told Matt then that she would come up with a way to fix that "old boy" club.

"You're going to dive . . . tonight, Dulcey? Oh, no . . . no, no. That is *crazy*! It's after midnight. Your mother needs you back at the diner. It's pitch dark out there and there's no one to go down with you. I am *not* going to be part of this!" Matt struggled out of her grasp and walked out into the parking lot, kicking gravel as he went.

Dulcey followed him as she expertly gathered her glossy dark hair into her hand and slipped an elastic band over it to form a thick pony-tail. She reached for Matt's hand and stood facing him in the circle of the only light in the parking lot. "Why Matthew Moore, I'm not afraid of that little bowl of water in the middle of town. Are you? Or maybe it's the ghost of Liam Bennigan that's got you spooked. Is that it?"

"Dulcey, I heard Dmitri say it's more than a *hundred* feet down at the deepest end of that 'little bowl of water' as you call it. And I've seen signs all over the beach that *no* one is allowed to dive down there . . . it's even posted in the dorms. There's a $500 fine if you get caught, Dulce!"

Dulcey ignored Matt and disappeared behind the café's over-flowing dumpster.

She dragged out an old speed limit sign she had sprayed a luminous white. In bold black letters, she had painted the words:

Dulcey was here. Labor Day Weekend, 1993

"You're nuts. I *refuse* to go along with this. You'll have me kicked out of school before it starts!"

"You know, for a preacher's kid, you sure are boring. One of the tamest I've met." Dulcey put her arm through his and stroked his wrist. "All I'm asking you to do is to wait for me on the beach, Matt. I'm trying to be at least *that* careful . . . to have someone know I'm down there for a few minutes." The light glanced off her intense green eyes, and Dulcey's jaw twitched.

Matt paced around the parking lot for a few more minutes, kicking things as he walked. Dulcey waited near her car, unruffled and serene, her arms folded over her chest. "You are so stubborn!" he said as he circled around toward the passenger's side of Dulcey's 1974 canary yellow Volkswagen Beetle with the exposed engine in back.

Dulcey smiled triumphantly as she unlocked her car doors. Matt offered a last feeble objection. "Why can't you wait until tomorrow so someone can dive with you? Even *you* said divers *never* dive alone."

Matt watched her throw her little victory sign on top of her scuba gear in the backseat of her car.

"Matt, if you're with me, I won't be diving alone, will I?" she tried again. "You know, since I *am* going to do this, it seems to me that you care more about getting kicked out of school than you do about me."

"Dulcey, I do care," he said, his voice softening. "It's just that I'm new here. What if something went wrong? I don't know who to call. I don't even swim very well so I couldn't go in after you."

Dulcey slid under the wheel and Matt sat on only half of the passenger seat, his feet still on the ground outside. Dulcey showed him her fancy new car phone mounted on the dash of her car. "See, Matt, if something happens, you just punch the speed-dial button, then the number one for my Mom or two for the police station. And—heaven forbid! I've even got Dmitri on number six. Well, six is actually the dance school but Madame could get Dmitri in an emergency. He lives in the apartment right there at his mother's school." Dulcey leaned over and gave Matt another kiss on the side of his angry face. "Any other questions?"

"Yeah, I'm wondering why you have the police station already programmed on your car phone. You must get into trouble all the time," he said miserably.

"Look, Matt, Chief Farley is the closest person I have to a father. He and the guys at the station bought me this car phone, okay? It's like I have the Chief and eight or nine uncles who carry guns and are on call all the time. Two of the guys are even divers; *they'd* know what to do," Dulcey said softly as she caressed the back of his neck. "Besides—the lake is very romantic this time of night."

Matt looked helpless against the forces operating on him. Finally, he folded his big body into the little passenger seat and Dulcey started the car, skidding happily through the parking lot toward Quarry Street. As she reached the end of the alley that separated the diner from the Ace Hardware Store, she caught sight of Hannah Dennison stomping up the front steps of the police station.

"What did I tell you? Miss Hannah has her hands full with that feisty little brother of hers. Every time their folks are out of town, she ends up having to bail him out of some jam. Ooooh . . . she does not look happy."

Matt slid down in the seat and kept his hand over his face like a cocked baseball cap. "Come on, Dulcey. Let's get this thing over with so you can get back and help your mom close the diner tonight."

CHAPTER 2

Hannah struggled to open the huge oak doors of the police station. She managed to pry one of the massive doors open a few inches so she could slide inside. As she approached the counter, she caught sight of herself in the glass that separated the foyer from the police officers' desks and realized she looked like Alice in Wonderland entering a strange place full of disagreeable characters. Her small hands were clenched into smaller fists, one of them containing the huge, jangling key ring. Setting the keys on the counter made Officer York look up from the paper work in front of him. Hannah, embarrassed, gave York a cold smile. He was new in town and had just started attending her father's church. The Dennison family's livelihood depended on the good opinions of others. After all, who would buy the product they were selling if it didn't work for them? *Gabe's arrest is not going to impress the York family,* she thought bitterly.

"Hello, Officer York. It seems you've all been very busy tonight keeping the citizens of Griggsberg safe from all the thugs in town," Hannah said coolly. "The chief tells me my brother is one of them."

Hannah could see that York was struggling not to laugh at her. She knew that he was either thinking words like *cute and precocious,* or *arrogant smart aleck.* She was used to both reactions from the adults in her world.

"I wouldn't worry too much, Miss Dennison; it's more like we are trying to prevent thuggery here in Griggsberg. We wouldn't have much to do if we just waited around until the youth of this town turned into full-blown criminals." He smiled kindly at her and motioned toward Gabe who was sprawled on the olive green vinyl couch at the side of the foyer.

"Oh, good. I thought he was actually behind bars," Hannah said, real relief in her voice. She walked over and stood looking down at her sleeping brother. Despite the brilliant fluorescent lights and the annoying static of the dispatcher's radio, Gabey slept like an angel with his cheek sweating against the plastic couch cushion. His dirty socks and sneakers were piled in a heap on the floor as if he were in his own family room in front of the television. Hannah didn't like the fact that he looked so relaxed.

She sat down on the couch and fingered his baby-soft, sun-streaked hair that fell in lovely, well-cut waves. An ancient ceiling fan breathed down on them, trying in vain to stir the early autumn air, humid from the recent rain. For several moments, Hannah watched Gabe's long lashes sleep-fluttering against his flushed cheeks. No wonder his face appeared in the church advertisements. The striking beauty and assorted talents of her family were often used to call attention to the Church on the Hill. There was even a big billboard on the highway at the edge of town with her family's picture emblazoned on it. It read, "If your family is important to you, grow closer by worshipping at the Church on the Hill. Sunday Services at nine A.M. and seven p.m. Wednesday Prayer Meetings at seven p.m. All faiths welcome." *Humph*, she thought as she gazed at Gabe. *My whole family ought to be arrested for false advertising.*

Hannah tried to wake her brother by dangling one of his smelly socks under his nose. He didn't budge. "Get up, jailbird. It's time to go home!" she said loudly in his ear.

Realizing where he was, Gabe grabbed his socks from Hannah and stuffed them into his back pocket. Looking dazed, he struggled his sneakers onto his dirty feet, then stood to follow his big sister. "Hannah?" he whined as his rescue got underway, "Can we stop on the way home and buy some Doritos?"

"Don't even think about Doritos! I should leave you in this place and let Mom and Dad bail you out tomorrow or a week from now!" Hannah scolded in maternal tones. *Doritos! Being picked up by the police hasn't bothered him a bit,* she thought. Then Hannah stopped for a moment considering that a night in jail might actually be just what Gabe needed. She weighed the possible value against the certain scandal of leaving Gabey in the clink for the night. After Rosa brought him his biscuits and gravy in the morning, the whole town would know about Gabe's brush with the law. She shook the idea out of her head and hurried Gabe toward the front doors.

"Hold on, Hannah. We've got to talk!" Chief Farley called from the back of the station, "I've got that paperwork on Gabe that we need to . . . "

Hannah and Gabe, pretending not to hear, pushed out the front doors to escape his questioning. The chief caught up to them just outside the doors and spun Hannah around to face him. The three stood awkwardly together at the top of the eight steps in front of the station. Gabe favored Farley with his best grin, "Thanks for lookin' out for me, Chief. I owe you one."

"What you can do for me, Gabe, is to stay out of trouble." Farley sighed and nudged Hannah out of the glare of the station's light. "Hannah," he said gently, "You need to keep Gabe in at night. This is not just a teeny sneak-out thing. I don't know exactly what he's doing, but Gabe's been getting into real trouble. Every time your folks go away to one of these church deals, we pick Gabey up downtown. Griggsberg's not like it was when you guys were little before we got the lake and the college—it isn't a sleepy little town anymore. We've got some major carousing on the weekends and it'll be worse when school starts up again next week."

"Oh, Chief, it's still summer . . . sort of . . . *all* the kids run around in the summer!"

"Gabe's too young to be out at night . . . downtown. Unsupervised. It's not healthy, Hannah."

Hannah looked up at the chief. When she was younger, she envied his two daughters, and even now she wished she had someone to tell her which end was up. Her own father's guidance had come to her from his pulpit. Like everyone else, Hannah knew her father regarded her as self-sufficient and capable, a sort of child terrarium— once planted, she never needed to be tended again. Hannah had received the same sermon from him that he provided all his church members every Sunday.

"Chief, you know how things are. Gabey just gets restless. He gets away from me. I was reading and I thought he was in bed. Let's just hope it's a phase," she said in the most grown-up voice she could muster. "And thanks . . . for being there," she added as she steered Gabe down the crumbling steps and headed down Quarry Street toward the Bluff.

CHAPTER 3

Instead of heading directly to the beach, Dulcey humored Matt with a quick detour through the town. She turned left onto Main Street away from the front entrance of the campus and drove down the modern cobblestone road. Antique gas streetlights alternated with stately oak trees forming an archway of leaves and light through the middle of town. Matt gazed appreciatively at the three- and four-story Victorian homes that had been restored to their original splendor during the renewal of Griggsberg. Built by wealthy farmers at the turn of the century, college professors and owners of thriving businesses now lived in them. The studios of Madame Karanaeva's School of Ballet occupied the largest Victorian at the corner of Main and Fourth Street. On Main and Sixth, they passed the Monastery Restaurant housed in the quaint little church that had been pastored by the Dennison family before they built the Church on the Hill. Dulcey turned off Main and drove through the quiet neighborhoods adjacent to Main Street.

Eventually, Matt seemed calmer and Dulcey headed for the beach. As they drove down the jumble of campus streets, Matt slumped lower in his seat every time they passed a group of students. Dulcey was sure his friends had warned him about her. *He's definitely in over his head,* she thought with a smirk.

Finally, Dulcey turned left onto Deep End Cove Road which ran along the backs of twelve lovely summer homes, their fronts facing the lake and a beach of pristine white sand that had been imported from Mexico.

"Mayor Lockhart's house is the only one with a dock, so he lets everyone use it," Dulcey explained as she drove through an opening in a high hedge that served as a gateway to his estate. The mayor's home was made of aspen logs and had a porch lined with cozy wicker furniture that ran down the length of the house.

"Where's the mayor?" asked Matt, peering at the darkened house.

"Lockhart's got property in Florida—goes there about every other weekend. A nurse stays with his mother when he's out of town. The chief thinks Lockhart will move down to Florida after his mother dies—says he has a whole other life in Coral Gables. The Lockharts still have some family around these parts and the mayor's mother says she doesn't want to move to Florida. He's just sort of keeping things familiar for her until she passes away. People in town think Jack Lockhart's a near saint the way he looks out for his mother. He couldn't lose an election if he tried."

Once they were beyond the hedge, Matt couldn't take his eyes off the Church on the Hill that stood on the Bluff directly above them now. Its huge, stained glass windows featured a two story-high figure of Christ carrying a lamb the size of Dulcey's Volkswagen. The windows dominated the sky above the town, their reflection color-fully spanning the lake below. On Sunday mornings, the stained glass reflection shone on the people in the church sanctuary, bathing them in a rainbow of soft colors. But each night, interior floodlights lit up the scene so the people in the town below could enjoy it. Dulcey chuckled at Matt, knowing full well that he felt Christ's eyes boring into him, enslaved against his will to a crazy woman's dangerous plan. *Preachers' kids. They always feel so guilty,* she thought.

Dulcey parked carefully between the dock and the mayor's boat shed, her front tires resting on the sand, her back tires on the grass of the mayor's meticulously kept lawn. Matt, who seemed resigned now to his fate as a helpless bystander, unloaded the heavy equipment from her back seat. Dulcey slithered seductively out of her jeans and sweater and stood there in her black neoprene wetsuit. She enjoyed the way Matt looked at her, knowing her years of dance training had shaped and toned her body to perfection.

"I need to get water in my suit and let my body heat warm it up before I go in," Dulcey said as she headed toward the water. Matt followed, carrying her rubber dive mask, flicking the lights on both sides to assure himself that they worked. Then he hauled her single tank and regulator, her buoyancy compensator jacket, a belt studded with lead weights, and her ridiculous metal sign to the edge of the water. Dulcey returned and sat next to him on the sand, allowing the water in her suit to warm.

Matt put both of his arms around her and gazed at the mysterious lake. "Tell me again about what happened to Liam Bennigan in this quarry."

Dulcey had told the story so many times that it no longer intrigued her. But newcomers loved to hear her tell the story because she had been there when it happened. Adjusting her voice to the appropriate tone of mystery that her listeners always seemed to require, Dulcey began to recount the familiar story. "It was a dark and stormy night in 1983—I was seven years old and living right here at the edge of the quarry. My mother moved here from Mexico with her father when she was just a teenager. Grandpa had worked limestone quarries in Mexico all his life and Liam had hired him as a foreman."

"And how did you come into the picture?" Matt asked.

"My mother fell in love with one of the quarry workers. They never got married, and he left her before I was born. We never heard from him again. We lived with Grandpa till I was nine. After Grandpa's eyesight began failing and he couldn't work as a foreman, Liam kept him on as a security guard in order to keep him on the payroll."

"So you and your Mom lived right here when this lake was a big dusty pit, huh?" Matt commented.

"Griggsberg was a really crummy place to live in those days. All those nice houses in town had gotten run-down and a lot of them were boarded up. Griggsberg was like a ghost town back then. So, anyway, at about five o'clock in the morning, my Grandpa was out in the storm making a security check when he discovered that the quarry was flooding. I vaguely remember standing at the front door with my mother watching the quarry fill up with water. I remember how the lightning lit up the Bluff between each crack of thunder. Mom had gotten up because she was worried about Grandpa: his eyes were so bad and the quarry was deep. She was afraid he would slip and fall into it so she always got up with him when he went on his night rounds."

Dulcey turned and pointed to a spot about twenty feet away. "The little house where we lived was just over there where the hedge is now. Eventually, they tore it down to build the new summer homes. Anyway, it had already been raining for several days. There were no workers scheduled to come in because it was Labor Day. By the time Grandpa saw the water, the deep end of the quarry was already under several feet of water and it was filling up fast."

"No one knew they were about to strike the water table?" Matt asked.

"Well, Ed Lawton, the geologist, swore for years that the water table was not anywhere close to being hit. He says it's *still* twenty feet below the quarry and he says the water that flooded the pit came from the Little Blue River behind the Bluff. He and Fiona Bennigan still claim to this day that there was some sort of conspiracy to flood the quarry with river water. But the mayor did an investigation and hired divers who said that the flood was caused by the water table being hit by the quarry diggers. Eventually everyone just got tired of hearing Fiona and Ed talk about plots and conspiracies. Ed moved away and Fiona is the bitterest woman you'll ever run into in this town. She still carries a grudge against everyone in Griggsberg."

"So, your Grandpa was on duty the night of the flood and all he could do was watch his job go under water, huh?"

"His and everyone else's in town. When Grandpa saw the water filling the quarry, he ran to the Lockhart's house to call Mr. Bennigan, to tell his boss that the quarry was flooding. Ten years ago, Mrs. Lockhart, the mayor's mother, lived back there on the banks of the Little Blue. She was a widow even back then. The Lockhart house was right next to the noisy rock quarry. Of course, she had the river to the front of her house so she didn't have to look at the quarry." Dulcey motioned behind the mayor's house and Matt could just barely make out the original ramshackle farmhouse through the trees.

"Okay, back to my ghost story," Matt urged her on.

"So after Grandpa called him, Liam came running down the hill from his house with his flashlight. You can still see where the quarry road used to be," Dulcey said, pointing to the base of the Bluff just above the lake. "Of course, the lake has eroded it away and it's just a path now, but Mr. Bennigan came charging down that road and down into the deep end of the pit. He hopped on his biggest quarry digger so he could save the most valuable piece of equipment he owned. But by the time he got it turned around and headed up the hill, the water had got hold of his back tires. And of course, the storm had been drenching everything for days so it was really muddy. My Grandpa used to tell me how helpless he felt watching Mr. Bennigan gunning that big motor trying to outrun the water.

Then Grandpa about had a heart attack . . . he sees Liam's wife, Fiona, and her two boys, Ian and Charlie, running down the quarry road toward Liam. Maura, Fiona's youngest, was just a baby then. By the time they got down near the quarry, Liam and the digger were completely under water and Fiona and her boys just stood there in the storm waiting for him to swim up out of the water." Dulcey stopped, remembering the story she had heard her Grandpa tell a hundred times. She could never remember which parts she had seen herself and which parts her grandfather had told her about.

"He never came up?" asked Matt. Dulcey knew he was trying to keep her talking.

"You know what happened . . . Liam's body had been dragged down under the quarry digger and wasn't found until the water stopped rising several days later. By then, the State of Missouri had dug an outlet so the water could flow into the Little Blue River on the other side of Bennigan's Bluff. Then they dug another channel on the deep end to connect the lake to the Little Blue at that end. Without the new channels, the town would have flooded. Overnight, that lake gave our shabby town of Griggsberg some brand new possibilities. The rest, as they say . . . is Griggsberg history."

"So has anyone ever seen old Liam's ghost?"

"Not his ghost exactly—but sometimes people see eerie lights just under the surface of the lake. Or sometimes just under the mist that rises off the lake on humid nights."

"Humid—like tonight?"

"Keep your eyes on the lake, Matt. You just might see what people call 'Liam's light.' They say the light is from Liam shining his flashlight trying to find his way to the surface."

"Creepy . . . " said Matt thoughtfully, staring at the lake. Dulcey laughed, knowing Matt thought she was now too scared to make her midnight dive.

"Okay, the water in my suit is warm. I'm ready!" she said cheerfully as she stood up.

"Hey, Dulce, if you drown down there, should I just have your body hoisted up to the Church on the Hill for your funeral?"

"Well, Matt, I'm a lapsed Catholic so you'll need to see if Father Thomas remembers me well enough to bury me."

"I didn't know you were Catholic." Matt seemed surprised.

Dulcey was more concerned with her equipment than by her possible watery demise or her religious affiliation. "Matt . . . I'm not anything right now," she said absently. "To me, religions are all the same . . . it's all GUILT . . . they all just have different holidays," she said, continuing her equipment check.

"Well, *I'm* the one who'll be stuck with the guilt if anything happens to you," Matt said and gave her face mask a gentle tap.

Finally, Dulcey seemed satisfied that everything was working properly and she staggered upright under her heavy equipment. It would be as light as a spring coat once she was in the water.

Matt made an exaggerated sign of the cross and pretended to pray for her. Dulcey responded by walking to the very end of the dock, performing a perfect scissors kick and splashing into the water. She treaded water for a moment, turning on her halogen dive lights and adjusting her buoyancy vest so that the water around her was at the level of her mask. Then she plunged down into the ink-black water.

CHAPTER 4

Dulcey allowed the weights to pull her down into the depths of the lake. The water in her suit felt deliciously warm against her skin. Though Shiloh was one of the cleanest lakes in Missouri, visibility was poor because the quarry water contained so much limestone silt. Even with her two powerful dive lights, she could see no more than five to six feet in front of her.

After swimming down about forty feet, her lights caught the eerie outline of the raised mechanical arm of Liam Bennigan's last ride. Fish swam by her mask and she remembered to be respectful of their rights to their watery kingdom. Using both gloved hands, Dulcey pulled her body down the length of the quarry digger's arm toward its eroded orange-colored cab. The metal sign trailed behind her, attached by its wire to her dive belt. She knew exactly where she wanted to hang it. The door of the cab was open wide, just as Liam had left it. The current had sprung its hinges in a forward position and the door could no longer be closed. Grasping the top of the metal door frame with both hands, she pressed her body into the cab and sat on the upholstered seat. She knew that every guy in her scuba class would want to sit on that seat, now covered with a layer of mossy sludge. She carefully unhooked the sign from her belt and reeled it by its wire inside the cab. Relishing every moment, Dulcey wound the wire first to one post and then the other of the cab's glass-less front window. It would stare mockingly into the face of every boy who sat on that seat.

Just as Dulcey finished placing her sign, she noticed a long yellow rope attached to a cinder block resting on one of the huge, man-tall tires just outside the cab. It was probably attached to a float marking the location of the quarry digger. As far as Dulcey was concerned, there was no reason for it to be there since it was illegal to dive around here anyway. And it bothered Dulcey's competitive spirit that some diver had placed it there. It detracted from her victory sign. Reaching outside the window, she easily untied the slick nylon rope and let the marker or whatever it was drift up toward the surface of the lake.

Satisfied with her work, she began to imagine Dmitri Karanaeva's face when he realized just *who* was the Queen of the Deep End. Although she would never let on to Matt, it was Dmitri's admiration she craved. The thought of winning the attention of Madame's extraordinarily good looking son had propelled Dulcey toward these dangerous depths. The ballet dancer from New York, injured in a car accident, had limped home to his mama several months ago to nurse his wounds. Although he was three or four years older than Dulcey, he was the biggest catch in town.

To support himself, Dmitri taught scuba diving at the college in the warmer seasons and managed The Monastery restaurant the rest of the time. As soon as his leg healed, he'd be back in the big time, dancing for the most prestigious dance company in America—the New York City Ballet. Dulcey didn't know just how she would manage it, but she planned to go to New York with Dmitri Karanaeva.

Thinking about Dmitri had made Dulcey careless. Instead of going out of the open door, she decided to exit through the large window at the front of the cab. Its glass had long ago been broken out; a few remaining shards and some broken strips of metal protruded menacingly. As Dulcey attempted to clear the window, she felt a sharp pain at the base of her neck. Her startled cry temporarily dislodged her regulator and she gulped water for a second or two before she located her air source and stuffed it back into her mouth. She willed herself to tread water as she removed a glove and felt the sharp metal that had inserted itself between her tank and her back. She could feel the jagged edge of the metal through her wet suit and felt a rush of adrenaline into her body as she realized her danger. A sudden movement could rip her wet suit and the extreme cold could put her into hypothermia. Or the metal could sever the hose that delivered the precious oxygen to her lungs. Dulcey whimpered in her throat, biting down on the rubber mouthpiece to keep it in place. She remembered Dmitri cautioning against panic and hyperventilating, which would use up her oxygen quickly and prevent her mind from thinking clearly. She leaned forward slightly, gingerly, hoping the piece of corroded metal would break away from the window. Instead, it pressed further into the base of her neck, ripping a small hole in her suit. She shuddered as the warm water around her body escaped from the tiny hole. The piece of metal, like a claw, seemed to be reaching for her, holding her tightly. She glanced at the lighted dial of her depth gauge and saw that she was at sixty-six feet—nearly three bars of water pressure.

Her next thought was to unhook the tank and try to surface without it. But Dulcey knew her lungs were small. A rapid ascent would send her body into decompression sickness. *Remember to breathe out. Not just in.* Dmitri's words floated toward her in her mind. *Lung barotrauma—lungs could explode if I don't breathe out!* She could feel the beginnings of a squeezing sensation in her ears and her sinuses. She knew she could not hold enough air in her lungs to allow her to rise to the surface slowly. *How long would Matt wait to call for help?* She had been too proud to give him details. She had said it would take only a few minutes. She had been down for twenty-two minutes. Would he know when to go for help? She hadn't really thought seriously about needing help so she hadn't specifically told him *when* to worry.

Dulcey could feel her core temperature dropping as cold water gradually seeped into the small hole in her suit. She tried not to think of Liam Bennigan in this very spot, ten years before, trying to survive the advance of the cruel water around him. Would she die as he had, trapped by this hideous, useless beast of a machine? Dulcey had been squeezing her eyes shut tightly to keep herself from seeing the horrifying visions that had been described by her grandfather. *I'm wasting precious time!* She forced her eyes open and found herself staring into the face of a huge black catfish with enormous rubbery whiskers, rushing toward her mask. Her startled movement scared him back into the depths of the lake and plunged the piece of metal more deeply into her neck. She knew her body would soon be in shock. With all her strength she pushed down and away from the metal. Its brittle grip broke like a frozen branch in a snowstorm, and Dulcey willed herself into a slow ascent toward the surface.

The rusty metal had cut a gash of several inches in her suit, and her body was rapidly chilling in the frigid water. She vaguely remembered that she needed to move slowly to the surface to allow her body time to adjust to the varying pressures. Blood trailed from the deep gash in her neck like tendrils of smoke from a new fire. She felt her strength seeping away and her mind becoming fuzzy. *Maybe I can get to my car phone,* she thought crazily. She fumbled for a moment with her dive belt as if her phone were clipped to it. *Was the chief's number one or two?* She remembered Dmitri was six. Then the thought came to her that Matt had her car phone. I hope Matt will call me soon. But . . . Dulcey stopped to squeeze her thoughts back into reality but her disjointed thinking persisted. *Maybe Dmitri should call me instead of Matt since he would know what to do.* Her thoughts tumbled in disarray like clothes in a dryer; she tried to grab them and make sense of them as they spun away from her.

Dulcey came to with a start. She realized she must have been unconscious for a while. How long? How much oxygen was left in her tank? She couldn't remember how to check the levels. When she became more fully awake, she saw her lighted depth gauge. *Still thirty feet down. I must have been moving laterally instead of vertically!* With great concentration, Dulcey moved her feet back and forth. After several seconds, she saw some sort of light just above her in the water. *Liam's light* she thought. When she became aware again, she realized she was near the surface of the water. Jesus Christ glowed softly above her through the last few feet of silt-heavy water. He and His giant lamb seemed to be encouraging her, waiting for her.

As she broke the surface of the water, Jesus reminded her to breathe slowly through her regulator. *Don't gasp . . . just breathe . . . don't gasp . . . just breathe.* For several minutes, Dulcey floated on her back, gazing at Christ. The lamb's expression seemed to be one of grateful relief. She breathed the oxygen from her tank slowly until her mind cleared. Then she remembered her neck wound and Matt waiting for her at the dock.

Still on her back, Dulcey moved her flippers slowly up and down, moving silently and painfully toward the dock. She kept the glowing

Jesus in front of her so she would head in the right direction. As she felt the cold shadow of the dock, Dulcey reached her hand out. But instead of something solid, she found herself touching something, *someone*, in the water. As soon as she had some ground under her, Dulcey stood and saw a form floating facedown in the water, sandy blond hair floating lazily around its immersed head. It occurred to her that Matt had seen her coming and was getting back at her for worrying him. But it was no time for jokes. She knew dangerous bacteria were coursing through her body from the corroded metal that had torn her flesh.

"Get up," she called weakly. "It's not funny, Matt. I got hurt down there . . . help me, Matt." Dulcey felt a mixture of fury and frustration when the form did not move. "Stop it. I need you!" she cried in a stronger voice.

"Dulcey?" Matt's voice came from the shore. "Who're you talkin' to?" He jumped in and sloshed toward her in the dark water by the dock. Together, they turned the figure over and stared into the bleached and bloated face of a human being. Its blue eyes were filmed over like poached eggs, the mouth open and contorted, tongue protruding like a sea creature from its shell. One end of a yellow nylon rope was tied to his ankle, the other end trailed into the water.

Matt screamed in a strange strangled voice. Dulcey, close to shock already, let out a long wailing moan, her mind blurry and out of control again. She took a few steps toward shore and let the blackness engulf her completely. Matt grabbed her and noticed the blood on her neck. Quickly, he unstrapped her oxygen tank and dragged her off the beach so she could lie on her stomach on the grassy lawn. He leaned down to make sure she was breathing and then scrambled toward Dulcey's car. Frantically, he felt along the dash for the car phone: turn signal, keys in the ignition, radio knobs—car phone. With trembling hands, Matt held the phone toward the overhead light to see the numbers. He punched the speed-dial button and the number two. Immediately, he reached the police station.

CHAPTER 5

Hannah and Gabe waited around the corner from the police station until Chief Farley went back inside. Then they got into the Taurus parked behind the station in the darkness. "Get in, Superman. Time for bed—for *real* this time," Hannah growled.

"Could we stop for Doritos, Han?" asked Gabe grumpily as he climbed into the passenger side of the car. As Hannah pulled onto the road, Gabe pulled out some change from his pocket, and four twenty-dollar bills spilled out onto the seat. Since Hannah was the only one entrusted with the grocery money, she was startled at the amount of money Gabe had. He glanced up at his sister as he stuffed the twenties back into his pocket. "Been savin' my money," he said cheerfully as he turned toward the window to avoid her eyes.

"From what job, Gabe?"

"I sold some of my old . . . stuff."

"What old stuff?" Hannah said, glaring at the back of his head, daring him to face her and lie to her.

"You know—uhhhh—that old bike with the high handlebars and the banana seat? I outgrew that bike years ago," he said, still looking out his window. "I rode it into town and sold it to some college guy."

"And just which college guy bought that old rusted bike from you—for eighty dollars?"

"I don't know him. I think he said he was a senior. He bought it for his kid brother back home." Gabe pointed at the 7-Eleven, the last store on Quarry Street. Beyond it, the downtown area faded into residences, then an empty field and the beginning of the woods near the covered bridge. "Come on, Hannah, stop at the store. I didn't eat dinner tonight."

Hannah veered sharply into the parking lot of the 7-Eleven more because she needed to stop the car than because she wanted to give in to Gabe. While Gabe was in the store, Hannah sat there, gripping the steering wheel, her foot still jammed fiercely against the brake pedal, the muscles in her legs shaking, feeling like worn-out elastic. As she sat there waiting for him, Hannah fought off her instinct that her brother was headed for deep trouble if he wasn't already drowning in it.

Gabe came back with his food, and Hannah drove home carefully; confusion and fear wadded up in her chest. An eery white mist had come up from the lake as it often did on nights like these. It seemed to hover over the water under the bridge and shroud them as they drove up the road on Bennigan's Bluff. Hannah looked over the lake to see if she could see lights—Liam's light. Years later, Hannah would remember the mist as a kind of omen of what was to come. Far below her, she could hear several screaming sirens. They made her worry more fervently for the little brother who was growing beyond her reach in a town that had already grown beyond her comfort level.

Gabe was sleepy again, subdued by a few bites of his Doritos and a bottle of chocolate Yoohoo. As Hannah reached the flat top of the Bluff, she passed Fiona Bennigan's once-magnificent Victorian home; its grounds occupied all the land on the right side of the road and down the back side of the Bluff for a mile by the river. The church and the other three hillside homes, including her own, were perched on the other side of the road, each with a breathtaking view of the lake and the town below.

Hannah slowed down as she saw a figure emerge from the shadows at the edge of the Bennigan property. Gabe saw him too and rolled down the window. "Hey, Ian, looking for me?"

Instead of answering, Ian scrambled up on the hood of the Taurus, then jumped onto its roof. Shifting his weight from side to side, he rocked the car violently throwing Hannah and Gabe alternately against the doors and each other. Then he stepped into the middle of the roof and his foot made a deep indentation in its thin metal. Hannah threw the car into a forward gear and pressed briefly on the accelerator. Ian lost his balance, but landed neatly on his feet beside the driver-side window.

"Driving without a license are we, Miss Dennison? What will Daddy say when he gets home?" Ian mocked, leaning into her window, "Is he out tending the sheep of the world again while his own darling lambs are home all by themselves?" He reached through the window and grabbed her braid, twisting it around his wrist and his stubby fingers, "I could keep you company in your big dark, *lonely* house, Hannah. Would you like that?"

Hannah pulled her hair out of his hands, recoiling from the face that filled her window. "You're a maniac, Ian. You ought to be locked up!" Hannah said angrily, restraining herself from pulling the car forward and running over Ian's feet. Ian had gone to Griggsberg High with Hannah and Gabe until he had dropped out as soon as the law allowed him to leave school. Fiona claimed she was home schooling all three of her kids, but everyone in town regarded them more as hermits than as home schoolers.

Hannah felt complete disgust for the boy who was her age and had been her neighbor for the past five years. "I wouldn't have to drive if my little brother hadn't been picked up in town by the police tonight. And what are you doing out here in the middle of the night unless you're up to no good? Move, so we can get home to *our* side of the hill."

"Oh, so now it's *your* hill, huh?" Ian grinned widely enough so Hannah would notice the tongue ring he had recently installed. He rubbed the metal stud against his teeth making a clicking sound. His foul breath made Hannah draw back further in disgust. The single streetlight farther up the hill illuminated a tattoo on his forearm: a drawing of an automatic rifle under the words Sinn Fein. Hannah had no idea what the words meant.

There were lots of things Hannah loved about living on Bennigan's Bluff, but having Ian as a neighbor just about negated them all. "You're such total bad news, Ian! I hate you. I hate what you're doing to my brother. You're a sorry excuse for a human being." Hannah felt bound by the steering wheel, cramped by the car. She wanted to spit her words directly into the boy's face. Jerking the car off the road and parking badly in front of her house, Hannah threw open the car door and met up with Ian in the middle of the road.

"You gonna tap dance on my face and hurt me, big sister?" Ian sneered, pointing to the tiny black dance slippers on her feet, thrusting his chest toward her as if he were preparing to fight Hannah, who was several inches shorter and just about half his weight. Gabe sat transfixed by the scene, cowering in the car.

Hannah stood her ground wishing she had worn her heavy Doc Martens so she could kick Ian and cause him some pain. "No, I'm going to yank that stupid tongue ring out of your mouth and let you bleed to death!" She crouched and ran at him, hitting him in the stomach, pushing him off balance. "You're like some kind of disease—and you're infecting my brother!"

"Everyone in town thinks you're so perfect," Ian retorted, unharmed. "If anyone lived across the street from you like I do, they'd know how fake that little act of yours is. You act so high and mighty. And you can't stand *anyone* who's the slightest bit different from you. You're the one who is sick and disgusting, Hannah. You're worse than that because you *pretend* to be so perfect!"

Hannah went for him again but gasped and backed away as someone leaped out of the darkness, punching Ian hard in the stomach, sending him skidding flat onto his back on the asphalt and loose stones in the road. It was Jared Spencer.

"Jared! Be careful. He carries a knife!" Hannah screamed, worried for her childhood friend.

Jared stood over Ian now, his bare feet placed vice-like on either side of Ian's head. Though Jared was all business, he looked vulnerable, clad only in the plaid boxer shorts he had worn to bed. "You gonna fight a woman, Ian? Is that how low you've gone?" Jared tightened his foothold on Ian's head, breathing hard, allowing sweat to drip into the miserable boy's face below him. "You gonna knife one of us? Or shall we just call Chief Farley and have him take care of you?"

Jared eventually allowed the boy to sit upright. Ian rubbed his temples and spat out some gravel, "I'm going to kick you off my land—all of you. You think you're better than everybody else!" He got up unsteadily and faced Hannah, his eyes fierce, wild, and dark as a Missouri tornado. "You too, Gabe," he yelled toward the car. "Shall I tell your sister what you've been up to lately?"

Gabe who had been trying to push the roof back into shape from inside the car, opened the car door and headed for home.

"Well?" Hannah called after Gabe, fear punching at her heart.

"You want to tell me now—or later? Or maybe everyone in town already knows and I'm the only one who doesn't. Is that it, Gabe?"

"Let's go home, Hannah," Gabe begged. "The neighbors are hanging out of the windows for crying out loud." He made his way steadily toward their front porch.

Jared moved toward Ian again, "You've done enough damage for one night, Ian. I think you'd better be heading home."

Ian looked beyond the three of them and saw Dan Spencer walking toward them. Dan was a bishop in the Mormon Church. The people in his church came from several small towns in the area just east of Kansas City. Everyone knew him as a strong man with certain unalterable ideas about life. Just the fact that he had seven kids and another on the way gave him a certain unquestioned credibility. Ian turned and sprinted toward his house, tossing a torrent of angry words over his shoulder as he ran.

Hannah composed herself, looking up at Jared's father, "Thanks, Dan. We had a little run in with Ian. Jared helped us out."

"Well, I was awake already. There's something going on down at the lake. Half the town is down there on the beach."

Grateful for the distraction of someone else's trouble, Hannah kept quiet about where she had been. Dan would find out about Gabe's run-in with the law soon enough from his sister, Darlene, the dispatcher at the station.

"Yeah, I've been trying to get hold of Darlene to find out what's happening at the lake." Dan turned away from them, pressing his portable phone to his ear. The phone worked as long as he was within thirty feet of his house. Darlene had put him on hold while she was dispatching the vehicles and officers and notifying the proper authorities about the incident at the lake.

Hannah followed Gabe, hoping Dan hadn't noticed that she had been driving. She would park the car in the garage before her folks got home from Dallas.

"I'm going to see that Gabe here gets into bed," Hannah said pointedly to Jared. "I may want to see what's going on a little later." She made a face and motioned towards the lake with her head to let Jared know he should meet her at the fort.

Hannah escorted Gabe authoritatively upstairs to his bedroom. He was emptying the last of his Doritos directly from the bag into his mouth. She didn't want to have to deal with him any more tonight. She was exhausted by the last few hours, her legs ached, and she wanted to talk to Jared without Gabe around.

After depositing him safely in his room, Hannah was relieved to see her brother flop on his bed, ready to give it up for the night. "Get some sleep. We'll talk tomorrow and you'd better come clean with me, buddy, because I am totally angry with you. I don't know where you got that money, but it can't be from anything good. I just can't keep covering for you and bailing you out all the time. The Chief will probably see Dad tomorrow about filing those papers. You're going to have a police record if you don't stop running around at night. Now go to sleep. And stay there!" Hannah closed his door firmly behind her.

Gabe thought for a moment in the darkness, smiling to himself, feeling fairly certain that Hannah would continue to protect him as she always had. After a few minutes, he crumpled the empty Doritos bag and tossed it on the floor, breathed out a long sigh, and fell soundly asleep. He'd had a busy night.

CHAPTER 6

Hannah raced downstairs, grabbed the binoculars from the hook by the back door and headed toward the fort. The little incident in the road with Ian, and the sirens at the lake had awakened both the Spencer family and the Silvermans down the hill. Marty and Esther Silverman stood at their back fence shining flashlights and speaking to JoLyn Spencer in low voices.

The expanse of water easily transmitted the sounds of students and residents clamoring around the officers who were examining a body that lay on the beach by the dock. Each new arrival on the scene was given a brief chance to identify the body lying under a thin foil blanket that had been placed over him by the police.

"Hannah, what's going on?" called Jared from the rope path above the fort. Jared's father, who had built the church and the new homes on Bennigan's Bluff, had supervised the construction of the fort from scraps of building materials left over from the construction surrounding them. The fort's structure had been reinforced over the years until it had finally met with the grudging approval of the mothers on Bennigan's Bluff. Hannah and Gabe had gotten in on the building five years before when they had moved into the new church parsonage next to the church. Over the years, they helped clear paths, string ropes, haul lumber, and hammer nails to create "Fort Bennigan." Though their mothers gave only reluctant praise for it because of their uncanny ability to foresee all of its possible dangers, the fort was treasured by the children who had built it.

As Jared made his way down the familiar path holding onto the rope railings, someone else called to them from Hannah's backyard. Jesse Candella, the church custodian who lived above the church offices for part of the week was peering down at them, waving to Hannah and Jared.

"Hey, Jesse!" Hannah called, feeling some comfort that he was there. She knew he would want to investigate the lake accident in case something was threatening his church. Jesse, now in his late twenties, had been born with Down's syndrome. In Hannah's mind, Jesse was as much a part of the Church on the Hill as the giant stained glass Jesus.

"Does Pastor Dennison know about the dead man?" asked Jesse who was beginning to preen in his largely untested role as guardian of the church.

"Dad's still in Dallas, Jesse. He'll know soon enough when he gets home tomorrow." Hannah hid her amusement at Jesse's total devotion to her father, a quality she herself had been steadily losing over the years since they had moved to the hill.

Even before the move, when the church was still plain old Griggsberg Community Christian Church housed in the little structure downtown, Jesse had been essential to the rhythms and the cycles of her world. To Hannah, Jesse was the true part of the church, set apart from its trends and fads, a touchstone against which she judged the rest of it. He had been trained over the years by his mother, Mary Louise, and Hannah's father to keep a watchful eye over the church grounds. He made sure the doors were locked, and reported any unusual occurrences to the pastor or to the police.

When the new church was built, Jesse had been given his own room right over the sanctuary's stained glass windows, where he lived with his big, yellow cat Cordelia. His apartment had its own set of panoramic windows overlooking the town below. Oddly, no one had quite understood the extent of Jesse's fear of heights and Mary Louise had sewed yards and yards of white sheets together to completely cover the bank of windows in Jesse's room.

Although it had taken him awhile to adjust to his room with the wasted view, Jesse cherished the microwave oven, radio, and combination TV/VCR that were now his. These were the symbols of adulthood. Being trusted with any of these on his own had taken him weeks of negotiation with his cautious mother. She feared that Jesse might put metal in the microwave or burn himself with hot liquid. Almost equally frightening were the television and radio and all the terrible images and ideas that she would no longer be able to censor or explain for him. In the end, Jesse had won his symbols of freedom. Mary Louise knew she had trained Jesse all his life to become independent, that she needed to allow him the "dignity of risk" as she put it. He should be allowed to hear powerful and sometimes frightening ideas and to do things on his own even if he made a mistake—even a very serious one.

"Hannah, should we call your dad now and get ready for a funeral?" Jesse asked, eager to be called into action.

"Not yet, Jess. We don't know whose church he belongs to. Maybe he's Catholic, and Father Thomas will need to bury him instead of us; or maybe he's Jewish, and the rabbi at the synagogue in Kansas City will want to have his funeral."

Although Jesse didn't know what a rabbi was, he knew Father Thomas from the interfaith meetings. Still, he seemed reluctant to pass up this rare opportunity to be involved in such a dramatic event. "Pastor Dennison should know—in case he's ours, Hannah. Will you call him in Dallas? Now, Hannah?" he insisted sweetly.

"Of course," Hannah fibbed to put Jesse's mind at ease. She was touched by his total faith in her father and in the role of the church; all of life could be organized and ordered within its rituals and observances. Hannah remembered that she had once felt that way too.

"Why don't you go on back to your apartment? I'll have Dad make a full report to you tomorrow," Hannah said in a low voice so that Jared would not overhear her giving Jesse direction.

Used to being the one who reported unusual situations, Jesse was encouraged and proud that he was soon to have someone report to *him*. He could relax until he was informed whose church the man belonged to. Besides, being near the fort made him uncomfortable, and he was anxious to return to level ground. After bestowing upon Hannah one of his trademark bear hugs, Jesse crab-crawled back up the few feet of steep path.

Hannah looked down through the binoculars at the scene below, trying to get a fix on what was happening. Several police cruisers were parked on the sandy beach that extended from the summer homes to the college. Hannah began to think about how the lake had changed her town. Being only five years old at the time, she didn't remember much about the flood, but she knew that her whole life had been different after the flood.

The *in-flooding*, as everyone referred to it, remained an unsolved mystery. At first, Fiona Bennigan had fought the town fiercely to reopen the investigation that had proclaimed the in-flooding an accident. As she watched rising property values around the new lake and the rapid development of the dusty quarry town into a lush summer resort, Fiona had become convinced that the quarry flood was no accident. She bitterly refused to accept that the lake had been created by an accident of nature and by Ed Lawton's poor geological research. For nearly a year, Ed had stayed in Griggsberg and tried to help Fiona with her campaign. But with a family to support, Ed had eventually found work at a mine in Elko, Nevada, leaving Fiona alone with her accusations.

Even before the in-flooding, Fiona and Liam, their three young children, and several other aging Bennigan relatives had lived a fairly self-sufficient life on the barren hill above the quarry. In winter, they were occasionally cut off from the town because of the treacherously icy, steep roads up the hill, and the deep snows that sometimes lasted for several weeks. They had learned to store food, use fuel-powered generators, and cook and heat with propane stoves, safely ensconced in their eighty-year-old, fifteen-room mansion on the quarry hill.

Because the quarry had been the major source of employment along with the surrounding farms in Griggsberg, the in-flooding of Bennigan's Quarry had changed the life of nearly everyone in town from that day on. Many people moved away, unable to support themselves. For others, life improved greatly as they established new businesses or sold land that had rapidly risen in value.

The citizens and elected officials of Griggsberg had learned to avoid Fiona, and regarded her as unstable, a loose cannon, a wealthy tyrant, a bitter ingredient in their new fortuitous circumstances. After the unemployed and unemployable had moved away from town, the only people who continued to suffer in the prosperous town of Griggsberg were the widow, Fiona, and her three children.

* * *

The fort offered the best view of the scene at the lake below. Hannah stood with Jared, surveying the scene. The rest of the Spencers were making their way down the slope to the fort. Jared helped his mother, JoLyn, down the rope path to the platform of the fort. She was seven months pregnant with her eighth child. Dan followed her with Jared's three little sisters in tow—first Elissa, then the twins, Laura and Leah, who were dragging their bed quilts behind them. Alyson, eleven, wore her huge bunny slippers. She and a slightly younger brother, Eric, had their arms full of snacks hastily grabbed from the kitchen pantry. They had assigned themselves the job of passing out potato chips, Oreos, and juice boxes to the troops. It was just like the fourth of July when the Bennigan's Bluff neighbors gathered each year at the fort to watch the fireworks.

"Darlene tells me the man in the lake is probably not from around here," announced Dan, covering the mouthpiece of the portable phone. "Farley's pretty sure he worked on the west side of Kansas City. They found a paycheck from a catering company in his wallet. He was still dressed in a uniform, so he must have come out here to the lake after work. Probably been in the lake for quite a while by the looks of him. The police have to wait till tomorrow morning to track down the catering firm owners."

The chief had told Darlene he hadn't seen this much community spirit in years. College students wearing bathrobes and carrying flashlights were milling around the scene. Residents who lived in summer homes near the lake were banding together in that strangely warm survivor's comradery that happens at house fires and car accidents. Perfect strangers were sharing blankets and hugging each other as they speculated about the dead man in the lake.

According to Darlene, Dulcey Martinez had found the body. She had been taken to the little community hospital for stitches and treatment for shock. Although she had lost quite a lot of blood, she was expected to pull through just fine. Matt Moore, a student at the college, had been with Dulcey. He had told the paramedics it had been the worst date of his life.

CHAPTER 7

As Chief Farley examined the dead body on the beach, he knew he was out of his league. Shoplifting, drunken fights at the town's single bar, and an occasional college prank were his forte. People didn't usually die mysteriously in Griggsberg. There had been a few farm accidents but the metal machinery that occasionally mauled, maimed, or murdered its owners never fled but stood there guiltily, often with plenty of evidence trapped in its teeth.

He turned to Officer York, who had recently transferred from a Kansas City police department. "York, what do you make of the cause of death? There haven't been any boating accidents and he obviously wasn't going for a swim in that waiter's uniform."

York, who had dealt with plenty of crime in Kansas City and had brought his family to Griggsberg to get away from it, was already one step ahead. He motioned to the Chief to kneel with him near the man's head, and spoke in confidential tones, "Chief, this is no accidental drowning, and it's no suicide."

Farley was anxious to shield the citizens of Griggsberg from York's disturbing speculation. He stood, hitching his holster belt authoritatively and addressed the gathering crowd, "People, we need to establish a police barricade here. We ask that you step back about fifteen feet so that our officers can investigate this unfortunate . . . accident. We do not think this is a local man, folks. From a paycheck in his wallet, we know this man's name is Reggie Showalter. He worked on the west side of Kansas City, so it's unlikely that he's from here." After his pronouncement, Farley firmly guided several onlookers away from the hideously bloated body. They seemed reluctant to be removed from the strangely titillating scene.

York began roping off the area with plastic police tape. He had decided that this was now a crime scene and wanted to protect whatever evidence might have washed up with the body. The town's entire fleet of four squad cars and the remaining ambulance that was treating Matt for shock were circled around the body like a covered wagon train expecting an attack. Blue and red lights flashed, doors hung open, and radios crackled. Permanent residents, summer visitors, and college kids spoke in hushed tones on the perimeter of the scene. It was the most exciting thing that had ever happened in Griggsberg.

York knelt again by the dead man's head. He flipped back the foil blanket revealing the ghastly blue, inhuman face. York removed a wrinkled pair of latex gloves from a leather pouch on his belt, the same pair that the guys at the station always ribbed him about. Griggsberg officers were rarely required to handle body fluids. York gently turned the man's face to the side so the chief could see the blackened bruise that encircled his neck. "Straight-line ligature," York said, expecting the words to trigger recognition in Chief Farley's face. When they did not, York explained further, "He didn't hang himself, Chief. If he had, this bruise line would be slanted up toward the nape of his neck. This guy was throttled . . . strangled by someone."

Farley recoiled at the thought of the man's life draining out of him at the hands of a killer. Having grown up in this town, the chief had never become hardened to death and its effects on the living. He had never seen anything like this.

This murder had occurred on his watch, while he was responsible for the safety of Griggsberg. Had he gotten too complacent lately? Had he provided the growing town with the police coverage it needed? The chief pushed his administrative worries out of his mind and followed York toward the man's feet. Lifting the foil blanket again, and hiking up a soggy pant leg, York pointed at a long yellow nylon rope knotted around the man's right ankle.

"My guess is that he was tied to a heavy object which would now be at the bottom of Lake Shiloh. You know, like a rock or a cement block or something. These slippery nylon boating ropes don't hold a good knot. I think it worked itself loose, which is why we got to meet the guy sooner than his killer would have liked."

Farley felt dazed and rocked back on his heels trying to keep his emotions hidden from the onlookers. "How long do you suppose he was down there?"

"Well, if this had occurred in the winter, that body, even untied, could have stayed on the bottom quite awhile because the gases would take longer to expand enough to float the body. But during the warm summer, the body would bloat right away and would only stay down if it were weighted by something. His body's pretty tore up though, like fish had been nibbling it . . . it was probably down there a few months by the looks of him."

Farley was glad that York's former precinct had included a stretch of the muddy Missouri River. He knew this wasn't the first floater or the first homicide victim York had examined, and Farley was grateful for the new officer's knowledge. Farley straightened and surveyed the summer homes. The people who lived near the lake were good people, mostly Protestants. Everyone knew Protestants were some of the most low profile, unobjectionable Christians in the world. Fine upstanding people, community leaders, and respectable citizens. They were bankers, businessmen, and teachers who had small, sensible-sized families . . . they were the very definition of average Americans.

Farley wondered if the murderer lived right there among them, protected by a cloak of apparent decency.

* * *

Dan looked at his dozing family and figured it would be easier to let them sleep rather than rousing them to return to their beds. Just then he caught sight of Fiona Bennigan making her way to the Fort. Elissa Spencer saw her too. The little girl whimpered, ducking her head down below JoLyn's shoulder, sniffling and pointing at Fiona.

"So! I knew it! Almost ten years to the day. Trouble in the quarry. More trouble in the quarry . . ." Fiona Bennigan's strident voice could be heard before the rest of the family had turned to look at her. Fiona made her way toward them, holding the rope with one hand, and pressing a citizen's band radio to her ear. Fiona often seemed to forget that the Bluff was no longer her own. She had become a dreaded guest in the homes that had grown up around hers.

Dan had originally built the platform of the fort not as a child's playhouse, but to give Fiona a place to grieve for her dead husband. Several times, in the middle of the night, Fiona had stood in their backyard singing the melancholy Irish ballad "Danny Boy" in full voice, her arms outstretched, her tune carrying easily over the water to the town below. JoLyn would usually be the one to lead Fiona home to her own bed and her worried children.

Dan had finally realized that his family's newly built home was preventing Fiona from viewing the quarry lake from her own property. And so he had built a simple, sturdy platform for her so she could grieve for Liam as close to the lake as possible. Over the years, Fiona needed the platform less, and the neighbor children saw the structure high above the lake as the first stage of a hillside fairy-tale fortress. At the insistence of the childrens' mothers, it had first acquired a strong wall with a Plexiglas window. Later, a partial roof of corrugated tin, a tiny picnic table, and a series of roped paths emerged. Dan had seen the fort as a way not only to spend time with his children, but also to teach them the basics of his builder's craft. Jared and his two brothers were expected to work in their father's construction business someday, and Fort Bennigan was their training ground.

Tonight, the fort had again become Fiona's mourning place. "So, the quarry has taken another one!" she declared again, as much to herself as to the group. She squared her thin shoulders, clutching the front of her tattered, terry-cloth bathrobe; "I have had murder follow me from Ireland. Murder *belongs* in Ireland where there is something worth fighting for. There's not even a good reason for it in this country!" A breeze briefly lifted lank wisps of her strawberry blonde hair. She caressed the smooth, reddened skin on her cheek. A petrol bomb thrown at her by Protestants had scarred her face like the residue of an angry slap. Having fought for Ireland, her love for it had grown fierce and intractable. She would never let the Prods have it— even now, in her mind, she still fought its wars. She and her Catholic friends had lived on Falls Road. Her Protestant enemies had lived a few blocks away on Shankill Road. Hundreds of years of hatred had simmered between the warring sides. Fiona had refused to have her scar removed. Though few people could see the resemblance, she claimed it was the shape of Ireland and she would wear it proudly in honor of her troubled homeland. JoLyn and Dan knew that tonight, Bennigan's Bluff was once again Falls Road in West Belfast: Fiona was tense, alert and ready to identify the enemy.

"Come sit with us a bit, Fiona," said JoLyn warmly as she placed Elissa between the twins and went to stand near the trembling woman. Fiona and JoLyn were about the same age but Fiona had aged less gracefully through her years of unrelenting hatred and suspicion.

"No, JoLyn. I won't be resting tonight. Liam's ghost is calling from his watery grave! Look how it's lit up tonight . . ."

"Just the lights from the police cars," JoLyn reassured her. "Someone drowned in the lake."

Fiona moaned and leaned into JoLyn for support. "I've been expecting it. I knew something was going to happen and this must be it. You'll see!" Fiona broke from JoLyn's embrace and went to stand by the edge of the fort. "Liam wants vengeance. Liam and I will never let this town forget what they did. My husband died trying to save his quarry from the greedy, evil people of this town. There was no gun— or petrol bomb—but he was just as good as murdered!"

JoLyn shushed her children who were frightened by Fiona's sudden fury. Fiona stretched out her arms as if the townspeople who were tending to the dead man had gathered below to hear her haunting declaration. Then she paused for a moment, as if listening to a faraway voice. "He's asking me to try again, JoLyn. I'm going to see that he gets justice at last so that he can rest."

Fiona made her way back up the path, never really having acknowledged any of them. Dan watched her as she trudged back to her once magnificent house high on the Bluff.

Everyone was silent for a moment, considering the possible link between the body in the lake and the well-known history of Liam's terrible drowning.

"It really has been ten years, Dan," said JoLyn, rising awkwardly to her feet, adjusting her chenille robe over her pregnant belly, slipping her small hand into her husband's larger one for comfort. "We need to do something for Fiona. She's bound to be grieving for Liam right now—especially with this drowning. We need to make sure she doesn't get worse because of this."

Dan had been the one to console Fiona in those early days of her wailing fury. She had lapsed for a time into a demonic reverie of her childhood in Ireland. She had lost both parents in an act of terrorism in Belfast during "the troubles," as the Irish called them. The scarred young woman had made her way to America's heartland. She met Liam while working as a waitress and a singer of sad ballads in an Irish pub in the old Westport district of Kansas City.

Liam's parents had come to Griggsberg during the same time to protect their youngest son from the horrors of Belfast life. Liam's two older brothers had been killed by British agents for their role in an Irish Republican Army attack on a city bus. Sick of the killing and worried he would lose his one remaining son, Liam's father had brought Liam and his wife to the Missouri quarry owned by his aging uncle, Seamus Bennigan. No one with the name of Bennigan could ever be safe in Ireland. Over the years, Fiona had buried them all. At last she was alone with her three children, trying to live with her own torn-apart heart.

In Fiona's experience, death, maiming and murder had been perpetrated in the name of religion. Dan had a hard time convincing her to allow Craig Dennison to build his church on the Bluff. As for the homes, Fiona had requested that the architecture be similar to the historic homes in Griggsberg and her own home. Dan had designed the homes to reflect Victorian elegance with a dash of Charleston charm.

Ian, Charlie, and Maura Bennigan had all the material possessions imaginable. And yet all three children had become voluntary outcasts in an empathic embrace of their mother's fears. They had grown up with the conviction that their father had been killed so a lake could be created. The new Griggsberg had been built on the very dirt and water of Liam's shameful grave.

Darlene came on Dan's phone again, "Dan? Are the Dennison kids okay? They're home aren't they? Chief just radioed in and wanted me to make sure they made it home from the station tonight. Gabey was in here earlier. We're all kind of worried about him. The Dennisons are out of town again. They have no clue what he's into, and Hannah seems to shield him."

Dan covered the receiver and asked Hannah if Gabe was home in bed.

"He's home. He just had a little adventure in town tonight, that's all," said Hannah protectively.

"Safe and sound, Darlene."

"Gotta go, Dan. More calls. It's a small town, you know—everyone wants to be in on this. It probably won't even make the last page of the *Kansas City Star*. They've got much more exciting crimes than we do!"

"That's why we all live here, don't forget, Sis."

A safe place to raise a family, Dan thought to himself. *Remember?*

CHAPTER 8

Hannah awoke sometime before six o-clock. She had fallen asleep against Jared's shoulder. Jared was already awake talking to his father in low tones. The sun began rising and shedding light on the citizens of Griggsberg. The coroner's van had taken the dead man's body off the beach. A few students, perhaps too disturbed to return to their dorms, had formed little groups on the beach, talking, waiting for the comfort of daylight.

Alyson, a motherly little girl, instigated the family's retreat back to the house. She had wisely removed her bunny slippers as she herded the twins up the path to their backyard. Dan wakened his little Elissa who instantly recalled her encounter with Fiona. "Is Miss Bennigan still up there? Don't make me go!" she called out in sleepy fright. Dan swung her onto his broad back and JoLyn picked up the quilts and the remains of the snacks. Jared steered his pregnant mother safely up the path, stooping to pick up anything she dropped on the way.

Hannah too began to make her way home, wishing she could cuddle into a bed full of brothers and sisters, feeling immensely unsettled because she had not been able to talk to sensible old Jared about her troubles with Gabe. The commotion caused by the dead man in the lake had overshadowed Gabe's problems for now.

Jared returned to Hannah after putting his mother on safe ground. He put his arm around her waist and hoisted her easily up the cliff. Hannah noticed that Jared's strong forearm felt comforting to her, and for a moment understood why couples instinctively touch each other during times of stress.

Although he had hinted that he was willing to listen, Hannah was reluctant to fully explain Gabe's problem and the incident with

Ian in the road. She knew her father would feel exposed and vulnerable if the Spencers knew about Gabe's problems before he did. Out of respect, and an odd sense of competition, Hannah never spoke of her family's problems around Dan.

"Thanks again for being there when Ian threatened me tonight." Hannah bit her lip, wondering how much to tell Jared. "This thing with Gabe is really big. If I find out exactly what's going on, I'll have to deal with it myself. Mom and Dad just seem lost to us right now. They're just out of it. They have so much on their minds lately," Hannah said, sadness and fatigue in her voice.

"Do you realize how little sense that makes to me? It makes me furious that your folks put just about everything in their lives above you and Gabe. They have no idea what's important in life!" Jared said angrily.

"What's important? You think pastoring a church of fifteen hundred people is not *important*? How about running the most well-known children's choir in the country? And my mother's music camp is going to put this town on the map! My parents travel all over the country because they get *hundreds* of speaking and singing invitations every year. They have an important ministry!"

Even as she spoke, Hannah could see that Jared was not the least impressed with her defense of her parents, so she hit a little lower. "If my Mother had seven—make that eight—kids, she'd be home every day doing twenty loads of laundry and cooking up a storm too. My mother just used a little restraint in childbearing, that's all. Your mom has no choices, Jared. At least my mother has a life!"

Jared reeled and Hannah was instantly regretful she had let loose those words. He was silent for a long time, his eyes blazing. "You haven't got a clue, Hannah. You are such a victim in all this, you can't even see how you're being used. How Gabe is so . . . lost! How he's just screaming for help . . . a little parental involvement!" Jared's words hit Hannah like fists. Then he softened his voice. "I think that if Gabe is having trouble, it should be your parents' job to find out what it is and to help him get through this."

Hannah couldn't help but hear the maddening certainty in Jared's voice. Confused, still trying to convince him that her life made sense, Hannah looked steadily into Jared's face. "Gabe is *my* responsibility. He's my *only* responsibility. It's the least I can do to help my mother and father." She turned and began ascending the steep hill toward her home to escape Jared's absurd ideas about how families should operate. It was so archaic to think that her mother and father should give up their ministry to thousands of souls because of two children.

"You're dead wrong, Hannah. Gabe's only three years younger than you are. He needs his folks—not you!" Jared flung this last comment at her back as she closed the wrought iron gate of her backyard.

Memories of simpler times flooded Hannah's mind. She recalled being delighted with the happy chaos and constant commotion of the Spencer home. JoLyn gave after-school piano lessons, and the discordant but determined sounds of amateur musicians had often wafted over the fence. The Dennisons had suffered the bad music good-naturedly along with the Spencers for the sake of future art. Hannah had been a frequent guest at meals and family outings. She and Jared had spent endless hours talking as they helped build the fort on the side of the Bluff. After it was completed, they had spent more hours at the fort, gazing over the town, talking about life and their separate places in the scheme of it.

Dan appeared at the back gate. "Jared, better come in for breakfast, son. We've still got a good deal of work to do before school starts in a few days. We need to start in about an hour. You okay, Hannah? When will your folks be home?"

"They'll be home at noon today, Dan," she said, quieting in the warmth of his concern, touched by his protectiveness. As Jared and Dan walked toward their house, Hannah called out over her fence, "Hey guys, how 'bout I grab my sleeping bag and come sleep at your house like I used to?" Jared and Dan smiled, but neither answered. Hannah knew her innocent closeness to Jared had come to an end.

As she crawled into her bed at about six-thirty that morning, Hannah reviewed the events of the night. She thought about Jared and his straightforward sense of his life's direction. At sixteen, Jared was becoming an extraordinarily self-confident young man. His summer of construction work had muscled his body and contoured his face in ways that were strangely pleasing to her. Jared was working hard every day during the summer as his older brother, Neil, had done to save up money to go on a mission. Neil had been in Argentina for the past year and would not return home for another year. *Oh, Jared!* she thought. *Why did you have to be born a Mormon!* When he turned nineteen, Jared would leave her for two years. After he returned, he would leave her forever. He had always told her it would happen. He had been warning her—and perhaps himself—not to fall in love.

In Hannah's mind, it was the mission, not the church that seemed destined to steal Jared from her. She could never understand why in the world Jared and Neil would spend their own hard-earned money and take off precious time from their teenage years to serve their church—for no salary whatsoever. In her church, *everyone* from Sunday School teachers to window washers was paid. It never occurred to her that someone would serve in her dad's church without being paid. Strange. Dan, who had been in charge of his church as bishop for the past three years wasn't paid either. How could he do what her father did and run his construction firm at the same time?

Hannah was endlessly intrigued by the incredibly busy Spencer family and the few Mormons she knew in town. At the same time, she felt furious at all of them for their old fashioned obsessions with their families—especially the women—the way they denied themselves and gave up everything. Sure, they had great families. *But at what price?* Those great families were largely the work of the mother who sacrificed everything else in her life for the sake of her husband and children. No, sir! Hannah felt relieved that she had options and real choices in her life.

Her one little brother, she realized groggily, was more trouble than the seven Spencer kids combined. As Hannah drifted to sleep, she felt bathed in a stark loneliness. She wished her own father was home right now. But sadly, she recalled that the distance growing between them would have prevented her from getting his comfort anyway.

Life was becoming more confusing than ever just when she needed answers. Her own childhood was gone. Hannah's last thought before sleep was that she wished she could be someone's little girl again.

* * *

Across town in the little community hospital, Dulcey woke with a start. Rosa leaned over from the chair next to Dulcey's bed and caressed her daughter's face. "Bad dream? Your mama's here with you now. Go back to sleep."

"I hate catfish . . ." Dulcey mumbled, turning onto her side.

When she woke again, Matt was standing at the foot of her bed with a huge bouquet of yellow roses. "Hey—Queen-who-went-off-the-Deep-End—how're you doing?"

Dulcey smiled at her co-conspirator. Good old Matt. "Thanks for being there, oh King of the Beach—I guess you saved my life. Dulcey raised up on one good arm, gasping at the pain in her neck. Suddenly the scenes of the night before flooded back into her mind. Lying flat again, wincing, she asked, "Who was the . . . the dead guy?"

Rosa soothed her. "Don't worry right now, Dulcey. You can find out about him another day."

"No one knows so far," answered Matt. "His name was Reggie and he worked as a waiter in K.C." Matt shuddered. "I can't shake it either, Dulcey—his eyes were so milky white—and his tongue . . ."

Rosa interrupted. "Thanks for the flowers, Matthew. Dulcey needs to rest now. Come see her tomorrow, okay, Mijo?"

"Okay . . ." Matt seemed reluctant to go. He plucked a rose bloom from the bouquet and slipped it into Rosa's hair just above her ear. "A rose for a Rosa," he said and walked out the door, closing it quietly behind him.

CHAPTER 9

The airport shuttle swung into the Dennison's driveway just before noon. Hannah had just parked the Taurus in the garage and was in the kitchen pouring a bowl of Quaker Toasted Oats when her parents came up the sidewalk, wheeling their rolling luggage, loaded down with carry-on bags.

"It was fabulous!" said Miranda before the question could be asked. Her long, thick, auburn hair was tied back with a saucy black and white, polka-dotted bow. She tossed her matching luggage into a heap in the front entryway and turned toward Hannah as though she expected applause. Hannah, weary from the crazy night, munched on her Quaker Oats, gazing tiredly at her mother. Miranda Mallory Dennison was a vivacious woman of thirty-seven who could easily pass for much younger.

"Mom, please don't do the cheery thing on me this morning. I was up most of the night and I can't handle it," Hannah mumbled.

Her mother's mouth, carefully colored in Mary Kay's latest shade of Antique Rose, formed itself into an attractive little pout as she faced her daughter. "Well, aren't we grouchy today. Where's Gabe?" she asked, searching for a more pleasant child.

"Gabe's still sacked out from a night of fun and games." Hannah poured another bowl of cereal, glancing up to see where her father had gone.

Miranda wanted the latest updates. "Did Aunt Kate call? How about Louis? Did Ralph Jamison stop by with that keyboard?" Miranda seemed eager to rev up her life to its normal fast-forward speed. Hannah knew it was the only speed at which her mother felt fully alive.

"It's all on the answering machine, Mom."

"Oh, I wish my daddy could have been at that conference, Hannah. I tell you, Christians are getting ready to take over the reins of government. We are all getting so sick of the mess the world is in."

Until he retired eight years ago, Miranda's father had been a theology professor at the old Kansas City campus of MCC. He had died before the college had moved to Griggsberg. For the last few years of his life, he had patiently nursed his wife Layla who was developing Alzheimer's disease. Now in the advanced stages of the memory-slaying disease, Layla still lived at the All Faith Nursing Home in Kansas City. Her daughter Kate visited her every week. Miranda managed to make a painful visit about once a month.

Miranda's beauty was matched only by her talent. She could sing gospel music like a rock star. She had only to open the beautiful mouth that framed her brilliant white teeth and let out a perfectly pitched note to take any crowd or congregation as her willing hostages. Her 1973 Miss Missouri Runner-up smile had cost her father one quarter of his annual salary at the time. Crowds still went wild for Miranda Mallory Dennison. They clapped and screamed as she belted out her joy in Jesus, her disgust for the devil, and her gutsy grip on the gospel train going home to heaven. She was a Christian celebrity and she had very naturally married another popular Christian celebrity, J. Craig Dennison.

Pastor J. Craig Dennison soon wandered back into the kitchen with much less fanfare. He looked tired from his three days of delivering motivational speeches to thousands of young preachers who idolized him. When he wasn't speaking, he had spent hours in a political caucus strategizing with Christian politicians. Craig was a towering six feet four inches tall, with a face made up of intelligent, carefully arranged features softened by a broad boyish grin. At thirty-nine, he was definitely approaching his prime, and he was in demand all over the country.

"Dad, a lot is going on," Hannah reported tersely. "We've got to talk. Some *major* things are happening."

Hannah knew her father was often puzzled by what constituted a "major event" in her life. Raised in the jungles of South America by missionary parents, Craig Dennison had *truly* experienced major events in his life. He had grown up on the outskirts of the most primitive region of Ecuador. Craig's parents would have left him in the United States at a boarding school but decided to sacrifice his early education for a higher cause. Craig's incredible ability to learn the tribal dialects of the region was the key to reaching the primitive people. So Craig had gotten a different kind of education as he ran unrestrained in the wilderness of Ecuador.

Her father could spear a fish with a sharp stick and climb a banana tree barefoot by the time he was eight. At nine, he and his rain forest siblings were earning spending money and presents from road builders who were clearing the jungles of South America. The builders had taught the children how to light the fuses on sticks of dynamite that had been placed under the trees and rocks that stood in the way of new roads and fields. Hannah knew her father still remembered the jolt of adrenaline he had gotten every time he had lit a fuse on a stick of dynamite and sprinted for cover. No one could run like a kid from the forest.

Hannah's own childhood traumas and worries paled in comparison to her father's. "Okay, no one has been throwing spears at us or burning our village," Hannah conceded. "But there are some things you should know about."

Without pausing to listen to Hannah, her father pushed the playback button on the answering machine. Hannah winced as she heard Chief Farley's voice. "It's Farley here, Pastor. It's about six o'clock on Saturday morning. Just thought you ought to know we had an unidentified body wash up on the beach at about one this morning. Dulcey Martinez and a kid from the college found him. We don't know for sure if it's suicide or foul play, but it's not an accidental drowning. Let me know if you ever heard of him—name's Reggie Showalter. Seems to be in his mid-twenties, blond hair . . . worked for Christopher's Catering on the west side." The chief paused, then added, "Oh—and ask Hannah about last night. Give me a call."

Craig looked at his daughter who had stopped in mid-crunch to hear the message. "Gabe was roaming the streets last night and the chief picked him up downtown. You might consider bolting his window shut—or sawing off a few limbs of that elm tree by his window," she said casually, feeling somewhat vindicated in her claim of having had an eventful night.

Despite a possible murder not three hundred feet away from his home and the fact that his children had been alone when it was discovered, Pastor Dennison turned his attention to getting unpacked. Hannah could almost hear her father thinking, *Trouble will find me soon enough.*

Miranda, known as "Randi" to those close to her, continued to sweep through the roomy, wood-floored house that belonged to the church, shuffling through the mail, adjusting the braided rugs, and pausing to poke her finger into the soil of her potted houseplants as she went. "Forgot to water, Hannah. It was on the list," she said absently as she mounted the stairs, paging through the mail. Hannah followed her like a lady-in-waiting.

Gabe wandered out into the upstairs hall, still wearing the jeans and T-shirt he had worn the night before, "Hey, Mom, you're home," he said matter-of-factly.

"Gabriel! It's noon! Are you trying to make me think you're a teenager already! Be a love and carry up my luggage, sweetie. I'll never unpack it if I don't do it right away. Tomorrow's Sunday . . . " Gabe disappeared into the bathroom, slamming drawers and turning on the shower. Hannah knew it would be she who would eventually drag those suitcases up the stairs.

Hannah wandered out to the backyard and found her father standing by the fence, looking down at the lake and the town beyond. They had such a great view of everything from there. Many of the MCC students and their parents were using the long Labor Day weekend to move back onto campus, hauling suitcases and lamps and computers, trucking their stereos and mini refrigerators into the dorms, creating elaborate, fully stocked fortresses for the semester ahead of them. After the relatively calm pace of summer, sleepy Griggsberg would once again be teeming with the good children of Christian families.

Further west they could see the vast farmlands that stood between Griggsberg and Kansas City. Every year, more and more acres of that land would be turned into housing for the residents of Kansas City who craved peace, space, and safety.

"Probably a summer visitor . . . the man in the lake . . . don't you think?" Craig wondered absently as he gazed down on the campus. The college was made up of new, clean-lined buildings and green areas dotted with young trees that spread from Lake Shiloh to the downtown area.

Craig walked back to the porch and sat down on a lawn chair. Hannah knew he was torn between the silence of his backyard and the path that led to his busy pastor's office just a little way up the hill. "Tomorrow's Sunday," he commented. "Lot to do."

Hannah nodded, knowing the routine well. "Better get that sermon spiffed up," she said, giving him permission to go.

"Sermon's in my head," he said and looked at his daughter as if he were seeing her for the first time that day. "What's on your mind, Hannah? Gabe give you a rough time?"

"Oh, like a murder in the neighborhood is not enough to upset me a little," she said huffily.

"Now, we don't know if it was a murder. Could have been an accident or a suicide," her father said as if either possibility was far preferable.

"Fiona Bennigan's convinced that her husband's ghost is back to get revenge on *his* murderer. You should have seen her last night, Dad. She scared the little Spencer girls half to death. She's really losing it. I half thought she was going to toss herself down the hill into the lake to join old Liam. This whole town has gone mad!" She moved closer to him, hoping he would stay awhile of his own free choice. "Remember how it was, Dad? Remember the old church and how we all felt like part of a family? I don't even know most of the people at church any more."

"They know *you*," Craig offered.

"None of them *really* knows me. They just see me the way they want to see me. They all think I was born with all the answers when I'm more confused than any of them ever were. I have more questions and more doubts than any of them—but they like to see me as Miss Perfect. They *need* to think that!"

"They all admire you, Han. The way you handle your Sunday School class. All those little five-year-olds love being in your class. You're so good with them. *They* know you!"

"They're babies, Dad! They love anyone who pays attention to them. Sometimes I just want to tell them to run—so they can keep their sweet little child ideas about God and how the universe makes sense!" Hannah's usual composure began to dissolve as she got wound up in her thoughts.

"Hannah—you're upset right now because you had a rough night," he soothed.

"It's more than that, Dad. I have real doubts about everything. The more I study the Bible, the more confused I get. When those little kids in my Sunday School get older, the church will take their ideas away from them one by one—just like it's doing to me. I'm only setting them up for the big letdown when they realize their childlike faith doesn't match Protestant doctrine!" Hannah stood and walked to the edge of the porch.

Craig stood up, too, and moved toward the path. Hannah could tell how tired he was from his trip. She knew he felt even more tired as he faced his usually strong daughter who seemed to be coming apart. The cork had popped off and a crack had appeared in his child terrarium.

"We'll talk later," he said, stepping off the porch.

"We used to be able to talk any time, Dad! Now you're better at escaping!" Hannah watched him hurry up the path to the church through the little patch of woods. Suddenly, without thought, she found herself racing up the path. Standing in front of her father, hot tears began to roll down her flushed cheeks. "WHAT WILL IT TAKE TO GET YOU TO NOTICE ME!" she screamed.

"Hannah, I can't solve all your problems on a Saturday morning," Craig retorted. "What is it . . . what is it that you want from me?"

His simple question stunned her. *Was he asking her for the real answer? Was this her only chance to tell him what was in her heart?* Her eyes darted back and forth, her mind raced to find exactly the right words that would pierce his oblivion. "What I want," she began slowly, choosing only the words that would fit this rare opportunity to reach her father. "What I want . . . is for YOU to be . . . WHO YOU SAY YOU ARE."

Craig stared at his daughter for a full minute, then pushed past her and entered his office door. Because she was wearing her night-clothes, Hannah could not follow him into the busy church offices. She knew he had escaped from her again.

CHAPTER 10

Stunned and deeply hurt, Hannah walked back down the path toward her house. As she stepped into the backyard, the French doors above the porch roof opened, and her mother walked out from her bedroom onto the deck. She had changed into a brilliant blue Japanese silk robe. Her polka-dot bow had been replaced with a wispy scarf in the same striking shade of blue.

"What a glorious day!" she said, taking a breath of air as if she were a star making an entrance in a movie scene. Miranda seemed not to have heard the argument between her husband and daughter and called out, "Hannah, I am *famished!* I didn't dare *touch,* let alone *eat* that little cheesy airline breakfast. Anything in the house to eat?"

Hannah regarded her beautiful mother. Why couldn't she be "hungry" or even "starved"? Why was everything bigger than life just because it had to do with her? If anyone doubted that beauty was power, let him live in the presence of Miranda Mallory Dennison for a week.

Even her wigs were bigger than life. Every one of them matched her trademark fiery auburn hair. It seemed to Hannah that she could tell how important an event was by how big her mother's wig was that day. Her television wig was the biggest. It flowed past her shoulders in huge waves, the crown teased up into a windblown perfection.

Hannah gave in to her mother just like she did with Gabe. "The fridge is stocked. Want some turkey on dark rye?" Why couldn't she resist her family any more than the rest of the world could? She knew them better too—hidden flaws and all. But she still felt responsible for them.

"That would be a delectable treat, my love. Perhaps a dab of that German mustard with the little seeds would be just the thing," said Miranda, disappearing into her bedroom again.

Hannah finished making the sandwich just as Jared came through the gate and into the kitchen. He had come home for lunch and was still filthy from hauling topsoil that morning. Hannah knew his casual behavior signaled his desire for a truce.

"Hannah, police think it was a murder. No water in his lungs, and they found a yellow nylon rope tied to his ankle like his body had been weighted down. That Russian dancer guy, the scuba teacher, dove down and found a big cinder block near the old quarry digger in the deep end of the lake. Coroner figures the body's been under water since the beginning of summer. A bunch of people phoned in and remembered seeing a guy in a red waiter's uniform hitchhiking to Griggsberg back in May. The reporters are all over down there." Jared paused and helped himself to the sandwich Hannah had just made for her mother. "This kind of stuff doesn't happen in this town . . ." he said between mouthfuls.

Hannah, grateful for his forgiveness, pointed out to him how dirty his hands were, sighing loudly as if she were his mother. Then she made another sandwich with a dab of that good German mustard for the fabulous Miranda Mallory Dennison.

"Man, I hate how those little seeds get stuck in your teeth," Jared complained, probing his teeth with his grimy index finger.

"Do you have twenty minutes to do me a favor that will keep old Gabe in his bedroom at night? There is a certain tree limb under a particular window that needs sawing off."

"Anything to help the cause," he said, tucking the last of the sandwich into his cheek and pouring himself a glass of milk.

Hannah led Jared into the garage. As she lifted the saw from its hook on the wall, Hannah noticed something leaning against the wall behind a large piece of plywood that made her stop breathing and her heart start to pound; it was Gabe's rusty bike with the banana seat and the high handlebars.

* * *

"Hello, Pastor Dennison! How was the conference?" said the church secretary, Marge Crimball, sticking her head into his office. Craig was distracted and worried that his secretary had heard the nasty fight he'd had with Hannah.

"Fine. Fine, Marge. Any messages?" he asked with a weak smile.

"On your desk, Pastor," she said. "What else can I get you—a glass of ice and a Coke?"

"That would be perfect," he sighed, grateful for her efficiency and the way she anticipated his needs.

While the door was open, Craig could hear the choir singing a fragment of a song over and over in the practice room down the hall as they went over a difficult number. The Reverend Louis T. Talbott, the church's minister of music, was giving an animated pep talk to the choir members in an exaggerated Louisiana accent to amuse them and loosen the expression in their voices. They were practicing a spiritual from the early 1800s and he was begging them to ease off the enunciation.

Craig hurriedly greeted other staff members who were busy preparing for Sunday. He hoped they didn't notice how Hannah's words had unnerved him. Sunday was fast upon them all. He couldn't be thrown off balance when so much was expected of him.

Marge brought the glass of ice and Coca-cola within a few minutes, shutting his door behind her to protect him from the onslaught of staffers who craved a word with him.

Craig slid out his bottom drawer and withdrew a bottle of Smirnoff Vodka. An old roommate had told him that vodka had no taste, nor could it be detected on your breath—it did its job with the discretion of a spy. It was only the third bottle he had ever bought in his life but he found himself looking forward to it lately. As he drank, he knew the power of his worries would grow weaker, allowing him to do what must be done. The alcohol did a nice job of getting him through his busy Saturdays, and lately, it was what got him through his Sundays as well.

Sometimes he wished he could turn this whole religion business over to Miranda. She had been bred for this life. Schooled in its social nuances. Tutored in its politics. Randi was the engine that drove the whole machine.

His childhood in the jungles of South America had left him unprepared for the complexities of pastoring a superchurch and the public speaking he was constantly asked to do. After he had regaled his audiences with his entire repertoire of exciting missionary stories, he often felt he had little else to offer them. The theology and church doctrine, the stories of the Old and New Testaments that had held him enraptured in seminary seemed unimportant to the people who came to his church on Sundays. They wanted more of the other stuff. Bigger shows. More frightening stories. Frenetic music. If they didn't leave each service on an emotional high, they considered the meeting a waste of time. As with all thrill-seeking, it took more and better stimuli to keep it all exciting. Lately, he knew his staff had begun to feel the strain of their gargantuan efforts to keep the services entertaining and fresh. He sent them to seminars and training retreats to pick up new techniques. Each Sunday had to be bigger and better than the last. He couldn't stop the mounting pressure they all felt. After all, the people who wanted these things provided all of their paychecks. He felt like the wizard behind the curtain in the Land of Oz. Sometimes he wished he could just confess to the people in his church that all the bells had been rung and all the whistles had been blown—that he had nothing left in his bag of tricks.

"Randi on line one!" called Marge through the intercom.

"Hi, honey," said Miranda breathlessly, "I've got a solo at that wedding in K.C. tonight. It's for the Baldwins' daughter, and you know Don and Fran Baldwin are going to be big contributors to the music camp, Craig. Louis is picking me up right after choir practice."

"Okay, Miranda. But I wish one of us could stay home tonight. The kids seem strange to me."

"Our kids *are* strange, honey! I don't know where they came from sometimes. But it's Saturday, Craig," she said in her best Scarlet O'Hara accent. "Think about it on Monday, darlin'. Gotta go!"

Craig hung up the phone and turned Miranda's picture toward him. She was stunning. Even after seventeen years of marriage, he still felt awkward in her presence. The light that shone from her and around her was blinding at times.

He thought back to his college days before he had met her. He had been unprepared for his own reception as a freshman at the old MCC campus more than twenty years ago. He had learned quickly that Americans would unhesitatingly bestow power and privilege upon him simply because of his towering height and good looks.

At first he felt guilty whenever he was easily granted the social position that other young men worked for, craved passionately, and occasionally earned. But his guilt was interpreted as modesty and was quickly regarded as one more fine quality upon his heap of natural talents. He was often flabbergasted at the attention he seemed to generate no matter what he did or where he went. A poorly delivered joke still got a guaranteed laugh from his companions. Each of his badly prepared sermons in homiletics class was awarded an A for effort. Even the mismatched clothing he had brought with him from the mission field was soon considered chic and fashionably eccentric by his college mates. The exciting missionary stories about his family were well known by the students who had grown up hearing them. The students regarded Craig Dennison as a sort of Christian Tarzan reentering civilization, and were fascinated with his every move. America was a strange land. Craig had never fully adjusted to its odd social customs.

During his junior year, he was smitten immediately, as was every other male student, by the freshman daughter of the theology professor, Dr. Samuel Milton Mallory. Miranda Mallory had been runner-up in the Miss Missouri pageant and had graciously taken some time off before starting college to perform the duties of the real Miss Missouri who had developed mononucleosis toward the end of her reign. Miranda had delayed her education to appear at county fairs and old folks' homes and to greet the citizens of Missouri with her expensive smile and, when even slightly coaxed, to belt out her gospel songs for which she was growing famous.

In a state of disbelief at his good fortune, Craig Dennison had dated the lovely Queen Miranda during the remainder of his college days until he finally caught on that he was as big a catch as she was. The two married the day after his graduation and went off happily to seminary where he, of course, would study to become a minister.

The normal career course for a new seminary graduate would have been to take a position as an assistant minister in a big church with a full ministerial staff. Under the watchful eye of a seasoned pastor, the new minister would learn the ropes. Learning how to conduct weddings and funerals, calling on the sick and grieving, and counseling troubled members took some time and was best left to an experienced minister, who then gradually turned these duties over to his assistant until he could fly on his own. Only then would he be given his own church.

But Griggsberg Community Christian Church had come available right after his graduation and he and Randi were itching to go solo. They envisioned turning the declining small-town church into an instant overnight boom church. With Randi's voice and Craig's missionary stories, it would be the most exciting place to be on a Sunday morning. And that's just what happened. People began driving from miles around to attend the little church. Soon Craig was doing three services every Sunday because the church was too small to hold all its members at once. Miranda was in demand at every church conference and big event. Soon television found her, and her name was known all over the country.

Sure there had been offers of bigger and better churches, but Miranda wanted to live near her sister and aging parents. Besides, keeping the small church gave the Dennisons an unquestioned position of humility and selfless service. An entire town had been vastly improved by the mere presence of the good-looking pastor and his stunning wife. When the college moved to town, Craig knew he wouldn't have to leave Griggsberg to get a bigger church. He and Miranda would *build* the superchurch they had always envisioned for themselves.

When Hannah and Gabriel were born, they were scooped up into the warmth and familiarity of small-town life as well. Griggsberg had been a great place to raise a family.

Hannah was such a bright child. She had taught her own Sunday School class of kindergarten children since she was twelve years old. But Craig often regretted the day he began letting her use his library to research the religious questions that plagued her.

Craig remembered the time a few months ago when Hannah had come to his office to return a thick book about the history of Christianity. *The Council of Nicaea! That was what was bothering her that day,* he remembered. The decisions made at a church council that had met in 325 A.D. were bothering his adolescent daughter nearly seventeen hundred years later.

Craig remembered Hannah pacing up and down, arguing with him about the nature of God. Nothing about her had been smiling that day. "Why in the world, Dad, would we still accept a . . . a decision made by a bunch of guys . . . okay, they were church leaders . . .

called to a meeting by Constantine almost three hundred years after Christ's death? I mean, Constantine had an empire to run. He didn't want people to be fighting and disrupting everything. Emperor Constantine, a pagan who refused to be baptized because he still had a lot of murder and pillaging planned for later . . . *Constantine* calls these church leaders together to get them to agree on the nature of God and his Son, Jesus Christ! I mean, there he is, *forcing* them to agree so that they will quit rioting in the streets about the nature of God."

"But why is that so offensive to you, Hannah?" Craig remembered asking.

"Well, until the Council of Nicaea, people held very different ideas about who God and Jesus were. Jesus *was* God's son who came to earth. Jesus was a completely separate being from God. But some of these church leaders decided that Jesus actually was God. They did it that way so that Jesus wouldn't have a lower status than God. And *that* decision made Jesus his own father! And because of that decision, no one can understand who God is. God gave us these wonderful logical minds that we then have to *turn off* in order to understand the nature of God. No wonder people give up and stop believing!"

Craig remembered this discussion from his seminary days but had never seen anyone quite so upset by it.

"So the church leaders agree to a creed that states that God and Jesus are the same person . . . of the *same* substance . . . so that Jesus wouldn't be cheated out of being a god . . . and *that* led to this whole idea of the Trinity!"

"Yes, and that concept has lasted all these years, Hannah. And *not* believing it makes you *not* a Christian."

"Why? It's not in the Bible. Why do we *Protestants* still accept this idea? We . . . at least . . . would have been free to change the idea of who God and Jesus are! We're not bound by the pope! *We're* supposed to be *protesting* Catholicism. So why do we still go on preaching and teaching all those old ideas about God? We have the Bible. Why can't *we* just figure out who God and Jesus are for ourselves?"

"Hannah, I know you're trying to be a good Sunday School teacher. But your five-year-olds aren't ready to be taught the notion of the Trinity yet. You'll prepare them in little ways, and they'll be able to accept church doctrine when they're a little older." Craig frowned as Hannah dragged a coffee table over to his bookcase and hopped up on it to return the book to its place. "And get your dirty tennis shoes off my church magazines—that *Christianity Today* just came this morning."

Hannah had jumped down and looked at her father. "I don't *want* to prepare those kids to accept church doctrine. They already know— without any doubts—who God and Jesus are! When they get older, our doctrines will . . . will . . . you know what they'll do? They'll erase the face . . . of God!"

"Erase the face of God? Hannah, little children simply cannot *conceive* of the unknowable entity that God is. He is mysterious and incomprehensible. He isn't like us!"

"I know . . . 'he's without body parts or passions,'" she had quoted from one of the old Catholic creeds still used in Protestant services.

"So you see, sweetheart. He doesn't *have* a face," Craig had said, hoping she would drop the matter so he could return to the sermon he was preparing.

Hannah, however, was not ready to give up. "Then why does it say in Hebrews," she had come around to his side of the desk, taken his Bible out of his lap, and flipped through its pages. "Right here— in Hebrews, chapter one, verse three—it says that God's son was created 'in the express image of his person.' And here, in Genesis," Hannah paged back to the first book of the Bible and read, "And let us make man in our image, after our *likeness* . . . "

Craig remembered feeling weary at this point. How could he explain to his teenage daughter that she could not change the course of seventeen hundred years of church history? Sure, understanding the Trinity was a tough one. They used to joke in seminary about how they could lose their minds trying to understand it—or lose their salvation if they didn't believe it.

At last he said, "Hannah, I'm glad you're coming to your own adult realization that we humans simply cannot understand . . . the nature of God."

She had retorted, "Why not? It's as clear as day in the Bible. My five-year-olds understand it. We *look* like Him. He's our father. *It makes sense that we would look like Him.* His son Jesus looks like Him too. What's so hard about that?"

"Yes, and just like you're understanding how difficult these concepts are—those little kids in your Sunday school class will grow to understand them too. It's a part of the conversion process. They'll *grow* into it."

Hannah had not been satisfied. Again, she thumbed through the Bible to Matthew. "Here. In Matthew, chapter eighteen, verse three, it says, 'Verily, I say unto you, except ye be converted, and *become as little children,* ye shall not enter into the kingdom of heaven.'"

Craig had shaken his head. He remembered thinking that if Hannah didn't quit reading her Bible, he was going to lose one of his best Sunday School teachers.

"Dad, we're supposed to have faith like theirs . . . *not the other way around!* My five-year-olds have a total faith in God and in his Son Jesus Christ. Why should I spoil their faith? If I tell them what notions a fourth-century pagan politician named Constantine and his church leader pals cooked up for them to believe, they might as well start packing their little bags right now!"

"Sweetheart, trust me on something here," Craig said, toying with a pencil, trying to phrase his next thought carefully. He remembered it was a pencil because he had looked at its rubber tip and had wondered how in the world his church had managed to *erase* the face of God. "Hannah, the vast majority of Christians do not even know what their doctrines actually are. For instance, they pray to Jesus even though Jesus Himself taught in the Bible that we should address God, the Father. Or they believe they will live in heaven with their families when both Protestant and Catholic doctrines state that there are no marriage or family relationships in heaven. And believe me, most church members have never *heard* of the Council of Nicaea. Despite all this, they all seem to make the transition from their child-like faith to their adult faith just fine. A lot of things are like that. We put away childish ideas and accept more sophisticated ones as we become older."

"Only if they don't *think* about it, Dad," Hannah had insisted. "Why would they put away the absolute sure . . . logical . . . faith of a child and accept ideas about the Supreme Being of the Universe that don't make any sense to anyone . . . ideas that aren't even *in* the Bible?"

"Well, that's why we go to church. We go to church . . . to learn about these harder ideas and we . . . sort of . . . grow into them when we're ready."

"Or grow out of them! You act like all of these little five-year-olds are going to be in your congregation twenty years from now. The ones who think very seriously won't be. You get to keep the ones who don't question these ideas, or you hope you get a whole lot of *new* people who never had that childlike certainty about God!"

Hannah had always been blunt. She was taking her job as a Sunday School teacher far too seriously. She did that with everything she did. If she didn't do a one hundred percent job at something, she wasn't happy with herself. And while she was doing a bang-up job at whatever task she was pursuing, she made everyone around her miserable. *Oh Hannah!* Craig remembered thinking, *Why do you have to think so much?*

Maybe the old church *had* been better. Hannah had been too young to ask serious questions then. Things were simpler, more straightforward. Maybe he *had* lost himself when they had all moved to the hill. He couldn't remember the feelings and the zeal that used to drive him. Bigger and better shows: sound effects, explosions, rock bands. He took another swig of his vodka and Coke and wished fervently that he could pull the curtain aside, and reveal to everyone out there that there was no wizard.

CHAPTER 11

It was Sunday morning, and Hannah was at the church early to prepare for her Sunday School lesson. Through a window in the Sunday School wing, she could see Jesse straightening chairs like a meticulous host before an important dinner party.

"Hi Jesse!" she called as she let herself into the church with her own key. "Did you finally get to sleep Friday?"

"It was hard to sleep. I was waiting all Saturday to find out . . . about the man in the lake," he said, not looking at her, continuing to straighten the tiny chairs.

Hannah suddenly remembered her forgotten promise to have her father "report" to Jesse about the dead man. "Dad says he'll let you know what happened at the lake as soon as he finds out for sure," she lied. Laying her hand on his shoulder, she said, "We still don't know who he belongs to, Jesse. No one seems to know who he is."

She set up some Bible story pictures against the chalkboard in her classroom so she would be ready for her lesson. The little rooms always seemed so cold and unfriendly to her. At the old church in town, the peeling plaster on the walls was held on by scores of crayoned pictures taped to the walls. She had helped paint the little wooden furniture in the primary room every couple of years. Her Dad had shown her how to scrape off the excess paint from her brush so it wouldn't drip. She had even gotten to choose the bright color or combinations of colors that would be applied to each chair or table. Things were different now. The children at the superchurch had plastic beige stackable chairs with little foam pads on the seats.

"Got your new bulletin board hung up there," said Jesse. He had forgiven her. He made sure there was enough chalk, and bent down occasionally to pick up tiny specks of lint from the carpet.

"That's great, Jess. Hey, why don't you help me teach my class today? You're so good with my kids."

After having waited all Saturday for Pastor Dennison's promised report about the man in the lake, Hannah's invitation easily restored his sense of importance. "Sure. Want me to tell the kids about Jesus and stuff?" He began humming and tidying with more enthusiasm. "I'll tell them how that man in the lake went to live with Jesus, how about that?"

"That'd be great, Jess. And bring Cordelia. The kids love to pet her and hold her during your lessons," Hannah said as she heard another key in the lock.

Miranda entered the door singing in full voice, "How great thou a-a-a-a-a-a-rt! How gre-a-a-a-a-a-t thou art!" Her beautiful vibrato seemed to shake the windows of the Sunday School classrooms. She stood with outstretched arms, a box of sheet music at her feet, and her eyes closed as she finished her impromptu performance for no one in particular. When she recovered from the emotion of her song, she opened her eyes and saw Jesse and Hannah waiting patiently for her to finish.

"Jesse, my love! Would you be my big strong man and carry this box to the choir room for me?" Miranda swooped toward him and handed him the heavy box of sheet music. She turned smartly toward her daughter who was frowning at her for stealing Jesse from her. "Hannah!" she said in mock seriousness, "*This* is the day the Lord hath made. Rejoice and be glad *in* it!"

She kissed the top of Hannah's head. "These precious children that you teach, darling, are so fortunate to learn these sweet little gospel stories while they are young. And you are the person to teach them, Hannah. I've taught you and Gabe all of them." Without missing a beat, she steered Jesse down the hall toward the choir room.

Jesse returned a moment later, shaking his head. "Your mother, Hannah . . . she sings when she could just talk."

Hannah smiled and took his hand. "Jesse, you don't miss anything, do you? Just remember, she needs to hear clapping and she's got to *sing* so people will *clap*."

"Yeah, getting claps is her best thing," Jesse said absently as he made sure everything was in order in Hannah's classroom. "I'll be back after the service for the lesson, Hannah. I'll do it good."

Hannah entered the sanctuary from the pastor's entrance. It was early and only a few people had taken their places. Hannah stepped up close behind the woman playing the organ, "I asked Jesse to help me with my lesson. That okay?"

"Of course, dear. Jesse's so good with the little ones. I'm glad you asked him to help. I'll remind him right after he videotapes the service. You know how he gets caught up with the camera and forgets the next thing."

Hannah remembered the day Jesse discovered videotaping. The church had bought an expensive system to tape the services for shut-ins and to record weddings and pageants. Jesse immediately adopted the machine as his own and spent hours learning how to operate it.

After many hilarious first attempts that featured Jesse's face peering into the camera to see if it was on, he actually became quite proficient at the job. Now his job on Sunday was to tape the service and send copies of the tape out to the members who were too sick to attend services.

Hannah smiled, remembering Jesse's last birthday gift to her— one of his "wild animal" films as he called them. The label on the side of the video had read, "The Atfenchurs of Curdeelya." Jesse was a phonetic speller. The videotape was nearly two hours of Cordelia eating, grooming herself, playing with a small toy, and taking several long naps.

Jess had made one entitled "FIS" for her father. For several days, Pastor Dennison had laughed whenever he told anyone about the three-hour video of Jesse's fish swimming in the aquarium at his mother's house. The climax of the film had been the appearance of Mary Louise's hand sprinkling fish food on the top of the water. Jesse often said that videotaping was his favorite part of his job at the church.

Hannah took her usual seat near the front. Gabriel, looking smart in a new pair of Dockers, a denim dress shirt, and a flashy print tie slid in next to her. "Get the numbers up, Hannah?" He grinned making his usual Sunday joke about the job that had made her feel so important as a little girl.

"Yeah, some robot got my job and I got fired," she said referring to the large overhead projector that flashed the words for all the new upbeat songs on a giant screen at the side of the platform. Hannah smiled at Gabe despite the fact that the two of them had unfinished business. She leaned over and spoke seriously to him. "Gabe, you need to come clean about this weekend. When are we going to talk about where you're getting all that money and what you're *doing* when you run around downtown at night?"

"Shhhhh, sis. Service is about to start and we have to be good examples," said Gabe, folding his hands in his lap, looking angelic, nodding to the familiar faces of the hundreds of people who were now filling the large, sunlit sanctuary.

Mayor Lockhart always seemed to wait until the last moment to make his grand entrance, pushing his elderly mother in her wheelchair. The mayor nodded toward Gabe and Hannah and busied himself with the positioning of his mother in the special wheelchair section near the front of the church. After his wife had died nearly twenty years ago, the mayor had devoted much of his time to his widowed mother who had multiple sclerosis. He deserved all the blessings that had come his way lately after devoting his life to his ailing mother.

Mayor Lockhart had been one of the first to notice the opportunity presented by the new lake since his family property had been located at the edge of the quarry. After the lake was formed, Lockhart's luxurious log home had set the tone for property development around the lake. Soon there were quite a few expensive summer homes on the shore.

Jack Lockhart had moved away from Griggsberg when he went to college, and had become a civil engineering consultant for the State of Missouri. After moving back home to look after his mother, he had gotten elected to the Griggsberg City Council, then to the mayor's job just before the area had mushroomed into a prosperous college town. Jack Lockhart had joined the Church on the Hill after it was built, and the members made sure he never lost an election.

Miranda was thrilled when Lockhart had donated the old Lockhart homestead and all the land by the river to be used for her church music camp. For years, Miranda had been beating the bushes for funds to develop the music camp for underprivileged children from Kansas City. She believed the power of music could change their lives forever. Ground was to be broken next summer. It was all Miranda could talk about sometimes.

Gabe and Hannah sat up straight as their parents took their seats on the platform. Hannah had watched her mother's face every Sunday for fifteen years, and she knew that something was wrong.

While the choir was singing the rousing spiritual led by a very animated Reverend Talbott, Miranda slipped out of her seat and went down the back stairs toward the pastor's study. Instinctively, Hannah knew her mother needed her.

"Stay here, Gabe. I think something's wrong with Mom."

Hannah slipped out of a side door and down a flight of stairs, then followed the corridor to the church offices. The door to the bathroom stood open, and Miranda was draped across the toilet. Her hair had come loose and Hannah gathered it and held it back for her as she vomited violently. "I saw your face go white, Mom. Let me take you home."

After she had lost the last of her breakfast, Miranda slumped against the wall of the bathroom. Her pale yellow dress was soiled, her mascara had dripped toward her chin. "Oh yes, baby. I need to go home. I felt this way in Dallas a couple of times, too. I guess I'm getting the flu or something. Help me back home. You go out the door first. I don't want anyone to see me like this." She stood up and took off her tall high heels. "No way can I walk in these," she said as she handed them to Hannah.

Hannah made sure there was no one in the hall and led her mother out the side door and down the path toward their home. Once in the backyard, Miranda stopped and clutched her stomach, "This is awful, Han," she said weakly. "I need to get into bed."

As Hannah tucked her mother into bed, a feeling of dread came over her. Her mother was not one to let the flu sneak up on her. She never would have sat on the platform if she had been getting the flu. This was something very different. Just like with Gabe, Hannah's instinct told her there was more to this sickness than a virus or bacteria.

CHAPTER 12

The last week of summer was an unusually quiet one at the Dennison house. Miranda had seen Dr. Williams on Monday and had been strangely silent for several days, offering unsatisfying answers to her family about the nature of her illness.

Hannah caught sight of Gabe disappearing with Ian and Charlie into the Bennigan's underground tornado shelter the boys called "the Bunker." Hannah noticed that Ian had taken to dressing in army fatigues and an old black beret that he claimed had been his uncle's when he fought with the Irish Republican Army.

Fiona had bought her children everything that money could buy, including a top-of-the-line computer that was now housed in the bunker. The boys spent hours engaged in elaborate military fantasies over the Internet with people from all over the world.

Hannah had begged her parents to keep Gabe away from Ian.

"Hannah," her father had said, "Gabe is growing up in the best of both worlds. In the middle of civilization, he has an incredible wilderness area to explore. He's learning self-sufficiency and independence just like I did."

"But Dad, you didn't hang out with a deranged boy like Ian," Hannah had countered vehemently.

"Well, better he learn to hunt and fish with Ian than sit home and watch television."

"How about Little League and scouting—you could get him interested in something besides television," Hannah had begged.

"Those are a city kid's substitute for the *real* games of survival . . . and . . . the wit sharpening challenges of a childhood in the wilderness," her father had insisted. "Besides, it wouldn't be Christian to keep Gabe from associating with the Bennigan boys."

As far as her father was concerned, Bennigan's Woods offered an ideal place for his son's boyhood.

* * *

As she went to her room on Friday afternoon, Hannah could hear her parents shouting at one another in their bedroom down the hall.

"It's not what I want," Miranda was sobbing. "It just happened."

"So what's next? What do you expect from me?" Craig said, his voice a mixture of anger and pain. "I'm already at my limit with what I can handle. I'm a poor preacher . . . not the president of a corporation!" Her father paused and his next words stunned Hannah. "These are the 1990s, Miranda; you could end this pregnancy and no one would ever have to know. Women do it all the time."

Hannah couldn't bear to eavesdrop and stomped noisily toward her room, closing her door forcefully. Hearing her, Craig crashed out of the bedroom, raced down the stairs and out the front door. Miranda sobbed on the bed. After a few minutes, Hannah went quietly to her mother's room and stood there until Miranda noticed her.

"I'm pregnant, Hannah," Miranda said miserably, her voice an octave lower than usual from straining her voice.

"Dad's not too happy about it, I gather," said Hannah quietly. Miranda gathered herself into a little ball on the bed and wept with abandon. Hannah could never remember her mother looking more terrified. She looked smaller and younger, as if she had slipped backwards into time.

* * *

School was a welcome relief for Hannah. She often left the house early in the morning while it was still dark in order to have a good, brisk three-mile walk to school. She even talked Madame Karanaeva into giving her a key to the ballet studio so she could stretch and work out a bit on her way to school.

"I thought that was you, Hannah," said Madame one morning as she came down the stairs from her apartment on the top floor. Her characteristic limp was always more noticeable in the morning before she had warmed up her muscles. She cradled a mug of coffee in her long, graceful hands. You were here even before the sun came up this morning. Or perhaps you never left last night?"

"I came in about five this morning, Madame," Hannah said sheepishly. She had hoped her ballet mistress would not realize how much time she had been spending at the studio. The old studio had become a haven for Hannah. The smell of Murphy's Oil on the wooden floors and the tattered ballet posters tacked to scuffed walls were an unchanging and safe part of Hannah's life. Several of Madame's ancient battered toe shoes, stained with blood from broken blisters and excruciating technique, hung above the mirrors as a reminder of the suffering that the art of dance would require of its students.

After Madame had been hired by the college to teach dance, she had insisted that her studio be located in one of the magnificent old Victorians downtown. It must have "the spirit of the dance," she had insisted. When her college students complained about the long walk into town for their lessons, Madame would reply curtly, "Ballet cannot be taught inside cold concrete walls in a soulless, spotless space. And, walking into town for ballet lessons, *especially* in the winter, is part of my discipline." The college was lucky to get such an accomplished artist and dared not suggest that she join the mere mortals on campus.

"Do you sometimes crave the pain of your training, Hannah? I know this need. Your muscles stretch with that delicious tangible ache and you feel alive all over. Is this not true?" said Madame, sipping her coffee with an amused expression on her thin, still-beautiful face.

"Yes, I do crave the way it makes me feel. And your voice, the discipline at the barre . . . I need that right now. My life at home is confusing and I need what I get from dance. I feel this is my true home right now," said Hannah, who had never confided so much in the woman who often seemed rigid and cold to her students.

"I too have had pain from life. I used to let it work itself out through my dancing," said Madame Karanaeva, her lovely Russian accent flavoring each word. "I have always let my pain *inform* my movements. That is what drives me toward . . . well . . . perfection!"

"Have you been happy here, Madame? After living in New York and being so important with the ballet there?"

"Happy? Happy." She let the word drift through her as though it were an unfamiliar term. "A refuge is not necessarily a happy place, Hannah. If it protects and shelters, it serves its purpose. I do not ask more from this place."

"Is that why your son is here—because it's safe?"

Madame drew back a bit at the directness of her student. "Dmitri was injured in a terrible car accident. He lost his closest friend as well. He will fly away as soon as his leg—and his heart—are healed." She thought a moment. "So, yes, I guess this is a healing place—a safe place—for him as well."

"Thank you for understanding, Madame—about the key."

"Ever since you were seven, Hannah, you have held back some part of yourself. This time of hurting is lonely for you but it will make you beautiful. It will purify you, my love," said Madame with uncharacteristic tenderness. "Have you noticed how merciless I have been with you in class?"

"Yes, I took your attention as a compliment. I was trying to live up to your expectations," said Hannah.

"That has not gone unnoticed. You must abandon yourself to the music now so you can ride this thing—whatever it is. Letting yourself go is something you have rarely done, Hannah. You have talent but not the *terror* that it takes to become a great dancer."

"Terror?" Hannah said. "I am only terrified that I will not be able to do what you are trying to teach me."

"That is exactly the terror of which I am speaking, Hannah. I knew that terror in Russia, because if I did not learn the technique, I did not dance! Here in America, you little girls get to dance as long as mummy and daddy pay for your lessons. Too often, my students do not get to the terror. And those who don't, never truly dance."

Hannah was silent. She felt as if she had stumbled on a new way of seeing a part of herself. In choosing the studio as her refuge, she was running *to* something beautiful, not merely away from something awful. Hannah found herself appreciating that part of her that had finally chosen to express itself.

CHAPTER 13

Reggie Showalter had only worked for Christopher's Caterers for two months, so no one at his work had known where to look for his family. All the Chief could find out was that Reggie Showalter had been twenty-six years old and was originally from Wichita, Kansas. His mother had died when he was fourteen, and he had helped his dad run Showalter's Granite, a quarry and mining supply business that eventually went bankrupt. His sister, who was two years younger than Reggie, had married very young and moved away from Wichita. People recalled that Reggie had run away after his sister had left home. Their father, Howard Showalter, had always been an alcoholic, and after losing his business he had been chronically unemployed. Several people suggested that Howard could well have joined the ranks of homeless wanderers across the country.

So Farley asked the coroner to cremate what was left of Reggie's body. The last piece of information the chief got was a form from the coroner's office stating that the young man had been HIV positive and had the first signs of a fully active AIDS virus. Farley was grateful that he and York had used the gloves when examining poor Reggie's body.

* * *

Chief Farley knew that Reggie Showalter was the victim of murder. It troubled him a great deal that few people in town seemed to care who might have murdered him. In fact, after it was determined that the stranger had AIDS, it was most everyone's opinion that he had probably been spared an even more painful death. Why search for the merciful murderer?

The chief had never really investigated a real murder in Griggsberg before. Of course, Fiona Bennigan had tried to convince him that Liam's death had been a murder, but the mayor had called and warned him about the widow's mental state. Mayor Lockhart asked that the chief be gentle with Fiona in her grieving state, but not to let her get things in too much of an uproar.

The dead man in the lake haunted Chief Farley's dreams. According to Rosa, Reggie was haunting Dulcey as well. Rosa said her daughter's dreams were filled with frightening images of enormous black-whiskered catfish, a quarry digger that chased her and tried to run her over, car phones and dead bodies swirling helplessly in the depths of the lake—and Reggie's horrid opaque eyes staring at her through milky, dimly lit water.

During his dive, Dmitri had found Dulcey's sign wired to the quarry digger and had reported to the chief that Dulcey herself had probably untied the yellow nylon rope that had fastened Reggie's body to the cinder block at the bottom of the lake. Dulcey's plan to impress Dmitri with her daring midnight dive had turned into an embarrassing display of teenage foolishness.

Despite the fact that no family member mourned Reggie Showalter's death and no citizens were pushing him to solve the crime, Chief Farley had done his best to question every resident of the summer homes by the lake and a good many citizens as well. He had pursued every lead that presented itself.

Herb Sumner, a soybean farmer who lived on the outskirts of town, had offered the best lead. He said he had given Reggie a ride into town back in May, and the young man had seemed distant and worried. On the way into town, Reggie had fumbled with some sort of old envelope containing a yellowed newspaper article. There had been quite a few stories about the quarry flood, but Sumner believed it was the one with the picture of Mayor Lockhart standing in front of the new lake. According to newspaper archives, the story had run in the Kansas City Star on Sunday, September 8, 1983. But no one in the department could guess why Reggie had that clipping or whether he had come to Griggsberg because of it. Lawrence Bitner who owned the variety store remembered that Reggie bought a Mars candy bar and a can of Sprite and had asked where Deep End Cove Road was.

Bitner had given him directions. The mayor had been home on the Saturday Reggie had come into town, but had neither seen nor talked to the young man.

Even though Reggie had been thrown away both by his family and by the people in the town where he had died, it bothered Farley that someone had gotten away with murder. It ate at him and woke him from his restless dreams at night. Now he knew that Dulcey too tossed and turned and worried that a murderer lived in their town and would never be discovered.

He remembered that Rosa had found Dulcey at the dock one night staring at the Jesus in the big stained glass window of the Church on the Hill. Rosa had begged her daughter to come home. "Let Jesus find him, Dulcinea," she had told her daughter. "You ask Jesus to find this very bad person, and you get on with your life."

The search for Reggie's murderer had gone nowhere. In mid-October, the mayor asked Chief Farley to stop questioning the residents. The citizens wanted to return to their normal lives. The people of Griggsberg wanted to forget the murder—if that was what it was. They began to believe that Reggie himself had tied the yellow rope to his ankle and then to the cinder block. Wouldn't his horrible sickness be a motive for taking his own life? He had grown up around a quarry—perhaps he had searched for one to die in, and the clipping had led him to Griggsberg.

It amazed Farley that people could get on with their lives so quickly despite the possibility that someone who lived among them might have taken someone's life. They regarded the victim as an outsider. He was not from Griggsberg. Not from the college. Not from a good family. And all this questioning and speculating was giving their nearly spotless town a bad image. Despite the chief's pestering, the mayor refused to authorize a special investigation because there were no funds to carry it out . . . especially when no one wanted it. The cold hard fact was that no one in the world really cared about Reggie Showalter . . . no one cared except Dulcey Martinez, whose dreams he haunted.

* * *

During the last week of October, Chief Farley was at the Ace Hardware Store buying some wood screws to fix the drawer in his desk when Dulcey came in. Farley had known her long enough to recognize the aura of mischief about her. He watched her kneel on the floor next to a huge spool of yellow nylon rope and begin to measure off yards and yards of it, counting to herself.

"Hey, Dulce. What're you up to?" Farley said quietly so as not to startle her.

"Thirty-eight, thirty-nine, forty . . . hey, Chief," she said, preoccupied with her work. "Did you get the press release I put on your desk this morning?"

"Yes, I got it but I thought it was just an assignment from your journalism class. You didn't really send your press release to all those Kansas City newspapers and television stations did you?"

Dulcey's eyes flashed and her jaw twitched. Farley had his answer.

"I'm just doing my part as a citizen of this community. I want my paper to keep the heat on the criminal element in this town," she said in a cool tone.

"Criminal element? Dulcey—you're the editor of your high school newspaper. You should be covering the harvest ball and the band concert coming up. You should be doing stories about homecoming and the latest music—not the murder of Reggie Showalter."

"Well, I can see you don't have the big picture here, Chief," said Dulcey, hauling the loops of yellow rope over to the cash register. Raymond Meeks who had known Dulcey all her life trusted that she had measured the rope accurately.

"And what big picture is that?" asked Farley, putting his six wood screws on the counter. Ray waved his money away. He was doing his part as a citizen as well.

"I don't care if this story runs in my paper, Chief. I want it to run in the Kansas City papers. I found the body. No one has found the murderer yet. Maybe a little publicity will cause someone to make a mistake or maybe even move out of town."

"Yes. It'll also make our town look unsafe . . . like its police department doesn't care about catching criminals."

"Chief, this isn't about you. I've seen you working this case. You're at a dead end. The mayor won't give you money for a special investigation, so I'm giving the police department a little boost. And by the way—the other part of the big picture is that I can't be a dancer forever. When my body gives out or I don't make it to the big time, I've got to support myself, don't I?"

"So you figure this press conference will give you a little exposure for your future career as a journalist—that it, Dulcey?"

Dulcey picked up her bag of rope and headed toward the door. "This press conference is the way we journalists conduct business. Okay, Chief? I'll see you at three-thirty this afternoon by the dock," she said, laughing at the look on his face. "Come watch us pros in action."

Farley sighed. He guessed this was the way Dulcey was conquering her fears and silencing her nightmares. He'd support Dulcey in this—even though the mayor was going to be hopping mad when he found out. He'd let Lockhart worry about the "image" of Griggsberg . . . *a safe place to raise a family* . . . and all that.

At three-thirty, Farley drove down to the lake. He was stunned to see more than a hundred people at the dock where Dulcey had called her press conference. There were news reporters from all the major Kansas City media, about fifty kids from the high school, and quite a few townspeople and college students joining the crowd.

Luckily the mayor was in Florida, but Farley was sure he'd be furious when he saw what Dulcey had been up to. He reminded himself that this was good for Dulcey. It would help her get on with her life and make her feel she was doing something to catch Reggie Showalter's killer.

"Thanks for coming today," Dulcey said into an electronic bullhorn with the words Griggsberg Police Department written on the side.

Blast it, Dulcey! The chief hadn't given her that bullhorn— Darlene had probably loaned it to her, and it made it look like Dulcey had the blessings of his police department.

"From the press releases you have received, you all know why I've asked you here today. I want you to put the murderer of Reggie Showalter on notice that Griggsberg has not quit looking for him or her."

"We know you were the one to find the body, Miss Martinez. What were you doing scuba diving alone after midnight?" yelled one of the television reporters who had done some sleuthing on the story. He had talked to Dmitri Karanaeva that morning.

"I was killing time before my mother's diner closed. I had to help her wash pots at one thirty in the morning. I admit, I took a risk diving in Lake Shiloh but I'm certainly glad that body didn't wash up on shore when the little children of this town were playing on the beach." The reporter, Jim Stott from KCMO television, noted how skillfully Dulcey had turned his question into a statement that made her look good.

"Why do you think Reggie Showalter was murdered?" shouted someone from town. "A lot of us in town think he killed himself because he had AIDS!"

"I have read the autopsy report," said Dulcey calmly, "and the same yellow nylon rope that was used to tie Reggie's body to a cinder block was used to strangle him. The type of straight mark on his neck indicated foul play—*not* suicide."

Farley saw Matt Moore approach the crowd from the direction of the dormitories. He had heard that Matt's parents had tried to get him to come home to Tulsa after he and Dulcey found the dead body. "Maybe Griggsberg isn't safe after all," was the argument they had used. Matt had compromised by agreeing not to see Dulcey any more. Farley could see that he was still interested in her by the way he was looking at her.

"What I'd like you all to do," said Dulcey into the bullhorn, "is to keep this investigation alive until Reggie's murderer is found. I believe the person who killed Reggie lives right here in this town. He or she could be in this crowd right now—on the faculty at MCC, or a student, or the guy who works at the video store, or the girl who does your hair. Don't you want this person caught?"

Several people from the crowd yelled their support. They wanted their town back. They wanted this thing to be over.

"I'm asking all of you to join me in wearing a length of yellow rope on your ankle until the killer is caught! The mayor of this town has refused to order a special investigation. Sure it's expensive, but who are we as people if we don't care whether there is a murderer living here among us. Are we afraid to arrest him and punish him? Do we let him go free because Reggie was sick? Why are we afraid to find out the truth? Reggie Showalter came into town alone in broad daylight on a Saturday afternoon in May. We all know everyone in town and would have noticed another stranger. Many of you noticed Reggie, didn't you? I believe it *wasn't* a stranger who murdered Reggie. It was someone who lives right here in Griggsberg." Dulcey kept speaking into the bullhorn as she handed out twelve-inch lengths of yellow nylon rope. She pulled up the bottom of her Levis and showed everyone how the rope could be tied on one's ankle. Immediately the image grabbed hold of the townspeople, especially the students from the college and the high school. Even a few reporters took a yellow rope and began tying it on an ankle.

Farley watched Matt Moore push toward the front of the crowd. Soon he was standing on the dock next to Dulcey taking the megaphone away from her. "I'm Matt Moore from the college here. I just want you all to know that I was with Dulcey the night we both discovered Reggie Showalter's body. If you had seen his bloated, hideous body like we did, you wouldn't forget it either. Let's find this killer so Griggsberg can be the kind of town it used to be—a town of God fearing, decent people!"

Dulcey grinned as Matt took a yellow rope from her and fastened it on his ankle. Farley knew Matt was hooked on her again. *Dulcey sure was something.* He shook his head and got back into his patrol car. He needed to have a word with Darlene about just who was in charge of the equipment belonging to the Griggsberg Police Department.

As Farley pulled onto Deep End Cove Road, he saw Hannah standing by herself watching the crowd at the dock. She turned away from him and began walking quickly toward the beach between two of the summer homes. She had seemed so depressed lately. Hannah had always been serious, but lately she seemed sad and withdrawn.

Farley's daughters, Andrea and Crystal, had reported to him that Hannah and Gabe seemed really standoffish at school. Hannah wasn't dating anyone. She wasn't in any of the clubs this year, and Gabe seemed to only hang out with that weird neighbor of his, Ian Bennigan, after school.

Chief Farley had heard from his wife that Miranda was pregnant and he decided the kids weren't adjusting to the prospect of a baby in their home. Miranda herself had not sung at church in some time, and the whole congregation seemed to miss her presence. Though the music was great and the services well attended, Pastor Dennison seemed out of sync with his flock. His sermons had a wistful, abstract quality to them. Eventually the assistant pastors took over the preaching. No one seemed to know what to do for the Dennison family.

CHAPTER 14

Hannah walked along the beach, crossed the covered bridge, and trudged up the hill, kicking the crisp fallen leaves that covered the road. She was walking everywhere these days so she could have time alone, and enough quiet to think.

After listening to Dulcey's press conference, Hannah felt particularly sorry for herself, wondering if anyone would care if it had been she who had washed up on the beach. *Probably not,* she had decided. As she neared her house, Jared burst out of his door like a wild horse and yelled, "Hannah! Mom had the baby last night—it's a little girl!"

How Jared could be ecstatic about another human being to compete with the rest of earth's miserable souls was beyond Hannah. Unenthusiastically, she allowed Jared to steer her into his house.

"When was she born?" asked Hannah as Jared dragged her into the house.

"About two this morning. The midwife left early this morning and I just got home from work."

"I wondered why I didn't see you at school today," Hannah said. Noticing the exhausted, worried look on his face, Hannah realized that Jared had been waiting for her to get home from school. He needed her, and as soon as she saw the condition of his house, she knew why.

"Dad and I were up all night and I took over for him at the building site today." Jared hung his head and leaned against the wall. "Hannah, please help me. Look at this place." He pointed toward the rest of the house like the specter of death pointing toward hell.

"Oh, my goodness," said Hannah reverently as she walked through the biggest mess she had ever seen in her life—it looked like the aftermath of a five-day slumber party. She walked into the family room, marveling at the dirty plates laden with half-eaten sandwiches and shriveled pieces of cheese. Potato chips had been ground into the carpet; lampshades were askew; cupboards and drawers hung open. There was a bleach stain on the carpet in front of the couch. Next to the stain she saw a sponge and a spray bottle of kitchen cleaner with the words "Now with Clorox bleach!" on the label. Above the cacophony of television voices, Hannah could hear the newborn baby crying upstairs and several wracking coughs from the bedroom down the hall. "Who's sick?"

"Eric and the twins have some kind of flu. I stuck them in the twins' room down the hall so the baby wouldn't get sick. All three of them have been in there since last night."

Hannah walked through the living room. The two long couches and the loveseat were denuded of the pillows that fit along their backs. Clothes and blankets were strewn on the floor. A forgotten board game and a thousand-piece puzzle with just the edges in place covered the two low tables. Magazines, notebooks, videos, robes, slippers, crayons, and sheets of paper were scattered in front of the fireplace. Ashes were strewn out on the carpet and marshmallows congealed on green sticks freshly torn from a tree. A spoon from JoLyn's good silver set rested in a near-empty can of split pea soup. A trail of Kleenexes led down the hall into the twins' bedroom. Hannah followed another trail of fun-size Baby Ruth wrappers to the downstairs bathroom and found Elissa sitting regally in the empty bathtub lined with all the pillows from the living room couches, watching *The Young and the Restless* on a little portable television. Elissa paused to note Hannah's presence and popped another bar into her chocolate-muddy mouth. Next to the tub stood a big paper bag with a warning written in black marker. "THIS CANDY IS FOR HALLOWEEN. A DEADLY CURSE WILL FALL ON ANYONE WHO TOUCHES IT BEFORE THEN. Signed—Management." *Well, management is taking a maternity leave and her corporation has collapsed,* thought Hannah. She felt a surge of guilt at her odd sense of satisfaction that JoLyn's usually well-run home had dissolved into chaos. It was like noticing a run in the stocking of a super model.

Hearing sobs coming from the kitchen, Hannah found Alyson scraping eight blackened grilled-cheese sandwiches off a large electric grill. "Hannah!" she shrieked running into Hannah's arms. "Everyone is so hungry. I used all the bread and cheese to make grilled-cheese sandwiches. I turned my back for a minute to make a salad and they all burned up."

Hannah held Alyson and patted her back. "Shhhhh, we'll fix it." The smell of carbon hung in the air. "No one is a perfect cook at the age of eleven," she comforted.

"It was the third thing I cooked today. *Everything* burned," Alyson wailed.

Jared tossed the burnt sandwiches into the trash can. As he lifted the full trash can liner out, Hannah saw the burnt fish sticks and blackened macaroni shells that had preceded the little squares of crumbling asphalt into the trash.

Jared sighed and looked at Hannah helplessly. She smiled as her gallant soldier stood there in the middle of a war zone holding his muscled arms out like a broken action figure.

"I need a hug too," he said.

Alyson released her and Hannah gave Jared a long, comforting hug. *It is good to be needed,* she thought as she prolonged the embrace another minute for her own sake. She felt an enormous rush of respect and compassion for Jared as her arms encircled his tired body. "You're exhausted, Jared. You were up all night and you worked all day. Go on and take a nap and I'll get things under control."

"I was in charge and I just couldn't do it. I failed."

"We all need help sometimes, Jared."

Jared shuffled off to his room and Hannah got busy on the house. She ordered pizza from Domino's while Alyson found some cash to pay for it in her Mother's secret hiding place behind the good dishes. Then the girls went into the bathroom to dethrone the soap opera queen from her comfortable digs. Alyson replaced the couch cushions while Hannah ran a warm bath for the chocolate thief. While Alyson scrubbed chocolate off Elissa's body, Hannah microwaved three mugs of Campbell's Chicken and Stars and took them on a tray to the quarantined flu victims.

"Hannah!" cried Laura and Leah. They looked like refugees from a third-world nation sitting in a sea of used Kleenex. The twins looked worse than Elissa had; their hair was matted and their nightgowns smelled like sweat and Vicks Vaporub. On television, two women were fighting in front of an audience while two big men tried to pull them away from each other. The title at the side of the screen read, "Today on Jerry Springer—My Mother Stole My Boyfriend." Hannah flipped it off and handed each of the girls a mug of soup.

"Where's Eric?" Hannah asked.

"I'm right here," said a muffled voice from the depths of a twisted sleeping bag. Eric coughed violently as he rifled through the pile of medicine on the floor beside him: two half-empty bottles of NyQuil with caps encrusted in green syrup, an empty box of Contact Cold and Flu capsules and an economy-size jar of Vicks. He chose the NyQuil and gulped several swigs of it straight from the bottle before Hannah could pull it away from him and hand him the soup.

"Eric, you're going to overdose on that stuff!"

"Better to be unconscious than feel the way I do," he mumbled, slurping the soup and dozing off to sleep again with a couple of pasta stars stuck to his wet chin.

Hannah knew something had to be done. The three of them had been in this germ-infested room long enough, but letting them loose would endanger the baby. She snatched a large beach bag from the girl's closet and began stuffing it with clean clothes, Disney videos and what was left of the NyQuil and Vicks.

"Are we going to the beach?" the girls screamed, jumping on the bed and making the Kleenex jump like popcorn in a hot skillet.

"Better than that. You're going to spend the night at my house," she said, handing each of the girls the pillows off their beds. "Come on, Eric, grab your sleeping bag and come with us."

Eric did as he was told, hoping for rescue from the nightmare he was living.

Hannah led the parade of coughing children next door to her house. "Gabe! Come help me."

Gabe appeared at the top of the stairs and took in the scene. "Did the baby come? What's wrong with these guys?"

"Yes, it's a girl and her sick siblings need a place to stay until they're healthy again."

Eric, two years younger than Gabe, tried briefly to rally in that macho way boys do. But soon he gave up the pretense and collapsed on his sleeping bag in Hannah's room. The twins giggled and threw their arms around Gabe. They'd had a crush on him for months.

"Just pop this *Little Mermaid* tape in and they'll be fine," Hannah said, handing him the video and the beach bag.

"Good thing Hannah did her annual cleaning last week or you wouldn't have wanted to stay in her room," Gabe said as he carried the twins toward the television set.

"My room looks like a sterile field next to the Spencer's house," Hannah said. "Where's Mom and Dad?"

"They're in Kansas City—some fundraiser for the music camp."

"Tell them I will be spending the night at Spencer's, okay? They need me over there. Desperately. It'll take a week to get their house back to normal. Can you handle things till they get home?"

"Sure, sis. See you tomorrow."

Hannah grabbed all the root beer from the refrigerator and made her way back to the Spencer's home. She noticed three unfamiliar cars parked along the street. One had a Domino's logo on its roof. Inside the house, a woman was cleaning the kitchen. Another was picking up dirty clothes. Hannah could hear a load of wash already started on the side porch. A teenage boy was running the vacuum cleaner, and a young girl was stacking the videos and books.

Alyson explained the strangers as she carried the pizzas to the kitchen table. "I called Mom's visiting teachers and got some help over here. Jared and I could have handled everything if Eric and the twins hadn't gotten sick."

Dan came downstairs, looking rumpled but happy. "Hannah, the pizza was a great idea. Alyson would have had us all eating little squares made from truck tires!"

Alyson blushed and nudged up against her father. "I'm starved. Come on, Hannah, have a piece," she said, lifting the lid and releasing the aroma of the pizzas into the kitchen.

Hannah sat down. "Did you notice that I took your flu victims over to my place, Dan? Gabe's keeping the girls entertained over there. I don't think they're as sick as Eric is."

"Good thinking, Hannah," Dan said around a bite of pizza. "I called Darlene and she said she'd pick them up tomorrow morning. Thanks for thinking of the baby."

"How's JoLyn?" Hannah asked, reaching for a pizza slice.

"She slept most of the day when she wasn't nursing the baby. But she just had a shower and she'll be down shortly. Did you see baby Janelle yet?"

"Janelle. That's a beautiful name," said Hannah. Alyson took one of the boxes of pizza to see if the volunteers were hungry. Hannah sat with Dan, counting the chairs on both sides of the long table. "Twelve chairs. By my count, you still have two chairs left over. You wouldn't want them to go to waste would you?" she teased Dan, biting into her pizza.

"No, no. Those will be extra. Janelle is the last. JoLyn and I always knew there would be eight spirits coming into our home. We picked her name from the first letters of the other children's names. She'll be sort of a bookend."

"Finally. A period at the end of the sentence."

Dan picked up her tone, "And you think it's a very long sentence. Kind of a run-on sentence—the kind you have been taught in honors English to avoid writing, am I correct?"

"You've been talking to Jared."

"I don't need to talk to Jared. A lot of people feel the way you do, Hannah."

"That the world is overpopulated?" she asked.

"Yes, that's the general sentiment these days," said Dan reaching for another slice, "The thinking goes that a truly responsible couple will have only two children to replace themselves on this earth when they die. That way the population won't grow."

"Gosh, Dan, I didn't know you had heard about zero population growth. Most people just look at your family and figure you don't watch the news," she said, grinning.

Dan wound a long, stretchy band of cheese around his finger and popped it into his mouth. "We Mormons are a bunch of idiots, aren't we?" He laughed, his tired eyes dancing.

"Well, not idiots exactly. Just uninformed," Hannah said, wondering if she had gone too far. "Of course, people make mistakes. My mother is pregnant with a mistake right now. It happens."

"That baby your mother is carrying is no mistake," said Dan, serious now. "Your brother or sister will have a mission on this earth the same as everyone else. No one's life is a mistake, Hannah. Everyone has a purpose in being here. Everyone is here to reach his or her potential. Not more than his potential—but *exactly* his potential, whatever it may be. The purpose of a family is to help spirits fulfill their divine mission here on earth. Families are designed to support each other—even after this life—as each member grows physically and spiritually."

"It all sounds so logical, Dan. I never heard anyone say it just like that."

"Look at my kids, Hannah." Dan leaned back in his chair and pointed the tip of his pizza slice toward the family picture on the wall behind him—the one they had taken just before Neil went on his mission. Hannah looked at it with admiration. All nine of them wore matching denim shirts and were seated in various poses on the Fort. The photographer had taken the picture from the hill behind them and had captured Lake Shiloh and the town beyond. They looked almost too good to be true in that picture. "My kids are going to be *solutions* to the world's problems, not *causes* of the world's problems. They're the good guys. The world needs as many of them as it can get," Dan said quietly as though he were speaking about something sacred and holy.

Hannah considered each of the Spencer kids in turn. They were normal kids with regular human faults. She'd seen them squabble over chores and homework. Jared had a quick temper. Eric was bright but he struggled in school with ADD. JoLyn and Dan had to hire specially trained tutors to help him with certain school subjects. Alyson was painfully shy. Neil tended to be overly competitive for Hannah's tastes. The twins would probably make a career out of their cuteness, and Elissa was a touch spoiled. But they were good people. They tried hard. None of them was cruel or selfish or dishonest. They weren't arrogant and they were who they said they were.

"A while ago, you said you knew eight spirits belonged to you. I thought spirits just developed along with bodies. What did you mean?"

Dan was silent for awhile, caressing the edge of a Domino's napkin. "I hesitate to tell you about that," he finally said.

"Why ever not?"

"When your father hired me to build your house next to ours, he and I got to talking one day. He made me promise not to tell you about these things or try to influence you in any way on the subject of religion."

"Influence me!" Hannah said, "Dan, I have a mind of my own. Do you think I don't think about these things and read about them on my own?"

"No, it's not that. It's just that your father has a right to teach you his own tradition. I have that right in my family too."

"But Dan, this is the stuff I think about and read about all the time. I look for answers in literature and in the Bible, and I read books from my father's library. I'm sixteen years old. It's only natural that I ask questions and think for myself. Why would my father prevent me from asking questions?"

"I know, Hannah. But I made a promise to your father and I have to honor it. Your family and mine are Christians—we follow the teachings and example of Jesus Christ—but we have very different beliefs about the nature of God and the purpose of life. Just like our conversation a moment ago about the premortal existence. You had never heard of it before. That knowledge was lost to the world centuries ago."

"The premortal existence," Hannah said slowly. "Plato talked about that. But why haven't I heard more about it?" Hannah was pacing now, straightening the twelve chairs as she walked around the kitchen table. "Dad said that Mormons are 'benighted Christians' and you only think what your prophet tells you to think."

"A lot of Protestants and Catholics think that about us. In Bible times, I'm sure a lot of people argued over whether prophets like Ezekiel and Daniel and Isaiah were speaking for themselves or revealing the word of God. Conversations like this probably took place whenever the prophets spoke—or when Christ spoke for that matter. Members of my church believe that God is working through prophets again to ready the earth for the coming of His Son, Jesus Christ."

"It's like you're speaking a different language, Dan," Hannah said angrily. "I can't begin to think like you do about prophets and the premortal existence. Where's the evidence? How do you know you aren't talking gibberish?"

"Hannah, this is exactly the conversation your father was trying to prevent. Now that's enough. When you are an adult, you and I can talk about these things if you wish. Or you can talk to Jared or JoLyn about it then. But I promised your father, and I have to end this conversation now. Please try to understand."

Hannah felt a confusion of emotions like moths caught inside a lampshade. She could either escape or burn herself up on the light. She chose to escape. As she swung her dance bag over her shoulder, JoLyn came in with the baby.

"The house looks so nice, Hannah. Alyson told me all about how you rescued her and Jared. You are an absolute saint!"

Hannah leaned over JoLyn's shoulder to look at the baby. "She's beautiful. Congratulations to you both. Another spirit fresh from heaven."

"Fresh from the presence of God, Hannah. You can still see the light when they first . . . " JoLyn stopped talking when she caught the expression on her husband's face and felt the strained silence as Hannah put on her coat.

"Be patient," said Dan as he walked Hannah to the front door. "Legally, you're still a child."

"No, Dan. I am an adult wearing the costume of a child. When will people stop treating me as if I can't decide things for myself?"

Dan thought a moment. "Maybe it's the other way around, Hannah. Maybe you are a child who has had to wear the costume of an adult." He gave her a brief hug. "Be a child for a little while longer. You have time."

"Either way, I'm so well disguised—even I don't know who I am."

"We love you, Hannah. Those two extra chairs are for you and Gabe—any time you want, okay?" said Dan. As he opened the front door, a man stepped in carrying two bags of groceries and a container full of new cold medicine. "Hey, Brother Beals, what's this?" said Dan.

"Kelly's coming right behind me with enough casseroles for the whole week from the Relief Society," said the man as he pushed past Hannah with his bags.

"Good night, Dan," Hannah said, wishing she could erase the worry on his face. She had no right to be an additional burden on him tonight. She smiled, blew him a kiss, and turned before he could see her tears. "I love you too!" she called.

Dan waved to her and closed the door of his home and its newly restored order. Hannah felt an intense longing—a ragged ache in her soul—as though he had also closed the door on her first glimpse of an orderly universe.

CHAPTER 15

Hannah stood outside in the chilly night air. Her family thought she was at the Spencer's; the Spencers thought she had gone home. Her bedroom was full of sick, coughing children. Unwittingly, she had won a whole night for herself. She walked back down the hill into town. *Until I decide where to go, the walk will do me good,* she thought.

It was about eight-thirty when Hannah let herself into the studio. Madame was spending the evening as usual with Thalia and the grandchildren. Thalia's husband traveled on business nearly every weekend and Thalia often asked for her mother's help when he was gone. Madame would be back bright and early on Saturday for a full day of ballet classes.

Hannah breathed in the familiar smells of the old house. The stairs creaked in all the right places as she ascended to her lovely hideaway on the second floor. Feeling exhilarated at her freedom, Hannah peeled off her jeans and sweater and snuggled into her familiar frayed tights and a threadbare leotard. She slipped on her oldest satin toe shoes that fit her feet like surgeons' gloves. Over these and most of the way up her legs, she smoothed on her warm wool leggings with the holes of hard work in them.

Hannah had an overwhelming desire to hear the perfectly intertwined melodies of Pachabel's *Canon in D*. She had performed her barre warm-ups for eight years to the graceful strains of the great classical piece. Her body longed for music and movement.

At the first chords of the *Canon*, her brain immediately switched to an intensely focused attunement. Her muscles knew the movements of the warm-up with a memory separate from Hannah's consciousness. The music moved her arms in slow graceful stretches. Then it quickened, cueing the same exquisite leg lifts that she had performed since she was seven years old. Even in her absence, she could hear the gentle tapping of Madame's antique ivory-head cane as she emphasized the counts of the music.

Hannah choreographed a dance that would heal and soothe her soul. She caught the reflection of her face as she came close to the mirror. Her expression was blissful. She was in charge of something somewhere on the face of this terrible earth. Just as JoLyn had been in charge of her baby's birth, Hannah was in charge of her body now. She was in charge of whether or not the music played and whether or not she would move this way or that way. She would decide when to turn and when to bend; when to raise her arms; when to leap. She alone would ride the music as she pleased. *Releve, pas de chat, pirouette, arabesque, chenet, chenet, chenet, chenet.* Hannah danced for hours as the tape played all the classical selections that had been a part of her life since she was a small girl.

It was midnight when she realized she actually had not thought about where she would stay the night. She had been dealing with each moment as if it were her last on earth. She had danced until she was exhausted and time had not mattered; perspiration glistened on her skin; her leotard was wet from the hours of effort. Finally, Hannah sat on the floor, breathing heavily, bending her torso over her outstretched legs in the silent room.

After awhile, Hannah went to the little observation room where the mothers could watch their budding ballerinas in the studio. She stretched out on the dilapidated old couch, threw her coat over her shoulders, and fell asleep immediately.

The next morning Hannah felt rested—lighter somehow. She tidied the observation room, straightened her clothing and went downstairs. As she reached the first-floor landing, she saw Dmitri Karanaeva backing out of his apartment, keys in his hand, the Griggsberg Gazette in his mouth.

Hannah stopped for a moment while he locked his apartment door. "You must be Dmitri . . . " She had seen him in town but had vowed never to talk to him. She didn't ever want to be one of his adoring Griggsberg groupies.

"Ohhhh. You startled me!" Dmitri said, looking at his watch. "It's not even six yet. What are you doing here?"

"Just an early morning workout," she lied, pushing past him and through the front door.

"Oh, really . . . " said Dmitri, looking at her appraisingly. "You're Hannah Dennison, aren't you?"

"How did you know my name?"

Dmitri laughed. "In a town of under ten thousand people—and with that awful Jesus staring down at us all from your father's church—did you honestly think someone would not know who you are?"

"You think our Jesus is awful?" she said, hurt. "No one has ever said that before."

"Doesn't mean they haven't thought it," Dmitri replied, walking down the front steps with her. Noticing the wounded look on Hannah's face, he tried to lighten the mood. "Why don't you come see the restaurant? I'll bet you've never set foot in it."

The Monastery was two blocks down Main Street and Hannah had worked up a bit of an appetite in the frosty morning air by the time she and Dmitri mounted the familiar front steps.

"How about a bagel for breakfast?" Dmitri said as he opened doors, turned on lights, and led her to the kitchen. Hannah remembered it as the former choir room just off the sanctuary.

"A bagel sounds great. Thanks," said Hannah as Dmitri fished one out of a plastic restaurant bin on the steel kitchen counter.

"I didn't even ask you yet . . . what *were* you doing spending the night at the studio?"

Hannah blushed. "Well, I probably shouldn't have been there. I just *needed* to be there. Did you ever feel that way about a dance studio?"

"Well, since I practically grew up in dance studios, if I wanted to get away or have an exciting change of scenery, I'd have gone to your house to see how a *real* family lives."

Hannah rolled her eyes at the irony. "You wouldn't want to know," she said.

"Come on, I'll show you around," Dmitri said, leading the way to the dining room, formerly the church sanctuary where Hannah had spent much of her childhood. "I got the whole scoop on the Dennison family when I took the job as manager here. Turning a church into a restaurant wasn't real popular with some folks, I hear."

"Well, it's just that *some* of us felt that this was a holy place—you know, where sacred things happened. But the building was so small that no other church wanted it—so it went commercial."

"It's a great location, near the campus and all. It's packed for lunch and then again for dinner. Thank goodness we don't do breakfast." Dmitri gestured around the large room, "Well, what do you think?"

Hannah was pleasantly surprised. The sanctuary where her father had preached for the first ten years of her life was nothing like she remembered it. The painted plaster had been removed to reveal the bricks underneath, with ancient mortar squeezing out between them, a chalky residue splattered over the old red color. A huge chandelier with gas candles dimly lit the room to create a hushed, peaceful atmosphere.

"See why they named it The Monastery? It's a really nice space. It makes you feel contemplative, doesn't it?" Dmitri said quietly, visibly enjoying Hannah's first experience of the refurbished church of her childhood.

Hannah moved toward the platform with the old stained-glass window behind it. The old church pews had been sawn in half and butted up against the walls to create booths of varying sizes. The original red velvet cushions were holding up nicely.

"It's beautiful," said Hannah, with something like gratitude in her voice. "I thought I would hate it. But everything is still here; it's just used in a different way."

Dmitri stepped up on the platform where the pulpit had been. "I guess your father stood here every Sunday," he said, and turned from her as if to face the congregation. "Were his sermons good or did he put his flock to sleep?"

"Oh, they were good, all right. Especially his stories of the mission field. He's pretty famous for some of those," Hannah said. "His other trademark is being able to make a metaphor out of just about anything. He could find something symbolic in everything from a child's cut finger to . . . to laying a new tile floor."

Amused, Dmitri asked, "So give me an example of how he would use a tile floor in his sermon."

"Let's see . . . that story had something to do with my parents laying new linoleum over floorboards they hadn't swept carefully. There were little, sharp rocks under the tile and eventually they pushed up to the surface and ruined the new floor. You know . . . like secrets and lies that eventually push up and find the light of day . . ."

Hannah frowned at the blank expression on Dmitri's face. She sat down at the organ that was still at the side of the platform. "Mary Louise sat here every Sunday of my childhood. I used to sit next to her and turn the pages of her music. But my feet just dangled in the space above the pedals. I was so little back then."

"See, there's a reason to come back to the places of our child-hood. It reminds us how far we've come—how much we've *grown*." Dmitri had a look of mock triumph on his face, "There—I did it. That's something your father might have used in one of his sermons."

"*Exactly* the kind of illustration he would have used," Hannah said, turning to look over her shoulder. There it was: the old hand-made hymn-number holder. Several of the plastic numbers were still in the holder, but now they indicated the price of the daily menu special instead of page numbers. "I don't believe this is still here," she said, smiling at Dmitri. "Of all the memories I have of this place, putting those silly plastic numbers in that wooden holder is one of my fondest. We never sing those old hymns any more. We've traded them in for all the upbeat ones—it's like a pizza parlor sometimes. We even have a bouncing ball on our overhead projector."

"I don't think I've ever sung a hymn in my life. Sundays were matinee days at the theater. It was a two-show day just like Saturdays were."

"We grew up so differently."

"Yes, but it seems to me that we spent our Sundays in pretty much the same way. I watched my parents perform on a stage every Sunday, and you watched your parents perform on a stage every Sunday. There. We do have something in common," he said, watching her slide into the booth nearest the platform.

Suddenly Hannah felt that she had reclaimed something of herself. Lately, her life had been a series of mysteries and dangling questions. Here, in this room, she felt she remembered some of the answers. "Dmitri," Hannah said as a sudden thought struck her, "are you hiring help right now?"

"We are doing just that—but you've got to be sixteen."

"I will be next month, on November thirteenth. What do you think? Do you think I could work for you?"

"Well, let's see. You'd have to be a hostess and be in charge of seating people. You're too young to wait tables." Dmitri looked at her, shaking his head. "Before five minutes ago, I don't think getting a job had even entered your mind. Am I right?"

"But I could do this," Hannah said vaguely, lost in her thoughts. "Dmitri, I *need* to do this right now. What do you think?"

"Aren't you the Dennison who vowed she would never set foot in this place because we were . . . let's see . . . how did you put it? 'Destroying a sacred place with commercialism?' Isn't that what you said, Hannah?" Dmitri said, pretending seriousness.

"Well, I did say that—a few years ago—but I guess I was grieving over this old place. I loved it here. It was where I belonged."

"Tell you what, Hannah. I could use you as a hostess. I think you'd be good at it, providing you agree to comb your hair a little neater, and quit spending the night in ballet studios. Deal?"

Hannah instantly put her hand to her hair, blushed again, and pushed him playfully. "Don't you tell anyone about last night—people will get the wrong idea."

"Look, you wander around here a bit and get your bearings while I tackle that paperwork. I've got some deliveries coming to the back door in a few minutes. You decide if you want to apply for that hostess position, and I'll give you the forms. Just stop by the office—the one with the window overlooking the dining room. I believe you church people called it the 'crying room,' right?" Dmitri poured himself a mug of coffee, leaving her to wander through the restaurant.

Lord knows I need somewhere to go, she thought to herself, pushing open the door to her old Sunday School classroom in the basement. There on the wall, behind a row of plastic bins labeled Flour and Sugar was the painting of Christ sitting on a hillside amidst a sea of desert wildflowers. Aunt Kate had painted it on the wall at child's eye level so that the children in the room would feel that they were sitting at Jesus's feet. Peering over one of the clouds in the sky, a smiling old man with a white beard seemed to be observing the earthly scene below. Even her Aunt Kate who never went to church had imagined that God had a face.

Hannah stood quietly in the little room grasping for something at the edge of her mind, her eyes clenched shut. Soon memories began to rain down over her, a waterfall of images drenching her. When she opened her eyes, Hannah wondered if she had grown bigger than the truths she had learned in this room. Or had everything in this place from her childhood been too small to sustain her during the journey of her soul?

CHAPTER 16

In early December, four days before Griggsberg High's Winter Prom, Tim Ledbetter jumped into the air to score the winning basket against Independence High. When he collided with the floor, he tore all the ligaments in his right knee. Hannah, who had been cheering for him from the stands, made a mental note to exchange the boutonniere she had bought him to wear to the dance for a bouquet of hospital flowers. She took her formal—bought with her first paycheck from the restaurant—back to Macy's in Kansas City and moped around the house for the rest of the week.

On Friday night, Hannah, still sulking, answered the phone.

"Heard your date's in the hospital," came the voice.

"Jared?"

"Want to go with the best-looking guy in the junior class?"

"And who might that be?" Hannah asked innocently.

"Don't push your luck, Princess. I heard you're a desperate woman who needs a date for tomorrow night. I'm offering my excellent company and my personal chariot for the event."

"Will your dad's truck have a full or half load of lawn fertilizer in it when you pick me up?"

"In anticipation of the requirements of my royal date, I have already unloaded my father's truck and washed out all the residue of the foul stuff. Have I met your standards, M'Lady?"

"Pick me up at seven, Ben Hur, and you'd better be wearing something other than that tool belt of yours," Hannah said, giggling at Jared's stilted language. Jared was anything but stilted. She also remembered vaguely that he hated to dance.

"Only the best for the Lady of the Bluff," he replied gallantly and hung up the phone.

Sweet Jared! thought Hannah. *When did he start calling me 'Princess'?* She didn't care. Her heart began to race, and she stood in front of the hall mirror in a state of amazement. Her face looked lit up—all because a boy she had known since she was ten was taking her to a dance. She had pounded nails with him, hauled rocks with him, shoveled dirt with him, laughed and cavorted with him—but she had never danced with him.

At six-thirty on Saturday night, Hannah was drying her hair when the doorbell rang. *When has Jared ever been early for anything?* Hannah wondered, throwing a robe over her slip, and opening the front door. There stood Eric up to his ankles in the six inches of snow that had fallen the night before.

"Meet Jared at the fort at seven-thirty," he said through chattering teeth.

"The fort? Are you sure?"

"Just following orders, ma'am," said Eric, saluting. "Oh, and he said to wear socks and warm boots and that down ski jacket of yours no matter how dumb it looks."

"Okay, Eric. Tell your strange brother I'll be there."

"Too late—he left a while ago in Dad's truck."

"Was he dressed for the dance?"

"He was wearing Neil's choir tuxedo. And I helped him with his cucumber bun."

"Cumberbund."

"Yeah, that. Dad cut his hair last night, and Jared even scraped all the dirt out from under his fingernails. He looked kind of nice—smelled good too."

"Thanks, buddy. You'd better get back inside or you'll freeze."

A few minutes later, Hannah had finished curling her hair in long, loose tendrils. She stepped into the pale blue, lace and organza gown her mother had worn in the Miss Missouri pageant twenty years before. It was hopelessly out-of-date and smelled like the cedar closet where it had been stored—but it would do. The empire waistline accentuated Hannah's figure. "Om-peer" her mother had pronounced the style as she brought it out of the closet after Jared had called. "Empire is that tall building in New York City, dear."

Whatever it was called, Hannah was glad it fit and that Miranda had not already donated it to the Salvation Army.

An hour later, Hannah found herself standing on the platform of the snow-covered fort, wearing the elegant gown accented by two pairs of Gabe's wool socks, leather hiking boots, wool dance leggings, and the big puffy down jacket that made her look like she was standing inside a stack of inner tubes. Under her wool mittens, she wore her mother's white, formal gloves that reached past her elbows, almost to the cap sleeves that cupped her shoulders. One silver-satin, high-heeled shoe peeked above each of the side pockets of her bulky jacket. She was glad her meticulous mother had not been home to see her daughter's ensemble for the evening.

As she stood there looking over the frozen lake, wondering what on earth Jared had cooked up, she heard a distant motor like a chain saw or a lawn mower. After another minute, she saw a figure riding a ski-mobile coming toward her, a plume of dry powdery snow kicking up behind it.

"Jared?" she called as the figure stopped twenty feet below her, turned off the motor, and dismounted. The cold silent air between them sparkled with falling snowflakes.

"Juliet?" came Jared's answer. "But soft! What light through yonder window breaks? It is the east, and Juliet is the sun."

Hannah laughed at the lines all honors English students were required to memorize. In her best Juliet voice, she answered, "O Romeo, Romeo! Wherefore art thou, Romeo?"

Jared knelt in the snow and leaned his head to the side with both gloved hands under his cheek. "See how she leans her cheek upon her hand. O, that I were a glove upon that hand, that I might touch that cheek!"

Hannah closed her eyes for a moment and recalled more of the lines. "Romeo—deny thy father and refuse thy name; Or, if thou wilt not, be but sworn my love, and I'll no longer be a Capulet . . . Romeo, doff thy name . . . for that name is no part of thee—Take all myself!"

The two of them were silent for a moment, embarrassed—the air between them electric with surprise. *Are we quoting Shakespeare or . . . talking to each other?* Hannah wondered, pacing on the platform of the fort, grateful that she could not recall any more of the words from the most famous love scene in history. "I'm cold. And I can't remember anymore!" she called down to him.

"Okay," said Jared, rising and dusting the powdery snow from the knees of Neil's choir tuxedo. "I'll come get you. While I'm coming, you get your corsage out of the cooler. I hope it's not frozen."

Hannah lifted the lid of the cooler the kids used to chill sodas in the summer and found a wrist corsage made of six red rosebuds nestled in a bed of baby's breath. She had forgotten to buy Jared a boutonniere. "It's beautiful, Jared. Now how am I supposed to get down there?"

"How do we get down here in the summer?" he asked.

"On the elevator rope?"

"Why not? Just wait till I come get you, and we'll go double like we used to when we were kids," he said, his voice muffled by the snow-laden shrubbery on the banks of the Bluff.

"This is crazy!" She laughed with delight as Jared led her carefully down the Bluff a few feet to their old jumping rock. A swimming hole much shallower than the rest of the quarry lake had been created by the submerged quarry road on their side of Lake Shiloh. Hundreds of times on hot summer days, the two of them had reached the lake below on a rope pulley contraption they had created and attached to the underside of the fort. Counterbalanced by a huge quarry digger tire, the rope was designed to send them spinning off the rock, down to the lake below. Just before the tire hit the fort above them, the kids on the Bluff always let go of the rope to plunge into the deliciously cold water.

Hannah placed her feet on one side of the disk of plywood secured by the knotted end of the rope, and Jared placed his feet on the other side. "I always wanted to do this in the winter," Jared said, his big gloved palms covering her hands to make sure she was holding on tightly. "I've scraped together about three feet of the softest powder you ever landed on."

Without letting her consider a moment longer, Jared pushed off with a banshee scream and the two of them reeled down the side of the Bluff, releasing their hold at the same moment, tumbling into the pile of snow. The two of them laughed hysterically and threw snow on each other, then climbed off the snow pile, stomping wildly to warm themselves up.

Jared led Hannah to the snowmobile and bowed low. "My chariot, madame," he said gallantly.

Hannah gathered the yards of frothy organza over one arm and straddled the back half of the snowmobile's padded seat. Jared placed a duffle bag containing something heavy and angular on the seat in front of her, and hopped on the little vehicle.

"Where did you get this thing?" Hannah yelled into his ear.

"Belongs to my cousins," Jared yelled back.

They sped along the snowy lake for awhile, then Jared stopped on the far side where his truck was parked on the beach.

"Why are we stopping?" asked Hannah, disappointed. "I was having so much fun."

"Don't you want to go to the dance?"

"What dance?" said Hannah, grinning. "Besides, I lost one of my shoes somewhere—I'd have to dance in these hiking boots."

"I was hoping you wouldn't want to go," Jared said. "Look inside that bag."

Hannah unzipped the bag and the steel blades of two pairs of ice skates glinted in the moonlight. "Skates!"

"Borrowed those from my cousins, too."

"But how will we skate when there's snow on the ice?"

"You don't give me much credit, do you?" Jared answered, roaring back over the lake and stopping near a metal scoop contraption sitting on the ice. "I spent the whole day with that little snow plow attachment making a path through the snow. Come on—put on your skates!" he said, digging them out of the bag.

Hannah gasped in amazement as she noticed a long path that looped and curled over the surface of the lake, then disappeared under the covered bridge. "I don't believe this—it must have taken you all day to scrape that snow off!"

"I got about a quarter mile down the river until I came to a big tree that had fallen across it."

"Well, let's go!" said Hannah, hitching up her evening gown and lacing up her skates. Soon they were gliding over the icy path, chasing each other, and racing in the moonlight. They ducked under the covered bridge and skated down the river until they came to the tree that extended across it. Just in front of the tree, Jared had cleared a round skating area that looked like the top of a birthday cake with a flute of snowy icing around its edge. He had also built a fire ring on the bank of the river and left a can of lighter fluid and some logs next to it. Boy Scout Jared built a quick fire and the two of them warmed themselves next to it.

"You think of everything!" Hannah said with real admiration.

When she felt warm, Hannah slipped off her down jacket and wool mittens and hung them on a tree limb. "I want to see if ballet pirouettes work on the ice," she said, positioning herself down the river a bit to get a running start. She got up some speed by the time she entered the circular area, then quickly tucked her arms in as she would to perform a pirouette. Jared pulled out a small camera from his pocket and began to snap pictures of her skating, sliding, and falling on the ice. After numerous tries and gales of laughter, Hannah taught herself to spin gracefully, head back, gloved arms crossed dramatically in front of her chest, her long, flying curls lost in a whirl-wind of blue. Jared crouched on the ice, watching her, snapping pictures from every angle.

"Come on, Jared, let's dance—a pas de deux!" called Hannah.

"A pas de what?"

"A step for two!"

Jared joined her, and the two of them skated together, making up steps and spins. "You didn't know about me and Mikhail Baryshnikov?" boasted Jared as he lifted her over his head and then dipped her toward the ice as he imagined the great ballet star would do. "I taught him everything he knows."

"I believe it—sort of!" came Hannah's voice from somewhere near his feet. Her hands were extended out in front of her just in case Jared dropped her headfirst on the ice.

"Hey, I almost forgot! My camera has one of those delayed timer attachments. We need some pictures of us together—they'll be worth a mint after we're a famous skating couple." He spent a moment positioning the camera on the trunk of the tree, and they snapped five or six shots of themselves together for their imaginary future fans. For the last pose, Jared held Hannah in a dip with her chin inches from the ice, her blue gown rippling in the breeze, the blades of her skates glinting next to his ear.

"We'll have the best Winter Formal pictures of anyone," Hannah said.

"I think we're having a better time than anyone, too."

"Absolutely," agreed Hannah, "And for someone who hates to dance, you are doing a pretty good job—and *liking* it too."

"Dancing is way more fun on the ice."

After warming themselves by their fire again, Jared and Hannah smothered the flames with armloads of snow. Then they skated back under the covered bridge to the lake. For hours, they laughed and skated over the paths Jared had created on the icy surface of the lake. Then they hopped back on the snowmobile and skimmed over the snowy part of the lake until they'd had enough for the evening.

Minutes before midnight, Jared and Hannah found themselves sitting on the same side of a booth at Rosa's, sipping hot chocolate, then sharing a plate of biscuits and gravy. They left the diner as their friends started coming in from the dance for a late-night snack. Neither of them felt like explaining to anyone why they never made it to the dance. Besides, neither of them really *could* explain why they had wanted the night alone to play, and talk, and just be with each other.

Capulet, Montague, Hannah thought. *A night of truce.*

Hannah's sides were aching from laughing all evening by the time Jared took her home. At her front door, she looked into the saddest eyes she had ever seen, and knew instantly how Juliet had felt. Jared held her for several moments on her doorstep, and Hannah buried her face into the front of his jacket to save them both from the kiss that would undo them completely.

"Thank you for the most romantic night of my life," Hannah whispered.

Jared struggled a moment and swallowed hard, "If I didn't believe what I believe—and you didn't believe what you believe—I could love you."

"Love me?" Hannah echoed, searching the face of her childhood friend.

"I already do love you. I think I always will . . . because you're part of me." He reached into his pocket and brought out her silver shoe. "I took this . . . because I really didn't want to go to that dance. I wanted us to make a memory together. To have . . . for always."

Cinderella took the shoe from her prince. She knew it fit like a glove—and also knew she and Jared would never fit like that. Hannah

sighed; a ripple of melancholy made her heart feel tender. "Good
night, sweet Jared." She kissed his cheek and turned to go into her
house before he could see her tears.

On the other side of the closed front door, Hannah slumped to
the floor in her still-damp evening gown. A few more lines from the
final act of *Romeo and Juliet* came to her mind.

"Eyes, look your last!
Arms, take your last embrace! And lips, O you
The doors of breath, seal with a righteous kiss."

Capulets, Montagues. Mormons, nonmormons. Protestants, Catholics.
Jews, Arabs. Warring clans—all of them, she thought miserably. She
knew clearly in that moment that she did not belong to the clan of
her birth. And just as clearly, she knew Jared truly belonged to his.
Why was it all so important? Wouldn't it be better if there were no clans
at all?

CHAPTER 17

At a quarter past eleven, Hannah had finished filling the little tray of salt and pepper shakers at the hostess station and was preparing to lock the front doors of the restaurant. Only a few customers lingered over their dinners, speaking in low companionable tones. Occasional ripples of laughter spilled out of their booths as the low light cast an atmosphere of restful privacy over them all. It was late January and The Monastery felt even cozier with the wind whipping fiercely against the windows.

Tired waiters, dressed in their brown monk costumes, wiped down tables, tidied the condiments, brushed crumbs from the velvet seat cushions, and occasionally paused to eat from a plate of fried vegetables the cook had set out for them. The bartender visited each table briefly giving a last call for drinks before he set about closing down the bar and restocking the wine bottles on the huge wall next to the stained-glass window.

After two months of working at the restaurant, Hannah had grown to love this quiet time at the close of her shift. There was something honest and satisfying and *basic* about feeding people who were hungry. She thought of the mural in her old Sunday School classroom downstairs which she often saw while retrieving condiments and restaurant supplies. It made her think of the loaves and fishes that Jesus had used to feed the crowds. Even Jesus had realized that he needed to feed people before they could think of spiritual things.

Hannah had begun to see this new use for the little church of her childhood as less commercial and even a bit mystical at times. Marriage proposals had been made here, anniversaries toasted, graduations celebrated, loves found and lost, plans made and changed. Along with every meal, the meat and drink of individual lives were consumed within these walls.

Just as Hannah moved toward the big entry doors to lock them for the evening, they suddenly swung wide and her Aunt Kate stepped into the restaurant, and took her coat off. Kate was a tall, handsome woman who was impossible to ignore when she entered any room. Eight years older than Miranda, she was as different from her sister as apple butter was from caviar.

Tonight Kate was dressed in one of her trademark, ankle-length muslin dresses of her own creation. A black, richly woven cashmere shawl was thrown dramatically over her shoulders; silver and turquoise handcrafted earrings trailed to her shoulders, setting off her graying auburn hair, which she wore down her back tonight. She wore only a touch of makeup on her flawless, almost translucent skin; but it was her deep, blue-green eyes that gave her face the color and drama that was Kate.

She stood facing Hannah in the foyer, holding her arms out wide like a mythical waterbird preparing for flight. Hannah wiped her hands on her skirt, and walked happily into Kate's warm-winged embrace.

"Where have you been? I haven't seen you since Christmas, Aunt Kate. Have you been gone or on a project? I'm so glad to see you," Hannah cooed, nestling in Kate's strength. The only time she had ever truly felt like a child, even during the years when she really was a child, was while she was wrapped in one of Aunt Kate's hugs.

"All of the above, Hannah. Tonight, I've just come from a gallery showing in Kansas City. And as far as my absence is concerned, your mother isn't exactly making me feel welcome at your house these days. She's been hell in a housecoat, hasn't she? Well, that baby's coming in a few months whether it's an 'inconvenient time in her life' or not. Have you got everything ready?"

"I don't know. Mom's in bed so much, I can't imagine that the nursery is ready . . . and I've been gone a lot . . ."

"If your mother hadn't been so depressing at Christmas, I would have offered to do the baby's room." The more Kate talked about her sister, the more intense she became.

"Well, Kate, never mind Mom, you can come see me any time now that I have a place of my own," Hannah said, indicating the restaurant as if it were her first apartment. "Doesn't this place look vaguely familiar to you, Kate?"

"Yeah, the *place* looks familiar, but *you* don't." Kate held Hannah away from her and looked at her quietly. "You've been trying not to go home—and you're not eating right. Come on, let's have a big fried dinner and some of that *Sinfully Delicious Strawberry Cheesecake* I saw on the menu last time I was here. You have two pieces, okay?" Kate laughed the hearty laugh she used when she was insisting on having her way. "Dmitri!" she called across the restaurant in her naturally loud voice. "Okay if I sit here at this booth and try to revive one of your employees with some high-fat food tonight? She's wasted away since I saw her last."

Hannah grinned at this sudden concern for her well-being. As they ate the heaping plates of food that Dmitri brought them, Hannah wondered how this woman could possibly be a blood relative of her mother. Aunt Kate had been the black sheep of the family. While Miranda had been sashaying down beauty pageant runways in the late sixties and early seventies, Kate had been leading anti-war rallies with friends from the Kansas City Art Institute. She and her hippie art student friends organized flower children festivals by the fountain in front of the Nelson Rockefeller Museum of Art. Folk singers, runaway teenagers and itinerant peace activists regularly slept on Kate's couches and floors.

In time, Kate had settled down and taken a job in the art department at MCC. The Mallory sisters had become famous in their own separate circles. Over the years, they had developed a cautious relationship across the miles of their differences.

"I wonder if Grandpa Mallory is pleased with the way his daughters turned out," Kate mused. "I get to thinking about that sweet old man every time I think about your mother—especially with a new baby coming."

"Don't you think Grandpa is just a bunch of atoms and energy dispersed randomly into the universe by now?"

Kate put down the zucchini stick she had just dipped into ranch dressing, and turned her whole body to face her niece. "You surprise me, Hannah. Your father has taught you every Sunday about what will happen to you after you die. But you don't believe a word of it."

"Maybe I don't," Hannah said, a bite of cheesecake balanced on her fork. "Sometimes I think the whole idea of heaven is a real great public relations tool to keep people coming to church. It buys them a seat on the shuttle . . . "

"Remind me not to have you speak at my funeral . . . " Kate said. "You ought to know better than that."

"Just because I am the daughter of a man who talks about heaven every seventh day of the week?"

"No . . . because I would have thought you would have a little reper- toire of personal experience by now to draw on—some direct spiritual encounters that whisper into your ear that earth life is not all there is."

Hannah put down her fork and looked at Kate. "Direct encoun- ters? Have you been going to seances or something?"

"Seances! All right, now you're making me mad. I feel like I'm talking to someone who has no faith at all."

Hannah thought a moment. "Maybe you *are* talking to someone who has no faith at all. And, by the way, my faith definitely IS shaped by my experiences. Just look at what those experiences have been lately—Gabe's too. We base our ideas on what we see every day—not what we hear on Sundays!"

Hannah felt sadness settle over her. Kate changed the subject. "By the way, how is Gabe doing?"

Hannah shook her head, and felt instantly guilty over her neglect of him lately. "He's getting so crazy, Kate. He wanders around at night downtown, and Mom and Dad don't even care. I've told them that the police pick him up every time they're out of town—and they said he's just being a boy."

"You sound so bitter, Hannah. Honey, I've been in la-la land, too. I've been completely out of the picture and I need to get back in touch with you two," Kate said with a quiet determination that unnerved Hannah.

"Yeah, Aunt Kate, we could be your latest cause or something. You could be the president of the 'Save Hannah and Gabe Foundation,' Hannah said, pushing her cheesecake away, her stomach roiling, tears stinging her eyes.

"That's enough sarcasm, young lady; I won't let you speak to me in that tone," replied Kate with a raw edge in her own voice. "I came tonight to find out what's going on in your life and I won't be made to feel guilty for not coming sooner. I came as soon as I could." Kate always knew when she was being manipulated. "You know I don't do guilt, Hannah," she said, putting her arm around Hannah's tiny shoulders and wrapping her shawl around her niece.

"I'm sorry, Kate. When I think of my family, I just feel so *helpless.*"

The last customers had left some time ago. The lights were off except those in the foyer and the floodlight that shone through the stained-glass window behind them. Dmitri had given them a nod of understanding as he let himself out of the self-locking door. Kate and Hannah sat with plates of half-eaten food on the table in front of them, and a tightness between them that felt heavy and complex.

"When I look at my mother, about ready to give birth to another human being, I want to scream, 'Take care of what you've already got!'" Hannah realized she had held that tortured little speech in her mind for weeks, and it had finally spewed out of her mouth like a big drink of spoiled milk. "I'm so afraid this baby is going to be the last straw on a load she can barely carry as it is. I heard Dad ask her to get rid of the baby, Kate."

"No. Your father would never . . . "

"I heard it myself, Kate. He said no one would ever find out if she got rid of the baby. In fact, if I *hadn't* heard him say that, he would have probably talked Mom into it."

"That's so hard for me to believe . . . " said Kate, tearing a piece of bread into smaller and smaller bits.

"I guess he feels this new little baby is going to cramp his lifestyle. He might have to cut down on his speaking engagements or change a diaper or something. I don't know what's the matter with him—I just know he has left us!" Hannah was sobbing with complete abandon now, her shoulders shuddering from the effort of this unfamiliar emotional release. Kate let Hannah use her shawl as a giant handkerchief to wipe her tears.

"You're really lonely and confused right now, sweetheart," said Kate taking her into her arms, rocking her, stroking Hannah's hair and brushing the sweat-soaked strands off her neck. "Oh, Hannah, life has a way of getting better just as you think it will fall completely apart! You're too young to know that I'm speaking the truth. But you'll know, you'll know. Just have faith . . . " Kate comforted her.

Hannah could no longer hear her words, but had felt safe enough with Kate to give voice to her anguish. After Hannah cried her throat dry, she laid her head on Kate's shoulder—gathering strength to leave her sanctuary and go home.

CHAPTER 18

Miranda took to her bed often during the last few months of winter. The gray days and her growing belly had left her without her normal frantic energy, and finally she had given up her hectic schedule completely. She and Craig had been telling everyone that Dr. Williams had sent Miranda to bed for the remainder of her pregnancy. It was a lie, but it kept the church members from pestering them about the pregnancy.

Today was a particularly warm spring day in the middle of April. Miranda was feeling jealous that Craig had gotten to fly to Washington, D.C., to attend a Christians United rally. The Christian right was finally getting a head of steam. Every Christian in America could almost taste the sweetness of being so close to real political power. And there she was—at home, in bed, four weeks of pregnancy left to endure.

Miranda had thrown open her French doors to catch the breeze, but even the warm spring air did not inspire her. She stretched out on her bed, glaring wretchedly at the svelte models in her women's magazines. *Will I ever wear size six again?* she wondered miserably. During the Dallas conference, she had slipped away to Saks and had bought an exquisite chartreuse suit made of one hundred percent pure silk. That was the week, back in September, that she had discovered her pregnancy and developed the terrible morning sickness.

Her first humiliation was having to cancel her appearance on the *Glory to God* show with Reverend John Avery Holton and his wife Tina. Millions of Americans were tuning in to the Christian network these days. The Christians of the United States were finally making a stand against the godless politicians that had taken over the country in recent years. Miranda would have been a part of that had it not been for the wretched, violent nausea that had accompanied her early pregnancy, and the flattening lethargy of these final months.

She felt a wave of stark loneliness. The piles of magazines strewn on the king-sized bed were causing more anxiety than distraction. The spring air had given her a slight sense of well being, and she found herself craving action, or some company.

She heard Hannah down the hall in her room getting ready for her Saturday shift at The Monastery. "Hannah! How about bringing me some of that wonderful raspberry tea!" she called, hoping Hannah was within earshot. She had educated her entire household about the benefits of raspberry tea. JoLyn had given her the rest of her stash the month before, enthusiastically extolling the benefits of the herbal tea for toning the uterus and preparing it for the difficulty of labor.

In Miranda's mind, anyone who had voluntarily birthed eight babies was a certified, bonafide expert on the tricks of successful childbirth. She had welcomed JoLyn's wisdom about herbal tonics that promised to reduce the amount of labor she would have to endure, and help her regain her famous figure as quickly as possible.

Miranda heard Hannah racing down the stairs on her way to work. The two of them rarely spoke these days.

Just as Miranda had resigned herself to a lonely afternoon with her magazines, the door to her bedroom burst open, and Gabe pushed in backwards carrying a wicker tray. A shiny black teapot decorated with yellow bumblebees sat next to two matching mugs. Gabe had even picked a handful of red tulips, and had arranged them pleasantly along with bits of bright-green spring grass in a jam jar full of water.

"If I have some of this raspberry tea with you, I won't get a womb or nothin', will I?" Gabe said disdainfully as he set the tray down on the pale pink satin comforter in front of his mother.

"Gabey! How perfectly sweet of you. You would actually sit here and drink a cup of tea with your fat old mother on a perfectly fabulous spring day? I thought you were going camping at the river with Ian today."

"I'm going. I just heard you call Hannah and since she had to work, I thought I'd be the one to help get your uterus in shape for the big event." Miranda had never heard Gabe talk about the baby as if it were really about to be born.

"I would like nothing better than to have a tea party with my handsome son on this fine spring day," Miranda said, suddenly cheerful. "And I'm fairly sure that men can drink potfuls of raspberry tea with no chance of developing unwanted anatomy," she said as she poured tea for both of them.

Gabe blushed and looked out the window. "I've been hoping you'll have a boy. With Dad gone all the time and all—we need another guy around here." He looked over at his father's side of the bed, nicely made up as it had been for several months now.

"Your dad just couldn't get any sleep with me getting so big, and with my tossing and turning every night. He gets a better night's rest in the guest room," she said, toying with her mug of tea.

Miranda looked around her bedroom. Evidence of a male was sorely lacking in their home. Craig had not chosen the cream-colored wallpaper embossed with a feminine pink and gold pattern, nor the elaborate brass four-poster bed covered by the mountainous pink satin comforter. The pillows behind her back boasted yards of ruffles and lace. Everything in the room looked as if it had been imported from the royal bedroom of some long-dead European princess.

Miranda knew Gabe hated the ridiculous upright telephone by her bed. He had told her it made her look like a bad actress in one of those films with subtitles. He had bought her the latest streamlined model for Christmas, a cordless phone in his favorite color of candy-apple red. She had left it in its box in her walk-in closet. Men just didn't understand color coordination.

"Oh! I nearly forgot. I've had an appointment with Mayor Lockhart in my planner for more than a month to talk about the music camp. I have to call him and cancel that meeting. I'll tell him I'm in a delicate condition these days and need to rest and have the soothing comfort and conversation of my adorable son today."

Gabe smiled at her and flopped contentedly on the satin bedspread, idly flipping through a few women's magazines as she made her call to Jack Lockhart.

The Church on the Hill Gospel Music Camp was Miranda's crusade in life. She and Louis Talbott had auditioned hundreds of inner-city kids and selected the most promising for the traveling choir. Aunt Kate and some of her art students had painted an old school bus in rainbow colored stripes with gigantic black musical notes bouncing all over it. Eventually, the bus became so well known that the choir of inner city angels had been nicknamed The Music Bus.

Once a week for practice and almost every weekend for performances, Talbott drove the gaudy bus with its squeaky brakes and periodic muffler explosions, briefly stopping for Miranda on the way down the hill. When she heard the bus, Miranda would fly out the door, shouting dinner instructions to Gabe or Hannah, and board the psychedelic bus for another raucous church concert or television appearance. The kids were cute but the only time they could be controlled was when they were singing at the top of their lungs which is what they did all the way to their appearances and every time they boarded that bus. Miranda thrived on the commotion and potential disaster involved in every bus ride.

Miranda was talking excitedly to the mayor now. "I'm getting Reverend John Avery Holton to put the choir on his *Glory to God* program," Miranda paused, arranging the bedclothes around her. "Of course he'll pay the expenses! Are you kidding? They'll be a drop in the bucket compared to the donations he rakes in after my kids appear on his show!" Miranda was silent a moment. "Besides, he owes me an appearance after my unfortunate cancellation last fall. We're nearly at goal, Jack. You and I need to settle this land thing so people will know this camp has a place to be built. *Then* you'll see the donations come in, Jack."

Miranda's face now wore her warring crusader expression. Gabe had seen brave men bend and crumble when fixed with Miranda's unremitting demands for money or favors for the music camp.

Gabe sighed and slipped out her bedroom door as his mother began taking notes and searching for some mislaid papers at the side of her bed.

The raspberry tea grew cold.

* * *

Grabbing his already-packed duffel bag and his camouflage-patterned sleeping bag from the garage, Gabe raced across the street to Ian Bennigan's house. He went through their side gate toward the back of the hill and down a grassy ramp to the underground bunker. Even on a glorious spring day, Gabe knew Ian would be underground plotting to overthrow the world in one of his imaginary war games.

Gabe gave the secret knock on the heavy metal door and Ian called out, "Get in here! The Cubans have their missiles pointed toward Griggsberg. I've just located them with the radar and it looks like some action today, boys." Ian spoke in an urgent, serious tone as if he were speaking to a secretive cluster of commandos in a White House situation room. His expensive IBM computer rested on a table against one wall of the underground room that had been blasted out of the limestone hill. The bunk beds he and Gabe and Charlie had built lined another wall. Militia and gun magazines were stacked on shelves. Army surplus equipment hung on hooks.

Two four-wheelers were positioned near the door. Ian had already loaded them up with camping supplies and secured the gear to the bikes with brightly colored bungie cords.

Gabe had heard the stories. In the sixties, Ian's Uncle Seamus had been involved in actual town meetings that were called to discuss how to protect citizens in the event of a war with Cuba. Seamus Bennigan went to the meetings more to protect his quarry business than to help the cause. He had no intention of putting his machines to work on some cockamamy scheme to turn the tunnels in the Bluff into fallout shelters. Let Castro shoot off all the missiles he wanted; Seamus had a business to run, and expensive marble to mine out of those tunnels.

Ian licked a gummed-back gold star and placed it on the map over Lima, Peru. The stars on the wall map indicated all the locations Ian regularly contacted over the Internet. There were stars all over his world map.

When he saw Ian engrossed in his computer fantasy, Gabe became irritable. "Ian, it hasn't been this warm since last summer! Let's get the bikes and go down to the river. It's late afternoon already and we won't be able to find our trotline in the dark! I bet we got a ton of big fat catfish on that line just waitin' to be fried up in that ol' skillet!" Gabe, now motivated by his own pep talk, pulled Ian away from his keyboard and tried to drag him over to the all-terrain vehicles.

"Sometimes you just don't understand how certain world conditions might make it *inconvenient* to suddenly go camping!" said Ian testily as he shut down the computer. He seemed to have to forcibly wrench himself away from whatever dark plot he had been cooking up with the other anti-social, hermit teenagers he had met on the Internet.

"No one would DARE start World War III on a beautiful spring day like today," Gabe said, trying to move Ian toward the door. "It would be . . . let's say . . . *un-American* to go to war when the trotline's full, and it's warm enough to sleep out all night, and we got two motor bikes already packed up with camping gear. Right, Ian?"

Gabe backed the bike that actually belonged to Charlie out of the door and up the grassy ramp that led to the woods on the backside of Bennigan's Bluff. Charlie rarely used the bike, lacking the adventurous temperament possessed by both Ian and Gabe. Ian took his time repositioning his supplies and adjusting the straps that held them on the bike. Gabe tried to be patient. After all, he could never own the equipment and have access to the exciting wilderness property without a Bennigan.

Fiona Bennigan was very strict about keeping people off her land, so the boys were virtually the sole possessors of Bennigan's Woods. The rusty metal "no trespassing" signs nailed high in the trees had kept the college students away ever since Fiona had taken several of them to court. She had even taken Esther Silverman from across the street to court for taking a walk in her woods.

"Yeehah!" Gabe screamed, revving up the ATV loudly before letting out the clutch. "Let's get those fish and cook us up a mess of 'em!" he yelled over his shoulder at Ian.

The boys careened down the side of the hill on trails they had forged themselves. Gabe headed toward the river, looking for their favorite camping spot. A ragged red bandana tied to a tree on the far side of the river marked the place where the boys had rigged up the trotline several days before.

"It's loaded!" Ian called. The fish seemed to reconnect him to the vigorous reality of the woods. He carefully lifted the line full of fishhooks from which nine or ten fat flopping catfish and a couple of bluegill were suspended. "Look at how those two cats got hooks in their backs. They didn't even take the bait and we got 'em!"

Ian had finally shaken off his morbid Saturday melodrama and seemed to be enjoying the wilderness adventure. "Throw those bluegill back; they ain't worth frying up," Ian said pointing to the two smaller fish.

"Lookey here, we got us a big old long garfish with his snappy little shark teeth. Can't eat him neither. Toss 'im back!" Gabe and Ian both knew perfectly well how to speak proper English but often lapsed into what they imagined to be an earthy Huck Finn, mid-Missouri butchering of the language as part of their mountain men behavior.

Ian disengaged the hook from the toothy mouth of the long, crocodile-like garfish and tossed it back into the river. Melting snow and a recent spring rain had swollen the river, and the boys had to be careful not to fall into the strong current.

"Get the skillet out of the tree. There should still be some Wesson Oil and a bag of corn meal from last time," Ian called to Gabe as he placed the flopping catfish into a burlap sack. The boys had hidden various supplies in a dead oak tree that hung over the river so they wouldn't have to haul so much equipment.

Gabe had already piled up the kindling around some torn-up newspaper to start the fire. The boys now followed an automatic ritual to prepare their dinner. They had become proficient in the ways of the wilderness since they had begun the camping expeditions two years before.

"I brought some soda pop and Doritos," called Gabe over his shoulder as he rooted around in the hole of the tree for the skillet and the bag of cooking supplies.

"And I rolled us a big old joint," said Ian. "Hey! We've got to start digging up the garden plot for this year's crop of Mary-joo-wanna. We've just about sold all the dried stuff from last summer," Ian taunted Gabe with anticipation. "We're gonna have ourselves a night, huh?"

Gabe tended the fire and threw some logs on it once it got going. The fire grew into high licking flames as the sun slipped down behind the woods. Streaks of pink and yellow briefly appeared above the trees, then faded into a denim-colored sky.

The boys had developed a fascination with fire. Rather than building a simple cooking fire, they always stoked it until it blazed wild and high. They were mesmerized by the heat and power of it.

Gabe and Ian were silent while the fire was at its height. As it began to die, they tended to the skinning, gutting, and battering of the fish.

Gabe pulled off the catfish whiskers and the sharp pectoral fins with a pair of pliers. The boys left the heads on as a part of their manly ritual. Only women would bother cutting off the head so as not to eat a creature with its dead eyes staring at them. This was their time. It was what they needed to feel like themselves again.

When the fire had died down to a few glowing embers and a spitting flame, the boys set a heavy grate on the stones in the fire ring. Soon the Wesson Oil was sputtering and the catfish were sizzling away as a violet darkness fell upon the woods. Ian made up some more blood bait—a mixture of liver, corn meal, bubble gum, and Ivory Snow dish soap. He put the little bloody clumps of fish bait on the hooks of the trotline and set the line down deep in the cold water for tomorrow's catch. Then he joined Gabe by the fire. The boys poked and turned the fish until they were crispy golden delicacies bobbing in the hot oil.

"Did you bring paper towels?" asked Gabe as he noticed the feast was nearly ready.

"Do I ever forget the details?" said Ian as he unrolled the towels to soak up the grease of the fish while they cooled. Gabe opened a giant bag of Doritos and popped open the two cans of tepid root beer. The boys reveled in the sensuous meal they had won for themselves.

The temperature grew colder as the heat from the ground dissipated into the chilly night air. The final night rituals began. Ian lit the hand-rolled cigarette and took a slow drag. Then Gabe took a puff and coughed self-consciously, handing it back to Ian. The fire was tame now; it had burned itself low. Ian stirred it with a big stick and threw on another log to keep it going.

Gabe felt the warmth of the fire on his face, and the chill of the night at his back. He belonged in these woods. The rules were simple; he and Ian made them up as they went. The boys grew sleepy and spread their sleeping bags out next to the fire. They undressed in a fog of sweet smelling marijuana.

As Gabe drifted off to sleep, he considered how thoughtful God had been during the creation of the world. Although the people he made caused each other constant heartache, God had also created a little plant that could help deaden the pain of existence.

CHAPTER 19

One month later, Kadence Kathryn Dennison was born. Everyone who knew the Dennisons held their breaths hoping this baby would pull the family out of the isolation and depression that had surrounded them during Miranda's pregnancy. Kadence was a miracle. Hannah was amazed at how her new baby sister changed everything for the good. Named after a musical term, Kadence was a wonder child, smiling and chortling early, observant of everything around her. Right from the start, she cast a magic on the Dennison family that none of them could have anticipated. Aunt Kate had been right: just as Hannah had thought things would never be right in her family—things got better.

Kadence reached her developmental milestones with a peculiar, unselfconscious grace and ease. She walked at nine months, and had a pet name for everyone by the time she was eighteen months old. Her eyes were what people noticed first—large, deep-brown eyes framed by long, thick eyelashes. She had a halo of hair the color of butter that exploded from her head in exuberant, unmanageable ringlets.

The Dennisons soon learned that the congregation would not tolerate her banishment to the church nursery. During every church service, she was passed around from member to member, her rare crying benevolently tolerated. She was walked in the halls by doting church members and often played with her toys on the platform, or snoozed peacefully in her baby carrier during her father's sermons. She had become a symbol of everything that was right in the world: an omen of God's favor upon their community, an instrument of healing.

Hannah and everyone else noticed that Pastor Dennison began to turn down speaking invitations in favor of staying home. His sermons were filled with compassion and eloquence. His prayers were long and poetic expressions of gratitude. The congregation left every Sunday strangely motivated to live good and righteous lives.

The Dennison home life settled into a peaceful routine. Though reluctant at first, Hannah had allowed her mother to give her tips about applying makeup and wearing more flattering clothing. She had consented to driving with Miranda all the way to an expensive salon in Kansas City to have her hair cut a few inches shorter, styled into silky layers, and highlighted with subtle blonde tones. The two of them talked and laughed like school friends whenever they were together.

Although Hannah never quit her job or her lessons, she worked and danced less—and lived more. When she wasn't studying, Hannah's social calendar was full. Though she dated several of the boys in town, she reserved the deepest part of her heart for the one boy who would never be hers.

All Hannah would ever have of Jared was their night of ice dancing. She had framed the photograph of Jared holding her in the dramatic swan dive, her chin just inches above the sparkling ice, their broad smiles illuminated by the light of their campfire. Though he lived next door, it was as though her childhood friend now lived in an entirely different solar system. A wistful ache came over Hannah every time she saw him. And when he saw her, he would wave and turn away from her. She would hurry into the house and close the door, afraid of what she might do or say.

But at least there was a home to go to. For Gabe too. The Dennison household could finally compete with the thrills of Bennigan's Woods. To Hannah's relief, Gabe no longer seemed interested in camping with Ian, or hanging out with him and Charlie in their sinister underground bunker.

Bennigan's Bluff seemed to be split down the middle into parallel universes—each home a separate planet. The Dennisons were thriving and feeling grateful for all the good things that had come their way. Neil Spencer returned home from his mission, and the Spencer family began to focus on getting Jared ready for his. The Silvermans entered the joyful land of grandparenthood as Alan and his wife had their first child.

On the other side of the road, Fiona's boys traveled deeper into their strange fantasies. With their single devotee gone, the Bennigan brothers had begun inviting a succession of oddball teenagers to spend time in the bunker. Some traveled great distances to learn what Ian and Charlie believed, and to see the amazing, Armageddon-proof underground bunker they had heard about over the Internet.

Hannah noticed how her brother had immediately brightened after breaking his association with the Bennigan brothers. He was almost sixteen now and had no burning desire to protect anyone from imagined military threats. Hannah smiled whenever she recalled the thumbs-up Chief Farley had given her at church one Sunday.

Miranda seemed more aware of the needs of both Gabe and Hannah, despite the amazing amount of attention she showered on the baby. She had turned over her long list of responsibilities including the entire concert schedule of The Music Bus to Reverend Talbott. She, in turn, took over his duties as the choir director. Miranda seemed to thrive on the light schedule of choir practices that could be scheduled conveniently into her routine.

The plans for the music camp on Mayor Lockhart's property had been finalized. By the time Kadence was two, twelve log cabins had been completed, and the old Lockhart farmhouse was being renovated.

Miranda and JoLyn became inseparable. In warm weather, Janelle and Kadence were treated to side-by-side stroller rides down Bennigan's Bluff. The mothers talked about mother things; the babies babbled at each other in time to the rhythm of the wheels.

Janelle and Kadence were referred to as the "Bennigan Babies." Extra latches were installed on all the gates that led to the fort to keep the toddlers from attempting an independent visit to the magical place. A gate was created in the common fence between their back-yards so they could go back and forth easily. Swings were strung up at the Dennison home, and a little blue plastic wading pool appeared at the Spencer's. The two little girls chased fireflies together on warm, humid Missouri nights, delighted in a mutually owned collection of Disney movies and picture books, and were traded back and forth by their nap-needing mothers. Janelle's toys and clothes could be found amongst the child rubble at the Dennison home; Kadence's stuff was regularly forgotten at the Spencer's.

* * *

But this time of happiness turned out to be an interlude, a parenthesis of calm between troubled times. An empty space on a bookshelf lined with the volumes of Griggsberg's secrets and unresolved tragedies.

Even Dulcey Martinez, who was in Kansas City studying journalism at the University of Missouri felt the change. The yellow rope around her ankle began to bother her. *Reggie maybe. Asking me to find his murderer.* She called her mother frequently asking if everything was all right. She called Dale Farley wondering if anything was happening in town that would explain her unsettled feeling. He told her there had been no new information to help find Reggie's killer. Dale knew Reggie still haunted Dulcey. He felt he had let her down by not finding the killer.

From time to time, Dulcey or one of her sympathizers did something to keep Reggie's memory alive. The week before Christmas, a front-page photograph showed the door of Mayor Lockhart's office decorated with a wreath made of yellow nylon rope. The reporter from the Gazette had snapped the picture before the angry mayor had torn it off his door. A month later, several street-light poles in front of City Hall were wound with yards and yards of the yellow rope. Citizens began wrapping yellow nylon rope around their mailboxes and sending lengths of it to the mayor by mail. Several times, he'd find a knot of the rope on his car door or on his antenna. Eventually, the mayor grew weary of the public's fascination with yellow rope, and hired a part time investigator to reopen the nearly four-year-old murder case.

The quarry under the lake seemed restless too. On such nights, Darlene got calls about lights under the water. 'Liam's light' the townspeople whispered. Fiona moaned, lying in her lonely bed, "He's restless—tired of waiting." The wind outside her window whined and cursed, calling her to remembrance.

Miranda and Craig began to miss being in demand around the country. Miranda worried that people would stop asking her to sing and that the music camp would suffer because she let herself slide into oblivion. So when Kadence turned three, a real little person who could travel without a truckload of baby paraphernalia, Miranda and Craig began accepting engagements around the country again, taking Kadence with them on the road. Gradually, they were traveling as much as they had been before Kadence was born. By the time

Kadence was four, Miranda discovered that her baby could sing, and Kadence suddenly became a Christian celebrity in her own right. When the Dennisons traveled, they left Hannah and Gabe behind so they would not miss school. At least Gabe had Hannah who attended MCC and lived at home.

Soon after his parents started traveling again, Gabe resumed his nocturnal wanderings. Because he was over sixteen, not even Chief Farley seemed to care when he was downtown at night. Hannah watched helplessly as her brother became one of the lost boys who leaned on alley walls sharing cigarettes, or sat in Ian's bunker listening eagerly to tales of conspiracy and the imminent demise of the world as they had always known it.

It was as if the whole town were holding its breath waiting for something to happen.

On Easter Sunday, 1999, something did happen—and the whole country focused its attention on the little town of Griggsberg, Missouri.

CHAPTER 20

At 12:37 in the morning on Easter Sunday, Hannah locked the church doors. Gabe was asleep. Her parents and Kadence were out of town, but would be home in time for services. Hannah had just finished arranging hundreds of pots of Easter lilies, lilacs, and yellow daisies all around the church in preparation for Easter services.

What was it that Gabe had tried to tell her before she had gone over to the church that night? Hannah thought back to the conversation she and Gabe had just before she went to arrange the flowers:

"You really want to know what's going on, Hannah? If you're the least bit interested, you can get all the information from Dad's personal file cabinet. The key is in his desk drawer."

"And what were you doing snooping through Dad's file cabinet?" Hannah asked absently.

"I was trying to find my birth certificate so I could get my driver's license a few months ago. And right next to G for Gabriel, I stumbled on a file labeled Hezekiah . . . "

"Doesn't Dad usually file his sermons in another cabinet?"

"Yes—but this file was not about some sermon."

She noticed that Gabe's face looked blotchy and contorted as though the contents of the file had caused him deep grief for a long time. "Gabe, I've got to get going. I promised Mom I would arrange the flowers for tomorrow, and there are hundreds of them sitting there waiting for me in the foyer."

"Well, after you're finished, you might just want to take a look at the Hezekiah file. I hadn't planned on telling anybody about it—ever. But it's just been eating at me, Hannah. Eating my insides raw. And if you don't get around to looking at the file, you can read all about King Hezekiah in Second Kings 20:20."

"Why can't you just tell me what you found?" asked Hannah. Gabe's little game was growing tiresome.

"Hannah, what's in that file is so big—it will change our lives forever," Gabe said.

Hannah looked at her mysterious brother whose face belied the load he had been carrying. It was true. His boyishness had left him during the past few months. He seemed to Hannah in that moment like an old, old man.

As Hannah walked down the road toward her house thinking about her conversation with Gabe, she heard the sound of heavy vehicles rumbling up the road. She watched, bewildered, as a parade of dilapidated cars and trucks rattled over the floorboards of the covered bridge and up the hill. Hannah held her watch up to the streetlight . . . 12:42 in the morning. *What is going on?*

Every one of the vehicles was turning into the grassy area below Ian's bunker and parking near the fence that ran alongside Bennigan's Woods. Hannah estimated that at least ten cars, trucks, and vans were already parked in an orderly row next to the fence. Another seven or eight vehicles were coming over the bridge and up the hill. Nearly all of them were rusted out and ready to fall apart. One car had no hood or trunk. Another had been in a serious accident; part of its undercarriage was scraping against its tires. *What kind of people drive these vehicles? They all belong in a junkyard!*

Fiona was in Nevada and wouldn't be back till Tuesday. The Spencers were at a church camp out in the Ozarks to watch the Easter sunrise. Jared had been on his mission for a year. *I wish you were here!*

Hannah sighed, remembering her promise to Fiona to keep an eye on Maura. At fifteen, Maura had never been left on her own before. Wearily, Hannah stood on the porch of the Bennigan home and rang the doorbell. She rang it over and over until she saw Charlie coming toward her from the bunker.

"What do you want, Hannah? We're kind of busy right now," he said, looking impatient.

"What's going on, Charlie? Who are all these people?"

"What business is it of yours, Hannah? This is private property. Ian and I told the Spencers and the Silvermans about it but I guess Gabe didn't tell the Dennisons like he was supposed to. Ian and I have rented out the woods to a bunch of guys we know. They're in some paint ball club and they needed some new terrain. They paid us real good money and they'll be out by Sunday night."

Hannah sighed audibly, hands on her hips, tired of having to endure the unpredictable lifestyle of the Bennigans.

"It's our land, Hannah. You don't have no rights on Bennigan property," said Charlie, trying to project an authoritative air.

Hannah was reluctant to move off the porch. "Well, I promised I'd keep an eye on your sister until your mother gets back home. Now get her down here so she can sleep at my house. Tomorrow's Easter. Ever hear of Easter, Charlie? It's what religious people do to remember the resurrection of Jesus Christ. Anybody ever teach you about that, Charlie?"

"Sure, I know all about Easter. It's all about new beginnings and starting over and all that. Some people celebrate with sunrises, others celebrate with up-rises . . . isn't that right, Hannah?" Charlie smiled and seemed to enjoy watching Hannah squirm at the joke she didn't understand.

"Well, you and your weird military geek buddies better not be shooting off paint ball guns in the morning and ruining our service. You tell Ian I said that!" Hannah said tersely, wishing she could put a stop to this ridiculous event. *Why on earth would these people plan something like this on Easter?*

"You got no rights on this side of the road, Hannah. You know that. In fact, you only got your church and all that property because my daddy got murdered. He's not here to protect Bennigan land! It's up to Ian and me now," Charlie said in his man-child voice. He was parroting the ideas he had heard from his brother and mother all his life. But Hannah knew Charlie wasn't as sure of that old accusation as Ian and Fiona were.

"Get Maura out here, Charlie. She shouldn't be over here with all these strangers. I hope you had the sense to make a rule about drinking. My goodness, paint ball guns and drinking together. I can see a real disaster happening if you didn't think of making some rules!" Hannah was pushing against the front door trying to go in and get Maura. The door was locked.

"What we do on our land is our business, Hannah. Now go on home—Maura's fine where she is!" Charlie shouted at her, glancing toward the bunker. At the sound of his brother's shouting, Ian emerged.

Suddenly, it dawned on Hannah that Gabe would never let all this excitement happen just across the road without him. "Is Gabey over here, Ian?" She could tell by his face that she was right. "Get him out here, Ian. I want him home!" Neither brother moved. Hannah knew she would have to see for herself what was going on and where Gabe was.

"You're still callin' him Gabey, Hannah. He's seventeen years old. When are you gonna let him grow up?" Ian called as Hannah marched down the road toward the makeshift parking lot where groups of men and a boy about Gabe's age gathered equipment from the rattle-trap pick-up trucks and cars. They all seemed deadly serious and strangely quiet. They spoke in low whispers and seemed uncomfortable that Hannah was standing there watching them. She smelled the smoke of campfires and could see the tents and gear scattered around the closest one. If Gabe was in those woods with those men, she would have to call Chief Farley and have him go in there and get him. Hannah had not seen one woman in the group, and the idea of going into the woods by herself seemed like a risk she shouldn't take.

Hannah had just about made up her mind to call the chief when Gabe emerged from the woods near the bunker. At first, she had trouble making out his form because he was wearing a black stocking cap, a dark green sweatshirt, and pants made out of army camouflage material. She had never seen him in these clothes before.

"Hannah? What are you doing here?" he said nervously. Ian stood behind Gabe with his hands on Gabe's shoulders as if he too were Bennigan property.

Then Ian shoved the boy toward his sister. "Gabey, you'd better go on home with your big sissy. She's probably worried about you. Just like old times, huh? Your folks are gone, so big sister's in charge. Go on, now. We don't want her worrying, do we?" Ian said in the slimy tone of voice that Hannah detested.

"What is going on here, Ian? Is this one of your crazy war fantasies?" she said, grabbing Gabe as he came toward her, a defeated expression on his face.

"Not a fantasy at all, Hannah." Ian's voice was irritatingly calm. "And in case you're thinking about calling your surrogate father, Chief

Farley, please be informed—since Gabey forgot to tell you—that Charlie and I have a permit for this event. From the Chief himself. Even though it was on my private property, I felt it was wise to inform the police department of this camping event, and here are the papers that says the local law enforcement agency is *aware* of what's going on here." Ian's voice was still calm as he held out the document so Hannah could examine it. Ian seemed able to control the sarcasm in his voice more than usual as if he had begun to enjoy this encounter.

Hannah turned to leave. "Well, take care of Maura, Ian. Send her over if things get out of hand."

"Maura's all right, Hannah. She's fast asleep in her own room. And, by the way, I'm twenty years old now, same as you. Don't you think I can take care of my family? You really have no rights when you're talking about Maura. I'm not letting her go into the woods while these people are here. Believe me, I'm way more capable of protecting her than you are." Ian's voice had a cold edge to it as if he were reminding Hannah whose territory she was on and that his congeniality had a time limit.

"Just make sure these maniacs are not running through the woods pretending to kill people while all of us *sane* people are celebrating Easter at that church three hundred feet up the road. Can't you see what hideously poor taste it was to plan this pretend war on Easter? What were you thinking?" Hannah had always spoken to Ian in this same clipped, impatient manner. But tonight, despite Ian's soft tones and unusual restraint, she felt she was pushing him to the limit of his tolerance of her.

Ian took a step toward her, his fists clenched, barely containing the violence that was causing him to shake visibly, "Get off my land! You hypocrites can celebrate Easter all you want. Just give me and my family what's ours!" Ian said, sheer hatred accenting his every word. "How dare you make me feel less than human on land that bears my family's name! It's Bennigan land that props up your way of life. Very soon you will understand what evil acts have cursed this place. I will *make* you understand!"

Hannah's whole body chilled at Ian's words. No one in the world hated her as much as this man did. His eyes glowed with it; his body trembled and pulsated with it.

Ian straightened and backed away from Hannah as a group of men came toward him, seeming ready to assist him if he but gave the word. As Ian turned to join his comrades, he spat, "Just give me what my father was murdered for!" His eyes shone wildly in the headlights of another broken-down car limping up the side of the hill.

Hannah felt her stomach clench in a sickening grip as she ushered Gabe off the Bennigan's property. She felt Ian's piercing stare at her back. Even the fact that Gabe was being cooperative gave Hannah the feeling that this night was harboring evil—as if something dreadful could and would happen.

Hannah wished the Spencers were home or that Jared would come home from his mission. Jared would know what to do. She longed for him now with a fierceness she had never felt before.

The parallel universes that had split Bennigan's Bluff down the middle had come together again. Both sides of the hill faced each other in a fierce, fighting stance.

CHAPTER 21

Six hours later, Easter morning dawned bright and clear. A cartoon-blue sky dotted with plump, Pillsbury-dough-boy clouds obliterated the night's events from Hannah's waking consciousness.

Suddenly the memory of Ian's angry face sprang into Hannah's mind. She flew out of bed and threw open Gabe's door. He was there in bed, still asleep. There was a note on the chair next to his bed.

Hannah—

Tell Mom and Dad I'm sick and I may not make it to church today.

—Gabe

It wasn't like Gabe to fake an illness to get out of church, so Hannah figured he really was sick and shut his door softly. She went to the window at the front of the house to check out the goon gathering across the street. There were about twenty-five old, rusted cars and trucks parked in neat rows next to the fence. Their occupants could neither be seen nor heard in the woods. *Good, keep it that way!* declared Hannah to Ian in her mind. Then her father's car caught her eye as it emerged from the covered bridge. She saw him slow down to a crawl as he surveyed the unusual parking lot of unfamiliar vehicles lined up next to the woods.

"You're home early!" Hannah greeted her weary parents as they came in the front door. "And yes, they've got a permit for a paint ball war or some such crazy thing at the Bennigan estate. I checked it out last night." Her father and mother looked rumpled and exhausted.

"How exciting," said Miranda absently. She had obviously been dozing in the car because her makeup was smeared, and she looked groggy. "Everything always happens when we're gone!"

"Well, since you're gone so much, of course everything always happens . . . " Hannah started to chide her mother but was quickly upstaged by her sister, energized by Easter.

Kadence had slept soundly from Columbia and was raring to go. "Come on, people. I have a solo today. Mary Louise is meeting me at 8:30 sharp to help me warm up my voice."

"Okay, let's get ready for church," said Miranda laughing, allowing herself to be dragged upstairs by her adorable daughter.

Hannah rolled her eyes and went to fix everyone breakfast.

* * *

Easter Sunday at the Church on the Hill was always an elaborately staged pageant of spring colors and smells. The glorious fragrance of the lilacs filled the church and burst out into the parking lot when Hannah opened the doors. She was pleased with her arrangements of Easter flowers in their shiny lavender ceramic pots, a huge mint-green bow fastened to each one.

People who hadn't come to church all year were decked out in new clothes, greeting each other as if they had been there faithfully every Sunday. Many people walked from the town in their Easter finery.

The eight children in the KinderChoir were easily identifiable, looking like hand-dyed Easter eggs nestled around the foyer. Each of the four girl singers wore a mint-green bow in her hair and the four boy singers, less enthusiastically, sported mint-green bow ties. Several women fussed over their children like nervous stage mothers, wiping off imagined breakfast stains, straightening already-straight ties and bows. All the fuss and bother would be forgotten as soon as the children started singing in two-part harmony and melodic rounds, their magnificent voices filling the cavernous church with the spirit of Easter morning. Only Miranda Dennison and Louis T. Talbott could coax such a sweet performance from mere babes. It was their gift to the world.

Jesse, too, had on a pink shirt with a mint-green bow tie. Miranda had insisted that he place his video camera right on the platform again this year to get the best shot of the singing children for the shut-ins. He was busy placing the video camera tripod near the organ when Kadence and Mary Louise came in from the choir room. Kadence was clearing her throat softly and humming the words to her song, glancing over the music as she had seen Miranda do hundreds of times. Kadence could barely read, but musical notes and symbols on a page somehow made perfect sense to her. Hannah's heart melted at Kadence's pure intention to do well on her solo.

"Hey, Kadence, I'm going to get a close-up of your face when you do your solo, okay?" Jesse said, visibly proud of his importance in today's performance.

"Just be sure to get my good side," Kadence said, briefly glancing up from her music.

Hannah was quite certain Kadence had no idea what a "good side" meant, which made her quip that much cuter. It was true: this child dripped cuteness. Few human beings could resist her charming impudence.

As nine o'clock approached, Craig Dennison, freshly showered and renewed, walked through the pastor's entrance onto the platform, shaking hands with the various ministers who were already seated. Then all eyes swept toward Hannah's mother as she approached her place on the platform, radiant in a pink lace, Donna Reed-style shirt-waist dress with a tight patent leather belt at her waist. Never one to be left out of any color scheme, she wore a mint-green orchid on her white lace, low-cut lapel. She had re-curled her auburn hair and no one could have guessed Pastor and Mrs. Dennison had spent three hours getting to the services that morning.

Hannah was seated on the front row in order to give the evil eye to any of the rowdier five year-olds from her Sunday School class. She also had a series of signs that Miranda had made with words like "Smile!" illustrated by a large happy face with a wide toothy grin on its face for the nonreaders, and the word "Quiet!" with a happy face saying "Sh-h-h-h-h-h-h," a finger to its pursed lips. Hannah thought these signs were ridiculous but her mother had insisted that she use them when needed.

Mary Louise began the prelude music and people relaxed into the plush benches and the warmth of the sunlight streaming through the towering stained-glass windows. All of the flat land around Griggsberg would be reminded of what day this was as the chimes played familiar Easter hymns, drawing attention to the Church on the Hill on this glorious spring Sunday.

The children's choir was first on so that they could be dispatched to sit with their families for the rest of the service. No amount of shushing or sign-waving from Hannah could keep these five-year-olds quiet for an entire service. Better to strike while their irons were cold. The attention from the congregation would only warm them up as the service went on. Then there'd be no hope of containing them in some semblance of order.

Hannah's father welcomed the congregation, and the children took their places at the front of the platform. Their first three numbers went without a hitch. The hours of practice had payed off. Then it was Kadence's turn to sing "Christ the Lord is Risen Today." There was no fear in her sweet face as she placed her music on the tiny music stand next to her mother's larger one. She flashed Mary Louise a dimpled smile and bobbed her head slightly to indicate that she was ready to begin.

Mary Louise played the first few chords of the hymn and Kadence launched into the difficult aria in her crystal-clear, natural soprano voice. She enunciated her words as she had been taught, and remembered to smile and to breathe at the places indicated on her music sheet. The congregation sat spellbound as they recognized the rare gift the child had been given. Many of them had tears streaming down their cheeks as they sat mesmerized by Kadence's angelic face framed by her soft caramel curls.

Jesse trained the video camera on Kadence's face, which seemed to glow with the intensity of her song. Hannah knew her mother was silently calculating how many videotape copies Jesse should make after the service and who should receive each one. Pastor Dennison sat with one hand over his eyes listening to the sweetness of Kadence's song without the distraction of everyone's reaction. Reverend Talbott, too, sat enraptured by the sound of Kadence's voice, silently mouthing the words and musical phrasing he had helped Miranda teach her.

As Kadence finished the last note in perfect pitch, the audience broke out in applause, rising as one to their feet. It had truly been a moment to remember.

Reverend Talbott stood at the podium waiting for the applause to die down, a look of utter joy on his face. Just as he began to speak, there were several shouts from the back of the sanctuary and the sound of heavy, running footsteps. The atmosphere in the building darkened. The congregation gasped and watched in horror as three masked men in camouflage uniforms carrying guns ran toward the platform. Talbott seemed stunned. Pastor Dennison got up and stood next to Talbott. Church members screamed. The children on the platform shrieked and tried to run to their parents but were stopped by their fear of the men running toward them.

Two masked men took up positions in front of the children on the platform, training their automatic rifles on the congregation; a third man wearing a black beret bounded up the steps and shoved the two ministers away from the microphone. The man's voice matched his fierce, angular face. "Do as we tell you and no one will be hurt!" he said gruffly to the congregation. Several more church members screamed; others sat in shocked silence. Several masked men dressed in various types of combat uniforms walked authoritatively down the aisles of the church pointing pistols at the startled members, the soft carpeting muffling the awful sound of their boots.

Margaret Cappoletti who had been a shut-in for most of the year clutched her chest, her face contorted with pain. Her husband fumbled through her purse for her medicine. Lawrence Bitner motioned for his family to flatten themselves under the church pew, others around them followed. The eight children on the platform, who had seen enough television to know those guns were used for killing people, began screaming for their parents. Kadence stood still behind her little music stand, her mouth open in shock, looking at her mother who was staring wide-eyed at the intruders. Suddenly Miranda grabbed Kadence and stood between her and the man on the platform. "What do you want from us?" she asked in a loud, clear mother-lion voice.

"No one move!" said the man in the beret again, ignoring Miranda. "I promise you, if you do as we say, no one will be hurt!" A masked man standing in front of the platform wearing beige Desert

Storm battle fatigues motioned for the soldiers to take up positions on the outside aisles of the church.

"There are men posted at all exits of this building. We are very serious about our demands and have no distaste for shooting any of you hypocrites!"

Hannah sat staring at the man ten feet in front of her in the place where her father usually stood. Nothing about him was familiar . . . but his words were. Ian had used the word "hypocrite" the night before. There was no doubt now what the event in the woods was all about. She glanced over at Chief Farley who had his cell phone to his ear, shielding himself from view behind the seat in front of him. York sat near the aisle several rows behind Farley, crouched down low, doing the same.

A short burst of automatic gunfire ripped through the air. It struck the ceiling, and bits of plaster rained down on the panicked crowd. York screamed as a soldier used the bayonet on the end of his rifle to dislodge the cell phone from York's ear. The side of his face exploded in blood, and his phone skittered to the floor. The gunman motioned for York's daughter to pick it up and hand it to him. She trembled and whimpered as she handed the man her father's phone.

"Pass all of your cell phones to the aisles!" shouted the leader with the beret into the microphone.

The children in the choir became hysterical. Nicole Myers lay on the floor, kicking wildly, screaming for her mother. Sarah Bitner threw up. The twins, Callie and Bryce Kline, held hands and screamed in unison. Kyle Framington stood in wide-eyed shock, his mint-green bow tie dangling and moving slightly as he swallowed great gulps of saliva. A wet stain spread on the crotch of Tucker Larsen's Sunday pants. Mikey Calvert began to breathe heavily, patting his pockets, searching for his inhaler. Hannah ached to go to them. Their innocence was profound and strangely beautiful against the backdrop of dark madness in the room. Calmly, Hannah stood and looked at the children, and held up both signs, "Smile" and "S-h-h-h-h-h-h." Some of the children straightened and obeyed her direction. The others continued to scream.

Jesse sat in shock next to his mother on the organ bench. His video camera continued to record, its red light indicating that it was picking up all of the mayhem going on in front of them. The man in the black beret noticed the camera was on and tore it from the tripod. Unraveling the videotape from its casing, he wound it up and stuffed it into the pocket of his soldier's jacket. Then he moved toward the children. "Who's in charge of these little ones?" he demanded. "Are you their teacher?" he asked Hannah who was still standing, holding the absurd little signs.

"Yes, I'm their teacher . . . where's Ian Bennigan? I want to talk to him. Where is he and what is this all about!" Hannah said, trying to keep her voice steady. Her certain knowledge that Ian was behind this made her feel somehow responsible for not taking more action the night before. She had been fooled by Ian's lie about why the men were in the woods.

"What do you men want?" came her mother's voice, strong, matching Hannah's.

Realizing his wife and daughter were trying to engage the man in a dialogue, Pastor Dennison stood in front of the man, towering over him. "What do you men want? Money? I'm sure the people in this room would be happy to give you whatever you want. How much do you want?" Craig's voice was forceful but it squeaked around the edges as he tried to stay in control of himself. Sweat began to pour from his forehead as he surveyed the heavily armed soldiers who had commandeered his church building.

A voice shouted from the congregation. "I am the police chief of this town! What are your demands?" Chief Farley stood and walked toward the soldier on the platform, ignoring the two gunmen whose assault rifles were leveled at him. Farley raised his hands, calming the gunmen. "I do not bring my firearms to church with me—I am unarmed." Farley said as he continued to move up the steps toward the leader. His wife and daughters screamed from the crowd, begging him not to go up on the platform. He turned briefly to his family and motioned for them to get under their church pew. York was moaning, blood flowing freely from his torn ear. His wife, Lonnie, took his tie off and held it up to the side of his face, her hands shaking as she tenderly examined his face.

As Farley approached the man, the leader yelled to Hannah, "You! Sunday School teacher! What's your name?"

"Hannah Dennison," she said, her teeth clenched in disgust for this man who held her children at gunpoint.

"So you're Dennison's daughter. Perfect. I want you to take these kids up to the room at the top of the stairs where your retarded custodian lives. These two soldiers here will escort you. Your complete cooperation is essential. The phone line up there is cut so don't even think of trying anything."

Farley spoke to the leader while two masked men moved toward Hannah and the children. "I want you to guarantee the safety of these children. These parents need to know their children will be safe with your soldiers!" Farley shouted.

"Relax, Chief. I'm only thinking of the children. They'll be less frightened if they're not in this room. This is adult business!" He leaned toward the microphone and said, "The children will be safe with Miss Dennison. No one will be hurt if you cooperate."

"What about Mr. York over there? How can we believe you do not intend to hurt us after what your man did to him?" Farley said, his voice steady, respectful, yet indignant.

"He tried to use his cell phone. I asked you to cooperate, not try to get in the way!" the leader shouted into the microphone. "We don't need any of you adults here. In an orderly fashion, row by row, you will be escorted to your cars and you may go home to your Sunday dinners. Our demands are simple and we will be finished very soon if they are met."

Judy Cline, the twins' mother, rushed toward the platform screaming, "What about our children? You've got them going upstairs with Hannah and those crazy men with the guns. Let them go or I'm not moving!" she shouted, advancing on the leader, a mother animal acting on sheer instinct.

The man laid his M16 across the podium and withdrew a small .22 caliber gun from his belt. He aimed quickly and shot Judy once in the shoulder. She screamed in pain and fell to the floor, her blood staining the carpet beneath her. The shot stunned her but she shook the fist of her other arm angrily at the soldiers. "LET THEM GO, YOU MONSTERS!"

Mark Cline ran toward his wife, not caring what would happen to him. "What is it you want? You're madmen! You've got our kids! You've shot my wife!" Cline was sobbing, holding his wife. Another church member knelt beside them and applied pressure to her oozing wound. "MADMEN! YOU'LL HANG FOR THIS!" Cline continued to shout.

Farley was at the microphone now. "Mark, put something on your wife's wound, keep pressure on it and get her to the hospital. These men are allowing all of you to leave. Let me do the negotiating. I'll watch over the children. Hannah will be with them. They trust her. Don't make things worse! You too, Lonnie. Get your husband to a doctor. These men mean business and I don't want to see any one else hurt."

"But our kids!" wailed another voice.

The man with the beret shouted again into the microphone, "You are endangering their lives by trying to get to them. Leave the building so we can get on with this."

"You should know," said Farley to the man, "I've already contacted the county sheriff. He'll be here with the National Guard any time now to put a stop to this."

"Good," said the man, pointing his .22 at Farley. "You saved me from having to call him myself. We've got the children now, Chief, so we've got *everything*. We don't need to hold the whole crowd. Too much of a headache . . . too many desperate folks to watch. No, the children are all we need . . . and three adults for good measure . . . no matter how long this takes," said the man with perfect confidence in the plan that was unfolding.

"What does Ian Bennigan have to do with this?" asked Farley, hoping to keep the man talking to get as much information as possible.

"The Bennigan Brothers are in charge of this whole operation. They've been planning it for more than a year. They've been calling it the Easter Rising—just like in Ireland, 1916, when the Irish tried to get their land back from the English. Hope you know your history, Chief. This is history repeating itself," said the man smugly. "No more questions now. I've got to secure this area and get you down the hill. Since the phone lines are cut," said the man, grabbing the chief's cell phone from him, "call your cell phone number as soon as the sheriff arrives—that's how we'll stay in touch. Now get going!" the man shoved the butt of his gun into Farley's lower back as if to make sure the chief didn't think they had just had a friendly conversation. Farley fell to his knees with the crushing blow.

CHAPTER 22

The pain in Farley's back was excruciating for a few minutes. He stood on the platform trying to gather his senses, his knees threatening to give way under his body.

The gunman laughed and pushed the chief toward the stairs. "Escort the chief to his car!" yelled Farley's tormentor to the gunman who had just escorted the four ministers off the stand. "And where's Talbott and that imbecile janitor?"

"Handcuffed in the foyer, sir!" shouted the soldier whose voice belonged to a teenager no older than sixteen or seventeen.

As Farley was being led toward the front door of the church, he saw Jesse Candella and Louis Talbott cuffed and gagged in the foyer.

Their guard chuckled as Farley stared at them helplessly. "We gotta have some hostages that aren't too hard to kill for starters, Chief—a black man and a retard. These two will be the first to go if you don't meet our demands. Next, comes Ian's personal favorite—the lovely Miss Dennison. Don't worry—we're saving the kids till last." The soldier clicked his heels and gave a crisp Nazi salute.

"You're all Nazis!" yelled the chief as the soldier shoved him out the door of the church. Farley drove slowly down the hill, barely able to see from the terrible pain ricocheting up his spine. Masked gunmen in fatigues were stationed in a staggered fashion every twenty feet all the way to the bridge. Farley tried to assess their firepower as he drove past them. Each of the gunmen carried an automatic or semi-automatic assault weapon. As he drove past them, Farley identified an Uzi, three AR15s, several M16s, a Tec 22, a couple of AK-47s and an old German Luger. Some of the guns had bayonets affixed to their barrels. Farley shook his head at the sight of so much power in the hands of maniacs. Not only were the men armed with rapid-fire assault weapons, but most of them also had pistols tucked into their belt holsters or held at their sides. Several of them were the same kinds of weapons his own patrolmen carried—9mm Glocks. But most were Lorcins, the inexpensive guns involved in a lot of street crimes in the United States. They could be had for under a hundred dollars at just about any gun show . . . or over the Internet. Many of the men wore helmets and police-issue Kevlar vests over their fatigues. Bennigan's Bluff looked like the Middle East. *Thank you, second amendment,* the chief thought wryly, staring at the gun-toting terrorists. *So this is what some of us are doing with our right to bear arms.*

Despite his pain, Farley gathered as much information as he could. The gunmen wore numbers written on wide strips of adhesive tape wrapped around their upper arms. Farley noted the numbers 83, 89, 94, 98, 88, and 82 as he made his way through the gauntlet of soldiers. With the ski masks hiding their faces, Ian must have come up with the numbers idea to keep his men straight. *And to keep us from guessing the exact number in his army, Ian started with high numbers.*

As the chief passed the Bennigan's home, he saw the words SINN FEIN spray-painted on the side of the house in large, uneven black letters. He knew he had seen those words before but couldn't think where.

Farley noted that Ian Bennigan had set up a command post. A desk was positioned on top of the grass-covered bunker. Just as Farley passed the Bennigan's home, Ian emerged from the bunker, dressed in full battle gear, holding a two-way radio to his mouth. *He's living out his fantasy of commanding an army,* thought Farley. As the chief drove past him, Ian stood at attention and saluted him, a smirk on his face. At least it wasn't the Nazi salute like the soldier back at the church had given him.

Beyond the empty Spencer home, Farley could see Esther and Ben Silverman being led out of their house under armed guard. Ben had their cat, Muffin, under one arm and a painting under the other. Esther too had grabbed a few possessions as if they would never return: framed photographs off the wall, a scrapbook, and a bag of food for their beloved cat. Farley knew the Silvermans had lost their families in the Nazi concentration camps. *They must think it's happening all over again—right here in America,* Farley thought sadly.

Farley had always known Ian was capable of anti-social behavior, but he had never anticipated this level of insanity—not in his wildest dreams. Fiona had trained him well to feel justified in his hatred of the townspeople. Where was she? Was she even aware of Ian's plan or was she just as ignorant and unsuspecting as the rest of the town had been? Farley felt responsible for the chaos on the hill. *Why didn't I check out the campers last night, or conduct surveillance like they do in the city?* He knew the answer: the Bennigan Brothers had the right to use their private property as they chose. He couldn't have stopped it. They hadn't even needed a permit. The fact that Ian had asked for one was what had thrown Farley off. Ian had put up a smoke screen to deflect suspicion from the odd gathering. He had even promised to have everyone off the Bluff by Sunday night so as not to bother the neighbors. "In by 2 A.M. to accommodate campers who are driving in from out of state, and the event will be over by 10 P.M. on Sunday night," Ian had assured him with a polite smile.

As Farley approached the bridge, he was stopped by two masked soldiers. Several more gunmen were stationed at positions inside the covered bridge.

"You Chief Farley?" shouted the man holding the walkie-talkie. "Please inform your citizens and the sheriff that we will soon have a series of land mines in front of this bridge here and armed men positioned all along the back woods to prevent any crossing of the river. We have enough ammunition to last for several months and enough stored food and water to survive any kind of siege, sir. I have been instructed to inform you that as soon as our demands are met, we will remove our troops from Bennigan's Bluff and release the children and the three adult hostages." He leaned into Farley's car window. "Don't make this another Waco, Chief. As soon as the media gets here, the whole country will be watching. Don't put this town on the map by screwing this operation up." The soldier lowered his voice and continued with prompts from the voice on the walkie-talkie, "This is private property, and the Bennigan Boys want the whole Bluff back, including the quarry lake and all shore property. They lost this land to the murderers of their father and they want what is rightfully theirs. Ian Bennigan is prepared to prove his father was murdered in this quarry, and the State of Missouri will have no choice but to listen to the Bennigans's charges, make the proper arrests, and return all land to its rightful owners. Any questions, sir?"

Farley tried to mobilize his mind to make the most of this conversation, fighting to ignore the debilitating pain in his back. "Why the violence? The children! Why is that necessary?" he asked the man behind the mask.

"Because it works, sir. It's the only way to get justice sometimes. Every peaceful way has already been tried," said the soldier. He seemed to know the story well.

"What does Sinn Fein mean? Those words sprayed on the side of Bennigan's house?" said Farley pointing back up the hill.

"It's Irish—it means '*Ourselves alone.*' In the end, sir, that's all the American people have now that the government has become the enemy. The Bennigan Brothers have the right to defend themselves against an unjust government. They've got themselves . . . alone . . . to solve this problem . . . and they want their land back for themselves *alone*. It was taken by illegal seizure, and in the process, their father died. The patriots who have come to assist the Bennigan Brothers are prepared to die for a citizen's right to his own land and to receive justice when murder or manslaughter is committed," he said, the walkie-talkie still pressed to his ear. The soldier stepped back, maintaining a respectful stance. When he noticed a signal from the hill, he motioned the chief through the roadblock.

"How many men do you have?" Farley asked. The soldier ignored the question, perhaps smiling behind his mask at the Chief's attempt to determine the enemy's number.

"Move on through the bridge!" said the soldier, waving Farley on. Then he leaned into the chief's window again, "I hope we don't have to shed too much blood to make our point, sir. I sincerely mean that."

Farley was baffled at the professional, almost respectful, demeanor of the soldier. He was no street tough—sounded more like an accountant or a schoolteacher. This operation was well thought out. It was as if every possible scenario had been rehearsed and a counter strategy for every problem was already in place. Although it had taken the Bennigan Brothers a year to plan this act of terrorism, Farley had to respond—and respond correctly—in a very short time frame.

As he approached the police station, Farley saw several Blue River Sheriff Department cars and a National Guard truck. Help had already arrived.

CHAPTER 23

Dulcey Martinez was the rookie reporter at KCMO television in Kansas City, Missouri. Jim Stott, the station manager, had hired Dulcey right after her internship. He had remembered Dulcey from the press conference she had called when she was a brash high school newspaper editor. He had hired her because she had the makings of a top-notch reporter. And because she had a face the camera loved.

But so far, Dulcey had only covered traffic accidents and festivals and filler stories used for unexpected dead air. Her finest moment was her live report of a severe windstorm just north of Kansas City. She had given that report while holding on to a stop sign in gale-force wind—hair tossing about her face, rain pelting sideways—all the while standing as close as she could get to a downed power line that was shooting off hot sparks, whipping and rearing itself like a cornered rattlesnake. Later, she told Stott she was trying her hand at what she called "flying bullet reporting"—the kind of reporting made famous by Peter Arnett and Bernie Shaw. On January 19, 1991—at the age of fifteen—Dulcey had watched those two gutsy CNN reporters hunkered down in the dark behind the window ledge of a Baghdad hotel room, photographing live the first tracer bullets of the Gulf War. Ever since then, she knew she would pursue a career in broadcast journalism.

Sunday, generally the slowest news day, was her day to cover the news desk. At the moment the phone rang, she had been imagining how to turn Easter egg hunts and ham dinners into exciting news stories. "Martinez, news desk," she answered, leaning down to adjust the yellow nylon rope she still wore on her ankle.

"Dulcey Martinez?" said a male voice.

"That's me. What can I do for you?" Dulcey said, all business.

"Rob Niles—we met at the Sheriff's Ball a couple of weeks ago."

Dulcey remembered interviewing the nice-looking spokesperson for the County Sheriff's Association. "Sure, I remember you. What's up?"

"Something big is going down in Griggsberg. A major special. You know that little quarry town just east of here?"

"Know it? I grew up there. What's going on?" Dulcey was standing now, pen poised above notebook. She knew the words "major special" was a law enforcement term for an act of terrorism or a hostage situation.

"Some militia army's holding a bunch of little kids in that big church on the hill. Their only demand so far is to have the media present. It's real sensitive but they're the ones requesting coverage, so I think you guys will be safe covering this from the air. They want to keep the authorities *honest*—their words—while they make their real demands."

"I'm on it, Rob," Dulcey said, trying to sound professional, pushing aside her own worry about her mother and everyone she knew in Griggsberg.

After she reached Stott, he instantly set the gears of the media in motion. A moment later, he rang her back. "Okay, Martinez, I've got McCloskey firing up the Bell 430. You stay here and man the phones. Kevin Barker's going to cover this—with Taylor on camera. We'll have a ground crew over there in an hour."

"Barker? Covering *this?* Hold up a minute." Stott's line went dead and a moment later Dulcey appeared in his office, her reporter's bag slung over her shoulder. She planted her compact little body in front of him so he had to look at her. "Mr. Stott, I'm *from* Griggsberg. I know everyone in that town."

"All the more reason for you *not* to cover it. You'd be too worried about everyone to keep your distance and focus on the report," said Stott, trying to get out of his door.

Dulcey stood in front of him, nothing moving except her jaw. "Mr. Stott, on this story, I'm the best thing you've got. I can get to people and places before Barker finds the bathroom. The police chief of Griggsberg practically raised me. Nobody at KCMO is up to speed on this one but me."

Stott paused for a moment. "Okay, Martinez, I can see how you'd be good on this. Go with Barker. I'll let him know he's got the rookie because she's got connections," he said, looking into her eager face. "But if it gets rough—or dangerous—I'll have someone from the ground crew take your place on the chopper. You hear?"

Dulcey was already in full battle mode, checking her tape recorder, glancing out the window at the helicopter on the pad, its blades rotating as fast as the adrenaline was pumping through her body. She knew instantly why Stott had asked for the big Bell with its protective metal body instead of the smaller, all-glass Hiller used for traffic reports: he was sending his crew into a possible war zone.

"Don't be surprised if it's harder than you think, Martinez!" Stott said to her back as she headed toward the chopper. "Like being a surgeon operating on a family member!"

Dulcey didn't hear him. She was already out the door, ducking under the spinning blades.

CHAPTER 24

Hannah herded the children into Jesse's wide room that spanned the area above the sanctuary windows. The two men with the guns had been silent on the way up the stairs, preferring to let Hannah take charge of the children instead of frightening them any further. After they had shut her and the children into Jesse's room, she heard a padlock drop into a latch on the other side of the door.

Jesse's room had a bathroom and a microwave and a little cupboard stocked with bottled water, cans of Chef Boyardee, and his favorite flavors of Campbell's soup. Hannah knew that at least the little ones would have something to eat.

Cordelia greeted them at the door, arching her back, purring loudly.

"How many of you can be brave and take care of Cordelia?" Hannah asked.

The Cline twins immediately sat on the floor next to the cat and stroked her fur. Nicole suggested that they take turns feeding her. Hannah saw the wisdom of letting the children care for something other than themselves. She would be doing the same in caring for them.

Cordelia took a small cat treat from each child in turn, and drank some water from a ceramic bowl Mikey Calvert had filled for her. Then she took a turn in each of their laps. She was well-experienced in this kind of handling, being no stranger to Jesse's exuberant brand of affection.

After letting them tend to Cordelia for a while, Hannah positioned the kids in a line to use the restroom. Some had already wet themselves. She tried to comfort and reassure them despite the metallic taste of fear in her own mouth.

Turning on Jesse's radio, she found some music to calm them. As she adjusted the antenna on the radio, Hannah held back a fold of the curtain that covered the entire view of the valley. She could easily see the police station a few blocks beyond the lake and hundreds of people already lining the streets looking up at the Bluff. Several National Guard trucks were moving through the crowded streets. A KCMO news helicopter hovered above the town. Would this put Griggsberg on the map? *Waco, Texas—Oklahoma City, Oklahoma— Pearl, Mississippi—Padukah, Kentucky—Springfied, Oregon— Jonesboro, Arkansas. Would Griggsberg, Missouri be added to that list?* Ian and Charlie had gone up against society—had gone against its grain and were defying its laws and code of conduct.

It had been just over an hour since the gunmen had burst into the church. The Cline twins, Callie and Bryce, were holding each other, cuddled up in Jesse's big armchair, their faces vacant. Mikey Calvert looked pale. Hannah made sure he used his inhaler whenever his breathing became raspy.

The floor of Jesse's apartment was littered with little green bow ties and pastel shirts and dresses. Some of the girls took off their big frilly slips to get comfortable. Kadence and Nicole hung their Easter dresses in Jesse's closet and found a couple of white T-shirts to put on. Jesse's room looked like someone's backyard after the Easter eggs had been found and eaten, their colorful shells discarded and scattered about.

* * *

On the brief flight to Griggsberg, Dulcey had persuaded Kevin Barker to let her introduce the story. Knowing the town, the terrain, and the buildings, she had reasoned that she could give the report a good grounding. Since this was going to be a long ordeal, there would be plenty of time to share the reporting duties back and forth.

Ben Taylor's hand signal told her to begin.

"This is Dulcey Martinez reporting live from the little town of Griggsberg, Missouri. You're looking at the Church on the Hill situated on a hill called Bennigan's Bluff. We were informed that a little over an hour ago, during the Easter service at this church, gunmen . . .

as many as twenty or more . . . burst into the sanctuary and held the people of this church hostage. They have released all of the adults," Dulcey squinted to see the note Barker had written, "except three . . . and are at present holding eight very young children in a room above those stained-glass windows that you can see there at the front of the church."

Barker nodded his head encouragingly at Dulcey, taking notes on the report he was getting directly from Rob who was now positioned on the campus beach below.

Dulcey continued her live report, "The Reverend Craig Dennison is the pastor of the Church on the Hill, which was invaded by these masked men just over an hour ago. The church has a membership of about fifteen hundred. On an Easter Sunday, the church was most certainly packed with churchgoers. But it appears that the gunmen are holding only the eight children . . . and the three adults I just mentioned. Oh, look . . . Larry can you fly closer to those windows above the sanctuary there?" Dulcey asked, noticing movement at the windows.

Despite the presence of armed men on the hill below, Larry McCloskey maneuvered the chopper closer to the church. The gunmen wanted this news coverage, so he had to trust that they would not fire on the helicopter if he got closer to the hill.

"Yes, right there at the tinted windows . . . just above the stained glass, if you look closely you can see several children looking out at the town below. No doubt they are trying to spot their mommies and daddies down there. This is an incredible thing we are witnessing here, folks. The gunmen have not formally made their demands at this point. They are, in fact, waiting for media coverage, to keep . . . as the gunmen themselves have put it . . . 'to keep the negotiations honest.' We will let you know what they are asking for just as soon as they have made their demands known."

Taylor focused his zoom lens on the windows of the church. Looking at the monitor, Dulcey could see what the TV viewers were seeing. She noticed a movement of the curtains and a familiar face appeared. It was Hannah Dennison.

"At least one of the adults being held by the gunmen is Hannah Dennison, the daughter of the Reverend Craig Dennison. I grew up in Griggsberg, so I know these people. Keep your television sets tuned to KCMO, and as this story unfolds, I'll do my best to get you important information to help us all understand what is happening here in Griggsberg."

Barker smiled at Dulcey. "Good job!" he whispered, urging her to continue.

"Hannah Dennison, who is now with those eight child hostages, has been teaching the five-year-olds at the Church on the Hill since she was a young teenager. Perhaps this is why she is one of the three adults being held . . . because of her connection with those children." Dulcey paused to read Barker's notes. "The well-known music minister, Reverend Louis Talbott, is also one of the hostages. According to the sheriff's department, the church's custodian, Jesse Candella, is also being held hostage in the church."

Dulcey's heart galloped as she tried to take in the whole scene below her. Her biggest unanswered question was *Who are these men and what are their demands?* As the chopper cleared the backside of the church, she caught sight of Ian Bennigan standing on top of his grassy bunker. Suddenly, Dulcey knew what these men wanted.

Off mike, Dulcie said, "Larry, take the chopper over to that big house across the road—the biggest one on the Bluff." To Barker, she said, "Do we have a loudspeaker on this chopper?"

"Yes, but Dulcey, you're not thinking of talking to the gunmen are you? You can't be part of the story! We're covering this thing, not taking part in it!"

Dulcey wondered for a moment if Barker was afraid of the guns below, of the possibility of being commandeered by the masked gunmen.

"Kevin, I KNOW some of those gunmen. I grew up with some of them! I think I even know what this is all about. Besides, they're the ones who asked for media coverage. They want us here!" Dulcey stared hard at him. She knew Kevin Barker had no idea who he was dealing with.

"Ben!" shouted Barker, "Don't let her have that megaphone! Dulcey, this goes against everything in reporting—you're *affecting* the story if you talk to those gunmen. I'll see that you're *fired* if you try this!"

Larry McCloskey had already steered the chopper toward the big house on the hill. Ben Taylor, fastened to his safety harness, leaned out of the open side door, panning the scene so the viewers could see an aerial view of the Bluff. With his other hand, he handed Dulcey the battery powered megaphone.

Barker cringed, sweating and uncertain. He radioed Jim Stott at the station, helpless against the three renegade reporters, feeling like another hostage in the crisis on Bennigan's Bluff.

* * *

Three hours had passed now since the gunmen had taken over the Bluff. Hannah had fed the children some canned soup, and made sure they drank some water. She had found that by allowing the children to see the town below and to point out where their houses were, she could keep the kids connected to what was important to them. She had seen her Aunt Kate talking with Chief Farley in his command post on the beach. She knew the two of them would do whatever it took to put an end to this unbelievable nightmare.

Seeing the children at the window, some parents got the idea to write messages on bedsheets and hang them on the slanted tile roofs of the college dormitories that faced the church. CALLIE AND BRYCE—MOM AND DAD LOVE YOU! Mark Cline had carefully placed the banner on the roof, weighting its corners down with bricks. Judy Cline, her shoulder bandaged, stood on the ground below, waving to her children with her good arm.

Hannah and the children watched as a huge bunch of helium balloons with a poster attached to the strings proclaiming, "We love you!!" floated up over the lake and past the windows. News crews from all the Kansas City stations were the first to set up their cameras and microphones on the beach. A while later, Hannah saw national media trucks and RVs arrive with complicated satellite dishes and equipment mounted on their roofs. News reporters dressed in tailored suits improvised introductions and updates in front of cameras balanced on the shoulders of burly cameramen.

Hannah had seen Dulcey Martinez in the KCMO chopper and had waved at her on one of her fly-bys. She felt strangely reassured that someone she knew was in one of those helicopters.

Ian had obviously planned this whole thing for maximum media exposure—the innocence of Easter contrasting and heightening his treachery. The tall brass cross on top of the church had been draped for Easter with a length of long purple fabric representing Christ's royal robe. Hannah imagined it flapping in the brisk spring breeze on the roof above her—a flag of innocence.

Hannah knew the children's parents would be riveted to their television sets hoping for glimpses of their children. She held the smallest children up to the windows to make sure their parents would catch sight of them before it got dark. Some of the children threw up from the stress. Others curled up and put their thumbs in their mouths, retreating to the safety of infancy.

As the sun went down, campfires lit up the beach. Hundreds of people gathered together, keeping a vigil for Ian's helpless hostages.

At about midnight, Hannah fell into an exhausted sleep lying width-wise on Jesse's bed. She was holding Kadence as much for her own comfort as for her sister's. Nicole and Sarah had wedged their little bodies next to Kadence's. The twins slept fitfully in the over-stuffed chair, Cordelia draped contentedly across its back, one paw extended downward in a gesture of protection over the sleeping children. The boys slept on Jesse's sleeping bag near the bed.

Except for more and more frequent coughing spells, Mikey Calvert had been the quietest child of the group and was therefore the one Hannah worried about most. She knew he had been hospitalized several times in the past year. If Mikey had an asthma attack and could not breathe, she had no idea what she would do.

Just as Hannah dozed off, a frightening dream image filled her mind. She was lying on gravel in the road in front of her house. Ian was standing above her, his feet gripping both sides of her head. Blood and sweat were dripping off his body onto her face and bare arms, "You're worse than anyone, Hannah, because you pretend to be so perfect!" The nightmare vision woke her instantly. A cold dread crept through her body. The little girls in the bed stirred and reposi-tioned themselves. Hannah knew that if Ian were going to kill someone . . . he would pick her first.

CHAPTER 25

Chief Farley prepared for the biggest test of his life. He had set up a command station on the campus beach close to the covered bridge, and had pitched several tents provided by the National Guard for his officers. Darlene, still at the station, was directly wired into a dispatch board at the makeshift command post. Everyone knew this event would not be over any time soon. Since the demand for media coverage was the only one made so far, Farley had agreed with the sheriff that the media would operate separately from all government entities. Otherwise, the gunmen would accuse Farley or the sheriff of controlling the coverage.

Even before he saw her, Farley knew Dulcey would be on the KCMO chopper. He knew she worked Sundays and that no news manager in his right mind would prevent that little ball of fire from covering a story in her own hometown. The sheriff had instructed the media not to contact any law enforcement personnel except through Rob Miles. In some ways, Farley was relieved Dulcey couldn't pump him for information. He knew he would have had a hard time resisting her.

* * *

At about two in the morning, Hannah woke to the sound of footsteps on the asphalt roof above her. The soldier must have used a ladder to get up there. *Why hadn't he just entered the roof from the trapdoor in Jesse's ceiling?* It occurred to Hannah that the soldiers might not know where the trapdoor was. The storage room was the most logical place for the access door to the roof, but the architect had put it in Jesse's room to give him a fire escape.

Hannah went to sit by the door of Jesse's apartment. *Who is the gunman on the other side of the door? Why would he risk his life for the Bennigan's cause? How did he fall prey to Ian's scheme to hold eight innocent children hostage for a crazy personal vendetta that in no way could have involved this man?* She searched her mind for a way to appeal to the man.

"Sir? Could I have a word with you without you coming in here and frightening the children?" she said quietly, testing the waters.

"What do you want?" came the firm reply of the soldier guarding the door. The voice sounded vaguely familiar to Hannah.

"I have a child in here, Mikey Calvert, who has been coughing all night. He has very bad asthma, and I'm afraid the stress of all this is going to make him go into an attack where he can't breathe. Asthma is very serious, you know," Hannah said with concern in her voice.

"I know all about asthma. Used to have it as a kid. Went to the emergency room once with it."

"What if Mikey needed medical attention and he couldn't get it in time? He could die you know," Hannah pressed. "Wouldn't that be a really bad thing if you let one of these little ones die because they couldn't get medical treatment?"

"Yeah . . . that might not look too good. How about the other kids? How they doin'?" asked the soldier.

"Well, several of them are definitely in rough shape. A couple of them have been throwing up and most of them are still in shock, I think. I'd say it's only a matter of time before we have some really serious problems in here." Hannah tried her best to sound concerned but not dramatic lest the soldier think she was trying to put one over on him.

"I'll see what I can do, Miss Dennison." The soldier repeated Hannah's concerns to someone over his walkie-talkie. Then he said to her, "In case you don't know, we're waiting for Fiona Bennigan to get here so we can start these negotiations. She's being flown in from Nevada by the National Guard."

"Fiona knows about all this?" Hannah asked in disbelief.

"Well, no ma'am, she went out to Nevada to get a model of Bennigan's Bluff from the geologist who used to work for the quarry here. The model's going to be used to demonstrate how the quarry was flooded and Liam Bennigan was killed."

"Yeah, I know the Bennigans have been saying that for years, but I honestly believe the in-flooding was a natural accident," Hannah said.

"That's because you believed the official explanation, Miss Dennison. When we get the model and some documents Mrs. Bennigan recently found in the county recorder's office, you'll see how the flooding was no natural disaster. The Bennigans are making sure the whole nation is watching so the State of Missouri can't sweep this under the rug and ruin Mrs. Bennigan's case like they've done for the past fifteen years." The soldier seemed to appreciate this chance to talk, even though Hannah realized he was probably saying too much.

"Well, you seem to be almost an expert about this. How do you know all those details?" she asked her unseen captor.

"I've been following this case on the Internet, ever since the Bennigan Brothers started their web site. All of us here have been documenting the evidence of the murder and tracking down the ways the State of Missouri has covered it up to protect the perpetrators of the crime."

Hannah wanted to know more, but Mikey's cough reminded her of her purpose in speaking to the soldier. "Look. I've got to get back to these kids. A couple of them are whimpering for their parents. Can't you help me get some of them out of here? And by the way— what can I call you?" Hannah asked the soldier.

"Well, to tell you the truth, we've already met. I talked to you several weeks ago in the church parking lot. I'd been talking to Jesse, the custodian, when you came up and asked who I was. It's not my real name of course but you can call me Joe. Just Joe . . . okay?"

That's why the young man's voice had sounded familiar. "Yeah, I remember," she responded angrily, exhaustion and helplessness over-whelming her. "Please . . . please do what you can for these kids. Several of them aren't doing well and they need your help!" Hannah pleaded. "And I could use another adult in here to help me with them."

"I'll see what I can do," said the soldier who now had a name.

* * *

Miranda sat in Kate's kitchen Monday morning; dark circles shadowed her glazed eyes. Her movements were mechanical, and there was not a trace of makeup on her pale, blotchy face. Her two daughters were in the church. And Gabe had disappeared. Thinking he was sick, Miranda had left him in his bed on Easter morning. He hadn't been there when Craig had gone to find him during the evacuation of the church.

The worst possibility was that Gabe was with Ian. *As an innocent bystander or as a participant?* Miranda was struggling with the fact that the gunmen knew exactly when those eight children would be on that platform. They wouldn't have been able to pull this thing off if they had not known that one fact. If the children had been sitting in the congregation, their parents would have put their own bodies between the gunmen and their children. Only by getting the group of children away from their parents could this thing have worked.

Had Gabe been the one to betray the children? Could Gabe have done that? Would the monstrous thing he was a part of cause him to get physically sick the night before? If he was not on the hill with Ian, why hadn't he called Kate's house to let them know he was all right? In her heart, she feared the worst.

* * *

Craig sat in the tent next to Chief Farley. He had been there all night to offer what help he could to the law enforcement agencies. He sketched floor plans of the church, provided information about the children, described Jesse's apartment, and helped relocate the residents of Bennigan's Bluff. Miranda had given him the keys to the cabins at the music camp. The Spencers had returned Sunday afternoon from their Easter Sunrise service, and had fought their way through the crowds to find that their home had been taken over by terrorists. They were staying in one of the cabins. The Silvermans had another. Some of the church's ministers who lived out of town occupied another. Television reporters and several deputies had asked to use the others.

* * *

As far as Craig knew, only Hannah, Jesse, Louis Talbott, and the eight children were still on the hill. Gabe was nowhere to be found. When Craig had gone into the house on the way down the hill to get Gabe, he had found his bed neatly made, his nightclothes carefully folded at the foot of his bed. Never in Craig's memory had he ever known Gabe to fold his nightclothes.

* * *

Farley spoke into the radio clipped to his shoulder and then to Craig. "Fiona has just arrived from Nevada. She's got Lawton with her. You remember Ed—he was the quarry geologist. Deputy says he's got some scale model of the quarry with him. Evidently, he's been working on this model for several years since he moved to Elko to try to figure out the in-flooding. He had called Fiona a few weeks ago to tell her about it, and she flew out there to see it. Evidently, that's why her boys staged this whole hostage thing . . . so the world would finally listen to their side of the story."

"Scale model? Fifteen years after the in-flooding, Lawton comes up with a scale model?" Craig said, growing visibly upset. "Why would anyone listen to him now?"

"Well, you're right. Fiona already lost the libel suit against Lockhart, and she's approached the attorney general of the State of Missouri several times asking for this new investigation. Seems Lockhart knows the AG pretty well, and has convinced the man that Fiona and Lawton are pure crazy."

"They are pure crazy and they're going to kill people to prove it!" Craig said, rising and pacing. Farley noticed Craig's face was pale and his hands were shaking. He knew the minister had not eaten or slept much in the past forty-eight hours. "Why don't you get some rest, Craig. This situation is going to go on for awhile. You're going to need to be on your toes for Hannah's and Kadence's sakes . . . and maybe Gabe's if he's on that hill," Farley said.

"What happens when Fiona and Ed get here?"

"Ian's calling a press conference," Farley said, wincing as he rose to a standing position.

"Why are we catering to the demands of terrorists?" Craig said, suddenly agitated, pacing more furiously.

"Can't tell you that. It's news. It involves free speech. Most terrorists are allowed to have their say even if they get nothing else. By the way, Fiona was as surprised as we were about what Ian and Charlie were pulling."

"Hard to believe she wouldn't have a clue that her own sons were planning this," Craig said.

The image of Gabe's neatly folded nightclothes flashed into Craig's mind.

CHAPTER 26

Farley had never had so many things to think of at once. Ian had specifically asked to deal with the county Sheriff and the National Guard in that order. He had requested that the FBI be kept out of the negotiations completely. Ian had recounted for him the details of how the FBI and the Bureau of Alcohol, Tobacco and Firearms had shot innocent people on trumped up charges at both Ruby Ridge and Waco. He said if he heard of any involvement from either the FBI or the ATF, he would shoot one of his hostages.

The chief was grateful that the National Guard was keeping the crowds under control. With each passing hour, cars streamed into Griggsberg. Finally, the Guard had closed all the roads leading into town and had set up a perimeter one hundred feet out from the hill completely around Bennigan's Bluff so that friend or foe could be more easily identified.

The chief allowed the families of the children to take the best spots on the beach near the Bluff. Mary Louise Candella, Jesse's mother, had claimed a spot under a huge oak tree close to the covered bridge. Someone had given her a kerosene heater and a lawn chair. Sheriff Atkinson had set up a small tent for her. Darlene had sent food from Rosa's diner to her several times. Even when Farley warned her about the land mines in the road next to her, she had insisted on staying to be near her Jesse.

Despite the military barrier, groups of vigilantes and lone Rambos attempted to swim the river and climb the hill from the backside of the Bluff, but had been shot at and turned back by Bennigan's soldiers. Some of these invaders envisioned themselves setting the children free. But most of them were there to lend their support to Ian and his men against the tyrannical oppression of the government.

They had been schooled in the details of Ruby Ridge and Waco and had been waiting for just such an opportunity to fight the U.S. government.

As soldiers from various militia organizations were caught and questioned, Chief Farley saw that most of Ian's sympathizers were fully armed, dressed in battle gear, and were wearing police-issue, bullet-proof vests. They were ready to do battle with law enforcement, having spent years perfecting their hatred . . . and their aim. They had learned about the Bennigans's plight on the Internet and they had come to support a fellow citizen whose demand for justice had been ignored for too long.

Just eight hours after the hostages had been taken, the chief encountered a woman from Kansas City who had already designed and printed five hundred T-shirts proclaiming, "I was at Bennigan's Bluff!" *That's the beauty of free speech combined with true blue capitalism*, the chief had muttered to himself. *Ahhhhhh, America. Land of the free.*

Darlene had printed a copy of Ian's web page for him. Ian's latest update—dated April 4, 1999—had ominously informed the world that he intended to get justice today in Griggsberg, no matter what it took—and no matter how many people he had to kill to get it.

* * *

Ed Lawton hadn't been back to Griggsberg in the fifteen years since he had left. As the Sheriff's car inched through the crowded streets of Griggsberg, Lawton couldn't contain his wonder at the way Griggsberg had changed. "Fiona, I can't get over this place. The college, the businesses—everything looks so new and so clean . . . " Even as Ed said the words, he regretted them. Fiona fingered the smooth scar on her cheek, and her strained, reddened face told him that she regarded every improvement to the town with undiminished contempt. "I'm sorry, Fiona. It's just such a shock to see it all at once." Ed kept the rest of his observations to himself as they drove up in front of Chief Farley's command post.

"My boys!" Fiona cried out. "And Maura! I need to talk to them." Farley helped Fiona out of the sheriff's car, handling her as tenderly as if she were his aging relative. "Mrs. Bennigan, we're in contact with Ian and Charlie. They've told us Maura's in the house, and she's fine."

Ed remembered how Fiona had always felt the chief had been in on the quarry flooding. She drew her arm back from him and stumbled toward the bridge. Her eyes were wild as she took in the crowds and the commotion at the base of Bennigan's Bluff. "All three of my children are on that hill! My boys have done all of this. Maybe Liam helped them!" Ed cringed, knowing Fiona's words were not helping her cause.

Suddenly Fiona bolted toward the covered bridge. Chief Farley and Sheriff Atkinson followed after her but seemed reluctant to step onto the road in front of the bridge. "Stop, Fiona! There are land mines in the road!" the Chief yelled.

A guard shouted, "Halt! Or you will be shot!"

Fiona stopped for a moment. Farley ran to catch up with her, grabbing her arm and holding her back. "Fiona! They've got mines in that road!"

She twisted her arm loose with a fury fed by her maternal instinct. "My children are on that hill and I'm going to be with them!" Farley grabbed for her again as she slithered out of his grasp and made for the bridge.

"Halt! There are land mines in the road!" came the voice of the terrorist on the bridge. Fiona ignored his warning completely and walked onto the bridge. The only sound was the simultaneous gasp of the onlookers.

"You get my boys down here right now," Fiona commanded the guards. "You tell them I've got Ed Lawton here and we're going to see that things get straightened out . . . " She seemed irritated when none of them moved. "Well, go on . . . tell them that."

One of the guards picked up the walkie-talkie and asked to speak to Ian. "Ma'am, I have orders from your son to keep you down here. It's too dangerous for you on the hill. He says to stay with the sheriff. He wants you to get Mr. Lawton's model set up, and then he'll tell you how to proceed," the guard said, a tone of trepidation below his firm statement.

"Orders? My son is giving his mother orders?" Fiona bellowed. Once again, she started to cross the bridge to go up the hill. Three soldiers moved into her path; one aimed his pistol at her. Fiona addressed the guards tersely. "My son is just about like this road here, boys . . . he'll tell you he's got land mines hidden just to scare you off . . . but my son is bluffing. He would no more handle a land mine than he would a rattlesnake with rabies!"

The soldiers stood their ground; several others took up positions behind them.

Fiona was shocked at the numbers against her. "Who are you people? How are you involved with my boys? This is family business. We're going to solve this on our own!"

"Yes, ma'am, we don't doubt that," the soldier said, leading Fiona out to the road that went to her house. "Look up there at your house. See those words—SINN FEIN? You and your sons are going to prove that Liam Bennigan was murdered. We're only here to make sure you don't get pushed around . . . that's all."

Fiona shielded her eyes from the sun with her hand as she gazed up at the words spray painted high on her house. As she read them over and over, they seemed to wield some kind of power over her. She visibly relaxed, absently touching her face, caressing her scar. "My boys have the Irish spirit. They will not be oppressed. Liam and I have taught them well . . . " With that idea in her mind, Fiona walked back down the road, through the covered bridge, and over the road with the supposed land mines buried in it.

* * *

Up on the bunker, Ian stifled a smile as he watched his mother storm over the road he had told everyone contained active land mines. Directly in front of the bridge, in full view of law enforcement, Ian had instructed his men to bury saucer-like contraptions he had bought from a crazy old World War II buff who lived outside Rumbar, Missouri. Ian radioed his men to assure them that the land mines were still activated, but that his mother's thin body had not been heavy enough to trigger the deadly devices. If Farley had followed her, he surmised, the mines would have gone off. Ian's explanation was accepted; no one knew how to disprove it anyway.

"Charlie! Get over here!" Ian motioned to his brother who had been stationed on the porch of the Bennigan home. "Mom and Lawton are here and we've got to move into Phase 2. We've got to get these television reporters to film the evidence of Dad's murder. You ready? You've got to tell Dulcey to go ahead and set things up so we can get this on the air."

Charlie and Ian had already asked Dulcey to call one of her press conferences. She had seemed willing, even eager to help them when she talked to them from the helicopter in the early hours of the siege. In addition to the KCMO crew, she was to pick top national reporters to film the conference. What luck that they had a local girl in on this! Even though neither brother had ever talked to her much, Ian had always felt that Dulcey was all right. As fellow Catholics, Dulcey and Rosa had always been misfits in this Protestant town, same as the Bennigans. If anyone could understand the Bennigans situation, it was Dulcey Martinez.

* * *

Mayor Lockhart took the phone call from Dexter Wright at his luxurious Spanish villa in Coral Gables, Florida. Councilman Wright was one of only a handful of people who knew how to reach him in Florida. After the call, Lockhart had sped to the nearest airport, cursing the second generation of Bennigans who would not leave the past alone.

Fifteen years ago, Fiona had smeared his name all over the Kansas City papers, and accused him at every public meeting she could attend. Finally, he had silenced her with the libel suit he had brought against her in a Kansas City court. In the end, Fiona had been forced to pay Lockhart damages of one hundred and fifty thousand dollars which he had very publicly donated to Miranda Dennison's Church on the Hill Gospel Music Camp. Jack Lockhart had won every re-election as mayor for the fifteen years since the in-flooding. Fiona's dementia and unfounded accusations had been well established in a court of law.

* * *

With all the media in town, Councilman Dexter Wright had realized the importance of having the mayor arrive in a car that lent some power to his image. Wright had borrowed his cousin's new silver Cadillac Seville to pick up the mayor from the airport. Reporters gathered in a feeding frenzy around the Cadillac as it pulled up to the command post, and Mayor Lockhart stepped out.

"Well, the Bennigan family has the town in an uproar again," Lockhart said, facing the reporters with a benevolent but weary smile. "They have been fighting this town for fifteen years over their allegations. A Missouri court of law has established that no wrongdoing was committed. Now, please! I have a serious situation on my hands and I'd appreciate it if the media would let the leaders of this town tend to their business." Lockhart batted his hands at the cameras as though they were bothersome gnats.

As he broke through the crowd of reporters, he caught sight of Ed Lawton shaking hands with townspeople he used to know. Suddenly the two men were face to face; the smiles on their faces vanished.

"What are you doing here, Lawton?" said Mayor Lockhart, keeping his voice low, hoping not to attract the attention of the reporters.

"Well, Mayor, Fiona and I just may have all the loose ends tied up, and I guess her boys want to make sure you don't railroad us again." Ed, too, spoke softly. "We intend to present our evidence in front of the whole world this time. Fiona's boys made sure of that."

"Fiona's boys are now terrorists, Mr. Lawton. I'll see to it that none of their demands are met. You know it's policy never to give in to a terrorist's demands." Mayor Lockhart could see the hungry look of the reporters who were crushing in on him and Lawton. He managed to raise his chin and plaster on a hearty smile just as the cameras began to roll again, "Okay, Mr. Lawton, I've got to meet with the sheriff and my chief of police right now to get this thing over with."

Mayor Lockhart followed Sheriff Atkinson and Chief Farley into the Griggsberg Police Station. There he was introduced to a tall, slender, gray-haired man who looked as though he had been born in a uniform. Al Benson, FBI Special Agent in Charge, and his crack unit of antiterrorist and hostage specialists had just arrived from Quantico, Virginia. Benson explained that they had known about the potential disaster for six months. In fact, one of their agents was on the hill at this very moment taking orders from the Bennigan brothers.

CHAPTER 27

"You knew this was going down for SIX MONTHS and you didn't tell anyone?" Farley bellowed after Al Benson described the FBI's infiltration of Bennigan's band of terrorists.

"Now before you start accusing us of moving too late, understand something . . . we are constrained by law and the constitution of the United States not to move too soon on a situation like this. We are not even allowed to monitor a group such as this—they have rights you know! But when Ian Bennigan described his accusations on his web site and finally *hinted* at a plan of action, a watchdog group reported it to the FBI, and we moved to infiltrate the group.

"But that was six months ago!" shouted Farley.

"Ever since the Oklahoma City bombing, every hate site, militia group, and potential terrorist group—and there are now *thousands* of these groups in the United States—has been watched by groups of individuals *not* associated with the government. The FBI can only get involved when the threats seem real. Remember, we can't arrest anyone for a crime they haven't committed. The Bennigans have been talking about their military fantasies for years to anyone who would listen. How could we be sure this paint ball gathering wasn't just a way to blow off steam?"

"Why didn't you let me know?"

"You couldn't have moved on them either. They didn't do anything wrong until they walked into that church. Ian never even let on to his soldiers what he was actually planning to do. He promised them that no one would be hurt and they would go home safely to their families if they would follow his orders. He never mentioned hostages or the Church on the Hill in any way."

"Unbelievable. I wanted to think those boys were so stupid and out of touch that their insanity would never amount to much." Farley put his head in his hands. "I thought their old wounds had scarred over. But I see now that they just festered under scabbed-over skin."

The agents went about their business, and Farley paced the station floor; his face a mask of despair, his mind whirling. Ian had been five years old when his father had drowned, the same age as those children being held at the church. How had he known that the five-year-olds would be singing? One name swam into his mind . . . it had a clarity that felt like certainty: Gabe Dennison. *Gabe would never have put his own sisters and parents and everyone he knew in harm's way to help the Bennigans.* Farley knew Gabe would do that only if he believed Ian and Charlie were justified—or if Gabe had been tricked into helping them.

* * *

On Monday at lunchtime, Rosa sent up a big tray of peanut butter sandwiches, plastic containers of macaroni and cheese, and several gallons of milk. In the late afternoon, the town's only McDonald's sent a Happy Meal for each child, and an adult meal for Hannah. Three of the children refused to eat anything. Others played absently with the little toy that came inside the Happy Meal. Hannah noticed Mikey Calvert didn't eat—he was too busy trying to breathe.

"Mister?" Hannah said through the door. She didn't know the day guard's name. "Mister? We've got to get Mikey Calvert to the hospital—it's his asthma!"

"We sent in his breathing machine this morning. What's wrong with him now?" the gunman asked.

"I don't know. It's just not enough—the color of his face doesn't look right. You have to do something!" Hannah's voice was frantic now.

"I'll see what I can do," came the reply. Static from his radio crackled from the other side of the door.

Hannah's bag had her name printed on it in large red letters. She wondered if her lunch would be something more edible than what McDonalds had sent the children. It was definitely heavier. She took her meal to Jesse's bed and looked in the bag to find a bigger hamburger—a quarter pounder—but everything else was the same as what the kids got. Why was the bag so heavy? Hannah took out the hamburger and the drink, weighing each item in her hand. Everything seemed to be of normal weight. But as she stuck her hand in to get the french fries, her fingers hit a very solid cherry pie carton. She unwrapped several layers of waxed paper and a small cell phone tumbled onto the bed. A phone number was written in red marker on one of the waxed papers.

Hannah took the phone into the bathroom. Her hands shook as she punched in the numbers. Someone answered the phone, but said nothing.

"Hello? This is Hannah!"

"Good. You got it, Hannah," said a voice she didn't recognize.

"Who is this?" Hannah caught her breath, wondering if some crafty reporter had set this up.

"Al Benson, Hannah," he said, declining to identify his authority. "Where are your guards?"

"Outside the door. They don't want to scare the children with their guns. Who are you?"

"I'm here to help you out of there. Chief Farley's right here with me," the voice of Al Benson said.

"Hannah? It's the chief. You okay?"

"Chief?" Hannah's body went slack with relief when she heard Farley's voice.

"We can't tell you too much right now over this phone, Hannah. But at least you've got a link with us. Don't call anyone or tell the kids you've got the phone. They'll all want to talk to their parents. We need this phone to be a secret and the line to stay open and secure, okay?"

Benson took the line again. "Hannah, the ringer is turned off but the phone has a vibrating attachment so you'll know when we're trying to reach you. Make sure you don't flip the ringer on or your guards will hear it."

"But I'm worried about Mikey Calvert." Hannah's concern was tangible. "He's not breathing . . . "

"Hannah, we already know about Mikey from the guards. Fiona got Ian to allow the KCMO news helicopter to land in the church parking lot to take Mikey off the hill. Ian wants only Dulcey and the pilot from KCMO because he trusts them."

"Oh, thank goodness!" Hannah said, glancing over to check Mikey's color. "He looks awful. He's just not breathing right."

"Hannah, listen carefully. We've got a plan to get *all* of you out of there. Are you with me?"

Hannah was quiet for a moment. "All of us?" she said, her hands trembling, tears stinging her eyes. "How?"

Your father told us about the trapdoor in the ceiling of Jesse's apartment. Instead of landing in the parking lot, the chopper will land on the roof of the church. You are to take the children up onto the roof instead."

"But there's a soldier up there!"

"Don't worry about him. We'll take care of him so he can't get in your way."

Someone else came on the line. "Hannah?" It was the chief, "If we don't get Mikey out of there, *Mikey* will be the one who is dead. Do you understand? We'll handle the guard."

"What's to keep the soldiers from shooting at us once we're in the air?" Hannah questioned, squinting her eyes and rubbing her pounding temples, trying to think of everything that could go wrong.

"I think we've got that worked out, Hannah. You'll see when the time comes."

"Okay, Chief. How will I know when to go to the roof?"

"You'll know . . . "

"How will I know? What if I go at the wrong time?"

"We're going to do this thing in about four hours, at 10 P.M.—so it will be dark and we've got time to pull it off—can't tell you much else right now, Hannah. Trust your instincts. You'll be fine . . . "

"But, Chief, what if . . . " The phone went dead.

Hannah went to Mikey to give him another breathing treatment. She hoped ten o'clock would not be too late.

* * *

Dulcey had made arrangements for the press conference in the morning—Tuesday morning—at her mother's café. It was a neutral place, cozy and non-threatening. It would set everyone's mind at ease, she reasoned. Rosa busied herself putting white linen tablecloths on the two long tables positioned down the center of the café between the booths. She planned to serve donuts and coffee to everyone before the press conference. Dulcey knew her mother would do whatever it took to help get the hostages off the hill.

"Miss Martinez? May we have a word with you?" said one of the strangers who had been stationed at the police station. Both Rosa and Dulcey looked up, but the man was motioning to Dulcey.

"Did you reach Hannah?" Dulcey said softly, following the man through the door to the police station.

"We've reached her. Ian has agreed to a parking lot pickup at 10 P.M. tonight—he wants his sister Maura to bring the little boy out when the chopper is on the ground, and he wants only you and the pilot on the chopper. He says Charlie will inspect the chopper as it flies over the church. Then when it lands, he will allow Maura to bring Mikey to the chopper. That way he won't have any deaths before the negotiations even start . . . and he can get his sister off the hill."

"But . . . " Dulcey looked expectantly at the agent. "But, what will *really* happen?" Dulcey herself had suggested a different plan. Of course, everyone was against it until she had come up with a way to get a cell phone to Hannah in the little cherry pie container. The plan had then seemed more reliable since Hannah could be prepared for the rescue.

"You sure you want to do this?"

Dulcey smiled. "You can bet my career as an ace television reporter on it!"

"Of course, your station manager and the other reporters have been told nothing of the rescue of anyone besides Mikey. They just think that since Ian knows you, he is willing to release the little boy with asthma. The bit about having Maura accompany the little boy was brilliant, by the way. That'll keep Fiona happy and get Maura out of there. It'll also keep the men from shooting at the chopper once the hostages are on board."

"Look, if something goes wrong on the roof . . . " Dulcey said, her eyes intense, jaw tight, " . . . you make sure you let everyone know that *none* of my guys at the station knew anything about this. You make sure everyone knows that this was their crazy rookie reporter's idea. Got it?"

"You got it. You're a brave young woman and I admire what you're about to do. If it works, you'll be a hero. If it doesn't . . . "

"I understand the risks. Don't forget whose devious mind came up with this plan." Dulcey found herself trying to cheer him up about the risks she was about to take.

"Is there anything else you want to ask about?" He checked his watch; it was eight-fifteen.

"Yeah, there is. I've been trying not to think about it. But everyone knows there's a soldier on the roof. Won't he stop the chopper from landing on the roof?"

"That's not your worry. Your pilot McCloskey was a crack soldier in Vietnam and he'll know what to do. We'd have sent one of our agents as the pilot, but Ian and Charlie have already seen McCloskey's face and wanted only him . . . and you, of course."

"Agents? You guys are FBI, aren't you?" Dulcey knew that information could get one of the hostages on the hill killed.

CHAPTER 28

Dulcey went back to her mother's diner, adrenaline coursing through her body. Lyle and Renee Calvert, Mikey's parents, had just come in. They had been told that Mikey would be off the hill and taken by ambulance to the hospital by ten-thirty—if everything went as planned.

The agonizing thirty-six hours since the children had been taken had been even more agonizing for the Calverts because of Mikey's condition. Dulcey noticed that Renee had tried to put on some makeup, but it was already streaked from new tears. Lyle looked grim and worried. Everyone knew the stress of the rescue could send Mikey into an irreversible asthma attack.

"Dulcey!" Renee cried as she saw her. When Renee was in high school, she had often been Dulcey's babysitter. Rosa joined them and the three women stood in a heart-wrenching embrace for a few moments.

"God has always been with my Dulcinea, Renee. You know this is true. My Dulcey can do anything and never get hurt." Rosa beamed at her daughter.

"Even when Dulcey was little, she always tested the limits. But she always knew where the edge was. I know you'll bring Mikey back to us," Renee said, giving Dulcey another hug. "We will pray for you."

Rosa scoffed, "If I had to get down on my knees every time Dulcinea was lookin' at some troubles, I would never get to my diner, Renee. You know that."

Dulcey squeezed Renee and kissed her mother on the forehead. She started to say something but decided no words were needed. It was time to get to the helicopter.

* * *

The guard outside Hannah's door changed at nine o'clock just as it had on Easter night. Hannah hoped it was Joe. She heard the daytime guard talk to his relief and then stomp down the stairs to go off watch.

"Hannah?" It was Joe.

Hannah spoke through the door, trembling. "Joe? Mikey's real sick. They're taking him off the hill; did you hear?"

There was a commotion and a loud knock at the door. Hannah knew more soldiers had climbed the stairs to Jesse's room. "Joe? Who's with you?"

Throughout the entire ordeal, Hannah had not been asked to open her side of the door. The soldiers had padlocked the other side. Being face to face with her captors was not a pleasant thought. As she heard the padlock slip out of the latch, she opened the door just an inch and saw Maura. Several masked men stood behind her silently.

"Maura! What are you doing here?"

"I'm here to take the little boy to the helicopter," Maura said. Her face was drawn as though she hadn't slept. "Ian and Charlie want me off the hill. My mother is waiting for me." Maura pushed past Hannah and stumbled into the room, shutting the door behind her. "Oh, Hannah! I can't believe this is all happening. Please believe me, I had no idea . . . Mom didn't know either." She collapsed in sobs and Hannah went to her.

"I never thought for a moment that you were involved, Maura. We're going to make it." She lifted the younger girl's face toward her. "We're going to be fine, Maura."

So this was how the children would be safe from Ian and Charlie. Their own sister would be riding on the chopper with the children. No one would dare shoot if Maura was on board, thought Hannah.

Suddenly, the cell phone vibrated in Hannah's pocket. Not wanting to test Maura's loyalty to her brothers, Hannah excused herself. "Well, I need to get Mikey to the bathroom before he gets on the helicopter," she said, searching the room for the pale little boy.

"Mikey—come here, sweetheart. Let's go to the bathroom, okay?" Once in the bathroom, Hannah answered the phone in a whisper. "Maura's here. Now what?"

"Is she alone?" answered the voice of Al Benson.

"The guard—I call him 'Joe'—is on the other side of the door, but Maura's in the apartment with me and the kids."

"Hannah," said Agent Benson, "Joe is actually one of ours. He is Special Agent Brett Ballard. You're in good hands—do what he tells you to do."

Hannah's mind raced between thoughts as she prepared herself for the rescue. She took Mikey by the hand, which was cold and white. "Did you go to the bathroom?"

"Couldn't," he said listlessly.

Hannah knew the little boy hadn't had anything to eat or drink in thirty-six hours, and who knew how long before that. "Mikey, we're going to get into a helicopter and go see your Mom and Dad. Okay? But you can't tell the other kids 'cause it's a surprise."

Mikey nodded. Looking dazed, he pushed out the bathroom door and went to sit on the floor by the closet.

* * *

Ian and Charlie had taken up a position in the parking lot of the church by nine-thirty that night. A twenty-foot extension ladder leaned against the front of the church, reaching its high roof.

"Charlie, it's time to go up on the roof," said Ian. "Let me know when the chopper takes off from down below, and make sure it's got KCMO on the side. You let me know if it's not—or if anyone besides Dulcey and that KCMO pilot is on it!"

Until now, Charlie's job had been to guard the Bennigan home from the porch and make sure Maura was safe inside. Ian knew his brother was anxious to have Maura off the hill so she'd be safe—and so he could see some real action. Pulling his mask down over his face, Charlie called to Ian. "What if the chopper is National Guard or Sheriff or some other news station, Ian?"

"Then do nothing but radio me and identify whose it is and how many people are on it, Charlie. You got that? I'll have plenty of guys on this side of the building to shoot it down if it's anyone else but Dulcey." He watched his younger brother climb the ladder.

"Charlie! Take cover up there. Don't be standing out in the open, okay?"

Charlie waved and then disappeared onto the roof. A few moments later, another soldier appeared and climbed down the ladder. "Man! That wind up there cuts right through you. It's the North Pole up there." The soldier stomped his boots and flapped his arms to return his circulation to normal. Ian directed him to take up a position at the side of the parking lot.

"Men, we have twenty minutes till touchdown. If this helicopter is *anything* but KCMO, we've got to take it down. Those are your orders."

* * *

Dulcey slipped into her old down jacket she had found at the diner. Her mother zipped up the front of it. "You bring back Renee's boy to her. And you bring Dulcinea back to *her* mama."

"Don't worry about me, Mama. Larry's one of the best military-trained pilots in the country. He was shot down twice in Vietnam."

"Shot down?" echoed Rosa, "Couldn't your boss find someone who *didn't* get shot down twice?" Rosa questioned.

"Oh, Mama—I'll see you in a little while." Dulcey waved at her mother and ran to board the KCMO helicopter.

"Let's go get those kids, Larry!" she said from behind his seat. None of the other news teams had been tipped off about Mikey's rescue. Ace reporter Dulcey Martinez took to the skies for the news scoop of the year . . . a lone reporter . . . with no camera.

* * *

Hannah's phone vibrated. She answered it in the bathroom with Kadence, the last of the children to use the toilet before the rescue got underway. The nameless voice instructed her. "Agent Ballard has instructions to take you and the kids to the roof just as soon as it is secured—within a few minutes. He will go first, followed by Maura, then Mikey, then the children. You will be the last to leave Jesse's apartment. That way no one gets left behind. Understood?"

"We're ready to go," Hannah murmured. Kadence's eyes grew wide as she saw the phone in her sister's hand. Hannah put a finger to her lips.

"Where'd you get . . . " Kadence whispered.

Hannah knelt down in the tiny space between the shower stall and the toilet. "Listen to me, Kadence. You have been my number one helper during this whole rotten mess. I'm going to really need your help now to keep the kids calm."

Kadence's eyes glistened. "I'll help you, Hannah. I'll stay right with you."

"We are going out on the roof and we're going to get those kids and us on a helicopter. Can we do that?" Hannah grabbed Kadence's hand and looked into her huge brown eyes, "Now go get dressed and help everyone else—but you mustn't say one word to the kids about the rescue."

Kadence shook her head, curls bobbing. Hannah watched her go out into the apartment, take Nicole by the hand, and whisper in her ear. Soon both girls were putting on their Easter dresses and helping the others find their clothes.

At ten minutes to ten, Agent Ballard unlocked the padlock on his side of the door. Hannah slid the latch open on her side. He took off his ski mask as he stepped into the room. The children stared at him, wide-eyed with horror. The Cline twins started sobbing, no doubt remembering what the soldiers had done to their mother. Hannah wrapped Mikey in a huge sweater that belonged to Jesse, then turned and locked the door to the apartment from her side.

Joe who was now Brett spoke softly to Maura. "There's been a change in plans, Maura. You and I are going to take Mikey to the roof and board the helicopter there, okay?" Brett tried to sound as off-handed as he could, busying himself with the ladder that led to the trapdoor.

"Okay, Joe," Maura complied.

Hannah realized that after all they had been through, some of the kids would refuse to go out into the frightening windy night with the man carrying a gun. She would be surprised if any of them would go willingly except Mikey and Kadence who had been prepared for the rescue.

Hannah knelt down so she was at eye level with the children. "Now listen to me. Am I your friend?" Several of the children nodded. "You do as I say and you'll be fine, okay?" She looked into each of their eyes in turn, noting which ones would be most reluctant to go through the trapdoor.

"What about Cordelia?" asked Callie.

"You're absolutely right. We need to take her with us. Would you and Bryce be in charge of Cordelia? You can take her to your house until Jesse wants her back. How about that?"

The plan temporarily calmed the twins.

CHAPTER 29

From the copilot's seat, Dulcey could see the familiar lighted Christ directly in front of the helicopter window; the lamb in his arms was as wide as the nose of the chopper. "Hello, old friend," she whispered, "I'm in another jam and I need your help again . . . " As the chopper hovered above the church, Dulcey looked down and saw a masked gunman on the roof emerge from behind an air-conditioning unit and speak into his radio handset.

McCloskey dipped the helicopter nose several times so the soldier could see that only he and Dulcey were inside. The masked man again spoke into the handset and motioned them over the church roof.

Suddenly, Dulcey saw another man burst through the trapdoor, hoist his upper body into the windy night, and take aim at the masked man in front of him. The terrorist fumbled for the pistol in his belt. The man at the trapdoor shot once, the sound muffled by a silencer. The terrorist went down, writhing, clutching his stomach, his gun and radio clattering to the asphalt roof.

Then Dulcey saw Maura push Mikey ahead of her out of the trapdoor and run across the roof with him. Just as Dulcey reached for the trembling little boy, she heard Charlie scream, "Maura! I'm hit! Help me!"

"Charlie!" Maura stopped, momentarily confused. McCloskey leaned out and yelled for Maura to get Mikey into the chopper. Dulcey leaned out of the side door and scooped up the fragile coughing child. Then Maura ran to her brother, lifting him, dragging him over the roof.

Dulcey jumped out to help Maura drag Charlie to the chopper. "Maura!" Dulcey screamed above the sound of the rotors, "I'll help you with Charlie . . . and we're taking *all* the children with us, okay?"

Maura looked stunned, her long hair blowing and beating her face in the wind. The two of them lifted Charlie into the chopper and covered him with a tarp to keep him warm.

Leaving Maura behind with Charlie and Mikey, Dulcey ran back over the roof toward the trapdoor to help Hannah and Brett rescue the children.

* * *

Brett, realizing the soldiers would soon be swarming the roof if he didn't take action, sprinted toward the parking lot side of the church, pulling his ski mask back over his face so he would look like Charlie. He grabbed the ladder and hauled it up rung by rung onto the roof. In the parking lot below, Ian and his men milled about in confusion. It appeared to Brett that they were unaware that Charlie had been shot or that the children were being rescued on the roof behind him.

By the time the masked figure had pulled the ladder up onto the roof, Ian knew something had gone terribly wrong. Leaving most of his men in the parking lot, he ordered two soldiers to look for another ladder and took four others with him into the church.

Ian and his soldiers tore frantically at the first office door, hitting it with Steelcase office chairs and rifle butts, finally bursting through, only to find the heavy, locked fire door at the bottom of Jesse's stairway.

When Dulcey reached the trapdoor, Hannah screamed to her, "Help me with the kids!" Brett stood guard over them, pausing to pluck each child from Hannah's arms through the trapdoor opening. As soon as four children had gathered on the roof, Dulcey ran with them to the helicopter.

Every child was screaming. Charlie, Maura, Mikey, and four of the kids were already on the chopper when Dulcey saw that Hannah was struggling with all her might in the space just inside the trapdoor.

The Cline twins were wailing hysterically, holding onto one another, creating a double-sized, flailing load of child bodies. Cordelia, a furry ball of teeth and claws in wild motion, was attempting to escape from her pair of small, screaming rescuers. Hannah could not convince the children that the gunman would lead them to safety.

Kadence was below them on the ladder, pushing the twins; Hannah was above, pulling them. Suddenly, Cordelia leaped out of their clutches, sailing past Kadence and landing on the floor of the apartment. Kadence gave the twins a mighty push but lost her footing and fell backwards to the floor, knocking all the air out of her tiny body.

When the twins emerged above the trapdoor, Brett wrapped his arms around both of their waists and hauled their writhing, kicking bodies to the helicopter. Hannah descended the ladder quickly to gather her breathless and then shrieking sister into her arms. Dulcey climbed down the ladder to help Hannah bring Kadence to the roof. Cordelia hissed at them from a corner.

As Hannah carried Kadence up the ladder and Dulcey assisted her from below, they could hear the soldiers cursing and bashing the steel fire door, trying to get to the apartment and to the escaping hostages. *If they break through the fire door*, Hannah thought wildly, *the flimsy door to Jesse's apartment will seem like cardboard.* Then, she knew, all of Ian's fury would be unleashed on the three of them.

Meanwhile Brett heaved the twins on board the chopper and yelled for Maura to hold them down to keep them from escaping back out onto the asphalt roof. Callie lashed out at him with her foot and Brett's radio flew off his belt and skidded out of reach under the belly of the chopper. Brett shut the sliding door and ran back to help Dulcey, Hannah, and Kadence.

Larry McCloskey could not believe the sheer terror aboard his aircraft. The children were screaming, Charlie was moaning loudly, and Maura was sobbing. He tried to follow the figures at the trapdoor, counting the seconds it would take for them to run across thirty feet of roof to reach the chopper. He couldn't understand why it was taking them so long.

Just then, McCloskey saw a masked head bob up above the roof at the far side of the church. The soldiers had found another ladder and were now using it to scale the church building.

In a matter of moments, the top of the church would be swarming with terrorists and their powerful weapons trying to prevent their hostages from fleeing. McCloskey made a split-second decision and rose up into the air a few feet above the roof so the gunmen would not have a clear shot at his windows. Brett too saw the soldiers racing toward the helicopter, and waved the pilot away. He and the girls were behind a huge air compressor and the gunmen could not see them. If the chopper flew toward them, they would be detected. There was no chance they would be allowed to board that helicopter.

* * *

Unable to break through the heavy fire door, Ian and his soldiers ran back to the parking lot and saw that the gunmen were aiming their rifles at the helicopter as it ascended and veered off over the lake. Ian screamed, "Don't shoot! My sister's on that chopper!" His men lowered their guns.

Ian seethed with revenge against Dulcey for tricking him into trusting her. A soldier brought Brett's radio to him from the roof, and by the number on its side, Ian knew that it belonged to the man he knew as Joe Dobson. And now he knew that Joe was either ATF or FBI.

As his soldiers watched, Ian flew into a rage, reeling from the quick succession of betrayals. "We were infiltrated!" shouted Ian to the men. "Where's Charlie?" he screamed. "Where's my brother!" As Ian gathered his men together, he asked them to remove their masks.

It was clear that Charlie was not among them.

* * *

Maura did her best to comfort the crying children, holding Charlie's limp hand under the tarp, not knowing if he was dead or alive. "Your mommies and daddies are waiting for you!" She too was buoyed at being reunited with her own mother and tried to pass her relief on to the children. "Soon you'll be home. Look down there— your mommies and daddies are down there."

McCloskey had been instructed that Agent Brett Ballard was in charge. Had he flown over to the side of the roof where Dulcey and the others were, he would have drawn attention to their location and made himself and the kids a better target. Nevertheless, he felt he had failed the four he had to leave behind. He was just grateful they were with a highly trained FBI agent. He prayed for their survival as he hovered over Griggsberg waiting for the sheriff's instructions.

* * *

"Down the ladder!" Brett whispered, closing and bolting the trap-door after they were once again in Jesse's apartment. "Get into the closet . . . and be quiet. I don't think they know we're in here," instructed Brett.

Hannah was down the ladder first, still carrying Kadence.

"Are we going to die, Hannah?" Kadence whimpered into her neck as Hannah carried her over to Jesse's closet.

Dulcey followed, dazed. Hannah pushed Jesse's clothes aside and helped her sister settle herself as far back against the wall as she could.

Brett was fairly certain that none of the soldiers knew that four people had been left behind. But it would be better to stay out of Jesse's apartment just in case the soldiers came to check the room or to use the trapdoor to get to the roof.

He motioned Dulcey into the closet, and then entered himself, shutting the door and turning off the light. The four of them trembled in silence, wondering if the apartment would be searched. "Use the cell phone and tell Benson what happened," said Brett to Hannah. He waited as she put her hand in her pocket.

"I must have dropped the phone somewhere!" Hannah gasped. She put her head on her knees and wept softly in frustration. They were her first tears and they seemed to spill out of her as if from an overfilled cup.

Brett readied himself in the dark, suffocating space, sweat pouring off his chin and down his neck. If anyone opened that door, Brett had his rifle already drawn and the safety off. Above Hannah's muffled weeping, they could hear the drone of the KCMO chopper hovering over the town. Seven of the children, at least, had escaped.

* * *

McCloskey radioed the Sheriff, "I've got Maura and Charlie Bennigan on board, sir. And seven children. Charlie took a bullet—

looks to be to his mid-section. Have ambulances on standby. And Sheriff?" he coughed and swallowed, "Dulcey's back on the hill. The pastor's daughters are with her and Agent Ballard stayed behind." It hit him how it might seem that he had carelessly left Dulcey and the other three behind. "Benson put me under Ballard's command, sir. It was Ballard . . . who waved me away from the church."

Sheriff Atkinson was silent for a moment. "You did well McCloskey. Ballard was in charge of that operation. We've got four ambulances standing by." He paused again. "Any reason to think Ian Bennigan knows he's still got hostages in the church?"

"The men on the roof seemed unaware of them," McCloskey's voice was nearly drowned out by the screaming of the children. "Where do you want me to put down? These kids have lost it—they're totally wigged out and they need their parents . . . immediately."

Al Benson got on the line. "McCloskey, put that chopper of yours down in the field just north of the police station. There are ten or twelve of those real tall, skinny Cyprus trees between the station and the field—you'll see it. The ambulances will shine their lights on that field. Not a word to *anyone* about the four hostages we left behind, copy?"

"Copy, sir." McCloskey flew over the police station, locating the field. "I see it. I'll be setting down in two minutes."

* * *

Kadence, who never liked tight spaces, got squirmy after about fifteen minutes in the closet. She moved her body along the wall to find a more comfortable position. As she drew her hand over the drywall to find more room, she felt a small, wooden door in the wall.

"Hannah," she whispered. "Feel where my hand is."

Hannah let Kadence take her hand and run it over the wooden panel. She pushed the little door outward and a rush of cool air burst into the cramped closet. Another precaution to keep Jesse safe—a passage into the storage room.

Brett whispered, "Here, take my light and see if anyone is in there." He unclipped a small flashlight from his belt and handed it to Hannah. Kadence slithered through the opening into the darkness. A cobweb brushed across her face and she inhaled sharply.

"Spiders, Hannah!" Kadence gasped, her hands flailing at the wispy filaments.

Hannah knew spiders were terrifying to her. "Just cobwebs, Kadence. Move on into the room so the others can come too. Hannah shined the small but powerful flashlight around the storage room that was nearly as wide and long as the sanctuary below it. She could make out racks of pageant costumes, clear plastic bags of Christmas decorations, wedding trellises, floral arrangements, backdrops, painted scenery panels, bags of old clothes, lumber, and several portable chalkboards on wheels.

Brett agreed with Hannah that it was safe for now and followed the three of them into the storage room.

* * *

Ian paced up and down in the parking lot of the church. His men whispered nervously among themselves. "I'm going to check on the condition of our two—count 'em—*two* remaining hostages." Ian seemed to be on the edge. Not knowing about the trapdoor was a serious tactical error. Even more serious was the fact that some ATF or FBI agent had infiltrated his army. It had been his best soldier, Joe Dobson, who had fooled him. Ian's chest heaved with bitter rage at having been tricked into trusting the man.

It had been such fun up until now—a game, a test of wills. He continued to examine the situation in his mind. Where was he going with this? How dangerous did he plan to become? What had happened to Charlie? Did he panic and board the chopper? If Maura had not been on that helicopter, would he have shot it down with eight children and several adults on board? If he had dropped it from the sky, what would have kept the sheriff and the National Guard from storming the hill? And most of all, without the children as hostages, would the world listen to the Bennigan's accusations of foul play and lies and cover-ups? Would Jesse and the music preacher provide enough leverage to win justice at last for the Bennigan family?

CHAPTER 30

Sheriff Atkinson watched the helicopter land on the field behind the police station. Because of the angle of the church roof, no one on the ground had witnessed the rescue of the children. At first, everyone on the beach thought KCMO was doing another in-air report on the situation. But as the word reached the families that their children had been rescued, the field swarmed with the parents of the children, a sea of aggressive reporters, and the people of Griggsberg.

The paramedics had already loaded Charlie into an ambulance before anyone had reached the field. It sped away with Charlie, Maura, and Fiona. Mikey and his parents were whisked away in another ambulance. The sheriff had instructed the remaining two ambulances to speed away to a Kansas City hospital with their sirens blaring as though they too contained victims.

The six remaining hysterical children were soon being hugged and kissed by their sobbing parents. The field behind the police station was sheer bedlam.

Sheriff Atkinson caught Miranda, Kate, and Rosa as they were about to leave through the back door of Rosa's diner. As he told them what had gone wrong with the rescue, the smiles left their faces. Miranda put her head down on her chest and wept. Rosa's face went slack, and Kate caught her before she collapsed to the floor.

"We believe all four of them are safe inside the church," Sheriff Atkinson said to Rosa, Kate and Miranda.

"SAFE?" Miranda raged the word. She flung her upper body from side to side like a caged tiger—hands clenched near her face—a cornered animal mother whose babies were in danger. "SAFE?" she spat again. "*Safe in the church* is the kind of thing someone would say *before* Easter Sunday of 1999!"

Craig came rushing into the diner. His hair was matted, his eyes wild and bloodshot. "Is it true? Farley just told me . . . " The sheriff silenced the four of them and led them to an empty office inside the police station.

"Ian has them, but he may not know he has them . . . right, Sheriff?" Craig asked when the door was shut behind them.

"We think Ian would have called us boasting about his new set of hostages if he knew they had been left behind," said the sheriff. "We think he would definitely use that card if he knew he had it. Now, you are all under strict orders not to tell anyone what happened. Your children's lives depend on it! I'm going out there and get the reporters to announce that everyone is off that hill, except Jesse and Reverend Talbott. We'll say that the three girls are wounded and are being hospitalized in Kansas City—that'll explain why they're not here." Atkinson looked into their pale, astonished faces, "Do I have your word that you will tell no one?" They nodded and left the room.

The sheriff approached the crowd around the now-empty helicopter. He found Kevin Barker and Ben Taylor in the crowd. "Barker! Did you hear what happened? Dulcey, Hannah, and Kadence were hurt. Did you see them before they left in the ambulance?"

"No!" Barker moved toward the sheriff, his notepad and pen ready, "I almost missed the whole thing. The children were in their parents' arms before we got here. What happened?"

"Gunshots. . . none fatal. They'll be okay. All three have been taken to Kansas City for treatment—I didn't even find out what hospital. It'd probably be better to keep their location quiet—with all the wackos running around," Sheriff Atkinson said.

Barker straightened his tie, ready to go on the air as soon as Ben gave him the signal.

Sheriff Atkinson encouraged him a little more. "Let everyone know they're off the hill and they're being taken care of. Make sure all the news outlets know what happened to them. They're heroes, Barker. You know that?"

"They sure are heroes. I'll get on it, Sheriff." Barker nodded to the sheriff and then to Ben, ready with his intro, waiting for Ben's hand signal.

* * *

The sheriff saw Mayor Lockhart hurrying toward him. Lockhart had been trying for hours to get the sheriff to order the reporters to leave.

"Now that we've got the kids off the hill," the mayor was saying, "why can't we get rid of this media zoo? I thought giving in to terrorists' demands was never advisable. So far we've done *everything* they want us to do. Now that those kids are safe, can't we run these reporters out of town?" Lockhart ran alongside the sheriff who seemed to be ignoring him. "Sheriff, you're new to Blue River County. You don't realize that we've been through all this with the Bennigans a hundred times. More media coverage isn't going to make it better for them . . . or bring Liam Bennigan back . . . or whatever it is they want!"

Sheriff Atkinson knew the power of the media as well as the mayor did. He'd been a scoundrel or a hero in the local news ever since he was elected sheriff. But one thing he knew for sure was that if you act like there's something that can't stand the light of day, the media hounds would be even more relentless when the scandal finally did show itself. Better to toss them a bone than to starve them and *then* show them some meat.

The sheriff stopped, his face just inches from Lockhart's. "Mayor, if this town has nothing to hide, then I'd suggest you just buck up under the scrutiny. If you shut down media coverage now, you'll look like you've got a broom in your hand ready to sweep some dirty secret under a big ol' giant rug."

"Okay, Sheriff," the mayor said, trying a new tactic, "allow the coverage of the hostage situation, but call off the press conference tomorrow morning! If the Bennigans have evidence of wrongdoing, they can go to a court of law like any other citizen!"

"They've been there, done that, Jack. And they're still not satisfied. After fifteen years of fighting with these people, maybe it's time we just sat and listened to them for a few minutes!" The sheriff stalked off toward his command post, knowing full well he had left Lockhart powerless and angry.

* * *

Hannah was relieved when Brett offered to take first watch in the vast, dark storage room. She and Dulcey had piled up some dusty draperies and bags of old winter coats to make a soft place to sleep. The girls had thrown some satin choir robes over themselves to keep warm in the drafty storage room. Within moments, Dulcey and Kadence were sound asleep. Their regular breathing soothed the terrors in Hannah's mind.

After an hour of tossing and turning, Hannah decided the welcome embrace of sleep was far from her. She crawled quietly over to the roll of carpet where Brett was sitting. A small, high window allowed a trickle of moonlight to fall on his face. His head was bent, his eyes closed, and his lips were moving silently. Hannah knew a prayer when she saw one. It touched her that a man with an AK-47 across his lap would think to call upon God for help. Soon Brett raised his head and seemed surprised to see Hannah awake.

"Do you mind if I join you?" Hannah asked.

"Can't sleep? You and Dulcey are going to have to stay awake tomorrow morning while I get some rest."

"Don't worry—I'm good at catnapping," Hannah said, sitting on the other end of Brett's rolled-up carpet. The two were silent for a while, lost in private thoughts. "Have you got a wife and kids who are worrying about you somewhere, Brett?"

"Yes, my wife's name is Shelly. And I have two little boys." Brett's voice caught for a moment and Hannah could feel his worry trapped up high in his throat.

"You seem so young to be doing this kind of work."

"Oh, not so young. I cut my teeth at Waco in '93. Saw four agents killed by gunfire there—and eighty of David Koresh's followers die in that horrible fire. Then I worked the Oklahoma City bombing. Nothing can compare to that. One hundred and sixty-eight killed—nineteen of them children. I guess as long as common ordinary citizens insist on fighting the federal government or taking hostages, there'll be jobs for guys like me."

"It's so odd to hear someone like Ian Bennigan accuse the government of oppressive acts against U.S. citizens. I've never felt so oppressed and frightened as I have since Ian's been in charge."

"Well, I'll tell you something really strange, Hannah. I've been undercover so long watching people who are in militias and in anti-government groups, I'm starting to understand how they think. Take Ian for instance—if it's true that his father was murdered and that his family lost a father and their land and their livelihood, who could blame him for thinking everyone is conspiring against him? I mean—they are! The only way this doesn't make sense is if the in-flooding really was an accident and all of the Bennigans' accusations are untrue."

"Like all those kids who shoot their classmates—they're not imagining things either. Their classmates really *do* hate them and make their lives so miserable they're willing to kill someone to stop it."

"In my FBI training, they called this the Stockholm Syndrome—when hostages start to identify with their captors and start to see things from the outlaw's perspective."

"If you had told me a year ago that I would be sympathizing with Ian Bennigan, I would have said you're crazy. But I want this thing to be over and I don't want to die—or any of us to die. I'm willing to be a little more open-minded than I have been," Hannah said, amazed at her own words.

"Well, now you know why we have terrorists . . . " Brett said, fingering the weapon on his lap.

"*Why* do we have terrorists?" asked Hannah.

"Because terrorism works," Brett said simply.

The two of them were silent for a long time. Finally, Hannah said, "I noticed you were praying a while ago. In your line of work, it must be hard to believe that someone's up there watching over us."

"Why do you say it must be hard?" Brett asked, moving to get more comfortable on the carpet roll.

"You see so much evil . . . because of your work. How could you believe in a God who allows something like this to happen—to innocent children, while they're in church—on Easter Sunday!"

"*Allows* something like this . . . " Brett thought a moment, "The way you put that sounds like this hostage situation just sort of fell from the sky. You have to remember that someone—a very troubled and angry someone—*caused* this to happen."

"But why wouldn't God stop Ian from hurting innocent children?"

"You know, right after the Oklahoma City bombing, people asked the same question about Timothy McVeigh. 'Why would God allow him to kill those innocent children along with all those innocent adults?' I heard it over and over. People kept saying that the bombing was proof that there was no God."

"It does make you think . . . about what God could possibly have been doing that day that was more important than protecting innocent people!" Hannah said in an angry whisper.

"As I understand how God works, He put Ian Bennigan and Timothy McVeigh here on this earth same as everyone else—with free agency—or free will as some call it."

"But they're just puny humans. Couldn't God stop a mere mortal from using his free will to hurt innocent people?"

"Well, sure He could. And God does intervene at times. But there would be no reason to give people free agency . . . free will . . . if God kept jumping in and interfering with the consequences of human action."

Hannah considered this for a long while. "So Ian chose to hurt us and God chose not to help us."

"He must have a reason why He's allowing this thing to play itself out," Brett said.

"So how do you know so much about God?" Hannah asked.

"Hmmmm. Well, I certainly don't know everything . . . but I've studied, and prayed and asked God to help me understand Him."

"Understand Him? My father always told me that it is not possible to know the nature of God . . . that He's 'unfathomable.'"

"I don't believe that."

"You don't?" Hannah was interested now.

"God is our Father. Why would He want to hide His nature from us?" Brett sounded so sure of himself that Hannah was beginning to get annoyed. He was sounding a lot like Jared. "We're His children, Hannah—*literally* His children. God can't very well expect us to love Him as a father if we don't know what He's like."

Hannah's mind was swimming. She had never heard these ideas before. Then she ventured, "Jesus is a lot easier to understand. He's definitely like us. He even lived here on earth for awhile…"

"Jesus is the son of God. You believe that, don't you? He is in the 'express image of His father.'"

"Hebrews, chapter one, verse three."

"You know your Bible," Brett complimented her.

"Yes—I do—but it doesn't help much. What I read in the Bible just gets cancelled out by Protestant doctrine." Hannah remembered a very similar conversation she'd had years ago with her father in this same building, three floors below.

"Catholic doctrine too," added Brett.

"So if you're not Protestant or Catholic—what *are* you?"

"I'm a Mormon . . . a member of The Church of Jesus Christ of Latter-day Saints."

Hannah was shocked into silence. No wonder he sounded like Jared. "But Mormons aren't even Christians—everyone knows that!"

"That's what people say—but what they really mean is that Mormons don't believe in the Trinity exactly like other Christians do. We believe that God and Jesus and the Holy Spirit make up a godhead: they're three persons with one purpose and one will. We just don't believe they are the same being."

"That's it?" Hannah asked, still in shock.

"That's the big one," Brett said.

"Ever since I was fifteen years old and read all about the Council of Nicaea and how the idea of the Trinity got started, I've had trouble with that too," Hannah admitted.

"Council of Nicaea—325 A.D."

"You know about the Council of Nicaea?" Hannah was truly amazed. She had never met anyone who knew about it besides her father. "You know, I've looked and looked, and I can't find the idea of the Trinity anywhere in the Bible."

"Not in there," Brett said. "The Bible's not an easy read. It came down to us through a whole lot of people, and it can be pretty hard to understand. But the idea of God and Jesus being of the *same substance* is just not there. Those ideas came a few centuries after Christ and after all the apostles had died."

"You're right. It's confusing. You can make the Bible say most anything you want if you try hard enough . . ."

"How come you don't know what Mormons believe—you've been living next door to Mormons since you were a little girl. The Spencer family goes all the way back to the beginning of the Church."

"My dad again. When we moved to the Bluff, he made Dan Spencer and his family promise not to talk to Gabe and me about the Mormon religion. He told them to especially stay away from me because I was confused enough as it was. Dan said he would never try to influence me. But he said if I ever wanted to know about it—I'd find a way."

"We Mormons respect a father's right to teach his own children his own ways."

"Well—I'm twenty years old—not a child any more. So tell me more—I've got plenty of time." Hannah smiled for the first time in three days.

Hannah and Brett talked all night long. Something about Brett told her he was not lying about the things they talked about that night. She had a feeling of peace and clarity as she listened to him answer the questions she had been asking since she was a young girl.

As the sun shone through the little window in the storage room, Hannah knew she had seen the face of God. It was just like she remembered it . . .

CHAPTER 31

By eight-thirty in the morning, Rosa had put out a huge urn of coffee and dozens of pastries from the bakery on the long tables so the reporters could get busy with the press conference. She was vaguely aware that she could have made ten times her normal daily profit from the café each day the hostage crisis continued. But instead, she had kept the help on overtime and provided free food and coffee for the law enforcement officers who used the diner as an extension of their headquarters. Rosa had also fed and comforted the bleary-eyed parents who had sat at the booths of her café while their children were imprisoned on the hill. Though her own child was still on the hill, she could tell no one. Instead, she pretended Dulcey was recuperating in a Kansas City hospital.

Kevin Barker was talking to Ed Lawton about the intricate clay model in front of them. Ben was jostling other cameramen with his tripod, trying to claim the best angle for filming the press conference. It was obvious by his craftsmanship that Ed had constructed his model according to surveyors' charts. He had included every crevice and contour, every rocky outcropping and core hole. Even the church and the four houses were represented, using photographs Fiona had sent to him.

The model of Bennigan's Bluff was riddled with tunnels that had been bored into her sides to find the precious pink marble with its unique pattern of impurities. Lawton had labeled the places where the rare marble had been quarried out of the side of the Bluff.

"So you're saying," repeated Barker, "that you believe the water table is *still* twenty feet below the quarry? And that the water that flooded the quarry came from the river behind the Bluff?"

"That's correct. Mrs. Bennigan and I believe that the quarry was flooded with water from the river that came through this tunnel here.

The tunnel goes through the Bluff and ends about fifteen feet from the river," said Ed, pointing to a bright blue river painted in acrylic paint on the plywood that supported the model.

"Fifteen feet of limestone just doesn't give way in a storm, Mr. Lawton," Barker said, straining to assess how much credence he could give the odd little geologist.

"That's our point exactly! Someone had to blast that limestone out so the river could flow into the quarry."

A few feet away, Rosa stood holding a platter of donuts. Suddenly, her heart started beating wildly. She put the platter down, and felt unsteady on her feet. As she stared at the model of Bennigan's Bluff, she felt transported back to the time she lived on the edge of the quarry. She heard thunder and felt as though she were standing at the door of her father's house with little seven-year-old Dulcey. The rain was pouring down in sheets. Her father with his poor eyes was out in the storm.

Then she saw it. In front of her—as though the model of Bennigan's Bluff were the actual Bluff fifteen years before. "WATER!" she cried, her hand flying to her mouth to stifle the unbidden shout. The diner fell silent; the reporters turned toward her to hear what she was saying. "Water was coming from this hole above Mr. Bennigan!" Rosa's eyes grew wide as she stared at the model. "The water . . . was pouring *out* of this hole and *down* into the quarry pit—from *above,* not up from the ground. I was there. I saw it!"

Ed walked over to Rosa. "You're Miguel Martinez's daughter aren't you?"

No one had referred to her as Miguel's daughter for so long it made Rosa gasp. "Yes, we lived here." She pointed to the edge of the plywood. "Our house was here near the edge of the quarry. We could not see the bottom of the quarry from our house! My daughter and I saw the water coming from here—high on the Bluff!" Rosa leaned over the model and removed the yellow pencil from her hair, causing it to cascade down her back. Using the pencil as a pointer, Rosa touched the core hole that would now be covered by the lake. "It was raining hard—you remember that, Mr. Lawton? But that water was like a waterfall coming out of the side of the Bluff and . . . " Rosa buried her face in her hands, realizing what she knew. "Mr. Bennigan got lost in all that water."

At Ben's signal, Kevin Barker gave an introduction and an update of the hostage crisis so his viewers would understand what was happening at the diner. Then Ben panned to Deborah Katzenbaum, an anchorwoman from CNN, who had agreed to be the moderator for the press conference.

"Ladies and Gentlemen," said Katzenbaum, ".Mr. Lawton and Mrs. Bennigan have called this conference to give an account of the flooding of Bennigan's Quarry fifteen years ago. An eye witness to the flooding—her memory apparently aided by this model built by Mr. Ed Lawton—has come forward with her recollections of the night of the flooding."

* * *

"Hannah, Brett!" Dulcey called softly, "Come watch the press conference with me—I got Jesse's television from his apartment."

Hannah and Brett made their way toward Dulcey and sat in front of the television set. Kadence woke up and cuddled near her sister as they watched the press conference taking place in Rosa's Diner in the town below.

* * *

Kevin Barker escorted Rosa to the podium. She straightened her uniform and smoothed her hair as she leaned into the bank of microphones. "When I saw this model of Bennigan's Bluff, I felt like I was there again. I lived with my father and daughter by the side of the quarry at the time of the flood. My daughter and I both saw the water pouring down like a waterfall."

"Couldn't the water have been heavy rain, Mrs. Martinez?" yelled a reporter.

"No, no. The lightning lit up everything and I could see the waterfall filling up the quarry, and poor Mr. Bennigan trying to save his big quarry digger!"

Lawton stood next to her pointing to the model. "Yes, exactly. If someone will just test it, we can prove that the water table is still twenty feet below the quarry. Rosa and her daughter are eyewitnesses.

They saw the water rushing through the opening—this core hole here—into the quarry."

* * *

Dulcey's eyes were riveted to the little scale model that Ben Taylor had zoomed in on for the viewers of the press conference. It was exact in every detail. "Yes! There was a waterfall coming out of that opening in the Bluff, Hannah. I saw it. My mother saw it. We tried to tell my grandfather about it, but his eyes were so bad, he couldn't distinguish the rain from the water pouring out of that hole."

"Are you sure?" Hannah asked. She caught her breath, listening to her own mind now. It was Gabe's voice saying, "When you're at the church tonight, go look at the file marked *Hezekiah* in Dad's filing cabinet. You'll understand everything. Or you could get the story right from the Old Testament—Second Kings 20:20." *Something about King Hezekiah,* she remembered.

"I need a Bible!" whispered Hannah.

"Christians," Dulcey said in an exasperated tone, her eyes still riveted to the television screen. "If you really need a Bible, I saw a whole stack of them over there in that carton."

Hannah found a box of thick family Bibles. Her father always gave one of them to every new member. She grabbed one, holding it near the light of the television, and quickly turned the pages until she reached Second Kings in the Old Testament. "Here it is . . . Second Kings 20:20," Hannah murmured. Her lips moved silently as she read the words.

On the television, Dulcey watched Ed Lawton at the podium in her mother's diner. "On behalf of the Bennigan family, I accuse the State of Missouri and the leaders of this town of covering up this evidence and concealing the identity of the person or persons who *deliberately* flooded the quarry, killing Mr. Liam Bennigan while doing so. The statement given by Rosa Martinez who is an eyewitness supports what we have been saying all along."

Lawton produced a file from his briefcase. "Also—under the Freedom of Information Act, we have learned that the lead diver hired by the State of Missouri was . . . Jack Lockhart, who was then and still is the mayor of Griggsberg! Mayor Lockhart, being a certified civil engineer with a specialty in water engineering, conducted this investigation and wrote the report himself. He then determined that the water that filled the quarry had risen from the water table beneath the quarry. The State of Missouri has continued to stand behind that report ever since, even though it was false and was made by a direct beneficiary of the flooding of the quarry!"

Another confusion of voices. "Mr. Lawton, what is the Bennigan family asking for now in terms of further investigation?"

"Two years ago, scuba instructor Dmitri Karanaeva reported to town officials and to Fiona Bennigan that he had entered the core hole and that it did indeed reach the river. But that was an unofficial dive—and we are asking for an *official, independent* underwater investigation in light of this information."

"Ms. Martinez, why wouldn't you have heard the noise if someone blasted out the tunnel to reach the river?" another reporter asked.

Rosa stepped up next to Ed, "For days before the flood, and especially that night, I did hear loud explosions—but I thought it was thunder from the storm."

"So who do you think blasted the hole to the river?" shouted another reporter.

Ed Lawton answered. "All you folks have to do is look at who has benefitted from the quarry flooding—the Church on the Hill, the college, the Lockharts—and you will have your prime suspects!" Lawton's hands were shaking now, his voice tinny and high with remembered emotion.

An NBC reporter shouted, "But you can't convict someone on that kind of circumstantial evidence!"

Ed Lawton pushed on. "Mrs. Bennigan also found documentation at the county recorder's office that shows that Jack Lockhart bought up all the land around the quarry in the year before the flood. Hundreds of acres of worthless dusty land around the quarry had been for sale for years—but no one wanted it. That land became prime real estate after the flooding."

"It's no crime to buy land!" someone shouted. "It *still* could be a coincidence!"

There was a commotion outside the door of the diner. The citizens of Griggsberg were carrying hastily made signs in front of Rosa's windows. "INVESTIGATE!" the signs demanded. Several cameramen rushed out the door of the diner to film the demonstration. The people of Griggsberg were walking up and down Quarry Street chanting, "DO NOT WAIT! INVESTIGATE!"

The residents of Griggsberg had borne the accusations for fifteen years. They knew the truth would set the town free . . . one way or another.

Pandemonium was brewing in the streets. The National Guard was brought in from the perimeter of the town to keep the people of Griggsberg calm.

But the people of Griggsberg were anything but calm.

CHAPTER 32

After the press conference, Ian Bennigan called the police station. He had a question to ask quite apart from what had been discussed at the press conference. Darlene patched him through to Farley. "Chief? What happened to my brother Charlie? Did your guys get him?"

"Ian, your brother Charlie was shot in the stomach and lost a lot of blood. Maura found him on the roof and got him on that chopper. Right now, he's in critical condition at a Kansas City hospital. Maura and your mother are with him." The chief was dog-tired, and his patience with Ian had worn away like paint on the wind-side of a barn. "Son, it's time to come down off that hill. It's clear to the people of this town that another investigation is needed. You've won that one."

"No! We will not leave this hill until justice is served! This is where we were fifteen years ago. Only this time, my *brother* lies dying instead of my father!" Ian's voice quavered with anger. "Everything stays the same until that investigation is finished and people are in jail for their crime!" He slammed the phone down.

* * *

Hannah sat stunned for a long time after the broadcast. The Bible in her hands lay open to the book of Second Kings in the Old Testament. She read it again by the light of the television: "*And the rest of the acts of Hezekiah . . . and how he made a pool, and a conduit, and brought water into the city . . .* "

Then she flipped to the dictionary in the back of the Bible and read: "*Hezekiah's Tunnel: an elaborate engineering scheme extending about 1770 feet through limestone rock, bringing the waters of Gihon spring inside the walls of Jerusalem to the pool of Siloam. Workmen dug from both ends in a zig-zag course until they met."*

Downstairs, in her father's locked cabinet, Hannah now knew there was a file labeled *Hezekiah* that would provide Ian with what he was looking for—evidence that would point to the person or persons who flooded the quarry. Evidence that would explain who drowned Ian's father. Evidence that could possibly drown her own father as well.

By one o'clock, they were all so hungry and thirsty, they were getting dizzy. Brett knew they needed water at minimum, food if possible. Taking his gun, he slithered back through the small doorway into Jesse's apartment. Several minutes later, he returned with cans of soup, a can opener, some bottled water and a pillow case stuffed with Jesse's videotapes for Kadence to watch. The television had a built-in VCR and Hannah was grateful that Brett had thought of a way to occupy her restless sister.

Hannah helped Kadence stack the videos next to the television. Taking care of her sister made her feel stronger. She couldn't allow herself to let up as long as Kadence needed her. "Look Kadence," Hannah said, noticing the labels on the videos, "Jesse has labeled these videos 'Baybe Brds'—one through twelve. They're probably some of his wild animal films. Why don't you see what those are?"

Kadence popped the video labeled "Baybe Brds--#1" into the VCR and was delighted with what she found. Jesse had held the church's video camera about twelve inches away from a bird's nest that contained three speckled eggs just outside his window. Soon a mother bird flew to her nest to sit on her eggs. The automatic time imprint read "May 9, 1993."

"You know how scared Jesse is of heights?" Hannah said, scooping out some room temperature Campbell's Cream of Mushroom soup with a plastic spoon.

"Yeah, that's why Mary Louise made all those curtains for him," Kadence said, slurping Spaghetti-Os from her can.

"Well, Jess probably wanted to watch those eggs hatch but he couldn't bear to look out the window!" Hannah smiled as she always did when she thought of Jesse.

"Jesse's so funny. I love that boy!"

"He's not a boy, Kadence. He's a man."

"Yeah, I remember. I love that *man*," she corrected herself.

The food was helping them feel normal. The press conference had given them hope. And reading Second Kings 20:20 had put Hannah into the deepest dilemma of her life.

Brett and Dulcey constructed a makeshift shelter to hide the light from the television from the view of anyone entering the storage room. Brett positioned three portable chalkboards around them to serve as walls. Dulcey laid several long wooden boards across their tops. Working quietly and carefully, Brett and Dulcey threw bags of costumes, choir robes, old coats, and Christmas decorations made of fake pine boughs over the whole structure to hide the light and muffle the sound of the television. The more junk they piled on their little house, the safer they all felt.

Kadence sat transfixed, watching the mother bird feathering her nest with down plucked from her own breast. Hannah was touched by the mother bird's sacrifice of her personal warmth to keep her eggs warm high up on that chilly window sill.

According to the time imprints, Jesse had let the camera run for two to three hours every afternoon at roughly the same time periods on twelve different days. He skipped Wednesdays through Fridays because he was at his mother's house on those days.

The camera also picked up the daily life of Griggsberg—a young girl sunning herself on the beach near the dock, the mayor trimming the hedges in front of his porch, people grilling steaks on the patios of their summer homes. The video camera took in a view of Quarry Street to the west, part of the campus, and the town just behind the mayor's house. There was so much going on that Kadence sat quietly engrossed watching tape after tape throughout the long afternoon.

Hannah was grateful for the gift of Jesse. As always, his comfortable predictability had served as a touchstone in the midst of chaos.

CHAPTER 33

At the hospital in Kansas City, Maura and Fiona had just finished watching the press conference on the television in the waiting room. An armed guard had secured the room in case someone would discover the identity of the now-famous disheveled woman and her pale, frightened daughter who sat together on one of the couches.

Charlie was still unconscious in the intensive care unit, having just come through a grueling seven-hour operation to repair the organs that had been dashed apart by the bullet from Brett Ballard's gun. The bullet itself had lodged near Charlie's spine, and the doctors left it there, not daring to risk permanent paralysis by removing it. Fiona and Maura were allowed to see him for five minutes of every hour.

Fiona turned to Maura. "Rosa remembered the night of the flood. She's an eyewitness, Maura!"

"Yes, but I know Ian. He won't come down off that hill until someone is accused of flooding the quarry. I just hope he doesn't get to Phase 3 . . . "

"Phase 3? What is Ian planning to do, Maura?"

"All I know is that Phase 1 was taking the hostages, and Phase 2 was getting the press conference on television. Charlie told me he hoped they would never have to go to Phase 3. He said he hoped it would all be over by then. He wouldn't tell me what Phase 3 was—but it sounded like the worst thing of all. He and Ian didn't tell the soldiers anything because they said they couldn't trust them—and it was safer for the soldiers not to know."

"Couldn't *trust* them? My goodness, those men seem like they're ready to die for Ian and Charlie. Why wouldn't Ian and Charlie trust them?" Fiona asked, her head buried in her hands, fatigue nearly overpowering her.

"All I know is that most of those men don't even know each other, Mother. Ian had Charlie sit on the porch to make sure none of them came near me."

"But, Maura! These men will all go to jail for this. If anyone dies, even Charlie, they could spend the rest of their lives in prison. Why would they do that for Ian and Charlie when none of them trust each other?" Fiona was moaning now, her confusion and frustration mingling with her worry for Charlie.

"Charlie said they're all doing it for different reasons. He said a lot of them are doing it so people won't forget April nineteenth."

"April nineteenth? What's that supposed to mean?" Fiona asked wearily.

"Waco, Mother. The government killed all those people in Waco in that awful fire on April nineteenth. Then that McVeigh man blew up the building in Oklahoma on April nineteenth. And then some of the other men are hoping they can stay on the Bluff until April twentieth—that's Adolph Hitler's birthday. They wanted to take Ben and Esther as hostages, but Ian said the children were the best bargaining tools."

"Hitler? To honor Hitler's birthday? This is unbelievable. They know nothing about Ireland then—they're using Ian!" Fiona wailed quietly, finally understanding that the hatred on the hill was coming from each man for his own reasons. "Those men are . . . if they . . . what will they do, Maura?"

"Mother, look what they've done already. They'll do anything now. They've gone too far."

"Ian will die today unless this thing is stopped. He never planned on coming down off that hill. He must have known that all along. And he's got that retarded young man up there with him. And that preacher who sings so beautifully. He may kill them too."

"That's not all, Mother," Maura stood suddenly, eyes closed, hands clenched. She appeared to be climbing the inside of her skin. "I didn't want to tell you this. I don't know what you'll do."

"What—tell me, Maura," Fiona pleaded, then stopped, realizing why Maura hesitated to tell her. "You think I *want* Ian to do this thing? To take lives? To honor Hitler? To kill people and get himself killed?"

"You seemed almost proud of him, Mother. When Charlie was in surgery you kept saying that your boys have the Irish spirit," Maura offered softly, feeling for her mother's mood.

"I want this stopped! No one has been killed yet," Fiona rose to face her daughter as if seeing her for the first time in years. "It can still be stopped, Maura. No one is dead yet!" She fingered her scar which had blazed to a smooth redness. Closing her eyes for a moment, she drifted back to Ireland and the hideous killings she had witnessed. The petrol bomb exploding in her face, the screams of her neighbors after the explosion of the bottled bomb, the laughter of the Shankill butchers as they scurried away after delivering death and mayhem to her side of Belfast, to her people . . . to her.

"Hannah and Kadence weren't on the helicopter with Charlie and me and those children. Rosa's girl Dulcey wasn't on it either. And that man who called himself 'Joe'. He's with them still at the church. They got left behind." Maura was sobbing now. "They said on the television that those girls were shot and had been taken to the hospital—but Mother, they weren't on the helicopter. Ian's got them . . . but I don't think Ian *knows* he has them."

Fiona opened her eyes fully and knew what she must do. "You stay here with Charlie, Maura. Be here when he wakes up. Find out what Phase 3 is . . . if he can tell you. Tell one of the sheriff's men out there if you find out. I've got to go get my boy off that hill."

Within minutes, a sheriff's deputy was driving Fiona back to Griggsberg.

* * *

Miranda and Craig told everyone they were going to Kansas City to be with Hannah and Kadence. But instead, they had sequestered themselves in one of the jail cells at the police station to be near their children. Miranda could tell her husband was a walking time bomb; she was guessing he harbored a terrible secret.

"Craig, you've got to level with me. The lives of all three of our children are hanging in the balance. I know there is something you're not telling me. What is it?"

Craig sat down heavily on the side of the rock-hard cot in the jail cell. "Miranda, it's so much more complicated than you can even guess," he said, rubbing his eyes to clear his blurred vision.

"Well, it's time for you to lay it out for me, Craig. There isn't any more reason to hide anything. Whatever truth you know may be all we have to buy our kids their lives!" Miranda spoke with the clarity of her conviction. It was now up to Craig to make the pieces fit together.

"If it was just me, Miranda, I'd have told you long ago. If it was just me who would suffer, I would have gone to the authorities years ago."

"Craig, I know you have done something terrible; and that you may have done it for me. But if you had a hand in Liam Bennigan's death, admitting it will save our children!"

Craig stared at the cement block wall directly in front of him.

"There wasn't anything I wouldn't do for you, Miranda. You were my world—my whole world."

"Then be the kind of man I need you to be now, Craig." Miranda's voice was calm and low. She saw her husband as a dry leaf near a blazing bonfire. He was close to being consumed, waiting for the wind of truth to brush him into the ferocious fire. "Save our children, Craig."

"It's not that simple. If it were, I told you—I would have done it by now." Craig was staring into space, agony in his eyes. "Lockhart has threatened me if I make any kind of move. He's willing to do whatever he has to do to stop me from dragging him down with me."

"You're protecting yourself and Jack Lockhart—and throwing our *children* to the wolves?"

"Miranda, all of us will go down if I tell what happened. You, me, the kids . . . he has threatened our lives! Lockhart doesn't have anyone to protect. He has nothing to lose!"

Miranda walked out of the jail cell door, turning briefly to look at her husband through the cold steel bars. "Find a way," she said, and walked away

No bars could have imprisoned Craig Dennison any more tightly than the fear and dread he was feeling now. Everything was on the line. Miranda had walked away. The lives of everyone in his family were at stake—no matter what he did.

* * *

Fiona came in through the back door of the diner and asked Rosa where Miranda was. Rosa was serving a plate of sandwiches to a booth full of deputies from Blue River County.

"She's in the station," said Rosa, removing plates from another booth.

"Come with me, Rosa," said Fiona tersely, leading her through the door that led into the police station. Fiona whispered in her ear, "I know your girl is on the hill. We need to get Miranda. We need to do something."

Fiona saw Miranda coming from the back of the station, "Miranda, I know your girls are on the hill. Come with us—we're going to go get them," said Fiona softly. "We don't have much time."

"What's happened?" said Miranda, not resisting the two women, walking willingly with them out the front door, quickly, down Quarry Street, toward the covered bridge.

CHAPTER 34

"Use that Chevy truck to take these fifteen cans up to the church," Ian ordered two of his gunmen. "We've got to have some action right now, or we're going to lose this war. The chief thinks the press conference has solved his problems—that I'll come down the hill and give up just because they promised to investigate!" Ian helped the men load the cans. "No one is going to take us seriously unless we move into Phase 3, men! We'll wait until it's dark—it'll be a much better show against the night sky."

"What do we do now, sir?" said the voice of the youngest soldier when they were finished loading the heavy five-gallon cans from the bunker into the back of the pick-up.

"We take this gasoline up to the church and soak down every piece of furniture and every square inch of carpet in the place."

* * *

It was about six in the evening when the four hostages finished the last of the canned soup and the bottled water. Kadence was draped across Dulcey's lap. The bird videos had lulled her to sleep. Hannah sat next to them, the big Bible open on her lap, lost in thought.

Dulcey had been sitting for more than an hour with the remote control in her hand. She had seen something strange in one of the videos and was rewinding the tapes to look for it. She had been half asleep when she saw it. Only her subconscious mind had understood what she had seen on the tape.

Suddenly, Dulcey sat up and leaned toward the television, stunned at what she had just seen. She rewound the tape again.

"Hannah! Watch this!" Dulcey could barely keep her voice to a whisper as she stopped the tape so Hannah could watch the brief section again. "What are you seeing there?"

"I see a blond-haired man dressed in some kind of odd red jacket—like a uniform, maybe. He's walking toward Mayor Lockhart who is on the porch. Now they're in front of the porch. The man is handing the mayor something from an envelope. They're quarreling. Lockhart is twisting the man's arms behind his back—he's reaching for a yellow rope . . . oh, Dulcey!"

"The man in the lake!"

* * *

Hannah made her way toward Brett. She crouched near him so he could see her face. "Brett, I need you to go with me to get a file from my father's office. It's very important that I get it!"

Brett stopped a moment, sniffing the air. "We all need to get out of here. Do you smell that, Hannah? I've been smelling it for the last few minutes."

"Gasoline!" Hannah stood, suddenly realizing what they were facing. "They're going to burn the church!"

"So that's what Phase 3 was," Brett muttered, standing now, looking out the little window.

"Brett, they don't know we're here!"

"Yes. Either that or they do know we're here." Brett switched on his flashlight and shined it toward the stairway and the elevator. "We have to get out of here now!"

"Brett, I can't leave until I go to my father's office to get a very important file."

"A file? Hannah, we are now running for our lives—one match and we're dead! The longer that gasoline soaks into the sanctuary, the more fumes will build up. No file could be worth the risk we'd be taking."

Hannah moved toward the elevator. "This elevator goes right to my father's office. Get your gun and go with me. We can get the file and be back on the elevator in five to ten minutes."

Hannah stood there facing Brett. With her eyes, she begged him to trust that the file was worth the risk.

"Hannah, do you know what happens to an elevator in a fire? If we get stuck on that thing, we'll never get out, and Dulcey and Kadence won't even know what hit them."

"Ten minutes, Brett. This file *cannot* go up in smoke."

She had trusted *him* the night before. Could *he* trust *her* now?

* * *

Roy Sedgeworth had been sent into the church with the matches. His angular face had grown a heavy scruff of beard in the three days since the takeover of the church. Throughout the siege, he had worn his black beret, refusing the anonymity of a ski mask. It had been his life's mission to fight the United States government. If his face ended up on national television, so be it.

Sedgeworth had directed the initial stages of the operation, barking his commands over the microphone in the church, evacuating the frightened church members from the building, and wrenching eight screaming children away from their wailing, terrified parents. He regarded it as his finest hour.

Sedgeworth had agreed with Ian that the image of the burning church would certainly get the attention of the powers that be. Even though they had moved Talbott and the custodian to the bunker, no one in town would know that. It was beautiful. It was perfect. To light this church on fire was Roy Sedgeworth's destiny.

* * *

Something in Hannah's eyes told Brett the file was worth the risk. "Let's get Dulcey and Kadence and go get that file," said Brett.

"I can't take my sister down there, Brett. She and Dulcey will be safer up here until we get back. Then we can decide what to do when we're all together again."

Brett thought a moment, weighing the risks of their options. "Okay—give me a minute. I'll tell them to climb out onto the roof if we aren't back in fifteen minutes."

"But what if there are soldiers up there?"

"My guess is that with the church soaked with gasoline, no soldier is going to be standing on that roof. But, just in case, I'll give Dulcey some protection." Brett removed the 9mm Sig Sauer from his holster and inserted a new clip. Then he made his way carefully over the boxes and between the racks of clothing to the makeshift shelter.

"Dulcey, come out here," Brett said.

"Brett, where've you two been?" Dulcey had the videotape in her hand. "This tape is very important—we've got to get it out of here."

"*We're* going to be getting out of here—as soon as Hannah and I get something from her father's office. We'll just have to trust her on this one. Tell me about the videotape later. "

Brett saw that Kadence was still asleep so he lowered his voice. "We'll be back in fifteen minutes. If we're not, take Kadence and wait on the roof. They've got at least six helicopters down there in town. You'll be able to get someone's attention."

Brett handed her his pistol. "You ever shot one of these?"

Dulcey swallowed hard, taking the pistol into her hand. "Just show me how to get the safety off. I suppose I'll figure out how to shoot it if my life depends on it."

Brett showed her quickly how to take the safety off and how to aim the gun and squeeze the trigger. "Remember, give us the full fifteen minutes before you go up." Brett had another thought, "And Dulcey, if you think there's a fire in the church, go up on the roof immediately."

Dulcey slipped the pistol into one jacket pocket, put the video-tape in the other, and went to sit by Kadence.

Brett hurried back to Hannah.

Hannah and Brett rode down silently in the freight elevator, hearts in their throats. Hannah's gut ached as if she were already exposing herself to gunfire. Brett took up a defensive position with his AK-47 pointed dead against the elevator doors. After a moment, the doors opened uneventfully on the first floor near the church offices.

"This way," whispered Hannah as she stepped through the office door that Ian had battered down earlier when the children were escaping. "The key to the cabinet is right . . . "

"Someone's coming! Hurry!" Brett whispered, stepping between Hannah and the door.

Hannah's hands shook; the key momentarily refused to enter the lock. Finally it slipped in and the file drawer slid toward her. E . . .

F . . . G . . . H . . . She grabbed the file labeled *Hezekiah* and crouched behind her father's desk.

Brett stepped into the hall and saw a man raise his weapon.

"Traitor!" the man yelled at Brett, his finger on the trigger of his automatic rifle.

Instantly, Brett let loose a short burst from his own automatic and the man slumped against the wall, clutching his chest.

"Traitor to the people!" The man groaned, sighed, his life running out of him. "Stinking FBI . . . "

Brett sprinted back to Hannah who was shaking uncontrollably, her mind numb with fright. "C'mon, Hannah. Let's go! Someone's sure to have heard that gunfire!"

Just as Brett had feared, men in heavy boots were running down the hall toward the elevator and the church offices.

"Let's get outside!" whispered Hannah, motioning toward the door that led out of her father's study and into the woods between the church and her house.

In another moment, they were outside in the chilly darkness.

* * *

Ian examined the dead man in the hall. "It's Sedgeworth," he said angrily. Ian removed the box of wooden matches from the man's flak vest and handed them to the unarmed soldier standing next to him. "Here. You're our new fire starter. You're in charge of Phase 3."

"Whoever killed Sedgeworth is probably in the building," the other soldier observed.

"So, now we have a better reason to torch the place. We have a traitor in the building, don't we? If it's not FBI Joe, it may be someone else from the other side. In fact—maybe *you're* FBI!" Ian waved his rifle at the soldier menacingly.

"No, sir. I'm on your side all the way."

Ian realized the soldier was young, which meant he certainly wasn't a government agent. "I believe you are. That's why you're the new man in charge of Phase 3."

The boy soldier took the matches from Ian and the two of them dragged Sedgeworth's body into the sanctuary where it would be sure to burn. Having completed this task, Ian went on a rampage through the church offices. He threw files everywhere, opened drawers, tore photos off the wall, and smashed Marge's computer on the ground. He identified the pastor's desk by the photo of Miranda on it. "I have a feeling I might find . . . something to provide a little fortification . . . " Sure enough, in Craig's bottom drawer, Ian found a bottle of vodka. "Let us drink a toast to Phase 3, kid!"

"No, sir, I don't drink," said his new right-hand man.

"Okay," said Ian, "I'll drink your share."

"Yes, sir," said the boy respectfully.

* * *

Fiona, Miranda and Rosa walked down the road that led to the covered bridge. The structure was dark and quiet.

"Miranda! It's me, Mary Louise! What are you doing?" a voice called to them from under the oak tree by the side of the road. "You're all going up there, aren't you?"

Fiona looked at Miranda.

"That's Jesse's mother, Fiona. And Rosa, you know Mary Louise Candella, don't you? She and Jesse come into your diner sometimes."

"You come with us, Mary," said Rosa. "It's time for the mommies now. It's too late for anything else."

Mary Louise joined the three women on the road. "I almost went up there all by myself just an hour ago. For some reason, the guards left their post on the bridge, and they went off in the woods down that way."

"Well, there are probably still plenty more of them on the hill," Miranda said.

Mary Louise stopped for a moment, "Miranda, why are *you* going up there? Aren't your girls off that hill? I heard on television that . . . "

"Those were lies to protect the ones who got left behind," Miranda said, gripping Mary Louise's arm more tightly as they walked toward the bridge. "All three of my babies are on that hill! My two girls—and my boy."

Mary Louise looked at Rosa. "And what about Dulcey?"

"Don't you worry about my Dulcey," Rosa said, wiping her cheek with the flat of her hand. "God in heaven is watching my girl and the rest of our . . ."

Suddenly, Mary Louise stopped ten feet from the bridge. "The land mines! I watched those soldiers bury land mines right in front of this bridge after we were all off the hill. You can see this part of the road is all dug up."

Fiona scoffed. "Where would my boy get land mines? He's bluffing . . ."

The four women linked arms and walked together over the freshly dug dirt.

* * *

Hannah felt exhilarated as soon as the cold air of the night hit her face. "It's so quiet—I don't hear anyone." She held the file tightly against her chest. "This file is what Ian wants. I think it's the only thing that will settle this mess—and fifteen years of hatred and suspicion."

"I'm worried about the fire, Hannah. If those men light a match to that church, we won't have time to negotiate over this file. In fact, the church might be on fire right now. They may be trying to flush us out."

* * *

Sheriff Atkinson answered his cell phone.

"I don't know who you have up here, but we will be making short work of them unless you listen carefully," said Ian. The sheriff detected a slurring of his speech.

"We're listening, Ian. What is it that you want?" replied Atkinson.

"I want you to assure me that an investigation will be done and my father's killers will be brought to justice. Otherwise, I have a box of matches that says your people up here won't last the night."

"Ian, Rosa is willing to testify about what she saw that night, and Dmitri Karanaeva has called us and has agreed to testify as well. You were right, Ian. Dmitri said the tunnel goes from the quarry all the way to the river. He says about two years ago he told both Fiona and the mayor about it. He said Fiona was very excited about it, and the mayor said he would handle it."

"Well, the mayor sure did handle it, Sheriff. He made sure the information went nowhere!" Ian spit the words over the phone line into the sheriff's ear.

"Now, if you want our cooperation in this investigation, Ian, you will not set fire to the church." The sheriff paused, "In fact, setting fire to it will mean all agreements are off, okay? Ian? Ian?"

"I'll do whatever I need to do, Sheriff. I don't trust any of you. Until I see a signed confession or a statement that someone is in custody for flooding the quarry, I'll stay right here—with the matches in my hand."

CHAPTER 35

Miranda, Rosa, Fiona, and Mary Louise, arms still linked, walked up the hill in the dark. Miranda noted that there had been no guards to inform Ian of their presence. The whole Bluff was eerily quiet.

"Just what *are* we going to do when we get up on the hill?" asked Mary Louise.

Fiona answered, "You three go and find your kids. I'm going to go knock some sense into that boy of mine."

"Isn't it too late for you to be knockin'?" Rosa asked quietly.

"What else can I do?" said Fiona. "When your kids are in trouble, life doesn't mean anything anyway. Don't you all agree?"

"You're right, Fiona. Everyone is afraid to come up here because of the land mines. It's up to us," said Mary Louise.

"Maybe it's always been up to us," said Miranda. She paused for awhile, thoughts flickering across her face. "It's so strange. Here I am . . . walking up this hill . . . absolutely willing to lay down my life for my children, to . . . to do . . . whatever it takes to save them . . . ." she paused again, struggling with thoughts that seemed to condemn her. "Why was I not willing to do that before?"

The four women walked toward the bunker quietly, drawing strength from each other as though they were old friends.

* * *

Farley shouted at Darlene over his radio. "What do you mean? Four of 'em? Miranda, Fiona, Rosa—who's the fourth? Mary Louise? *Who* saw them? Why weren't they stopped?"

"The deputy who saw them said he was too far away to stop them, and he also didn't pursue them because of the land mines," said Darlene. Farley exhaled slowly.

"Well, don't this beat . . . " Farley pictured the four women walking up the hill and shook his head in disbelief. "An army of mothers . . . "

Sheriff Atkinson stepped into the headlights of Farley's patrol car, his face a mask of exasperation. "Don't tell me! I've already been informed—they just walked right up the hill!" Atkinson slapped both hands onto the roof of Farley's patrol car, "Just when we had this thing under control."

"What's to keep the soldiers on the hill from firing at those women?" Farley kicked at a stone, feeling a mixture of awe and anger.

"They'll be lucky if no one does. I came to tell you that Ian is planning to burn the church down . . . he called it Phase 3. What do you say we put a hook and ladder at the ready just in case?"

"Okay by me. No guards on the bridge. And there are obviously no land mines in the road since those women just walked right over it. What have we got to lose? Let's have two or three ready. And a couple of ambulances just in case. We'll park 'em behind the 7-Eleven so they can't be seen. We don't want Ian thinking he has to use them."

* * *

The four mothers approached the bunker. The man who was guarding the door got to his feet quickly. He sputtered, throwing his cigarette into the dirt, rising and fumbling with his rifle. Mary Louise saw Jesse inside the lighted bunker.

"Mom!" said Jesse. He seemed dazed, exhausted. "I was waiting for you!"

"And I was waiting for you!" said Mary Louise, tears streaming down her face, allowing herself to be swallowed up in Jesse's bear hug.

The surprised guard disappeared into the bunker.

Miranda and Fiona saw Ian walking down the road toward the bunker. His automatic rifle was up on his shoulder, and he seemed to be staggering. Fiona stepped out of the shadows and faced him.

"Ian," she said quietly.

Ian fumbled with his rifle, aiming it at the voice in the shadows. "Mother!" he said, lowering the gun, "What are you . . . "

"Never mind what I'm doing here, Ian. I live here. Same as you."

"Did you hear about Dmitri and Rosa?" Ian suddenly sounded like a little boy for a moment, coaxing approval from her. Fiona could tell he was drunk.

"Ian, I know all about the tunnel."

"You knew about the tunnel?"

"For two years. But it's what they call circumstantial evidence. It doesn't prove who made the tunnel, does it? It's just there. Filled with water."

"Of course we know who made the tunnel—just look at who got rich!" Ian was shouting his childhood lessons now, feeling the alcohol percolate in his head, waving his rifle around at unseen enemies. " "Lockhart and the Church on the Hill and the Dennisons!" Ian was out of control now. "The college . . . the mayor . . . the whole town. They got together and made the tunnel!" Ian was choking now, his voice hoarse and rasping, saliva gathered thickly at the corners of his mouth. Tears streaked down his dirty face.

"Shhhhhh. Shhhhhhhh," Fiona soothed, folding her son into her arms.

"Is Charlie dead?" he asked, gulping his tears.

"No, Charlie had surgery and he's getting well," Fiona continued to pat his back, motioning to Miranda to join them.

"Ian?" Miranda said, stepping out of the shadows. Ian shoved away from his mother and pointed his rifle at Miranda. Then Ian seemed to recognize Miranda Dennison. "Gabe's guarding in the woods, Mrs. Dennison. He was real mad at me once he figured out what my men were going to do at your church. He didn't have a thing to do with this—tried to stop it once he found out it wasn't really paint ball." He talked to her, still pointing the gun toward her face. Fiona held her breath. Miranda stood perfectly still, knowing Ian could fire if he was startled or angered.

"Thanks for telling me about Gabe, Ian," said Miranda.

"I tricked him into telling me all about your Easter service—about the kids singing and all. Where is Gabe anyway?" Ian asked.

"Oh, probably in the woods or hiding somewhere. Do you know where my daughters are?" Miranda fought the fear in her voice. She could tell Ian was not fully in possession of his senses and his reflexes. She spoke calmly and deliberately, staring at the barrel of Ian's gun. Twice in three days, Miranda had faced the muzzle of an assault rifle.

Ian's finger was on the trigger now. He squinted into the gunsight. Then he straightened, raising his head, apparently confused by her question. "Hannah? And Kadence? Aren't they with you?"

"Oh . . . sure . . ." Miranda said, pacing her words. "I'm so mixed up . . . they must be in town if they're not here with you."

"I thought you always knew where your kids were, Mrs. D. Don't you care about 'em?" Ian grinned at his joke. He sighed and let the gun momentarily wander off its target. Ian's sleep deprivation combined with the alcohol had made him docile and woozy . . . and unpredictable.

An unarmed, unmasked young man of about Charlie's age came hurrying down the road toward Ian. He held a box of wooden matches in his hand. He saw right away that Ian was surrounded by women who seemed very certain that they belonged there. "Sir?" he said in Ian's direction. "There's no one up at the church but me. Shall we carry out Phase 3, sir?"

Fiona put her hand out to the boy to silence him. "Shhhh. Shhhhh." She whispered to her son again. "What's Phase 3, Ian?"

Ian smiled, his eyes unfocused, swinging the gun wildly in the direction of the church. "We're going to get that old church off the hill, Mother. We'll have a much better view when it's gone. It'll be just us then. We'll burn the other houses off the hill too. Then it will be SSSSShin Fein! Ourselves alone—just us Irish!" He pulled the trigger and a burst of gunfire sprayed the Dennison's home across the street. Two of the front windows shattered. As the gun erupted in Ian's hands, Fiona and Miranda leapt for it. Ian struggled with them, but the alcohol had made him weak and uncoordinated. The stench of cordite filled the air as Ian, disarmed, lay on the ground sobbing.

The soldier stood in front of Ian, still holding the box of matches in his trembling hands for a moment. Then he dropped them, dashed toward the bunker, and disappeared inside. The whole hill was deathly still. Only one soldier remained, soaking the soil of his father's land with hot, bitter tears.

Miranda looked up at the spray painted words on the side of the Bennigan home. "Sinn Fein . . . " Miranda sighed.

Miranda went into the bunker and found Mary Louise untying Louis Talbott, "Louis!" She hurried to remove the silver duct tape from his mouth.

Louis indicated a small metal door in the far side of the bunker. "The gunmen went through there. It must be a tunnel to the river." He went to the little door and opened it slightly. Cool, damp air flooded the bunker. A distant sound of heavy boots on rocky ground could be heard far down the tunnel. Talbott immediately got on a cell phone the soldiers had been using and called the police station. "We're all okay—the soldiers are using a tunnel that leads to the river on the east side of the Bluff. Most of them left a long time ago—but you can still pick up the ones who just left!"

"We'll have someone watch for them!" came the reply.

Mary Louise whispered in Jesse's ear, "Why don't you go up to your apartment and tell your friends they should come down here, okay? The soldiers are gone so it's safe for them to come down now."

Jesse's face brightened, "My friends?"

His mother hugged him close to her. "Go through the woods and through Pastor Dennison's study. Go tell everyone they can come down now."

"And Cordelia . . . she can come too. I'll get Cordelia and *all* my friends," Jesse said.

"Tell them all to come here, Jesse. Tell them it's safe. Go! Run and get them!"

CHAPTER 36

Brett and Hannah were crouching silently in the woods near the church when they heard the gunfire. Then Brett saw someone coming toward them. He knelt and took aim at the approaching figure. "Halt—FBI! Identify yourself!"

Hannah gasped and put her hand instinctively in front of his gun. "Brett—it's Jesse!"

"Jesse? What are you doing here—who fired that gun?" Brett said, relieved to see Jesse.

"Is that you, Joe? And Hannah? Mom said to go to my apartment and tell my friends to come down here and to get Cordelia. The soldiers are all gone. Ian shot his gun but his mother and Hannah's mother took it away. Ian told the soldiers they could all go. They didn't even want their cars—they just left 'em and Ian's crying."

Hannah felt relief flood her body. She began to shake and her knees gave out. "They're gone?" she said. "You mean the soldiers have left?"

Brett knew exactly what Jesse was talking about. "There's a tunnel to the river somewhere. No one was supposed to know where it was until the last minute. That way no one could get caught and tell the authorities how to use the tunnel to come the other way—onto the hill."

"I know where—I saw them," Jesse said. "The bad men left through a door in Ian's bunker."

"He's right. It was part of the deal Ian made with his men. As soon as they reached Phase 3, the men could leave the hill through that tunnel. None of us knew what Phase 3 meant at the time. After we crossed the river and changed into the civilian clothes we had hidden over there, no one could tell us apart from anyone else."

"Let's go upstairs. Kadence and Dulcey must be terrified by now."

The three of them stepped back into the church. Brett insisted on going first, his gun still ready. The body of the man Brett had shot in the hall had been removed.

"All clear," he whispered to Jesse and Hannah. "Let's take the elevator. That's how Dulcey and Kadence expect us to come back."

"But Brett, you said fifteen minutes. You told them to go to the roof. It's been longer—they're on the roof by now."

"You're right, they'll be up there on the roof."

"Let's go," said Hannah.

"The roof?" Jesse didn't need to say more—the tremor in his voice conveyed his complete message.

"Brett, Jesse's terrified of heights," Hannah reminded him.

"Okay," said Brett, changing course in his mind. "Jesse, you stay in Pastor Dennison's study until we come back. We're going to go get Kadence and Dulcey, okay, Bud? And we'll bring Cordelia back to you."

"Okay, Joe," said Jesse, still using the name Brett had used when they had first met. "Joe?" He squirmed a bit and asked, "Are you a good guy or a bad guy?"

Brett smiled, "I'm a good guy, Jesse. You don't think Hannah would be with me if I were a bad guy, do you?"

"Oh, yeah," Jesse smiled as they disappeared into the church.

Jesse sat down for a few minutes in the pastor's chair thinking of all the things he would tell Pastor Dennison. The door to the office was completely ruined; they would have to get a new one. The heavy door to his apartment had been scratched and dented in. He sniffed the air and realized that he smelled a strange odor . . . *like when Mom gets gas at the gas station.* Jesse wandered into the sanctuary to find out why the church smelled like Ike's Chevron station.

* * *

When Craig Dennison heard from the sheriff that the soldiers were gone and that Hannah, Kadence, and Dulcey were with the FBI agent and would soon be off the hill, he knew what he had to do. Swimming in the silent dark water, he reached the bank directly below the fort. Using the rope the kids used to get to the lake, he climbed up onto the platform. The fort was littered with things the soldiers had left: camping equipment, wrappers from candy bars, jugs of water, dirty plates and mugs from his own house, two sleeping bags, and two sets of army surplus camouflage clothing.

Craig reached behind the little wooden cupboard and found a lighter tucked inside a pack of cigarettes in a wadded-up plastic bag. He had come upon Alan Silverman smoking at the fort once and had seen where he had hidden his cigarettes. Craig stuffed the lighter into his pocket and climbed up the rope path to get to the church.

Peering into the darkness of his office, he could see that someone had already tried to destroy it. Marge's computer monitor was smashed, lying on its face. The drawers of his desk had been up-ended—their contents in a heap on the floor. The photos on his desk and the ones from his wall were smashed, glass and frames broken and bent. His personal file cabinet had been opened and all the files had been tossed about the room. *No use looking for the Hezekiah file.* Craig picked up a folder from the floor and held the lighter to it. When it caught, he held the folder against the paper on the floor until the whole pile was blazing. Then he fled out the door to the woods.

Craig knew that the fire trucks were poised near the bridge to handle a fire. They would have the small blaze out in moments. He felt relieved that already the Hezekiah file had been consumed. Now it would be his word against Lockhart's—he and his family were safe.

CHAPTER 37

Even before he saw the flames, Larry McCloskey's instincts had told him something was happening on the hill. He had been hovering in the KCMO chopper above the town for several minutes. There! His eyes distinguished two figures crouching behind one of the big air compressors—Dulcey and a little girl. As he flew the chopper toward the roof of the church, he saw Hannah and Brett emerge through the trapdoor. He saw Hannah momentarily try to reenter Jesse's apartment and saw Brett pull her away. As he flew toward the church, he thought, *This time there will be no mistakes.*

As the KCMO chopper swooped toward the roof of the church, McCloskey watched in horror as the church's huge stained glass windows exploded outward like a Belfast petrol bomb, its force pushing the chopper backwards. Molten pieces of stained glass rained out and pummeled the chopper. McCloskey steadied the craft. Each of his arms and legs had a separate job to do. His feet worked the rotors, his right hand worked the joy stick, which determined the chopper's direction, and the collective leader in his left hand controlled the lift. It was like balancing on a ball underneath a set of rapidly spinning machete blades. With all his body parts working in unison, McCloskey shot straight up, and in moments he had set the craft down on the church roof.

Kadence and Dulcey were the first to get on board. Then Brett threw Hannah bodily onto the chopper and went back toward the trapdoor.

"What's he doing?" yelled McCloskey.

"It's Jesse!" Hannah screamed, the rotors were deafening with the side door still open. "We heard him just as we got to the roof. He said he saw a dead body in the sanctuary and had seen my father in his office. The door to the apartment was open and he was running up the stairs. But then we heard the explosion and nothing more from Jesse!" Hannah was sobbing against Dulcey who sat like a stone, her teeth chattering from cold and shock, one arm around Kadence, her other around Hannah.

Brett came running back to the chopper as black smoke began to roll out of the trapdoor. "I can't see him, Hannah!"

"Get in here!" yelled McCloskey, "We'll hover a minute and see if he comes up through that door. It's his apartment; he knows where the ladder is."

"But he's scared of heights!" screamed Hannah.

As soon as Brett's body cleared the chopper door, McCloskey lifted off a few feet above the roof. They were beginning to feel the heat of the flames that were blazing out like crazed demons through the shattered windows at the front of the church.

The hook and ladder truck from Griggsberg saw the fiery cue and raced out onto Quarry Street toward the covered bridge. Two rigs from Kansas City and two ambulances were close behind. Suddenly there was another deafening explosion. It had not come from the church but from the road in front of the covered bridge. *The land mines*, McCloskey thought. *Ian had not been bluffing.*

The huge steel fire truck flipped off the road in front of the covered bridge and smashed down on the tent the sheriff had given Mary Louise. The huge vehicle slid a few feet and came to rest at the base of a giant oak tree, its engine clicking and cooling. The two firemen on the back had been thrown free of the wreckage. Instantly the paramedics were opening the cab to get to the injured driver. One ambulance stayed with the fire truck wreckage, and the other raced onto the hill with the two hook and ladder units from Kansas City.

The mothers on the hill watched in stunned horror as the fire trucks raced by them toward the church. Miranda found herself running toward the church. "Our kids are still in there!" she screamed to the firemen. Mary Louise ran by her side toward the church. She had just sent her boy into the inferno in front of her.

* * *

McCloskey was about to head for the town when he saw a head poke up out of the trapdoor. "There's your man!" he screamed, heading back to hover above the trapdoor. "What's that in his arms?"

Kadence screamed, "It's Cordelia—Jesse has Cordelia!"

McCloskey was astonished to see Jesse stagger onto the roof clutching the huge, smoke blackened cat to his chest. "Can you land again?" Brett yelled above the sound of the rotors.

"That asphalt roof's no good. You see it starting to buckle over there by the cross? We'd crash right through."

Brett screamed again, "You got rescue lines on this thing?"

"In that compartment above the door—they're attached to a retractable arm. Open the door wide and swing it out."

In an instant, Dulcey and Hannah were helping Brett into the leather sling. Another sling hung loose from the metal clasp at the end of the rescue rope.

"I'm going!" Brett yelled. McCloskey positioned the helicopter exactly over the trapdoor. Dulcey pushed the button on the winch, and the rescue line played itself out slowly until Brett reached Jesse.

Nearly overcome by the smoke, his face and clothes as black as coal tar, Jesse just stood there and let Brett put the harness on him. His head lolled to the side and his knees buckled, but Jesse continued to hold Cordelia against him.

"Jesse!" Brett yelled into Jesse's ear, "We need to get your cat onto that helicopter—can you help me?" Brett talked while he positioned Jesse in the sling. "We need to get her to the vet!" Jesse mumbled in agreement. After securing Jesse into the sling, Brett positioned the terrified cat like a collar around Jesse's neck. If Cordelia cooperated, she would ride safely between Jesse and himself.

McCloskey guided Dulcey in reversing the electronic winch to bring the men up toward the hovering craft. To keep the smoke from surrounding the men, McCloskey inched the chopper forward so that the two men now dangled high over the lake. Any abrupt movement could cause the line to begin to swing and make for a perilous reentry into the chopper. Even the tiniest movement of the chopper could mean several feet of dangerous swing for the two men on the rope.

The whole town gathered on the beach to watch the terrifying rescue. The light from the fire illuminated the night sky. Blazing

beams from the church tumbled down the side of the hill like canoes
on a river of molten lava. The crowd below could hear the crack of
collapsing ceiling beams and the crash of falling chandeliers and
flying glass. The asphalt roof bowed and the brass cross began to
topple. Sparks from the fire ignited the purple fabric hanging from
the cross. Its dangling fabric was instantly consumed as the cross fell,
disappearing into the ruined church beneath it. Chunks and bits of
melted glass sizzled and popped as they struck the cool lake below.
Jesus and his lamb blew into a million pieces and descended coldly
through the water onto Liam's quarry digger, covering the bottom of
the lake like newly minted coins.

The town gasped as if it were one body as Jesse and Brett dangled
high above the lake. Cordelia was frozen in fear, wrapped tightly
around Jesse's neck. Jesse's blackened face hung to one side, his arms
loose, his legs splayed out. Brett had one arm around Jesse's chest, his
hand on Cordelia's back haunches. As the winch brought the two
men close to the chopper, Brett reached for the door frame, and
Dulcey and Hannah pulled the two of them to safety.

A cry rose from the crowd below. Five helicopters were in the air
now, reporters with microphones, and photographers with heavy
cameras were leaning out of them, fastened to their own harnesses.

Inside the chopper, Hannah tended to Brett who was coughing
wildly, trying to get his breath. His entire body had been blackened
by the smoke. Jesse was unconscious. Kadence cradled his sooty head,
to which the frightened, whimpering cat was still attached.
McCloskey explained to Dulcey where the oxygen masks were located
as he flew toward the Griggsberg Community Hospital.

Moments later, all six occupants of the helicopter, including
McCloskey, were taken into the emergency room for treatment of
smoke inhalation. Cordelia was taken to the animal hospital.

* * *

Back on the Bluff, Fiona held Ian's gun while Sheriff Atkinson
approached her son to handcuff him. Ian turned to run toward
the bunker, but slipped and fell on the slippery grass. Sheriff
Atkinson easily handcuffed the weeping terrorist. Two National

Guardsmen placed Ian into an armored truck and drove him to the Blue River County jail.

* * *

In the emergency room, Hannah breathed the humidified oxygen and tried to think. The curtains parted and Miranda stepped into her cubicle carrying an exhausted Kadence, who was wearing an oxygen mask attached to a portable tank. A nurse wheeled the tank close to Miranda's chair and covered the mother and her sleeping child with a blanket. Miranda snuggled down into the chair with her youngest daughter, putting her hand out to soothe her older one.

Unable to speak because of the mask, Hannah took the manila folder from under her blanket and handed it to her mother. While Kadence dozed against her chest, her mother read the documents in the file. *The deed to the land for my Music Camp. Land agreements that made a lot of money for Craig. A surveyor's map of the quarry and the river with marks and notations on it. And a receipt from Showalter's Granite for dynamite—signed by Jack Lockhart.*

As Miranda read what was inside the file, Hannah read a thousand emotions on her mother's beautiful and tortured face.

CHAPTER 38

After breathing the oxygen for an hour and drifting in and out of a restless sleep, Hannah awoke in a darkened hospital room. Kadence was in the bed next to her, sleeping soundly. Her mother sat in a chair between her daughters, resting her head against the wall.

"Mom? Gabe knows about the file. He found it a few months ago when he was looking for his birth certificate. He tried to tell me about it, but I didn't understand what he was telling me."

"Imagine how tempted he must have been to let Ian have those documents," Miranda whispered, tears streaming down her face.

"I think he was being loyal to Dad." Hannah struggled against a tidal wave of emotions. "It's so awful to realize that the Bennigans have been right all this time!"

"I never had a clue about any of this," said Miranda, paging through the file. "The deed for the church property and the college property—all part of a deal Dad made with Lockhart," she said mournfully. "Showalter. That poor dead boy must have stumbled onto all of this too."

"What will you do with the file, Mom?" asked Hannah.

A large man in a khaki uniform suddenly appeared in the doorway. "Hannah Dennison?" he said respectfully.

Hannah had never seen the man before. "Yes, I'm Hannah."

"I'm Sheriff Atkinson. How're you feeling?"

"I'm going to make it I guess," Hannah smiled, her eyes darting to her mother, then to the file.

"I came to tell you how extraordinary you were with those kids. Every one of their parents wants to thank you for what you did. Most of them are doing pretty well because of how you handled yourself. You made them feel as safe as you possibly could."

"Thanks, Sheriff. They were my responsibility."

Miranda looked down at the file she was holding open on her lap and drew in a sharp breath. Casually she picked up a magazine from Hannah's bedside table, slipped it behind the file, and clasped it to her chest. Then she rose and walked toward Atkinson. "Sheriff, any word on my son Gabe? I know my sister Kate gave your guys his picture and everyone's been on the lookout for him."

"No, Mrs. Dennison, not yet. He'll turn up. We've got an all-points bulletin out on him and everyone leaving town is being checked at a sheriff's roadblock. It's the darnedest thing, though—of the twenty-five to thirty men we estimated were on that hill with the Bennigans, the National Guard has picked up only four of them so far. The FBI was using an infrared system to keep tabs on them. But when the gunmen used that tunnel in the bunker to travel a good distance into the woods before they crossed the river, no one knew the men were escaping. We only caught the four because Talbott alerted us about the tunnel and told us where to watch for them. One of the four men was Gabe's age but we knew by the picture it wasn't your son. I'm so sorry."

"Please ask those men in custody if they know where Gabe might be."

"We have, ma'am. They don't know much about each other. Seems Ian wanted it that way."

"Where did Ian find all those men?" asked Miranda.

"On the Internet. We figure Bennigan doesn't know their real identities either so he couldn't give them up if he wanted to. He told them if they'd do what he said, he could almost guarantee they wouldn't be caught by law enforcement."

"What kind of hoodlums are these monsters?"

"It's kind of hard to believe—one's a school teacher from Terre Haute, Indiana," said Atkinson, shaking his head. "The kid we picked up is from St. Louis. He came to town with his uncle who hasn't been arrested yet. The other two were brothers who own a gun shop in Wyoming—members of some kind of citizen's militia. It seems Ian was in control of everything up there on the Bluff and with the masks and all, they can't even identify the other soldiers by sight. Can't trace their vehicles either—all of them had stolen license plates. They just left them up on the hill. We may never find the men who got away."

"It's almost as if Ian never intended to take those men down with him. He could have been so much more ruthless," said Miranda.

"We were all saying the same thing. Ian could have hurt a lot more people than he did."

Hannah was suddenly furious at the admiration being expressed for Ian. "He's not an idiot! He knew that by keeping everyone alive, his own punishment wouldn't be as severe. He's not exactly a selfless hero you know!"

"Oddly enough, that's what he's become to a lot of people out there," said Atkinson. "For every person who considers him a monster, there's another who considers him a hero—that he did what he had to do in the face of an oppressive government."

"Oppressive government?" Hannah said, bewildered by an array of images in her mind. She thought of government employee Brett Ballard risking his life for her and everyone else. And how Ian had been able to pull this whole thing off because the government had respected his rights. Using the Internet to find others like him, and gathering those blood-thirsty strangers in the woods behind his house was not against the law . . . he was within his rights. Ian's rights had even allowed him to purchase assault weapons. His rights had protected him every step of the way while he tore apart the lives of everyone he knew.

"He's no hero, Sheriff," Hannah said at last, thinking of the terrified five-year-olds and how long it would be before they would trust anyone again. How easily the rescue could have turned into a deadly disaster. Her deepest thoughts could find no physical voice. Miranda and the sheriff were silent for a while, communicating respect for the horror Hannah had faced.

Hannah suddenly became agitated and began to gasp. Miranda moved to her daughter. "Hannah? You all right?"

"I was just remembering Charlie and the man who died in the church. Even though it was Brett who shot them, Ian is to blame!" Hannah fought against the horror filling her mind, realizing she could descend into the madness of the past few days, and lose herself completely.

"Here, Hannah," a nurse said, coming into the room with a

syringe. She adjusted the oxygen mask over Hannah's face, and injected the needle into her arm. "Breathe slowly into your mask and try to calm your thoughts. We held off as long as possible, but we're going to need to give you a sedative now."

Miranda noticed the sheriff walking toward the door to leave Hannah in peace. "Please let me know the minute you hear anything about my boy," she said to him.

Hannah struggled against herself and then allowed the oxygen and narcotic to infuse her body with calm. Miranda stroked Hannah's hair, tears running down her cheeks, making clean tracks in the dirt and soot on her face. She leaned close and whispered, "We'll get through this, baby. We'll work things out."

Miranda called the chief at the station and asked him to meet her outside the hospital at six o'clock so they could search for Gabe when the sun was up. He told her the National Guard had been all through the woods and had found no trace of him.

As she sat in the darkened waiting room near the hospital's front entrance, still clutching the file, Craig walked in. He stared at the file in Miranda's hands for a long time before he seemed to convince himself it was real. He put his weary head into his big hands and wept his heart out. Miranda felt torn between compassion and rage toward the stranger who was her husband.

"Craig, Chief Farley and I are going to look for Gabe. As you struggle with what to do tonight, let me leave you with a thought . . . a true story from our life together . . . one that you told during a sermon back in our little church on Sixth and Main."

They sat quietly in the dimly lit waiting room, Craig's eyes still on the Hezekiah file.

Miranda continued, "Do you remember the linoleum that we laid all by ourselves in that horrible little kitchen we used to have?"

Craig looked at his wife's face, trying to find meaning in her words, gauging her mood.

"Do you remember how we were so excited about laying down that brand new sheet of linoleum that we didn't spend a whole lot of time cleaning the floorboards before we laid it?"

Craig was exhausted. He was having real trouble following

Miranda's story.

"It looked so perfect after we glued it down," she continued. "We had cut it perfectly and it was so shiny and new that it brightened up our little kitchen right away. But after I washed dishes at the sink for a few days, standing there without my shoes like I always do, I started feeling a couple of bumps under my feet. A few days later the bumps were even more noticeable and they hurt my feet when I stood on them. We realized we had covered over several tiny sharp rocks when we laid that linoleum."

Craig seemed to vaguely recall the story, and began to connect it with what was happening to them.

"A few more weeks of walking on the linoleum and those rocks pushed almost clear through. Remember?" Miranda continued quietly, holding Craig's gaze with her eyes. "I remember we wished we hadn't covered them over, because after they worked themselves up completely through the tile, they left holes, and all our work and our lovely little floor was ruined."

Craig sat still, letting the story remind him of better days. "There are a few of us around here who have covered over some pretty sharp rocks."

"And now that our beautiful floor is ruined, we need to pull it all up and start again." Miranda touched her husband for the first time in days. "And Craig, some of those rocks are mine as well. They don't all belong to you . . . "

The Reverend and Mrs. J. Craig Dennison held each other for several minutes in the deserted waiting room. As the sun came up, Miranda tenderly placed the file in her husband's hands and walked out of the hospital to look for their son.

CHAPTER 39

Miranda and Chief Farley walked all through Bennigan's Woods, sifting through the remains of the siege, kicking apart cold campfires, examining articles left behind by the soldiers, looking for something of Gabe's.

They came across a little clearing in the woods that had been dug up for planting. A shed stood to one side. Miranda opened the door of the shed and saw a kerosene heater and a series of shelves made of screening on three of the walls. Several of the shelves were still littered with the remains of dried plants. The chief came to look at it, sniffing the plants. "That's how Gabe made his money. He wasn't buying marijuana from those college kids—he was growing it, drying it and *selling it* to *them*. From the time he was twelve."

"And he and Ian were no doubt smoking it as well," Miranda said wearily.

As the sun shed its morning light on the eastern fields behind the Bluff, Miranda saw a red bandana tied to a tree on the far side of the Little Blue. An empty Dorito bag lay next to a cold campfire. "He's here," she said quietly with a mother's certainty.

Miranda and Dale Farley saw that the trotline had been cut in half. The far side floated with the current, a fat catfish caught on one of the hooks. The chief waded into the river and pulled up the rope on the closest side. He asked Miranda to turn her head—but she refused.

Every hook had gone deeply into Gabe's lovely face and his lanky teen-aged body as he had wrapped himself around and around in the long fishing line that had spanned the swiftly moving stream. It looked as though Gabe had just laid himself in the river and let the current hold him down.

Miranda had known all night that her boy was gone from her. Even as she and the other mothers had walked up the hill, Miranda's heart had ached toward the woods like a maternal compass seeking its true direction. She knew. She simply knew that a boy like Gabe could not do the things Ian was capable of doing. And if he did do them, he couldn't live with himself.

And then there was the Hezekiah file. It had been Gabe who had discovered it in Craig's personal filing cabinet. A boy like Gabe couldn't live with what was in that file either.

Miranda held Gabe on the side of the Little Blue River, picking the hooks out of his skin one by one, rocking him, holding his sweetness to her one last time. The chief finally left her to get help. Miranda stayed behind, sitting by the river, singing softly into her boy's ear.

CHAPTER 40

After leaving Hannah's room, Sheriff Atkinson made his way down the second floor corridor of Griggsberg Community Hospital. He thought he had come to tell the occupant of each hospital room how grateful he was that he or she was safe and how well they had held up during the terrible ordeal on the Bluff. Instead, each of Ian's victims revealed more and more elements of a story that was far from over. When Atkinson visited Jesse's room, Mary Louise took him outside in the hall and told him that Jesse had regained consciousness several times. Each time, he had said, "Mom, why did Pastor Dennison set our church on fire?" She knew her son. He was not hallucinating, and he was not lying.

"Is it possible that Reverend Dennison set the fire?" asked Mary Louise. "Ian didn't do it; I was standing right there with him when the church went up in flames. The soldiers had all left by the time the fire started. Why would the pastor do that, Sheriff?" asked the woman who had been asked to endure far too much in the past three days.

"I don't know, but I'm going to find out," Atkinson had responded.

Dulcey Martinez was in the next room. He thanked her for her heroic efforts on behalf of the hostages. Then Dulcey leaned over, slipped a videotape from under her pillow, and handed it to him. "Go somewhere right now and watch this tape, Sheriff. Don't watch the birds in the foreground—watch what is happening at the mayor's house. Go! Before it's too late!"

The sheriff asked a nurse to show him to a conference room where there was a television and a VCR. He was astonished at what he saw in the background beyond Jesse's birds. At four o'clock that morning, Sheriff Atkinson made three videotapes from the original, swore out a warrant, and arrested Jack Lockhart for the cold-blooded murder of Reggie Showalter.

After viewing the incriminating tape at the Blue River Sheriff's station, the miserably defeated mayor made a full confession of his crimes—including the involvement of Reverend Craig Dennison. By eight o'clock, the sheriff had gotten a warrant for the arrest of Craig Dennison. He suspected that not only had Craig assisted in the flooding of the quarry, but he had burned the church to hide the evidence that would implicate him.

The stone-cold, unsolved murder of Reggie Showalter suddenly burst into a blinding flurry of answers—and along with it, the Bennigan family's accusations of foul play were looking more and more accurate.

A few minutes after the warrant for Craig Dennison's arrest came through, an investigator called saying he had finally located the father and sister of Reggie Showalter. The detective had used the hostage crisis to get nationwide coverage of the unsolved Griggsberg murder case he had been working on for years. His plan had worked. Reggie's father, Howard Showalter, had seen the story about his son's mysterious death and had called the investigator's phone number at the end of the report. The sheriff immediately flew Howard Showalter in from Pennsylvania, and Reggie's younger sister, Ann Rawlins, from Wisconsin.

A grieving Mr. Showalter confirmed to Sheriff Atkinson that in July of 1983, he had sold dynamite to Jack Lockhart and Craig Dennison. Reggie had been sixteen and had worked with him at Showalter Granite at the time. Mr. Showalter remembered that Lockhart had signed the receipt. As a certified water engineer, Lockhart could legally buy the dynamite. During the transaction, Showalter claimed, Lockhart and Dennison had shown him a surveyor's map of the quarry and the river. He had shown his customers exactly where to place the dynamite in an existing tunnel to blast out the remaining rock between the quarry and the river.

Reggie's sister, Ann, recalled that in September of 1983, she and Reggie had come across the article about Lockhart in the Kansas City Star during a visit to their grandmother who lived in Kansas City. The article contained a picture of the mayor and his statement about how he was struggling to rebuild the town after its biggest employer, Bennigan's Quarry, had been accidentally destroyed and its owner killed. Ann remembered Reggie getting very excited about the situation.

"How did you know that Reggie was excited about finding that article, Mrs. Rawlins?" questioned the sheriff.

"He kept saying he knew he was 'onto something.' First he cut that article out, and then he went through a stack of newspapers on Grandma's porch and found another one about that quarry flood. A couple of days later, he cut a story out that had a picture of Mrs. Bennigan. It was all about how the quarry flood was no accident and how no one would listen to her."

"What did he do with those articles?"

"He saved all of them in an envelope and kept saying it was his 'Ace in the Hole.' He didn't even tell Dad about it—I got real worried that he was up to no good. I didn't understand what it was that was so important about those news stories."

The investigator set a file of clippings in front of Ann, and right away she picked out which ones Reggie had saved. As the sheriff and the investigator read them in sequence, they could see why Reggie realized he had damaging evidence against Jack Lockhart. Afraid that his father would alert the police, Reggie had kept the articles to himself and made plans to someday blackmail the mayor of Griggsberg.

Sheriff Atkinson speculated that when Reggie contracted the AIDS virus, he had probably needed money desperately and had tried to get it from Jack Lockhart. Jesse Candella's video camera had captured Lockhart's enraged reaction to Reggie's blackmail attempt.

* * *

Just before ten o'clock on Wednesday morning, TWA agent Mia DeSantos handed a boarding pass to a tall, disheveled man wearing a Kansas City Chiefs baseball hat. She noticed his bloodshot eyes and the shaggy growth of beard on his face. He seemed distracted, barely looking at her as she asked him questions to make sure his ticket was in order. TWA Flight 146 to Miami would be departing from gate 23 in less than an hour. Then the man was scheduled to connect to American Airlines Flight 931, arriving in Quito, Ecuador at 10:10 P.M.

Between customers, Mia glanced at the tired man in the boarding area, clutching a small carry-on bag to his chest, his long legs stretched out in front of him. He had pulled the bill of his cap down over his face and seemed to be dozing. Occasionally, he would rouse himself and stare at the television mounted on the wall above him. Mia made a mental note to make sure the tired passenger wasn't asleep when she announced the boarding of Flight 146. Between customers, she watched the television broadcast.

"This just in," said the anchorwoman on Channel 3. "In an unbelievable turn of events in the ongoing crisis in Griggsberg, the seventeen-year-old son of the Reverend and Mrs. Craig Dennison was found dead early this morning. He drowned—in what appears to be a suicide—in the river behind Bennigan's Bluff where the hostage crisis took place."

Mia's passengers gathered around the television to watch yet another shocking update from Griggsberg. The hostage crisis and the layers of mystery and corruption in the small town had been all anyone had talked about since Easter Sunday. *Wait a minute*, she thought. *Dennison. Dennison.* She went to her computer terminal and called up the passenger list for Flight 146 by alphabetical order. As she was staring at the screen, Craig Dennison's name began to flash and a notice floated across her monitor: Use code 100 if this passenger attempts to purchase a ticket or receive a boarding pass.

Mia grabbed her hand-held radio and noticed that Dennison was no longer in his seat. A full head taller than the people in the crowd, she could see him standing right up next to the television. His mouth was open, his face contorted. His hat had fallen off, and he stood clutching his bag to his chest, eyes wide in unspeakable horror.

Mia pressed the security frequency and steadied her voice. "Code one hundred at gate two three." She kept her eyes on the man as he watched the television set. "Repeat. Code one hundred at gate two three."

The radio hissed and the dispatcher responded. "We copy you, gate two three. Keep subject in view please."

Another airline agent took Mia's place at the desk and Mia moved behind the crowd, watching the news report, keeping Dennison in sight. The live broadcast showed paramedics carrying a stretcher out of a wooded area roped off with crime scene tape. A weeping woman followed, supported by a police officer. Then the anchorwoman came on the air again. "It is still unclear how the death—the apparent suicide—of seventeen-year-old Gabriel Dennison is related to the events in Griggsberg during the last few days."

More and more airline customers crowded around the television as the anchorwoman continued her report. "The father of the young man, Reverend Craig Dennison, the pastor of the Church on the Hill is wanted for questioning. In fact—we have just received information . . . " She pressed her earpiece more tightly to her ear, listening. "There is now a warrant for Reverend Dennison's arrest. Anyone knowing the whereabouts of Reverend Craig Dennison should notify the Blue River Sheriff's Department or the Griggsberg Police immediately." A picture of a smiling, clean-shaven man filled the television screen. Mia saw little resemblance between the photograph of the minister and the tall, unkempt man who stood before her now; no one in the crowd recognized him either.

As the reporter commented on the arrest of Mayor Jack Lockhart in the death of Reggie Showalter, the boarding of flight 232 to Boston was announced and most of the crowd dispersed. Mr. Dennison turned away from the television, and Mia shuddered at the look on his face. At first, no sound came from his throat. Then he fell to his knees and crumpled in a heap on the floor of the airport lounge. "My son! My son!" he moaned, writhing on the carpet of the busy airport as strangers gathered around the tormented man.

Using her portable radio, Mia shouted another code that would summon both the paramedics and security. "Stand back, everyone!" she commanded in her firm, trained voice.

"It's him!" someone shouted. "That preacher from Griggsberg!"

"Are you sure? How can you tell?" someone else asked.

"He said 'My son!' just now, talking about the boy they found—the dead boy in the woods. It was his church . . . in Griggsberg!"

Craig Dennison appeared oblivious to the crowds and commotion surrounding him. "Gabey, Gabey, my boy . . . " he repeated. Violent, wrenching sobs shook his body, and he thrashed from side to side on the floor, lost in his private agony.

Mia assisted the airport paramedics in clearing a path to reach the man on the floor. Efficiently, they lifted Mr. Dennison, laid him on a rolling gurney and tightened the restraints over his heaving body. An officer read him his rights and placed him under arrest. Mia and a security guard walked quickly behind the procession of emergency personnel and officers, opening Dennison's carry-on bag, checking for concealed weapons or contraband. Mia noticed a passport, several thick stacks of American twenty-dollar bills secured with rubber bands, and a tattered manila file folder with the word *Hezekiah* written on its tab. One of the arresting officers took the bag from Mia and escorted Reverend J. Craig Dennison to a waiting ambulance.

* * *

Within minutes of hearing of Craig's arrest, Chief Farley found himself speeding toward the Blue River Sheriff's station. He had been told that Craig Dennison was being treated for shock. Farley wondered if he himself had entered some phase of physical shock. No sooner had he and Miranda discovered Gabe's body in the river than Atkinson floored him again with the news about the mayor's arrest in the death of Reggie Showalter. *And now this!* He wondered if there was a limit to what a human being could deal with before lapsing into some sort of protective unconsciousness. When he had heard about Craig, he knew where he needed to be.

When he arrived at the jail, Craig was already heavily sedated. The camera mounted on the wall, focused on the sleeping minister, indicated to Farley that Craig had been placed under a 24-hour suicide watch. The chief stood looking through the bars at the man who had been his spiritual mentor and friend. Then he wept bitterly over all the act of inhumanity he had witnessed since Easter morning.

CHAPTER 41

Three days later, several hundred people stood in a drizzling rain in the little cemetery behind the Monastery Restaurant. Miranda had asked that several of the rosebushes be removed from the long hedge of roses at the back of the cemetery to make room for Gabe's grave. Her son had loved those roses and had played under them during his childhood. In June, the roses would bloom again and shower their petals on the grave of her sweet and troubled boy.

The people of Griggsberg filled the cemetery, spilling out into the shimmering wet streets nearby. The crowd murmured and parted as Chief Farley drove his patrol car slowly down the street and parked near the cemetery gate. Under the Chief's watchful eye, a broken, hollow-eyed man got out of the car to attend the funeral of his son. Newspaper reporters posing as mourners snapped photographs until they were chased away by the indignant citizens of Griggsberg.

Miranda stood solemnly next to Gabe's casket, holding one of the funeral home's large black umbrellas over herself and her two daughters. Craig stood next to them in the rain with his head bowed, sobbing quietly throughout the service. Kadence took his hand and tugged him under the shelter of the umbrella.

After the brief graveside ceremony, Miranda had asked that a special song be sung—one that had private meanings for those who mourned for her son and for others. It wasn't a religious song, but an old Irish ballad about a boy who felt he had to go to war and leave his loved ones behind.

Oh, Danny Boy, the pipes, the pipes are calling
From glen to glen and down the mountain side.
The summer's gone, and all the roses falling.
It's you, it's you, must go and I must bide . . .

As the last strains of the melancholy song echoed against the walls of the cemetery, the chief escorted Craig to the patrol car. They drove past the mourners who stood in a line two blocks long to comfort Miranda and her daughters and to say a word to the woman who had sung the beautiful Irish ballad as only she knew how to sing it. Fiona Bennigan was clear-eyed and serene as she shook the hands of those who offered her comfort and their wishes that things would turn out well for her.

* * *

Later that afternoon, Al Benson stood by Brett Ballard's hospital bed reading from a report, giving him a rundown of the survivors. "Charles Bennigan is in serious condition—possible paralysis. We've got a serious head injury listed for that fire department driver. Only time will tell on those two. The little boy with asthma is home—doing well. Everyone from the chopper has been released except you and Jesse Candella. You two sucked down more smoke than anyone else—but Jesse is awake and doing fine. Hey, even the cat made it, thanks to you."

Brett smiled and gave his commanding officer a weak thumbs-up.

"You handled yourself well, Agent Ballard. Doc says you need a week or two to get your lungs working right. He says it's best if you don't fly right now so I'm bringing your wife and boys to you. They'll be here this evening to watch out for you while you recuperate. Then you can report back to Quantico, say by the twenty-third of April?" Benson asked.

Brett removed the breathing apparatus from his mouth to answer his boss, "I can be back to work by then." Then he coughed violently for a few minutes. A nurse came in, adjusted Brett's breathing machine and tried to shoo the FBI man out of the room.

Benson laughed at the feisty nurse. "Well, you just take it easy, soldier. I can see these people will take good care of you." He turned to leave and added, "You'll have my highest commendation for what you did up there on that hill, son. The FBI's fortunate to have you. I'll see you when you get back to headquarters."

* * *

Miranda, Kadence, and Hannah moved in to Kate's big Victorian house in town. They knew they would never live on the Bluff again. Kate made the care of Kadence her main task. Hannah had spent the days since Gabe's funeral quietly; and sometimes loudly. Mostly, she spent time alone, thinking and praying, or shouting her bitter anger to the heavens. She had failed to keep her brother safe. It had been her job. Or had it? At odd moments, she knew Gabe was all right. That she would see him again. And that he didn't blame her.

Almost equal to her anguish over her brother was the knowledge of what her father had done. Years of secrecy had hidden his despicable acts. And rather than setting it right, he had tried to escape and leave them to cope with the mess. He had become a stranger to her. Her mother could not offer much to Hannah. She spent whatever good hours she had talking to lawyers, visiting her husband, and selling everything they owned to raise money for his defense. Hannah found some comfort talking to her aunt, or just sitting quietly inside one of Kate's warm embraces, being a little girl again.

Sometimes she talked to JoLyn and Dan who stayed up several nights with her while she talked her heart out. She wrote Jared a long, rambling letter pouring out her anguish and rage to him. Jared's letter to her was full of understanding and hope and comfort. She began to trust his understanding of why there was evil on the earth and how it might all seem random and insurmountably cruel while it was occurring, but that there was a purpose. In fact, she had been sent here to earth for that very reason—to experience both the sublime and the abominable—and make her own free choice as to which side would claim her. Jared was solid in his position that it had not been Hannah's job to parent Gabe. She had been a child herself and was in no way accountable. Hannah didn't know how she could go another year before she would see Jared again. Her loneliness for him was nearly unbearable. And now she knew beyond mere hoping that she loved him deeply, completely, and that he loved her.

Hannah's friends circled around her, offering her what they could. Sometimes what she wanted to hear was their *offer* of comfort— comfort itself being beyond what most of them could give. Dmitri

never questioned where she was going when she headed to the basement of the restaurant. She had arranged the big sacks and tubs of
flour and sugar into a kind of sitting place in her old Sunday School
room. She wanted to be near Kate's mural on the wall, as though she
were sitting at the feet of Jesus asking Him to explain to her how to
go on with her life. A kindly God in His heaven gazed down on them
as they talked.

Madame gave her back the key to the studio on the second floor.
Often, Hannah found herself there dancing until she had nothing
left, and then collapsing on the floor, crying out her pain, wetting the
wood with her agony.

* * *

On April twentieth, Hannah and Brett and Brett's wife, Shelly,
were sitting on Kate's porch after lunch. Brett had been released from
the hospital earlier that week and had been staying in town, enjoying
his family while he recuperated fully. Hannah had been asking them
questions all morning long about temples and eternal families. The
answers Brett and Shelly gave to her questions sounded deeply
familiar to her—as though she were remembering them rather than
learning the answers for the first time.

Despite the overcast sky, the day was warm and seemed to draw
everyone out of doors. Brett's two sons were playing with Kadence in
Kate's front yard. Miranda sat in Kate's Adirondack chair on the front
lawn, writing quietly in her journal, pausing to watch the children
play.

Just after noon, Kate came out looking worried and handed Brett
her phone. Al Benson came on the line. "Ballard? I know I said I'd give
you till the twenty-third, but I called your doctor and he says you're
good to go. We've got a major special going down in Littleton,
Colorado. At about eleven-thirty this morning, a couple of shooters—
most likely students themselves—opened fire at Columbine High
School. We think they may have put homemade bombs all over the
school . . . I need you here. I've already sent someone to pick you up."

"I'm on my way, sir. You say this special is in Littleton? What kind
of town is that—pretty rough?"

"No . . . no. Just your average middle class town. Kind of like Griggsberg—you know . . . a safe place to raise a family and all that."

Brett tried to imagine what it must be like in Littleton, Colorado, where frantic parents were wondering which end of the gun their children were on. Either way—it was a parent's worst nightmare.

"I'll be there as soon as I can."

Brett handed the phone back to Kate and went to gather his family. Hannah watched him take Shelly tenderly in his arms, and then kneel on the sidewalk to talk to his boys. She watched them making promises to each other, trying to look brave.

EPILOGUE

On Good Friday, one year later, the survivors of the hostage crisis on Bennigan's Bluff gathered at Rosa's Diner. As Dulcey's airport shuttle deposited her in front of the diner, she felt that she was truly home. It was her first trip back since she had gotten her new job as a rookie reporter at WPIX, a New York television station—the biggest news market in the United States. Her manager told her she was no doubt the most famous rookie reporter in the world, and he was lucky to get her. Dulcey had always known she was headed for New York; she just hadn't known how she'd get there.

Chief Farley had asked Rosa to close her diner on Good Friday so that everyone could be together. He said that everyone needed to be together on this anxious anniversary.

For the past few months, Dulcey and the whole country had followed the trial of Craig Dennison. The charges against him had included manslaughter, criminal trespassing, arson, and fraud. A month ago, it had ended with a guilty verdict on all charges. Despite his excellent defense team, Craig had been given seven to ten years in prison by a judge who was outraged at his misuse of the public trust, and the devastation and deaths that eventually resulted from his crimes. Jack Lockhart's trial would begin in a few months. The charges against him included a second-degree murder charge in the death of Reginald Howard Showalter. The trial of Ian and Charlie Bennigan and the four terrorists who were caught would not begin for a long time. Their lawyers refused to go to trial until the guilt of both the mayor and the minister were first determined.

Dulcey greeted her mother and was enjoying the smells and sights of her childhood when the front door opened and a young woman with dark circles under her eyes walked in. *Hannah*. Dulcey felt a rush of compassion for the woman who had watched her family unravel like a piece of ragged fabric. The two of them embraced and wept, wiping each other's tears. "I could barely sleep all week knowing we were facing the anniversary of . . . what happened to us all," said Dulcey. "I'm so glad to be a whole year away from it."

"Me too. I'm glad you're home," said Hannah. Rosa came in from the kitchen and Hannah kissed her on the cheek. "Hello, sweet Rosa. Something's different about the diner."

"You are never gonna believe this, Hannah. Dan Spencer showed up last week with a whole crew of workers. They worked all night replacing my tile so I wouldn't have to close and lose business. They said that someone donated it, but I can't know who it is. Still blue and white squares—but look how shiny and new they are."

Dulcey added. "Isn't that weird, Hannah? The donor wanted it in by Easter for some reason. I mean, Mom's tile was ancient but—it was part of the charm, and not replacing it was one way she kept her menu prices down."

"Why would someone . . . " Hannah said.

The door to the diner opened again and Kadence and Miranda walked in.

"I am *famished!*" Kadence announced, flouncing into the room, knowing all eyes would soon be on her. "Dulcey! How's New York? I knew you were coming today and I wondered if you know anyone who would like to hear me sing in the Big Apple?"

Dulcey whooped with delight at the sight of Kadence. "You are stunning, Kadence Dennison. Look at that hair . . . " Kadence flashed her toothless grin proudly and shook her buttery ringlets. "And those missing teeth tell me you must be almost six now, right? Give yourself a few more years and I'll just bet the whole world is going to want to hear you sing."

"She's almost six all right," said Miranda, kissing Dulcey on the cheek, "Six going on sixteen," she said, holding Dulcey away from her. "Dulcey, you look wonderful. How have you adjusted to life in New York?"

"It's wonderful. I'm having the time of my life . . . but I miss you all. I really do," said Dulcey.

"There isn't a day that goes by that we don't think about you and pray for you," said Miranda quietly. Dulcey looked into Miranda's tired, sad eyes and the beautiful face now etched permanently with grief.

The door opened again and Jesse and Mary Louise entered.

"Jesse!" Dulcey ran to him. "How's my hero? How's Cordelia? Is she all right these days?"

"She's got eight lives left, Dulcey—same as me!" said Jesse, delivering a bone-crunching bear hug.

Mary Louise wrapped Miranda in a tender hug. "My stomach has just been in a knot all week. The chief says he's got something to show us. What could it possibly be?"

Dulcey surveyed the group of survivors. She never imagined she would feel so close and so protective of the people in this room. They had changed in her eyes and she knew she too was a different person than she was a year ago. *Of everyone here, it's Miranda who has suffered the most. Life for her has changed in the harshest way possible.* Rosa had told her that the church executive board had donated all the church property including the Dennison's former home to the Bennigan family. Miranda, Kadence and Hannah lived with Kate in her big Victorian house on Main Street. Through Fiona's generosity, Miranda now owned the Music Camp free and clear. She and Kadence would someday live and work there. But for now, after a year of grieving the death of her son and the tremendous strain of the trial, Miranda was just surviving from day to day. And on every one of those days, her mother reported, Miranda had rejoiced in Kadence. The little girl was her reason for going on, her reason to stay sane and to move ahead each day in her complicated life.

Rosa brought Kadence a vanilla milkshake in a big red tumbler, and the six-year-old scooted into a booth next to Dulcey to devour the delicious concoction.

"I once knew a guy who liked vanilla milkshakes," Dulcey mused.

Overhearing her daughter, Rosa hurried back to the kitchen. A moment later, the swinging door of the kitchen opened and Matt Moore pushed into the diner carrying a platter of chicken wings. He wiped his hands on his splattered apron and embraced Dulcey.

"Matt? How did you . . . are you working for my mother?"

"I owed her some kitchen time for all the cheeseburgers I ate here over my college years."

Rosa beamed at the surprise she had arranged for her daughter. Matt was now a television personality for a Christian network in Dallas, Texas. The son of a preacher man might still be a good match for her Dulcey.

"Something's different about the diner, Rosa," said Miranda, trying to pinpoint what it was.

"It's my new tile—donated by a . . . a . . . a . . . *nonymous* donor," said Rosa.

"Anonymous?" repeated Miranda, sitting perfectly still. "Just this week?"

"Yes, a few days ago. Do you know who gave me this tile, Miranda?" asked Rosa, setting a plate of vegetables and dip next to the platter of chicken wings on one of the long tables. She had decided it was both too early and too late in the day to serve her famous biscuits and gravy. And besides, the vegetables would please her daughter who was still so fussy about eating healthy food.

"Maybe I do know, Rosa," said Miranda, turning to Farley. "Chief? Do you know anything about this tile?"

"It was one of the reasons I brought you all here today, Miranda. Craig said you'd know what it meant."

The diner was silent except for Kadence slurping the remains of her milkshake.

* * *

Just before two o'clock, Farley stood to address the group, pausing to dislodge the napkin from his collar, using it to wipe barbecue sauce from his chin. "Folks, I have asked Officer York to bring the police van around so you all can see something really quite amazing. Fiona and Maura have created a place to remember what happened to . . . well . . . to all of us up on Bennigan's Bluff a year ago. A lot of people from the town did the work on it and they just finished up this week—especially for this occasion."

Silently, the group boarded the police department's van and York drove them up on the Bluff. Though the day was a bit chilly, the sky was a clear blue—the same bright color as Rosa's new tile. And there was not a cloud in the sky.

York parked the van in front of the Bennigan's home. Everyone noticed the scaffolds and ladders scattered around the property and knew that the Bennigan home would soon be restored to its original splendor on its perch high above the town. Fiona and Maura were waiting on the porch. The two women went to meet the people who had shared something that would weld their souls together forever.

"We'll take you up there," said Maura simply, putting one arm around Hannah's waist.

Matt walked with Dulcey. Kadence held Jesse's hand. Fiona joined Miranda, Rosa, and Mary Louise. The women were silent at first as they remembered walking up this hill together one year ago. Then Fiona spoke, "We all lost some things on this hill last year."

"And gained other things, Fiona," responded Miranda, taking the other woman's hand, tears streaming down her face now.

"I want you to know that everyone in town is welcome to come to this place any time. To remember what happened."

The group paused at a small sign carved in wood that read "Bennigan Memorial Park." Half of the church parking lot had been left as it was, but beyond the lot was a grassy expanse of land where the church had stood. Trees and flowers had been planted all over the park. Small colorful gardens dotted the newly planted lawns. Next to three of the gardens stood a hand-carved wooden bench displaying a single name. The first one was inscribed "Liam Bennigan." The second read "Gabriel Dennison." There was even one for Reggie Showalter. Roy Sedgeworth's widow had planted a weeping willow tree with her husband's name on a small brass plaque nearby.

Everyone separated into groups of twos and threes to walk the paths. Dulcey told Matt she needed some time to herself. She walked toward the wall at the edge of the Bluff near the place where her life had once hung by a thread. Nearby, a bed of red and white tulips, their heads bobbing in unison, surrounded a small wooden cross that rose from their midst. A length of purple fabric hanging from its crossbar undulated gently in the breeze off the lake.

Dulcey wondered about what the future would hold for all of them. *How do we move beyond what has happened to us?* She noticed that a long wrought iron fence had been set into the low retaining wall at the edge of the Bluff. Some of the stones were charred. It had no doubt been constructed of the limestone and pink marble salvaged from the ruined church. Dulcey read the words etched into the long stone wall:

Father, forgive them for they know not what they do.

Dulcey knew it had been among the last requests of the dying Christ who had been sent to teach the world about love. His words were a divine response to the human treacheries He had found on earth—as well as a plea on behalf of those who had committed acts of horror in the name of justice.

Dulcey bent near the cross, picked a blood-red tulip and held its trembling cup of petals in front of her mouth like a microphone. She had learned to love the feel of a microphone in her hand. Telling the stories of real people had become her singular passion in life. It had become her way of seeing the world and telling its truths, be they wretched or beautiful. In her mind, she imagined what she would tell the world about this place today.

This is Dulcey Martinez here again on Bennigan's Bluff. She walked slowly toward the wall at the edge of the Bluff, tulip petals close to her mouth, gazing steadily into the eye of an unseen camera. *It was not a simple match that destroyed the Church on the Hill one year ago. Greed, lies, fear, vengeance—smoldering emotions hidden for many years under the dry kindling of secrecy. In all, four men are dead, two are seriously injured, and eight are now in prison because of what took place in this town. The Church on the Hill itself was a lie. Its absence—a confession.* Dulcey shuddered at the memories and threw the tulip over the wall. It rode the wind down to the lake below and floated on its shimmering surface. *That was for you, Liam—and you too Reggie.* She turned, snugged the collar of her wool coat tightly around her neck, and watched the people of her childhood walking together on the paths of this clean, clear space.

Fiona walked along the wall toward Dulcey, gazing at the lake below. "Your son," said Dulcey softly, moving to stand by the woman, "was a quarry man too, you know—like Liam was."

"What do you mean, Dulcey?" asked Fiona, raising her head, wiping her eyes with the edge of her scarf.

"He was the digging instrument," Dulcey said. "He unearthed the darkness from the deepest quarries of all of our lives."

Fiona thought a moment, fingering the scar on her cheek, "Yes, yes. He did it for his father, Dulcey."

"What he did was wrong, Fiona—but yes, I know he did it for his father."

Dulcey and Fiona looked up as a fifteen-passenger Dodge Ram van came to a stop near the park entrance and a familiar young man jumped out. They saw that Hannah too was squinting her eyes against the sun as the figure swooped toward her, his beige trench coat flapping wildly behind him as he ran.

"Jared!" Hannah gasped in delight, running to him, throwing herself into his arms.

"Princess—I missed you so much!" Jared said, joyfully swinging Hannah off her feet and squeezing the breath from her lungs.

He was taller, leaner, and had a confident, steady gaze. Dan, JoLyn, and Jared's seven brothers and sisters got out of the van and came toward them. Dulcey realized they had probably just picked Jared up from the airport after his two-year mission. Soon the air was filled with the sounds of boisterous laughter, excited conversations, and the feeling of unquenchable hope that surrounds new love. Fiona and Dulcey hurried to join the good people of Griggsberg.

In the distance, a bell in the steeple of Father Thomas's church tolled three times to signify the moment of Christ's death. It would be Easter soon. It was time to begin again.

ABOUT THE AUTHOR

Jeni Grossman was born in Johnstone, Scotland, and grew up in Kansas City, Missouri. She holds a dual master's degree in Theology and Marriage and Family Counseling from Fuller Theological Seminary in Pasadena, California. She and her husband joined The Church of Jesus Christ of Latter-day Saints in 1985.

Jeni has worked as an organizer, publicist, legislative activist, family advocate, news writer, and newspaper columnist, and has used her writing and public speaking talents to promote her views on family values and the rights of people with disabilities. Her essays and articles have appeared in newspapers and magazines throughout the United States and Canada—though all these activities have been secondary to her role as wife and mother.

While writing her first novel, Jeni taught creative writing both in workshop settings and at Heritage Academy in Mesa, Arizona. She currently lives in Gilbert, Arizona, with her husband, Gary, who is on the faculty of Arizona State University. They have raised a remarkable son and daughter who are both attending college.

RACE AGAINST TIME

Chapter 2

"Sniper One to Command."

"Go ahead," said Al from the Command Post.

"I've got one suspect eastbound toward the administrative buildings. Looks like he came out of a manhole near the furnace area."

Our sniper teams had much of the compound covered, except for some blind spots in and around the tank farms that speckled the compound. For the most part, the suspects would be within our control as long as they stayed above ground.

"Copy, Sniper One. Details?"

"Copy. White male, balding, prison coveralls. No weapons in sight."

"Received, Sniper One," said Al. Snipers were a strange lot, very cool, and good at giving information quickly.

I looked briefly at the tactical position of my team. They were all taking advantage of available cover awaiting the suspect who was heading our way.

"The other one?" Al inquired over the phone

"Negative. Only one person in our view at this time," replied the sniper calmly.

I could see the man walking, coming right for the lot where we waited. He was indeed everything the sniper said he was.

"He's looking around," the sniper added.

He was skulking through the compound, swinging his head back and forth looking for an avenue of escape, not yet seeing us.

"We'll take him at the edge of the lot," I said in a whisper into my microphone.

He had several steps to go, and with each one my heart skipped another beat. Willing my body to relax, I took several deep breaths, waited for the suspect to reach the edge of the lot, and issued a loud and official-sounding challenge. "Police Department. Stop where you are and put your arms out to the sides." The suspect abruptly stopped, shocked at the voice that seemingly came from nowhere. "Any movement you make not directed by me will be assumed hostile." I repeated the practiced litany I'd said so many times in my career.

The suspect paused and looked as if he was about to acquiesce.

"His name's Ed," said Al over the phone, seeming to sense my needs.

"Turn around and face away from me, Ed," I said more softly. He did it slowly, indecision showing on his face like neon.

"Sniper Team One to Team Leader." I heard the phone traffic in my ear. "Another male has emerged from the manhole. He is approaching Owen's team."

"Owen, you got him?" Al waited for a reply.

"Negative," I answered. I held Ed at gunpoint and tried to sound calm. "I can't see the second suspect from here."

"Sniper One to Command." Sniper One's tone of voice had changed. In his voice, I heard the panic and fear that only a father must be able to feel. There were times when even a professional let the world in. His next words chilled me and cast an icy pall over the entire operation.

"Bad guy number two is holding a young girl hostage."

CHAPTER 4

The next morning, a wet autumn Saturday in western Missouri, I steered my big Dodge diesel towards the rolling line that sufficed for the horizon. The landscape was dramatically different from the towering mountains that surrounded my Salt Lake City home. Here the trees were mostly deciduous and were losing their colorful leaves, and the tall grass rolled on for miles and miles, interrupted occasionally by thick stands of barren shrubbery. The change in scenery satisfied me, despite the rain.

We spent most of the day visiting historical sights, and Julianna was really quite a good tour guide. As if it wasn't enough to watch her brush locks of burnished hair out of her green eyes, she also gave a concise and informed lecture at each spot. As indifferent as I was to Mormon history, I found some of it fascinating.

"Mormons experienced vicious opposition as well as unprecedented growth in Missouri," she said as if reading from a textbook. "The Mormons who settled this area were run out of the state on a number of tragic occasions."

"Run out?" I said.

"This area," we had stopped and were looking at a large open bluff, "was once Far West, one of the largest towns in northern Missouri. It was home to over five thousand people, mostly Mormons. They were burned out and massacred after the governor ordered their extermination."

"Extermination?" I wrinkled a brow.

"The official extermination order wasn't repealed until nineteen seventy-six," she said. "It didn't pay to be a Mormon in Caldwell County in eighteen thirty-eight."

"It's a wonder they survived to cross the plains in such numbers," I remarked, hoping to sound somewhat informed.

"A wonder, indeed, Mr. Richards."

"So whatever happened to those people who made life so miserable for the Mormons?"

"They assumed much of the Saints's property and went on living in Missouri—the pukes."

"Whoa, Julianna McCray, your language!" I exclaimed, amazed at Julianna's new vocabulary.

She straightened in her seat. "Forgive me, but the term is a well-documented, historical epitaph for Missourians of that period."

"Okey-dokey, artichokey," I said, shaking my head.

We continued driving east on a two-lane highway. I was admiring the undulating landscape and wondering why they didn't stay and fight for what was rightly theirs.

"Like it?" Julianna was looking out her window at the rolling, forested prairies.

"Sure. It's nothing like Salt Lake City."

"Rolling prairie. That's what I like about it."

"It's a change of pace," I said, wishing there were a mountain somewhere. "How do you tell which way is north without the mountain range for orientation?"

"Oh, yes. There's a trick that only we Missourians know about."

This would be interesting; I liked to hear about the local lore.

She went on, "Behind those clouds there's a big fireball in the sky."

I started to look out the window where she was pointing.

"That fireball usually goes from east to west each day." Her face was deadpan.

So was mine, until she started to laugh and couldn't stop. I eventually joined her.

We drove north for about half an hour and then east a couple hundred feet down a gravel road.

"This is it," Julianna announced as we entered a clearing cut by a small creek. "It's right over there, somewhere," she said pointing down a gentle slope to a small wooded valley.

"And what would that be?" I asked.

"My great, great, great grandfather was born here. The exact location and the incredible story about his birth is recorded in his mother's diary, and that is a story in itself, but things have changed too much for me to find the actual spot. I'll show you where I like to imagine it is."

I stopped the truck and we both got out. It wasn't raining at the moment, but the air was brisk.

Julianna walked around the truck to meet me. She glanced at my feet and wrinkled her nose in amusement. "You're still wearing those ridiculous thongs?"

"No. Flip-flops. What about it?"

"Never mind, Tourist Boy." She walked past me shaking her head and smiling. "My favorite spot is through that brush down along the creek bed," she said.

My camera hung on my neck, as usual, and I grasped the body with both hands to prevent the lens from swinging around as I slid down the embankment. Sticks and twigs pulled at my sweatshirt as I parted the thick brush.

Julianna waited above in a long sleeved T-shirt, apparently enjoying the fresh, brisk air.

"Take a picture," I heard her yell.

It was the golden hour, that hour just before sunset that photographers await, when the sun is low in the sky and its light is diffused in a golden, flattering hue. The fact that the cloud cover ruined all that bothered me not a bit, considering the intended subject of my photo shoot.

"Walk that way," I gestured. "I see the perfect picture. I want you in it."

The brush along the depression was impassable in places and the daylight filtered in through it. I wanted just the right angle, so I forced my way through the brambles to find the perfect place to stand. The branches were stiff and clung to my shoulders as I clawed my way through. What a stupid time to be wearing my flip-flops. One unfriendly branch took me across the face, hitting both my eyes. I suppressed a curse, owing to the uncommonly pure company I kept, and squeezed my eyes shut. Tears formed to quell the sting and I blinked them back.

"I'm blind," I yelled, making a joke of it in case she'd seen me walk headlong into the branch and start crying. She didn't respond.

"Give me just a few seconds," I hollered up into the clearing. My eyes had stopped watering, but were still blurred. I closed my eyes and gently rubbed them before I raised the camera and made a rudimentary aperture calculation. I wanted enough exposure to bring out the shaded areas and not wash out Julianna's face. I played with the settings, waiting for her to show up in the frame. She made her way down the slope to the edge of the creek and made a couple of modeling gestures before settling in for the picture. I took a little extra time gazing at her through the lens, pretending to make minor adjustments. Oh man, she was beautiful.

"Okay, say . . . rutabaga."

"Rutabaga?"

Holding the camera firmly, I eased down on the shutter release expecting to see a momentary flicker. Instead, the frame turned black for a moment as if the shutter was stuck. When the shutter finally snapped back, a different woman was centered perfectly in the frame, and Julianna was no longer there.

"What the . . . ? Excuse me," I said, peeking over the camera.

The woman wore a long, calico dress with a full skirt and a knitted wool shawl over her shoulders, looking like she'd just stepped out of an old-time sepia photograph taken at a county fair. She had one hand to her face, brushing at the wisps of red hair that spilled out from under a wide-brimmed bonnet while her other hand clutched at the shawl. Her hair was just the color of Julianna's, and there was something of Julianna in her eyes as well.

Her face was fair and she wore a pained expression, just short of tears. Reflexively, I snapped another photo and lowered the camera.

"Uhh, hi," I said. The woman did not answer, but stood in front of me, looking furtively at the camera and then at the bank as if she didn't know what to do. Whoever she was, she was scared.

"I knew I'd find you," she finally murmured.

I took a step in her direction before hearing what I unmistakably recognized as a gunshot. The sound of the shot echoed through the evening air and over the distant hills, but the report was not far off. I dropped the camera, letting it fall to my chest, and pulled the zipper on my fanny pack to expose my pistol. The handle of my gun went firmly into the web of my hand, as it had done thousands of times before. Pulling it from its hidden holster, I lunged for the woman and shoved her to the ground in the shadows of the thick brush.

"Where's Julianna?" I asked, but got no response.

Another shot broke the evening air as the sun dropped below the horizon, leaving only long shadows on the Missouri countryside. This shot was much closer.

"Hurry," said the trembling voice of the woman beside me. "It's my brother. They're killing him."